THE FINAL FLIGHT

A Bermuda Triangle Mystery

By

Tony Blackman

The Final Flight

This book is entirely a work of fiction. Characters, companies, organizations, agencies and the island St Antony in this novel are either the product of the author's imagination or, if the organisations, companies or agencies exist, then they are used in an imaginary way without any intent to describe their actual conduct or behaviour. Description of certain aircraft electronics have been altered to protect proprietary information. Mention of real aircraft incidents are all in the public domain.

ISBN **978-0-9553856-0-5**
   0-9553856-0-1

First Published September 2006
© 2006 by Anthony Blackman.

Published by Blackman Associates
24 Crowsport
Hamble
Southampton SO31 4HG
UK

Previous books by same Author

A Flight Too Far
ISBN 0-9553856-3-6/ 978-0-9553856-3-6

Flight Testing to Win (Autobiography)
ISBN 1-4116-4825-0

To Margaret, without whose ideas, enormous help, painstaking editing and continuous encouragement this book would never have seen the light of day.

This book could not have been completed without some expert help. I should like to acknowledge with thanks the support and advice I have received from some members of the Civil Australian Safety Agency and Airservices Australia particularly Nick King and Katrin Hewitt. Also Rob Foulkes of British Airways and John Coulson, Consultant to UK National Air Traffic System. I also received advice from many other people in the aviation industry and hope I will be forgiven for not naming them all. Any errors remaining in the book must be laid entirely at my door.

Antony L Blackman OBE, M.A., F.R.Ae.S

About the Author

Tony Blackman was educated at Oundle School and Trinity College Cambridge, where he obtained an honours degree in Physics. After joining the Royal Air.Force he learnt to fly, trained as a test pilot and then joined A.V.Roe and Co.Ltd where he became Chief Test Pilot.

Tony was an expert in aviation electronics and was invited by Smiths Industries to join their Aerospace Board, initially as Technical Operations Director. He helped develop the then new large electronic displays and Flight Management Systems.

After leaving Smiths Industries, he was invited to join the Board of the UK Civil Aviation Authority as Technical Member.

Tony is a Fellow of the American Society of Experimental Test Pilots, a Fellow of the Royal Institute of Navigation and a Liveryman of the Guild of Air Pilots and Air Navigators.

He now lives in Hamble and spends his spare time writing books and designing and maintaining databases on the internet.

CONTENTS

Quotations at the start of each chapter are from the poem 'Bermudas' by Andrew Marvell(1621-1678)

DRAMATIS PERSONNAE

Peter Talbert	Aviation Safety Expert, Narrator of Book
Mandy Arrowsmith	Peter Talbert's girl friend, a lawyer
Dick Bartholomew	Immigration Head, St. Antony
Fred Baxter	Doctor, Bermuda Police
Joshua Brown	Bermuda Police
Lionel Brown	Airport Manager, St. Antony
Susan Brown	Frank Westbourne's secretary
Adrian Cartwright	Hotel Manager, Full Moon Bay
Sheila Cartwright	His wife, Full Moon Bay Hotel
Harry Collier	Thompson Hotel Manager
Marion Collier	WAA Operations/Dispatcher
Chuck Curtis	WAA Radio Engineer
Lawrence Darling	Commercial Attaché, UK High Commission
Francis Devere	FAA Oceanic controller
James Donald	SATCO Bermuda
Dora	Peter Talbert's help
Greg Fairclough	Chief of Paragon Flt. Ops.
Claudio Fernandez	Westfield Insurance Guard
Mick Flanagan	WAA Chief engineer
Brian Fletcher	AAIB Avionics specialist
Jim French	First Officer VP-WAL
Martin Frost	European Aerospace Flight Control specialist
Bob Furness	Head AAIB, UK
Robert Gagin	Westfield Insurance Guard
Ron Gibbons	WAA Chief Pilot
Wendy Greengrass	Charlie Simpson's boss at Westfield Insurance
Tim Hardcastle	SATCO St. Antony
William Hatton	SATCO Barbados
Bill Hudson	Captain of VP-WAL, the lost aircraft
Jane Hudson	Bill's wife
Jessica	Honeywell FMS Programmer
Samuel Justice	Immigration, St. Antony
Ted Linklater	ATC St Kitts
Henry Livingstone	SATCO, Antigua
Phil Mancuso	Head of WAA's Bermuda station
Mike Mansell	CrossLink Insurance
Ben Masters	Police Head, St. Antony
Brian Matthews	Flight Reporter

Chris Mattinson	Radar controller, St. Antony
Jack Maynes	Supervisor, New York Center
Jimmy Morrison	Millionaire, CEO Paragon, house in Bermuda, owner of paintings
Samantha Morrison	Jimmy Morrison's wife
Tom Mullard	WAA Avionics Mechanic
Dr Newhouse	SRG Doctor
Roger O'Sullivan	Westfield Insurance Guard
Kim Petersen	FAA Certification Engineer
Max Postwick	Honeywell FMS manager
David Roberts	RN Lt. In charge of operations room.
Wally Roberts	SATCO Port of Spain
Steve Rodriguez	Ex Honeywell programmer
Tom Sampson	Manager of hangar building firm.
Jim Sanderson	BA First Officer to New York
Martin Saunders	Head of Cleaning, St. Antony airport
Gunter Schmidt	EASA Controls Engineer
Richard Sebble	Head Customs Inspector, St. Antony
Charlie Simpson	Insurance Investigator, Westfield Insurance
Cindy Smart	Reporter, St. Antony Announcer
Philip Smith	World Underwater Surveys Search co-ordinator
Rupert Stanton	Doctor, St. Antony
John Southern	Hull Claims Insurance Surveyor
Margaret Springfield	Greg Fairclough's girl friend
Philip Statler	SATCO St. Vincent
Matthew Stephenson	LIAT MD
Simon Stevens	EASA Certification engineer
Paul Thomas	WAA Avionics Mechanic
Walter Thompson	Aviation. Week Reporter
Robin Trethowen	Senior European Aerospace Engineer, Hamburg
Steve Watson	United Training Manager
Rick Welcome	St. Antony policeman
Jack Wellings	AAIB Inspector
Frank Westbourne	Owner and CEO, West Atlantic Airways
Pamela Westbourne	Wife of Frank Westbourne
Daphne Williams	Director, Drake Williams Secretarial Agency
Guy Wostenholme	Bermuda Met Forecaster

ACRONYMS

Acronym	In full
AAIB	Air Accident Investigation Branch
ADS	Automatic Dependent Surveillance(position reporting)
AOL	American On Line
ATC	Air Traffic Control
BA	British Airways
BAA	British Airports Authority
CAA	Civil Aviation Authority
DME	Distance Measuring Equipment
EASA	European Aviation Safety Agency
FAA	Federal Aviation Administration
FMC	Flight Management Computer
FMS	Flight Management System
GESS	Galileo European Satellite System
GPS	Global Positioning System
ICAO	International Civil Airline Organisation
ILS	Instrument Landing System
INMARSAT	International telecommunications company
LIAT	Leeward Islands Air Transport
PAPI	Precision Approach Path Indicators
RWA	Royal World Airways
SAE	Society of Automotive Engineers
SATCO	Senior Air Traffic Control Officer
SRG	Safety Regulation Group, Civil Aviation Authority
VOR	Visual Omni Range directional beacon
WAA	West Atlantic Airways

THE CARIBBEAN, ST. ANTONY AND BERMUDA

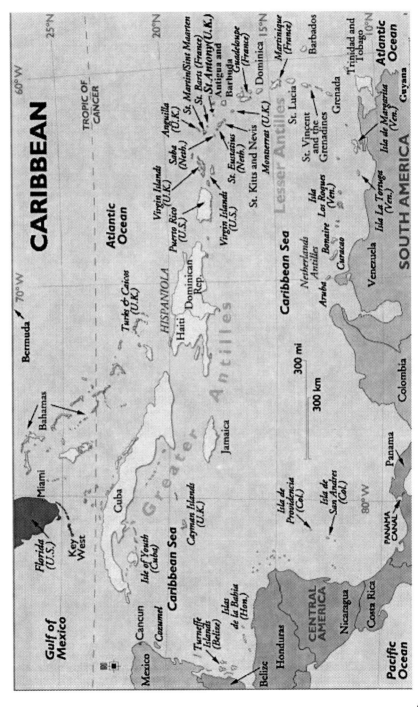

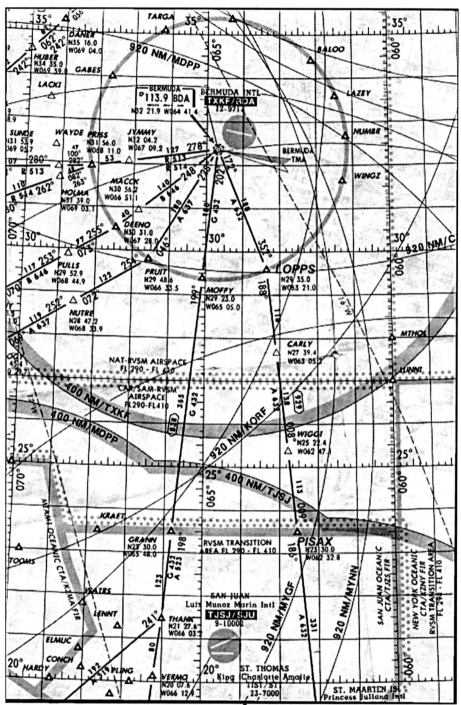

Tracks shown are magnetic, 10⁰ greater than true track

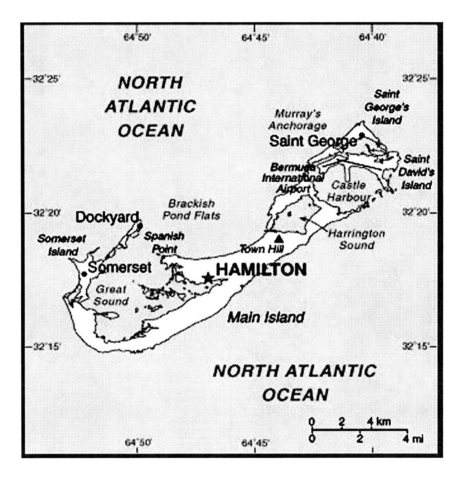

BERMUDA

The Final Flight

PROLOGUE

'Where the remote Bermudas ride
In the ocean's bosom unespied'

Bill Hudson put his car in the parking lot reserved for airline staff. The weather was overcast, a ceiling of 2,500 ft., with a 25 mph westerly wind. He collected his uniform jacket, hat and navigation bag from the back of the car and walked towards the buildings. He moved slowly trying to keep cool with the temperature of 90°F and a humidity of 95%. In all his years flying for Leeward Island Air Transport in Antigua and now West Atlantic Airways, based locally in St. Antony, he had never known weather quite like it. Luckily, hurricane Angela had missed the island to the West by about 100 miles so that the southerly winds had only been up to 50 mph but that was quite enough to cause extensive damage to some of the poorer housing in Cape Harbour. The hurricane in May was incredibly early and, amazingly, it had been category 3 on the Saffir-Simpson scale with winds of 120 miles an hour. The global weather really did seem to be changing but Bill was not convinced it was entirely due to the world's population.

Though Angela had gone by two days before, the weather still had not returned to the dream climate of the Leeward Islands, sun and clear skies. Before leaving his home overlooking the sea near Farways, Bill had looked at the Weather Channel on the piped cable TV. Thank goodness the hurricane had reduced in intensity and was now down to category 1 and forecast to become a tropical storm. It had been tracking North East in the last thirty six hours so that the centre was now about 120 miles east of Bermuda, which was just as well since Marion, the operations girl, had called him unexpectedly this morning and asked him to take a load of freight to Bermuda. He wasn't too pleased since it was his twentieth wedding anniversary and he had planned to take Jane to Full Moon Bay as a surprise. He hadn't even been on stand-by but Marion had told him that apparently Jimmy Morrison, the billionaire boss of the Paragon Corporation, had specially asked for him. She said that it was going to be a very lucrative charter so he couldn't very well refuse, since he knew how important it was for all of them to keep the airline profitable. Why Jimmy wanted him he couldn't imagine. He had only met him once and he certainly didn't want to repeat the experience.

He entered the complex of single story airline offices next to the control tower and decided to go straight into the met office before going into West Atlantic Airways operations room. As he entered the room he was surprised to see Jim French looking at the weather charts.

"What are you doing here? I thought you were on holiday in the States."

"I should have been but because of Angela and the weather the other day my flight was cancelled and I decided to postpone the whole trip. I'm your first officer to Bermuda this evening."

Jim was a relatively new pilot with West Atlantic Airlines. He had lived in St. Antony for some time and previously worked for the flying operations division of the Paragon Corporation which was based in St. Antony. When Jim heard there was a vacancy for a pilot in WAA he had applied straightaway and not surprisingly the chief pilot, Ron Gibbons, had hired him. Jim was a very experienced pilot but apparently had got fed up with the unsociable hours of Paragon. Airline Training in Miami had given him very high marks on their European Aerospace 412 aircraft training course and Bill found him an excellent First Officer. He'd be a very good captain the moment there was a vacancy.

"Great. What's the weather like?"

"Well we've got the landing forecasts, the upper winds and the synoptic charts and it all looks good, but I think it's disgraceful the way they've closed the met office here and made us rely on these faxed charts. I know we can ring the forecasters in Barbados or Miami but it's not the same thing."

Jim took another look at the charts.

"Luckily Angela seems to be tracking North East and is expected to be about 125 nautical miles East of Bermuda by the time we land at 0100Z, 9 o'clock local time to-night. However, it's still a Force One hurricane so it's just as well that it's way off our track. They're forecasting a northerly wind of 30 knots for landing at Bermuda so we should be alright on Runway Three Zero. The weather will be overcast, a ceiling of 20,000 ft, no rain, a visibility of 10 miles and some upper cirrus. There shouldn't be much of a problem."

"Have you spoken to the forecaster, Jim?"

"No, not yet. I was waiting for you."

"Well, why don't you do that and I'll go in to operations."

Bill picked up his bag and left the office, nodding to Simon the clerk as he went out. The clerk was a local and Bill tried hard not to notice that there was still a resentment by the locals of the expatriates who came in to St. Antony and took most of the highly paid jobs. Of course there were notable exceptions, like Lionel Brown the airport manager, who did a really first class job.

Marion was behind the desk, waiting for him. She was definitely not a local. She was married to Harry Collier, manager of the new Thomson

Hotel near Hughes Point. They had two children and the older one, Luke, helped Harry in the hotel. However, Bill knew Marion disliked being on call twenty four hours a day at the mercy of every guest and preferred to work a roster with WAA. True she had to work nights occasionally but in return she got lots of days off to keep an eye on Sonia during the school holidays. She didn't like sending her daughter away to boarding school in England but there was nothing suitable on the island. Luckily Thomson paid the fees, not that the firm had much alternative if they were going to attract good managers.

"What's the panic to deliver the freight to Bermuda? Aren't these the paintings that have been sitting around in the air conditioned customs shed for five months?"

"Yes, Bill, that's the main freight but there are some other heavy crates to go. It does seem odd. However, if you're as rich as Jimmy Morrison I suppose you can do what you like. Frank told me that he quoted three times the normal price for the trip, because the plane would have to come back empty and Greg Fairclough agreed without a demur, though apparently he did ask for you and Jim French."

"I thought as a matter of principle we didn't like our charterers specifying who is going to fly the aircraft?"

"You're right, but in view of the price we got it was difficult to refuse Greg. He knows Jim well of course, and Jimmy apparently asked for you."

Bill thought for a moment.

"Why aren't Paragon flying the paintings up themselves? The crates aren't that big are they?"

"Well actually one or two of them are quite large. You know the crates are significantly larger than the paintings themselves and, of course, the paintings are in Jimmy's original frames so they can't get the larger ones through the doors of either their Gulfstream 3s or their 4. Anyway, even if they could the insurers, Westfield Insurance, have said the paintings must be transported by an airline with a proper Airline Operators Certificate. Greg said he tried hard to persuade Westfield that Paragon could do it but they wouldn't listen to him."

Greg Fairclough was the Chief Pilot of the Paragon Corporation and ran the Corporation's flight operations setup which was head-quartered in St. Antony. The Corporation was truly international with its head office in New York and offices all over the world. It was particularly strong in South America and so having the flight operations based in St. Antony was quite convenient, especially for Jimmy Morrison who had homes in Bermuda and Florida. The gossip was that Greg and Jimmy were pretty close and Jimmy seemed to leave the whole of the flight operation scheduling to Greg which, by all accounts, didn't always please the high powered executive passengers. Bill had met Greg but even though the island was small, particularly for expatriates, their paths didn't cross socially.

Marion was continuing to apologise for the short notice of the flight.

"Apparently there's been a very long legal case going on in New York contesting whether Jimmy Morrison really owns some of the paintings but, unexpectedly, the case has just been settled in Jimmy's favour. Customs will be pleased to see the paintings go since they're fed up with the insurer's guards hanging around outside the customs sheds. The guards aren't allowed into the sheds of course, but they've been sitting outside watching that the crates don't leave the building. They've got a security bleep on each piece of freight containing a painting, like valuable goods in a store, so that if anybody did take a painting out of the customs shed the guards would hear the bleeps."

Bill's high opinion of Frank Westbourne was confirmed by the story of the charter. Frank always did good deals and that was why West Atlantic Airways was doing so well. True they had lost one of their European Aerospace 412s a few months ago trying to come in visually from the South in a large thunderstorm. They had hit Crazy Peak. Fifty feet higher and they would have got away with it. Luckily the insurance company paid out, but they hadn't liked doing so since they said that the crew training was inadequate. Bill had some sympathy with the insurers, Hull Claims Insurance, though he would never say so out loud, since he thought Ron Gibbons, WAA's chief pilot, should never have made Malcolm Lazarus an airline captain. Airline Training had given him the lowest pass mark possible at the end of the Course. Bill suspected that local politics had played a part. Why the hell Malcolm hadn't waited for the storm to pass or landed at St. Kitts no-one would ever know. Forty passengers and four crew killed for nothing.

"Marion, what aircraft are we using?"

"We're using one of the European 412s, VP-WAL." She looked at him apprehensively. "But Bill, there's a problem with the fuel. The ground crew have put full fuel in the airplane."

"That's crazy, Marion. Who gave the instruction? I thought we'd stopped that happening. That must be the second time in a month."

"I've no idea. I can't get anyone to take responsibility. It's not a regular flight so the proper procedures weren't followed. They were told to fill it up with freight and someone filled it up with fuel. You remember last time it happened it was on a charter."

"Somebody ought to be disciplined. Are they going to defuel it?"

"Apparently they can't. They've got no empty tankers and maintenance want us to take it with full fuel. They know the aircraft is not fully loaded."

16

"But can we take full fuel, Marion? How much does the freight weigh?"

"Well Bill, by my calculations you can just get away with it. You will be limited by the aircraft's maximum structural take-off weight though you won't be far off the single engine climb limit with the high temperatures here. What shall we do? If we wait until to-morrow there will be an empty refuelling truck."

"Why are we carrying so much freight if we are just taking the ten paintings that I read about in the local press?"

"I've no idea but that's what the customer wants and he's paying us well."

Bill thought about it. It really made no difference to him if they carried far too much fuel. They would actually use a bit more fuel on the trip to Bermuda because of the weight of the extra fuel that wasn't needed but Jimmy Morrison had agreed to pay so much above the going rate for the job that they could afford it. He shrugged his shoulders.

"OK Marion. Leave the aircraft the way it is. At least we won't have to refuel on the way home." Bill hesitated for a moment. "I'm still a bit surprised that we are on the limit. The pictures can't weigh very much. What's in the other crates, gold bars?"

"Actually a lot of the extra freight is quite heavy though we have no idea what it is. As you say there are only ten masterpieces or whatever they are. By the way all the crates with the paintings in are marked with shockwatch and tiltwatch indicators to make certain that they are handled like eggs, so we are having to be very careful. It's not made any easier by the people from the shipping agents and the two security guys watching every move and urging us to be as quick as possible so that the paintings don't get damaged by the climate. My understanding from the shippers is that the paintings are actually protected from all reasonable variations in the climate and that even if a shower of rain comes along the paintings won't get damaged. However, the agents are very nervous and I can't say I blame them.

"The rest of the freight is proving very awkward to load. We've removed most of the seats and are lashing the boxes down in the cabin. We're only allowed to take one box out of the customs building at a time which slows things down but of course we're air conditioning the aircraft on the ground with a truck. In spite of all the difficulties we should be able to get you away by 6.30, 2230 Zulu."

Bill looked at his watch; it was 4.30 so they should be away in a couple of hours. He still felt uncomfortable about the cargo. For all he knew it might be dangerous material which was prohibited for carriage in aircraft.

"Marion, don't you have to say on the cargo manifest what's in the crates?"

"Yes and No. The cargo here is in transit so customs don't insist on looking inside, particularly as they get well paid for providing the storage. We're relying on the information from Morrison's shipping agent here in St. Antony. The documents say it's machinery and paintings. What happens in Bermuda is between Morrison and the Bermudan customs but I bet he's made sure that there won't be much duty to be paid."

"But how do we know we're permitted to carry the freight by air? We don't want a repeat of that ValueJet flight out of Miami some years ago when the oxygen cylinders caught fire."

"We just have to believe the shipping agent that it is machinery. I suppose we could insist on an inspection, if you like."

Bill thought about that for a moment. He really should insist on opening the crates. Then he had an idea.

"How did the heavy crates arrive? By ship or by air?"

Marion shook her head, looked in her directory, dialled and took up the phone. Bill heard her talking about the freight, presumably to the shipping agents. It took a long time, as many things did in the Caribbean. She turned to Bill as she finished the conversation.

"Apparently they were flown in from the States in a Lockheed C130 transport."

"Civil registered?"

"I don't know. Do you want me to find out?"

Bill felt a bit happier. At least the freight had come by air and it was most unlikely that a military C130 would have had freight for Paragon.

"No, don't bother. I give in. I suppose it'll be OK."

He could feel Marion still eyeing him nervously. She obviously had another problem for him.

"By the way there's no cabin attendant on the flight if that's alright with you. You've only got freight plus the two guards so Jim will have to shut the doors. I've booked the two of you in at Rock Cove. We get a good rate at this time of year and it's reasonably close to the airport."

"Not that place again. It may be great for golfers but as a night stop it's rubbish. To coin a phrase, Marion, all the staff are full of bullshit and have their hands out for tips all the time."

Marion grinned. "How you people suffer. You should be grateful I didn't put you up in the Bayview downtown. By the way, I'm not sure of your schedule to-morrow yet. We may just ask you to come back empty but we'll look around for a load of freight. You can't very well bring passengers as most of the seats will be here in the hangar."

Bill looked at the clock. They still had an hour and a half to go before the expected time of departure. Marion passed him the flight plan to look at. She had already put full fuel in the plan. He checked the weights, signed the plan and gave it back to her to file. She really was a superb dispatcher. She called the flight plan up again on her computer, sent it straight out from the machine to San Juan and New York Oceanic centers and to Bermuda. The computer also wrote a disk which she gave to Bill so that he could load the flight plan and forecast winds straight into his Flight Management Computers when he got to the aircraft. He put the disk in the special compartment of his nav bag and then looked out of the operations room window. The ground crew were working on the aircraft. He could see Chuck Curtis out there.

"Marion, what's Chuck doing out at the aircraft? Was there a problem?"

"Yes, Bill. Jim had difficulty with the VHF radio on the company frequency and he snagged it in the tech log."

There was a truck going out to the aircraft presumably with another crate. The truck was being followed by a car. At the aircraft the truck backed up to the front freight door and two men got out of the car. He guessed they must be the security guards. Jim came in from the met briefing room.

"I've spoken to both the forecaster in Barbados and the one in Miami. They're saying the same as the charts; the forecasts say that the en route weather will be no problem and also at Bermuda, with Angela well over 100 miles to the east. The upper winds will be westerly at about seventy knots. I assume we will be flying at 35,000 ft.?"

"That's fine Jim. I suggest we go out when they finish loading. You'll have to close the cabin doors as we're not taking a cabin attendant. We've got the two security men sitting in the back. There's time for a coffee if you like. Let's go over to the terminal."

They put their uniform jackets and hats on and then threaded their way through the corridors, finally emerging into the new terminal. The place was quite busy as the regular daily flights from Europe had just arrived. They found a free table in the coffee shop and put their bags down before getting their drinks. Jim took out a newspaper from his nav bag and started reading.

"The gossip says that Jimmy Morrison has a new girl friend and she is staying in Bermuda. I can't imagine the lovely Samantha will allow that."

"You're right. She'll probably arrange for her to be deported for not having a United Kingdom passport."

"But she may be a United States citizen, the papers only show her body, not her passport."

"In that case she'll be deported for not having a visa. Either way I bet Samantha will deal with Pussy Galore or whatever her name is. That lady is tough. Jimmy may be able to run a billion dollar corporation but he is no match for Samantha in marital matters."

"Have you ever seen Jimmy's house near Tucker's Town? It's said to be almost as big as Buckingham Palace."

"In fact I have. I had to deliver a special letter to him in person last month from his St. Antony lawyer. I wasn't sure I was allowed to do it as I suspect it is against the St. Antony Post Office rules but it didn't seem worth arguing. Jimmy's house is actually mock Georgian and very large but I regret to tell you it is probably only a quarter the size of Buck House."

"What was Jimmy like?"

"Since you ask, I thought he was very rude and rather frightening. I had to penetrate a security gate at the main entrance with my car and then three security screens in the house to get to him in his study. He was quite short, thin and immaculately dressed. He was smoking a thin cigar and by the look of the ash trays spread round the room it was not his first of the day. He looked me straight in the eye and reached out his hand for me to give him the letter. He glanced at the envelope, made sure it hadn't been opened and told me to help myself to coffee from a very expensive Wedgwood coffee pot on a side table that looked as if Chippendale himself had made it. I sat down opposite him expecting to have a chat after he finished reading the letter but instead he just looked at me as I drank my coffee. He already had a cup so I couldn't very well offer to get him some. The coffee was hot and it seemed to take forever to drink and all he did was to look at me. I decided that two could play at that game so I just looked back. I finally managed to swallow the stuff, scalding myself in the process. There was no smile and barely any acknowledgement of my presence. It was really rather unpleasant. He finally lifted up a telephone receiver and gave permission to the guards to let me out. I never want to go there again."

They finished their drinks and went back to the operations room. Marion smiled at them.

"The loading's complete and the security guards are already on the aircraft. I've called for the van to take you out."

What a super girl. She knew how hot they would get just walking to the aircraft in that humidity. They went outside as the van came up and, as they climbed in, the driver got permission on the radio to cross the ramp to the aircraft. Jim got out first, put his gear down and walked round the outside doing the external check. Bill climbed up the steps and put his bag next to his seat. The aircraft's auxiliary power unit was running so that it was cool inside and Bill enjoyed the air conditioned atmosphere. He had been brought up in England and had never really accepted the tropical climate though he loved the benefits of the heat when it came to

20

relaxation. He also knew that as one got older the joints were less likely to give trouble. To him, both Florida and St. Antony were prime examples of the extra life expectancy obtainable from a hot climate.

Bill took off his jacket and hat and went to the back of the aircraft. In fact they had taken the front twenty rows of seats out and lashed the boxes down to the floor. The two guards were sitting in the first row of seats. Bill didn't like the look of them very much, both bearded, tough eggs, and he was pretty sure they both carried guns. One looked a bit smarter than the other, a white Caucasian, and tried a smile. The other looked very South American; someone had told him he was Venezulean or Colombian. There wasn't much to choose between them. He wouldn't have liked to meet either of them in the dark. Presumably they were very good guards or Westfield wouldn't have hired them. It was no use fussing, he told himself, and went forward to look at the paper work. The passenger manifest showed Roger O'Sullivan and Claudio Fernandez. He hoped that the airline staff had checked them carefully or WAA would get fined by the Bermudan authorities. The load sheet seemed alright but he checked carefully that the centre of gravity was within limits with the freight as loaded and was again surprised to see how heavy the freight was. There just had to be more than valuable paintings inside some of those boxes. He wondered if the customs men had looked inside the crates though, as Marion had said, the freight was in transit so they didn't have to care. Thank God it was no business of his. He looked at the technical log to make sure that all the snags from the last flight had been cleared. There was nothing of any significance. Chuck had done the radio. He signed the log and gave a copy of the sheet to the mechanic. He looked down just as Jim was putting his mobile phone away into his flight bag and climbing up the steps. Bill went back on to the flight deck and sat down in the left hand seat. Jim put his bag by the right hand seat on the flight deck and went back to close the cabin doors. On his return he strapped himself in and started the checks.

Bill took the flight plan disk out of his bag and inserted it into the Flight Management System, then selected the load page on the left hand flight management box and started the load procedure. Once the data had been loaded into the computers the pilots had very little more to do in order to get the two navigation displays in front of them showing the planned route, because the disk had not only the filed flight plan but also all the forecast winds and waypoints. Bill checked that the expected arrival time calculated by the computers agreed with the printed flight plan time that Marion had given him. In fact they agreed exactly showing a landing time of 0105Z. Bill called Marion on the company frequency, 132.65.

The Final Flight

"West Atlantic Operations this is Alpha Lima, please confirm that the passports of our two passengers have been checked for correct visa requirements."

"Alpha Lima, both have United States passports, Operations out."

Bill was pleased that Marion had looked at the passports. He was slightly surprised to hear that Fernandez had a US passport since he looked as if he could barely understand English, but he knew from his frequent trips to Miami that the local population seemed to speak more Spanish than English. On the other hand, Westfield Insurance were hardly likely to employ non-US nationals considering the value of the paintings. Once more Bill was glad that it wasn't his problem. Jim called St. Antony tower on the ground control frequency of 121.9 MHz.

"Nelson tower, this is Victor Papa Whisky Alpha Lima. Request permission to start."

"Alpha Lima, this is Nelson please stand-by."

There was a wait of about five minutes.

"Alpha Lima, this is Nelson. Clear to start, change to 118.2 and call San Juan Oceanic for clearance."

Jim switched to the satellite radio.

"San Juan Oceanic, this is Victor Papa Whisky Alpha Lima, request clearance from Nelson to Bermuda."

"Victor Papa Whisky Alpha Lima this is San Juan. You are cleared as filed, upper amber 632 to Bermuda. Initial clearance Flight Level 100, expect 350 en route."

Bill liked clearances as short as that. He set the glare shield altitude controller to 100 and made sure that both flight management computers showed the same flight plan. There was no way they could disagree since the flight plan disk loaded both computers with the same data and if there was a disagreement a warning was given. Nevertheless, Bill always liked to double check. He called the marshaller in front of the aircraft, who was connected to the aircraft intercom system, and asked him if the aircraft was clear of all ground equipment. Satisfied, he started the right engine with bleed air from the aircraft's auxiliary power unit. The engine temperatures climbed and stabilised. He started the left hand engine and the moment ground idle rpm was reached he asked the charge hand to disconnect his intercom lead. Jim called the tower for taxi clearance.

Bill taxied straight ahead. That was the nice thing about not being parked at a finger from the terminal, there was no need for a push back and then having to disconnect from the towing vehicle. He steered the aircraft towards the new taxiway and the holding point for Runway Two Five. Thank goodness the St. Antony Government had finally spent the money and improved all the airfield facilities and taxiways. It had been needed for years since many of the tour companies had got fed up with the lack of facilities and moved away to more modern locations. Jim tested the satellite reporting equipment on the way out to make certain that the position of the aircraft would be transmitted automatically every 10 minutes to San Juan Center on the first part of the flight and every 5 minutes to New York Center on the second part. This was a relatively new technical innovation, both for the airline and for the Air Traffic System, but it made sure that the controllers who looked after the air space over the Atlantic, where there was no radar, could 'see' all the aircraft under their control when they were way outside radar cover in the middle of the Atlantic. The system was called ADS C, Automatic Dependent Surveillance, for no obvious reason, Automatic Position Reporting sounded much more logical to Bill. The C denoted the reporting was by satellite as distinct from ADS B where the reporting was via ground radar. It was part of the so called FANS, Future Air Navigation Systems, which again Bill thought illogical since the future was now. He got Jim to check the system was working.

"San Juan, this is Alpha Lima. Are you receiving our ADS?"

"Alpha Lima, this is San Juan Oceanic. We can see you on the ground at Nelson."

"San Juan, thank you for check."

VP-WAL reached the holding point of Runway Two Five and the two pilots could see an old 767, landing lights on in the gathering darkness, on three miles finals.

"WAA VP-WAL you will be cleared into position after the landing 767."

Jim acknowledged and as the Britannia 767 touched down with spurts of smoke from all the main wheels, Bill opened the throttles slowly and lined the aircraft up for take-off. He checked all his flight displays were normal and that the navigational displays were correctly lined up with the runway.

"WAA VP-WAL you are cleared for take-off when the runway is clear. You may climb as cleared to flight level 350."

Jim acknowledged the Tower again, reset the glare shield controller to 350 and called out the final checks for take-off. Bill opened the throttles halfway and released the brakes. The aircraft accelerated slowly at first and Bill opened up the throttles the rest of the way forward. The aircraft picked up speed, Jim checked that they had the correct take-off power and then called the airspeed out as the plane got faster and faster. He called 'V_1' as they were committed to go and not stop in the event of an engine failure, then 'rotate' as the aircraft reached the planned rotation speed, V_R. Bill nudged the side stick controller backwards until the aircraft reached the right attitude for climbing out at V_2 and then engaged the auto-pilot so that the aircraft would follow the planned track. The tower cleared them to Nelson approach frequency, 119.1, and the aircraft, controlled by the flight management system, turned right to capture the outbound track from St. Antony and then settled on the 358° True heading on Upper Amber 632 to Bermuda, climbing steadily.

"San Juan, this is Alpha Lima. Airborne from Nelson, on course Bermuda, climbing to Flight Level 100 requesting 350. Please confirm when you are receiving valid ADS data."

"Alpha Lima, this is San Juan. Cleared to 350, advise reaching. Will confirm ADS after next report."

Bill checked that the aircraft was on the planned track by looking at his navigation display. He noticed that the St. Antony VOR direction marker on the display was missing and no DME was being displayed. He tried to manually tune in the other VOR but he could hear and see nothing of the VOR.

"Jim, I can't get the VOR on either set and the DME is not showing."

"That's strange. I checked with Air Traffic that everything was working just before I left the operations room."

Bill decided to check that the fault was not in the aircraft's equipment.

"Approach from Alpha Lima. I can't get the VOR."

"Alpha Lima from Approach. Both the VOR and DME failed about an hour ago. Problem being investigated."

Jim adjusted his flight management computer and both displays showed the desired track.

"Luckily the VOR/DME doesn't matter Bill, the FMS uses satellites and the inertial gyros for calculating the position."

"I know, but you know I always like checking."

They were quickly in cloud at 3,000 ft. and Bill could see the intermittent glow of the navigation lights and the beacons. Jim got permission to change frequency and he called San Juan using their satellite transmitter receiver; reception was perfect. They came out of the low cloud at 6,000 ft. but the high cloud prevented him seeing the stars. The climb to their cruising altitude of 35,000 ft. took about thirty minutes and the aircraft levelled off automatically.

"San Juan, Alpha Lima. Level 350."

"Thank you Alpha Lima. We are receiving your ADS."

The aircraft was still in cloud and Bill looked at the weather radar. There was some weather ahead but not too much. Jim got out of his seat and produced some coffee and sandwiches. After 55 minutes the aircraft was at the latitude 23° 30' N waypoint, called PISAX, which divided the control responsibilities between San Juan and New York. South of that latitude was San Juan's responsibility, north of the latitude New York Oceanic was in charge.

"San Juan Oceanic, this is Alpha Lima, we are showing our position at PISAX, request permission to transfer to New York."

"Alpha Lima, this is San Juan, cleared to call New York Oceanic. Maintain 350."

Bill switched to the New York Oceanic satellite operating frequency. He noticed that the returns on his weather radar seemed to be increasing.

"New York Oceanic, this is Victor Papa Whisky Alpha Lima en route Nelson to Bermuda, position PISAX flight level 350."

"Alpha Lima, this is New York we see your ADS, check at LOPPS."

LOPPS was the waypoint where the aircraft would enter Bermuda airspace, another 366 nautical miles ahead which would take them 48 minutes with the forecast wind. Bill started to get concerned as he could see some strong weather returns ahead.

"Jim, look at that weather. We shouldn't be having anything significant on this heading."

"I know, it's very strange. Look, I've pulled down the stand-by compass out of its stowage to check, but it seems spot on allowing for 10° magnetic variation. Shall I call New York and get them to check the forecast weather en-route?"

"Good idea. Go ahead."

Jim switched his selector box to the satellite frequency.

"New York Oceanic, this is Alpha Lima. We are getting a lot of weather ahead of us. Can you check with met on the latest forecast? We were expecting high cloud and no weather on the route to Bermuda."

"Copied Alpha Lima. Stand-by."

Bill disconnected the auto-pilot and manually steered the aircraft between the weather cells but he started to get concerned as the cells got more and more numerous and it was very difficult to see a way through. He switched the ADS C reporting rate to the maximum of 90 seconds so that the controllers could check the aircraft's track more accurately. He put the seat belts sign on. He wished New York would hurry up with the weather. He looked at his watch. They had been flying for an hour and thirty five minutes and were now at the LOPPS reporting point, 180 miles from Bermuda. The aircraft followed the flight management system command and turned left onto 342°T direct to Bermuda and Bill steered the aircraft as best he could in that direction through the thunderstorm cells. Thank goodness they would be able to speak to Bermuda directly in about fifteen minutes.

"Alpha Lima, this is New York. We've checked with the forecaster and your weather en route is fine. There is still severe weather in the tropical storm but that is well off to your right."

The Final Flight

'New York, Alpha Lima. Copied your message but weather around us and ahead is very stormy and turbulent. Out'

Bill rechecked the stand-by compass against the navigation display but there was still no significant discrepancy showing 352°M. He wished he had been able to check the VOR radial as they left St. Antony even though nowadays, with the latest navigation equipment, it did not seem necessary. He tried to see the stars but they were hidden by the cirrus. The aircraft was back right on the indicated track but it was getting into some moderate to severe turbulence. He switched his VHF set to the Bermuda approach frequency, 119.1, and called Bermuda. There was no reply. He listened out but he could not hear other aircraft calling Bermuda which worried him since, even if they were further away than he thought, he should have been able to hear other aircraft at that altitude. He switched the number one VOR receiver to the Bermuda beacon, 113.9, but there was no signal. He tried the second VOR but it was no better. He tried looking at the Distance Measurement beacon but again there was no response. They were showing 160 miles out from Bermuda according to the navigation display. Bill asked Jim to carry on steering the aircraft through the cells but it was getting increasingly difficult to fly it. There were frequent flashes of lightning which were very disturbing.

Bill decided to look at the Global Positioning System position page on the flight management computer and was astonished to see the page was blank. There should have been a warning on the navigation display if the GPS was not working. He tried the Galileo European Satellite System, GESS, but that page was blank as well. What the hell was going on? He tried the inertial navigation pages. The information seemed alright but Bill was getting extremely worried. Thank goodness they had taken off with a full load of fuel. At least that was a stroke of luck. If they couldn't contact Bermuda soon he was going to turn straight round and return to St. Antony.

"New York Oceanic, this is Alpha Lima. We are in heavy weather with lots of lightning and severe turbulence. We should be 120 miles from Bermuda but we cannot raise them on the VHF and we cannot see Bermuda on our weather radar or receive their radio beacons. Will you please contact Bermuda and see if they can see us on their radar?"

"OK Alpha Lima. According to us you are right on track. Do you want descent clearance?"

"Not for the moment. We must get contact with Bermuda first."

"Alpha Lima, this is Oceanic. Advise when you have contacted Bermuda Approach on 119.1"

The lightning was almost continuous now and the turbulence was very severe.

"New York, this is Alpha Lima. Situation is getting very difficult. We are having to make quite large changes of course, to avoid the worst cells. We are still unable to make contact with Bermuda. The turbulence is getting almost uncontrollable."

"Alpha Lima, this is New York. Bermuda Radar advise that they cannot see you on their Radar. We see you 100 miles south of Bermuda on ADS."

Bill knew something was seriously wrong and not just with the weather. He decided he couldn't wait any longer despite New York telling him they were on track.

"Jim. Let's go home. There's something strange going on. Let's get out of here. Do a 180° turn. I'm afraid Jimmy is going to have to wait for his paintings and gold bars or whatever they are."

The Final Flight

CHAPTER 1

'Unto an isle so long unknown,
And yet far kinder than our own?'

Incredibly the aircraft had vanished. Apparently the crew had been talking to Oceanic Control when the plane had suddenly disappeared into the Atlantic without a Mayday call. That was all. Nothing more. Another accident statistic the world didn't need.

 Our breakfast was forgotten. Mandy turned off the radio.

"What do you think happened, Peter?"

I looked at her. She wasn't wearing very much but I wasn't complaining. It was her flat after all and she must have set quite a high temperature on the heating system. Just as well, as it was blowing a gale outside and the sea was breaking over the wall. It was May but it might as well have been February it was so cold and there was no protection from the southerly gale.

The BBC hadn't really said anything except that the aircraft was missing, presumably because the particular news item wasn't rated very highly in the scale of fatal disasters. They did mention that the R.A.F. were sending some aircraft to help in the search but the producer must have cut the rest.

"No idea. It could be so many things."

She put her coffee down. We were in the middle of a late Saturday breakfast and had been listening to the news.

"But you're the expert!"

"And that's why I'm not giving you an opinion. Stop winding me up."

"It's strange that it should be Bermuda. There must be something odd about the place. Aircraft always seem to be disappearing near there."

"I'm not sure that's statistically correct." Mandy didn't look convinced. "There have been some celebrated disappearances but they have occurred over a very long time frame and have been spread over a very wide area. As usual the media have just exaggerated the situation."

I paused. I had finished an accident investigation two months previously, which had got a lot of press coverage and had been exhausting physically, involving two flights to Australia in quick succession. I had been living with Mandy ever since the accident investigation had finished and our week-ends together were meant to be relaxing. During the week

The Final Flight

Mandy worked long hours in her solicitors' office and I was able to work from her flat thanks to the internet. Accident investigation wasn't really my expertise by training, though it looked as if it might become so in the future.. My education had been in electronics and I'd had to start using this knowledge after I'd had to stop flying when the medics said I had a heart problem.

I found I could not stop myself thinking of the fate of the aircraft crew and passengers, lost in the inhospitable waters of the Atlantic.

"I wonder if the newspapers have got anything about it?"

Mandy leant over and kissed my neck and I could smell that clean, after shower fragrance, in her hair. She felt me responding and then turned and walked slowly and seductively through the kitchen door to the hall outside and returned with a whole pile of papers which she dumped on the table. She selected the Telegraph but the way she handed it to me made me wonder whether I might be unpopular if I decided to read it immediately. We had been together now for about six months and I had got used to the idea that a first class lawyer could be very attractive sexually. As I reached out my hand to Mandy instead of the paper, she threw the Telegraph at me, grinned, sat down and started reading the Times.

I examined the paper. The Public Inquiry into the accident to the Royal World Airways 798 aircraft, in which I had unexpectedly become the star witness, had finally finished.[1] It had been reconvened after the Chairman, Lord Justice Thomas, and his two assessors had got back from Australia. The plane had crashed at Heathrow with 429 people killed and 101 injured and a further 38 people killed in cars driving along the A30. The paper gave the findings and recommendations of the Inquiry.

"The findings of the Inquiry have been very complimentary about you, darling. It says if it wasn't for you, the pilots would have been blamed, the real cause would never have been found out and other similar accidents might have occurred in the future."

"I wish the media would find some other news. The accident was five months ago. There must be other things to discuss."

"But Peter, the accident was the biggest ever and the findings have only just been released. It will be a long time before it is forgotten."

She was right but I didn't like the notoriety from the media, knowing how fickle they were. I hadn't realised there were so many different radio and TV channels. I refused interviews as a matter of principle since the producers always pasted and cut the interviews to suit the points they were trying to make, even when they said they wouldn't. Though I needed

---

[1] A Flight Too Far

the interview fees, I didn't want my face to become public knowledge; not that I could stop the papers printing their photos.

Thank goodness I had been able to escape down to Mandy's instead of being at my house in Kingston. Looking back at the Royal World Airways accident, I could see that I had been a bit lucky getting such an important assignment from the insurers. I had done a small job for Mike Mansell of CrossLink Insurance some months earlier, before the accident, and he had called me the morning following the crash to get me to protect their position. My two trips to Australia had enabled me to find out what had actually happened and it was very clear that my success in the investigation would bring me more business. I had certainly needed it at the time. However, it now looked as if my work load was going to go from famine to feast, with articles to write, specialist interviews, and more insurance jobs in the pipeline. It all seemed so unfair that such a terrible accident had propelled me to fame, if not fortune.

I searched through the Telegraph for news on the aircraft that had been lost going to Bermuda. There was nothing in the main columns but there was something in the stop press 'The Bermuda Triangle claims another victim.' Apparently the aircraft was a European Aerospace 412 owned by West Atlantic Airways and had just disappeared as it was approaching Bermuda. The aircraft was carrying freight and there were only four people on board. I started looking at the other newspapers.

Thank goodness Mandy always had a good selection delivered on Saturdays and Sundays. During the week I was having to go out every morning to get the papers since she bought what she wanted at the station, read them on the train and understandably never brought them home. There was no reference to the loss of the aircraft in the FT nor could Mandy find one in the Times. However, the Mail must have gone to press later than the other papers since it had managed to have the accident in the news. 'AIRCRAFT LOST IN TRIANGLE' with 'IS THE BERMUDA TRIANGLE A BLACK HOLE?' and there was some extra news that valuable paintings had been lost. I gave up looking any further. There was clearly nothing more to be learnt from the papers. I'd just have to wait.

"You know I told you that Mike sent me a large cheque," Mandy put her paper down "in final settlement. I think we ought to go away on holiday for a bit."

"You have to be joking. You've got a lot of articles to write and work to do. You would go mad if you weren't doing something useful. Anyway you need to keep on working. Your girl friends are very expensive." There was a pause. I could see Mandy thinking for a moment or two before continuing. "Where were you thinking of going? Japan, Singapore, Australia?"

I wasn't sure how innocent was the question. Mandy was a super lawyer and I always felt it was necessary to give her questions the consideration they deserved.

"None of those and certainly not Australia. I don't need the practice." I looked at her carefully. "Could you afford the time?"

"Wait a moment. Are you including me in? I'll have to consider my position, going away with a strange man. It's the sort of thing my mother tells me I shouldn't do. She calls you her sin-in-law." She paused reflectively. "I think I'd like to go to Australia. It might be quite nice. And I want to visit all the places you went to. You still haven't really told me all you did in Sydney. How did you persuade Liz to come to England to be a witness?"

She looked at me quizzically but then leant over and kissed me in a way that clearly suggested she wasn't intending to make a 'cause celébre' out of it. But then she was a very sensible solicitor and knew exactly when to stop probing. Just as well, as there was no way I could tell her what I'd had to do to get Liz, the girl who helped me solve the RWA accident, to come to England. I hadn't realised what a hard time investigators have.

"There's something worrying you, Peter. You are not concentrating on the papers and you are certainly not concentrating on me even though I'm right next to you. Is it that accident in the Atlantic?"

I nodded. I wouldn't admit it to anybody but the accident seemed very clear cut. For some reason the aircraft must have got involved in some bad weather, the crew had lost the place, the aircraft had got out of control and had dived into the Atlantic. Still, why was there no MAYDAY? It couldn't have been a fatigue failure of the pressure cabin like the Comet; apart from anything else the aircraft was relatively new. I tried out all sorts of other scenarios and then gave up. There were no facts to go on. Perhaps Sunday's paper would throw more light on the matter.

Mandy's flat was in Bournemouth, probably because she liked sailing. She raced in some of the faster machines when she could get some free time, otherwise she sailed in her own Moody 34. I was not too keen on racing and so far we had only been over to Cowes and Yarmouth on the Isle of Wight. I was looking forward to going over to France when the weather got a bit warmer. Her flat had certainly proved a good place for me to avoid the reporters. I stretched out and audibly relaxed. I might just as well enjoy this last week-end before going back to live at Kingston. As Mandy said, I had been working very hard ever since the accident to the RWA aircraft. Perhaps I did need a break. Mandy was reading the papers again. I took them away from her and she didn't complain.

We spent the rest of the day very quietly. It was before the tourist season and we went for a walk along the front towards Hengistbury Head. It definitely was unusual weather, cold and windy but the rain held off.

In the evening I took Mandy to dinner to Chez Dominique, a very nice French restaurant which had a small dance floor. Mandy put on a short dress with a low neckline which showed her figure off to perfection. The food was excellent and we enjoyed dancing to a sophisticated three piece band, saxophone, double bass and piano. We stayed until after midnight when they played the last waltz and Mandy danced very close indeed.

In the morning we took our time waking up and getting up. I could still smell the perfume in her hair when I held her close. She got up and disappeared to the kitchen.

The phone rang. I could tell from the ring that it was diverted from Kingston and was for me.

"Peter."

I froze. The voice sounded very familiar. I had heard it two months ago after a gap of five years.

"I've just been reading the final report of the Crash Inquiry. You were really marvellous."

Mandy was coming back and I put the phone down without saying anything, as I had done once before. She reappeared with some coffee which smelt superb, croissants and the Sunday papers piled high on a tray. I wanted to grab the papers but decided that Mandy would prefer it if we had breakfast first. Actually it was a sensible decision since I always found croissant crumbs tended to permeate throughout the bedclothes if one tried to read the papers at the same time.

"Who was it?"

"Oh, somebody trying to sell you double glazing."

"I thought I had stopped those calls."

"It was a foreign sounding voice. You can't stop the overseas ones."

I began to wish I had not had my phone calls patched through to Mandy's. When we finished breakfast I took the tray out to the kitchen and dialled 1471 on the kitchen phone to hear the calling number of the last phone call.

"Service Activated. Telephone Number Country USA 2021 413 5367 at 0805 GMT. Press 3 to return the call."

I made a note of the number and the time on a piece of paper and stuffed it in the back of the telephone directory to recover later. I was sure the call was from Diana, my missing wife of five years, though she sounded slightly as if she had been drinking. I wasn't sure what to do. I didn't feel ready to talk about it yet.

The Final Flight

When I got back Mandy had already opened the Sunday Times and that suited me since I wanted to read the Mail which had been very close to the 412 story yesterday. I didn't have to look very hard. On the front page was "TEN MASTERPIECES LOST IN BERMUDA TRIANGLE." Apparently ten paintings, all impressionists, were being returned to Jimmy Morrison, head of the Paragon Corporation, whose main home was in Bermuda. They had been on display in London in the previous year but had been delayed in St. Antony due to a court case. They were finally being taken back to Bermuda. The paintings were listed in the paper, goodness knows how in the time. Presumably the reporter must have been talking to someone who handled the exhibition at the Royal Academy. There was one of the Monet haystacks, a Monet water-lily study, a Monet outdoor scene, two ballet studies by Degas, a nude by Manet, a small portrait by Renoir, an unusual Toulouse-Lautrec, a landscape by Cezanne, finally another landscape by Pissarro.

The aircraft had been talking to Oceanic Control Center in New York and then all communication stopped. It had been roughly 100 miles South of Bermuda. The Royal Air Force were sending two of their Nimrod Mk 4 aircraft to search for the 412 and look for any survivors. The United States Navy were also sending two aircraft and a helicopter. The Royal Navy luckily had a frigate visiting Bermuda and it was on stand-by to join in the search. I looked at the other papers and the stories were similar.

"Peter, what do you really make of this Bermuda Triangle story?" Mandy had been watching me sifting through the papers.

"It's difficult to say anything definite. There are no real details in the papers. We'll have to wait a few days before we get anything significant. Aviation Week and Flight will have some more information by Thursday."

"Is it really a dangerous place to fly?"

I looked at her wondering whether she was being serious and came to the conclusion that she believed, like many people who had not investigated the stories, that there was something in the reputation that the area had for untimely disappearances.

"My love, I have to tell you that I am a disbeliever of such stories. I'm sure it is as safe to fly or sail in the Bermuda Triangle as anywhere else in the world. If there are any problems they will be caused by the weather, not by black holes or marauding aliens."

I wasn't sure that Mandy was completely convinced by my assurances as we got up and went to the Poole Yacht Club for a drink. I was getting to know quite a few of Mandy's expert yachting friends. On our return, I decided I'd better check Mandy's answering machine. There were several messages for me, mostly about the RWA accident, but there was one which got my attention. It was for me to call a Frank Westbourne in St. Antony in the Leeward Islands; the message was left at 12.05. I looked at my watch, it was just after lunch, 2 o'clock. Westbourne must have called me at 8 o'clock in the morning his time so he must be very keen to speak to me. I told Mandy about the call and she took my hand as I reached for the telephone.

"Peter, you know what he wants. He needs your help in St. Antony, right now." She looked at me. "Have you worked out what you are going to charge him?" I shook my head. "I don't think you should call him until you've thought through what your rates are going to be."

She was quite right. But then it was part of her job as a lawyer to think about fees. My standing and value in the profession had clearly increased enormously as a result of the Inquiry into the RWA accident. I really did need to decide my scale of fees before calling Westbourne. We talked it over and came out with a scale of fees far, far higher than I would have dreamt of charging. By myself I would have been swayed by the fact that the airline was quite small and only had a few Boeing 737s and European Aerospace 412s and couldn't afford very much. Mandy told me I couldn't afford to be a philanthropic society.

"This accident sounds like it has enormous insurance significance quite apart from the loss of the aircraft. Think of the value of the paintings. He clearly needs you urgently, judging by the time he called you."

We talked it over some more and then I called Frank Westbourne.

"Peter, thanks for returning my call. I don't think we've met. I'm the owner and chief executive of West Atlantic Airways. We have six Boeing 737-700s and five European Aerospace 412s or rather we had five. Did you see we lost one on Friday night going into Bermuda? It's a terrible tragedy and we have no idea what happened. I'm calling you because the insurers of the hull are saying that it looks like pilot error and that they are not going to pay us if it is pilot error again."

"I don't understand, Mr. Westbourne."

"Well we lost an aircraft making a bad weather visual approach into Nelson airport, here in St. Antony, about six months ago and I'm sorry to say that the pilot made a mistake. He should have waited until the storm had passed through. Very disappointing as it was our first local St. Antony Captain on the 412. The insurance company immediately put an exclusion in the policy which said that they would not cover pilot error accidents."

"That's a very difficult exclusion to police, Mr. Westbourne."

"Please call me Frank, Peter. I agree but they insisted and that's why I want you to come out and help us. The St. Antony Government has asked the UK Government for help and two Aircraft Accident Investigation Branch inspectors are arriving to-day, but even if they find the cause of the accident they won't be defending our position. I've read all the reports of the RWA Inquiry and, if I may say so, you did an absolutely outstanding job against all the odds. I need someone like you to look after WAA's interests. If you'll agree to come I only hope you'll be able to help us the way you helped RWA."

"I think you've got an unjustified expectation of my ability to help you. However the case does interest me. Who did you say your insurers were?"

"I didn't but they are Hull Claims Insurance."

I knew them alright. It looked as if they were going to have to pick up the tab for the RWA accident as a result of my efforts. I shouldn't think I was the flavour of the month with them.

"Frank, what actually happened on the flight?"

"It was a short notice freight flight, flying machinery and ten paintings, masterpieces actually, which belonged to Jimmy Morrison, who owns the Paragon Corporation. The paintings were insured by Westfield Insurance and the airframe, crew and passengers by Hull Claims. There were two pilots and two Westfield Guards on board. They took off for Bermuda and the flight seemed to be going alright but the aircraft apparently got lost, though New York Oceanic said it was on track according to the automatic position reports on the screens in New York. It sounds most peculiar and to be honest I don't understand it. That's why I want you to investigate on our behalf."

"The investigation could take some time, Frank. I think you should know what you are letting yourself in for financially if I come and help you."

"Look, Peter, I understand that in life you get what you pay for. I'm assuming that the investigation will take about a total of 30 workings days initially. You're quite right to raise the matter now. Nobody likes surprises. What are your charges?"

I gave him my fees which were additional to my direct expenses and he accepted straightaway without demur.

"When can you start? The sooner the better."

"Well I have to work in London to-morrow but I might be able to travel on Tuesday. From what you say I need to talk to New York Oceanic. It might make good sense for me to visit Oceanic on Tuesday afternoon before coming down. I would be with you then Wednesday evening. How does that sound?"

"Fine Peter. Let me know your flight details. I'll make a hotel reservation anyway."

Frank rang off and my mind was racing around trying to assimilate all that he had told me. It seemed a strange business. New York Oceanic knew where the aircraft was but the crew didn't and then it disappeared.

"That sounded alright, Peter. It looks as if you've got another job."

Mandy had clearly followed every word.

"Yes it does but I'm going to have to move if I'm travelling on Tuesday to New York. I'd like to talk to Bob Furness, AAIB. He's still the head of the Air Accident Investigation Branch at Farnborough. I also need to talk to Hull Claims to hear a bit about the accident."

"Why don't you travel Wednesday and be there Thursday?"

She was right again. It did sound more sensible. But it was difficult for me to think clearly because the earlier telephone call had given me a shock. The voice on the phone had sounded very like Diana.

"Peter, what are you going to do about an office." I forced myself to listen. "There's no question of your going anywhere, work or holiday, until you've sorted that out. You need a proper office and secretarial support. Whether you like it or not, you've become well known, notorious, famous, whatever word you like to use. You always wanted to be a consultant and now that you are going to be an extremely successful one, you need a secretary at the very least."

"You're right. I've been thinking about that. But you know the interest in the RWA accident will soon disappear. It would be premature to make any large investment until I get more long term business. I'm sure there must be secretarial agencies which will provide a service for me. Why don't I do some telephoning on Monday and choose one? I can then divert all my telephone calls to the agency when I'm away and take it from there."

"Sounds a good idea but you had better interview the agencies. Some of the 'hole in the corner' outfits just won't do for someone in your position. You need an agency with presence, one that has a reception area and also has occasional offices for meetings. It's going to cost you but, as I said earlier, you don't have any alternative if you are going to take on more work. Getting an agency and signing an agreement is going to take time."

"Yes, but at least an agency is not a lifetime's commitment."

I could feel myself getting slightly frustrated. Mandy was quite right, I did need some form of an office where people who needed me could contact me, leave messages and the like. She was also right that I would find doing nothing absolutely impossible. She had clearly got to understand me very well as a result of our living together. The Royal World Airlines accident investigation had certainly bound our relationship closer. I hoped, as I believed she did, that our association might be an enduring one but, unfortunately, any hope that our relationship could become permanent was problematical because Diana had left a big question mark over everything, particularly for me after the telephone calls.

The Final Flight

Diana and I had been married for several years. I was a pilot flying for Britannia when we first met but I had begun to suspect that she was being unfaithful to me while I was overseas. Matters came to a head one day when I got home after two weeks away on a trip to New Zealand and found there was no sign of her. I had tried everything I knew at the time to find out what had happened but without any success. Her parents had also tried very hard but they too had found nothing. The police, understandably, suspected me of getting rid of her since invariably the husband was the guilty person in these situations. They examined every inch of the house and kept on questioning me but they finally decided to leave me alone when they established beyond doubt that she had been alive three days after I had gone on my trip and that I really had been on the other side of the world. The police then, in my opinion for the first time, seriously started searching all their databases of missing persons, but all to no avail.

It was not long after Diana disappeared that I lost my pilot's licence because of my heart condition. I had appealed, since my own medical consultant had said it was a lot of nonsense, but in truth I had not been too worried since I got paid my loss of licence insurance in full and I had always intended to stop flying sometime and start using my electronic engineering degree in some way. I had managed to earn some money specialising in the training of airline pilots in human factors on the flight decks of new commercial airliners, but, until the RWA accident, I been finding business very slow going.

I had tried again quite recently to find some trace of Diana, when Mandy felt we could not progress our relationship any further without some more searching. I had spoken to Diana's parents as well as to the police but, as before, we seemed to be completely up against a brick wall. Mandy was torn between wanting us to live a normal life together right now and getting everything sorted out first. Not altogether surprising since she was a hard working City solicitor. When she was in the office she tried to make certain every angle was covered but I had noticed that her resolve seemed to lessen the further away she got from her desk. As things stood at the moment, in two years time it would be seven years since Diana had disappeared and I could have a divorce on the presumption of her death. Of course the telephone calls, if they were indeed from her, would re-open the whole situation and I clearly needed to find out if it was Diana who phoned, and what she was doing. I was in two minds whether to discuss the recent telephone calls with Mandy but decided I would try to trace the location of the last call first.

"Peter, you'd better go home right now and start sorting things out. Especially as you've been away so long," Mandy was being practical. "It's a pity because we were having such a nice week-end but you need to start thinking about what you ought to be doing. I'll take you to catch the 5.23 and you'll be home reasonably early. If you stay here to-night, which of course would be very nice, you'll start on the wrong foot to-morrow. There are bound to be things you need to do."

I didn't argue as there certainly was a lot to do. We brought our week-end to a close and I returned to my home in Kingston, carrying as much as I could of my clothes and the work I had been doing.

As I opened the door, the house smelt musty and unlived in which was a bit surprising since I knew Dora, my help, had been cleaning the place regularly. I turned on the heating, then cancelled the call forwarding and listened to the new messages on my answering machine which I had not cleared from Mandy's. There were a few messages sounding as though they might be new business. I made a note of them, ignored the rest and then got out my diary and the piece of paper with the number I had copied down on Saturday morning. It was a downtown New York City area code.

"Adelphi Hotel. How can I help you?"

I might have guessed. Unless I was able to examine the hotel register I wasn't going to make any progress and even looking at the register wasn't going to help since the girl told me, when I asked, that they had 350 rooms. The register would be on the computer but even with a printout I wouldn't know what I would be looking for. Still, if the voice was Diana it was a step forward, knowing that she was alive and was actually in New York on Saturday morning. Mind you, it was a strange time for her to call me, 3.05 in the morning Eastern Standard time. Maybe she had indeed been drinking which might explain why she called me. Before ringing off I got the hotel address and, looking at a map I had, it seemed to be in quite a good location in Mid Town. I started to tidy up my office and went to bed.

On Monday I walked to Kingston station, all muffled up as there was a cold wind, and caught the 8.15 to Waterloo. All the papers were covering the loss of the WAA 412 though there was nothing new, so the Bermuda Triangle angle was being worked overtime. The editors reminded their readers of the loss of the two Avro Tudors in the late 1940s, *Star Tiger* and *Star Ariel*, both belonging to British South American Airways, both disappearances never explained satisfactorily. In addition, other tragedies like the discovery of the derelict brigantine Marie Celeste were mentioned and the many United States aircraft that had disappeared in the area. By the time the articles had been written and read it was not too difficult to believe that there really was indeed something sinister in the area bounded by Bermuda, Florida, Cuba and the Caribbean. As I walked across Waterloo Bridge to the CrossLink Office in Holborn where Mike Mansell worked, feeling cold and looking at the cold and deserted Thames, I reflected that it would at least be warm in the Bermuda Triangle.

I told Mike about the call from Frank Westbourne. He looked at me thoughtfully.

"Peter, you are getting well known."

"Only thanks to you, Mike."

"Nonsense. As the lawyer said to you at the Inquiry, the harder you work the luckier you become." There was a pause. "Yes, actually I did hear a report on the accident. It sounds a very interesting case. You know these crashes which end up in the sea are always very tricky to sort out." Mike smiled. "Especially in the Bermuda Triangle. You know it is strange how many aircraft have disappeared round there." He paused again. "I expect St. Antony will be safe enough but leave me a contact number just in case. Anyway, I suppose I can always use your mobile number?"

I nodded and went on to explain my secretarial requirements and as I had hoped, Mike offered to help. He rang up the firm that provided secretaries to CrossLink Insurance and wrote down the four or five firms they suggested to him which provided the type of support I needed. He gave me the list and I decided to start inspecting them straightaway. Being an optimist I wondered if I would be able to choose one immediately, so that I could start using one of their offices to ring Bob Furness at AAIB.

Before leaving Mike I asked him about West Atlantic Airways. He got out a reference book and looked through some of his own notes.

"It seems a good airline and has been operating for over 20 years. As you know they use Hull Claims Insurance who are a first class firm but, like most companies these days, they won't pay up if there is the slightest transgression with the conditions in the policy. They had to pay for the one that crashed in St. Antony before and understandably they don't want to pay for another one. Airlines need to be absolutely meticulous with their paperwork and so there had better not be anything wrong with WAA's. Anyway, John Southern is the guy you need to talk to at Hull Claims. I'm sure he'll know what is going on. By the way Peter, do you know if they've found any wreckage yet?" He was obviously very interested in the accident.

"I've no idea. I'm going to sort out my office situation right now and then ring up Bob Furness to hear what he knows so far. Apparently AAIB have sent two people out to investigate. By the way, can I really approach Hull Claims Insurance, bearing in mind that, thanks to me, they will probably have to fork out a lot of money to RWA instead of your firm?"

"Of course you can. It's going to take a very long time before it is decided who pays and when. I'm sure John will talk to you, Peter. You forget that you are now a significant player in the aviation insurance scene. They won't be surprised at all to find you are being retained by WAA."

Mike gave me Southern's number and I left to go down the Strand to the first address he had given me. It did not have a very impressive interior and the entrance was down a not very salubrious side street. I had a job finding the next place down a small passage near the Law Courts and I didn't like the look of it. The third address was near the river in Farringdon Street, the Drake Williams agency, and it had the right feel straightaway. I saw the lady in charge of the organisation, Daphne Williams, and she showed me one of the rooms, the other four were being used. The reception looked efficient and we spent some time in her office discussing what I would need and she gave me some costings, which made my eyes water a bit. However, there did not seem to be much alternative if I was going to be travelling the world and having to keep things under control at home at the same time. She produced the papers for me to sign and asked me to commit to using them for two years with one year's notice but I didn't want that. She settled for one year and thereafter six months notice and we were on our way. Mandy had forecast that finding a suitable office would take a day or so but it had only taken a morning. Mind you, Mandy would probably have spent at least half a day poring over the legal agreement. I went into the empty room and called Bob Furness.

"Peter, how can I help you? The Sunday papers had a field day over the Inquiry as I am sure you noticed. You did alright but I got a caning, which I suppose I deserved in the circumstances."

It had been unfortunate, but the accident inspector Bob had put in charge of the RWA investigation had not done the job properly; he had been in financial trouble through gambling and had sold information to the press. Bob should have spotted what was going on. The inspector finally committed suicide which was an appalling tragedy for his family.

"Bob, I believe you're investigating the West Atlantic Airways missing European Aerospace 412?"

"Yes, Peter we are. The aircraft was registered in St. Antony and the St. Antony Government called the Foreign Office for help. It's been agreed that we're in charge of the investigation though I don't know who's going to pay for it. My budget can't stand it without some help, that's for sure. Anyway what's your interest?"

"Well, Frank Westbourne called me on Sunday morning and asked me to help them. I was going to rush out there but it occurred to me that I could get a lot of the background from you and from the insurance company. Would you mind bringing me up to date?"

"Not a bit. The aircraft, registration VP-WAL, was flying to Bermuda with a full load of freight, just two passengers and two crew. It took off at 6.30 local time on Friday night and the flight should have taken two and a half hours but it never arrived.

"Apparently the aircraft left St. Antony Approach frequency, called San Juan Oceanic and, for all practical purposes the flight seemed entirely normal. Of course there is no radar coverage for the flight out over the water but the automatic satellite position reporting, you know ADS, was quite normal showing the aircraft right on track. It was transferred to New York Oceanic and they too were receiving the ADS position reports showing the aircraft to be on the correct track. However, when the aircraft was about 180 miles out from Bermuda the ground radar could not see it, nor could Bermuda Approach talk to the pilots. The Bermuda controller called New York and asked them to check with the aircraft. Meanwhile the pilot seemed to be getting very worried. He remarked that they were flying into some very heavy weather and he could not see the island on the weather radar. After another fifteen minutes the crew were clearly becoming extremely concerned. They could not talk to Bermuda on the VHF radio, only by satellite to New York Oceanic and, apparently, the crew were having the greatest difficulty, flying in a storm with lots of lightning and severe turbulence. The aircraft was obviously lost even though, incredibly, its automatic position reports showed that it was just south of Bermuda where the weather was good. Suddenly all voice communication with New York ceased and no further ADS position reports were received. I sent Jack Wellings out there with Brian Fletcher, our avionics specialist yesterday. What I've just told you I got from them late last night."

"Bob, has there been wreckage anywhere?"

"No not yet, but it's early days. The Atlantic is so vast. Luckily the US Navy had a search aircraft at Kindley Field, Bermuda and they sent it out on Saturday and Sunday but nothing has been seen. Two Nimrods from Kinloss started searching on Sunday, so far without success. It looks as if the aircraft went straight in without trace. The wreckage is bound to start coming in soon, it always does. You know, seat cushions, dinghies, the odd life jacket, floating material and bodies."

"But Bob, the whole thing sounds ridiculous. You say the aircraft flew in a straight line to Bermuda but when it was nearly there, it wasn't there at all but somewhere else in the middle of the Atlantic? What was the total weather situation in the area?"

"Ah, that's an interesting question. There was this very unseasonal tropical storm. It had moved west from Africa to the Leeward Islands in the Caribbean south of Dominica, then veered north to go west of St. Antony and finally tracked north and east so that it was forecast to be east of Bermuda, Category 1, at the time they were due to land. The Miami weather men named the storm Angela being the first of the season. The winds were well over 100 mph as Angela started going north but were said to be just under a 100 mph at the time the aircraft disappeared. There seemed to be extensive associated storms swirling round the centre. The whole area was overcast with high cloud.

"Had the aircraft been on track there wouldn't have been any problem. However, they must have flown straight into the storm, goodness knows how. To be honest Peter, we have no clues at all at the moment. It just doesn't make sense. If the aircraft was flying in the wrong direction why did the position reports show it was on track? By the way, there is something else worrying us."

"About the aircraft?"

"Well about the European 412. It's a fly-by-wire aircraft of course, no control runs to the flying controls, just electrical signalling from the front of the aircraft to the control motors. It's a well proven system now, on civil as well military aircraft. All the latest Airbus aircraft, the Boeing 777 and the Independant 798 are fly-by-wire. However, the 412, like the 798, has gone for optical fibre connections instead of wires to carry the signals from the pilot to the control surfaces and we are concerned technically. It should be perfectly alright, in fact safer than using wires because it should be less prone to electrical interference but, nevertheless, it's a new development and so we have to be extra sure that it's not a factor in this accident."

"Who have you spoken to?"

"So far just the Safety Regulation Group of the Civil Aviation Authority at Gatwick. As you would expect they're very concerned. But you have to remember they only rubber stamped the certificate of airworthiness. It was certificated by a team from the European Aviation Safety Agency. We'll just have to see what transpires during the investigation. We really need the accident recorders at the very least to see what happened."

"That's going to be quite difficult isn't it, Bob?"

"Well I feel this accident is so important in view of the possible design implications that we just have to try to find the two recorders and, hopefully, the aircraft. The technology of searching the sea bed for wrecks has improved significantly in recent years, as you know, so we have authorised the firm that advises us in these matters, World Underwater Surveys Ltd. to get quotations and time scales to start searching. Nowadays there is a much better chance of finding the aircraft because accident data recorders have to carry sonar beacons which give the searching vessels a real chance to hear the noise from the beacon if they can get in the search area quickly."

"Why don't they have some means to make the recorders float as they do on the North Sea Helicopters? That would really solve the whole thing."

"The problem about that is that there would have to be some ejection mechanism to release the recorder when it hits the water and that would mean all the world's transport aircraft would be flying around with an ejection device which might go off when it shouldn't and damage the aircraft. It could cause more accidents than it would save. I believe that there is some work going on trying to ensure the recorders do leave the aircraft and float if an aircraft crashes into the sea but that's way in the future."

"Surely it is still very difficult to find a crashed aircraft, even with a beacon? The chances are that it will have split into small fragments when it hit the water, unless it was ditched, so it will be virtually an impossible task. How on earth can you hope to find anything?"

"I agree it is a long shot to find the recorders and hull but we have to try. Remember, if we can just find one of the recorders we should be able to make some progress in the accident investigation. Of course finding the recorders is only half the battle, we still have to recover them and that's where World Underwater Surveys come in. They advise us of the best way of getting hold of them. You appreciate that finding and getting the recorders is a battle against time?"

"Not exactly, I've never really thought about the problem before."

"Well the sonar beacons on the recorders can't go on transmitting for ever. They can only last for about a month and so if we don't find and recover them quickly the chances of ever getting them back are small. In the specific case of this European 412, I've authorised World Underwater Surveys to send a man out to Bermuda straightaway to help in the search and, of course, to decide what is really needed to actually recover the recorders and, hopefully, to find the aircraft. There is a frigate in Bermuda, HMS Broadside, which has a hydrophone on board tuned to the right frequency to hear the sonar beacon; it should be able to find the recorders providing they are not too deep. Trouble is that if the aircraft is in deep water it's still like finding a needle in a haystack even with a beacon. Unfortunately the hydrophone has to be towed because the acoustic noise from the ship itself drowns the crash recorder signal and the hydrophone can only be towed very slowly, 4 knots maximum, so searching for a beacon is a very slow business and the deeper the beacon, the closer the search tracks have to be. To be honest the success rates of these sonar beacons transmitting in emergencies have not been as good as we would like."

"Can't the Nimrod drop a hydrophone or even two in order to pinpoint the exact position of the recorder?"

"Yes Peter, it can. But it comes back to knowing roughly where the aircraft crashed so that the hydrophone will be able to hear the beacon. Unless some fairly exact position of the crash is known the Nimrod will run out of hydrophones before the beacon is heard."

Bob carried on.

"Now, what our Navy has done, very sensibly, is to set up an operations room in Bermuda. The whole area being searched is being controlled from this ops. room which is coordinating all the search operation, that is the US Navy aircraft, the Nimrods and, of course, the frigate. The problem Peter is where to ask the frigate to start searching. Should we believe the ADS or the weather people?"

"I would have thought you would have believed the weather people but I agree it's a real problem."

"That's my view also. The Nimrods are already searching in that area and the US Navy aircraft is tracking out south of Bermuda believing the ADS. We've got to get a lead quickly from the sonar beacons or from some wreckage or we'll never find the aircraft and the recorders. Things are made much worse in the Atlantic because of the depth and the weather. Operating a search which must, of course, be very accurate from an underwater navigational point of view, rapidly gets impossible if the weather deteriorates. If we have to resort to a towfish or a Remote Observation Vehicle, good weather becomes even more important."

"What on earth is a towfish?"

"It's a device, which as it name implies, is towed through the water by a search ship and uses sidescan sonar to survey the sea bed so that the operator on the surface can see the terrain of the sea bed and, possibly, the shape of the crashed aircraft. Of course the data from the towfish is only an indication. If we thought we had spotted an aircraft we would have to use a TV camera to check one way or the other. Hopefully, we won't have to use a towfish but just a hydrophone to hear the recorders. That's where World Underwater Surveys come in. They advise us what we need in the current situation. Once the accident data recorders have been 'heard' I would expect them to recommend a ship which has a Remote Observation Vehicle, ROV, with TV and the necessary underwater lifting gear to recover the recorders and also relatively large pieces of wreckage. Of course the ship would also carry a towfish in case it's needed. One of the problems in our work is that when we need a ship and equipment, we need it immediately and there are only a limited number of ships in the world that can do this work and they are normally on long term contract work. We keep portable hydrophone equipment at Farnborough and Jack Wellings took one set out with him but luckily it isn't needed immediately in Bermuda because of the Navy."

"Can't you use a manned submersible for the search, Bob?"

"Not really. It's true that in deep water the submersible is not affected by the weather but the endurance of the vehicle is very short and it has to be supported by a surface vehicle. Remember, accurate knowledge of position is vital and you can't use satellite navigation underwater."

"But then how do the submersibles manage to navigate, or the towfish for that matter?"

"Well the submarines are able to navigate for short distances on their own internal equipment but the accuracy soon degrades, so really it's a combination of the ship's position plus 'pinging' the towfish or the submersible with directional sonar from the ship so that the position of the underwater searching device can be calculated. Thank goodness for global positioning systems; in the past the positions depended on how good the ship's navigation officer was."

"Well Bob, let's hope someone finds the beacon very soon so that there's a chance to make the recovery."

"You and me both. I shall be very interested to see what World Underwater Surveys advise."

"Surely they're going to advise searching whatever the difficulty, because they get a percentage of the contract?"

"If we thought that we wouldn't have given them the contract to advise us. They're meticulous and always justify their advice in great detail. If they think we will be wasting our time they will say so. By the way, you do know that WAA lost another European a few months ago?"

"So I believe. What happened there?"

"Oh, that was a clear cut case of flying too low, trying to fly visually in bad weather. They lost forty passengers and four crew. We did the investigation on that accident as well. It was very sad. In fact we have only just issued the report. Would you like me to send you a copy?"

"Please. That would be great." I gave Bob the address of my new office. We chatted for a few more minutes but Bob was not able to add anything new.

"Bob, I plan to go out in a few days. Could you let your people know I'm coming and hopefully we will be able to exchange information?"

"No problem there. I'll tell them to expect you. They've got an office on the airfield and I'm sure Frank Westbourne will be able to take you round and make the introductions."

Daphne Williams put her head round the door just as I put the phone down.

"Can we get you anything? Coffee? How about a sandwich? We are getting an order together now."

It sounded good to me and I placed my order.

"Could you do something else for me? Could you ring Kelvin Hughes at Hainault and get them to send me, by first class post to-day to my home, two charts of Bermuda, one for the whole island and one for the east end? They don't have to be fully corrected. Would you also contact Jeppeson Sanderson either in Englewood Colorado or Germany and get them to send me c/o Frank Westbourne, West Atlantic Airways, Nelson Airport in St. Antony, Leeward Islands a complete aerial chart coverage of Latin America and the Caribbean, I think they call it a trip kit, they used to when I was a boy anyway. See if they can also send me a 1/1,000,000 aeronautical topographical map coverage for the area. If they can't, I'm sure they will be able to tell you where you can get them. They're probably obtainable over here even though they are US Government Charts but I'm not sure where."

This was better than being alone at home. I decided to call Frank Westbourne in St. Antony. He had just got in to the office. I told him what I was doing and that I would now be arriving in St. Antony on Thursday. Apparently the aircraft were still searching but there was no sign of any wreckage.

"Frank, have you alerted shipping to keep a look out for wreckage?"

"Well I've asked the people in London at Lloyds to send out an alert bulletin. There's just got to be some wreckage sometime."

"OK. I'll call you soon with my flight details."

One of the girls in the office appeared with my sandwich order and some coffee. I called Hull Claims and asked for John Southern.

"Mr. Southern, we haven't met. My name is Peter Talbert and I'm acting for West Atlantic Airways."

"Hello Mr. Talbert. Your name and face are, of course, well known to me because I was at the Inquiry two months ago when you were explaining why, in your opinion, the RWA accident was not pilot error. As you well know, you may have caused the insurance claims to move from CrossLink towards my company. Of course there is a lot of water to flow under that bridge yet. Anyway let's leave that to one side. How can I help you?"

"Frank Westbourne of WAA has asked me to try to assist him and before going out to Bermuda I thought it would be useful to have a chat."

"Fine, why don't you come round and see me? It's easier than talking over the phone."

We agreed to meet at his office in Mincing Lane. I called Mandy's office but she was busy and her secretary took a note of my new office number and address. I had plenty of time and the weather was bright, though cold, so I walked to Mincing Lane. Hull Claims Insurance was on the first floor. I gave my name to the man at the desk and sat down.

John Southern appeared and introduced himself. He was about sixty years old, thin, and he looked at me over stainless steel reading glasses.

"So Mr. Talbert, the RWA Inquiry's finally over?"

"Peter, please. Yes, thank goodness. Just as well as I plan to be in St. Antony on Wednesday or Thursday. What is your view of the situation out there?"

"Well Peter, the aircraft has clearly disappeared and must have gone into the sea somewhere. You know that this is the second loss of a WAA European Aerospace 412. We believe that the crew had some sort of system failure on the flight deck and that they had not been adequately trained to recognise the problem. We shall need a lot of convincing before we pay out. I shall be looking very carefully at their crew records."

"When are you going out?"

"I'm going out to New York this evening and will be in St. Antony to-morrow evening. We obviously rely on the AAIB to find the primary cause of the accident. The first one was clearly pilot error and I suspect the second one was as well, since they should have recognised the system failure."

"You may be right, John, but it is very strange that the position reports showed the aircraft being on course for Bermuda but the aircraft wasn't there. To put it more strongly, it's simply impossible. I just can't get my mind round the whole thing."

John reflected for a moment.

"Peter you may not want to answer this but surely the crew should have spotted that there was a problem?"

"Yes, I suppose we are on opposite sides but, as I am sure you appreciate, I only want to find out what actually happened. If it's pilot error, so be it. Anyway I can't answer your question, John. However, there's one obvious point. Have you considered that there could be something wrong with the aircraft, possibly a design fault?"

"That of course is always possible, but we have to rely on the certification authorities to validate the manufacturer's design and so far there's been no reason to doubt what has been done. The only new feature in the aircraft is the fibre optic cables to the control surface motors and we don't believe there's anything wrong there."

"John, we clearly need to understand a lot more about what happened. Of course it's bread and butter for the newspapers and the media to try to make everyone believe in the fantasy of the so called Bermuda Triangle. The whole thing seems mysterious, unbelievable, whatever word you like to use. The problem is that if we don't get some wreckage I don't believe we shall ever find out what happened. But of course finding wreckage won't be enough. What we really need are the accident data recorders and if we don't find them quickly then the chances of finding them become more and more remote. Bob Furness tells me he is getting their underwater search consultants to advise what is needed and when."

John looked at me quizzically.

"Frank is hoping that you will solve the mystery and hopefully persuade us to pay him for the aircraft, I suppose?"

"Yes, John, in a way I am sure he is. He naturally wants to be sure that his interests are considered. However, let me reassure you again, if the accident could have been avoided by the pilots then I would be the first to say so. In my view, this accident clearly has some unique features for which the crew may not have been specifically trained. The challenge for us is to find out what must have gone wrong and then judge whether the crew should have spotted the trouble and taken corrective action."

"Peter, I saw you in action at the RWA inquiry. I do understand your position otherwise I would not have invited you here. I'm more than happy to talk to you again if you feel inclined to keep in touch."

We talked some more about the accident and then I left, promising to call him from St. Antony with an update in a week or so. It looked as if he would have left St. Antony by the time I got out there, though he told me that he expected to be back again a week or so later. I wandered back slowly to Waterloo and went home to my house at Kingston, stopping to buy some essential supplies on the way. Everywhere was tidy except in my dining room/office because Dora, my help, was never allowed in there. I decided that that must be my job for the evening. However, there were ten messages on the answering machine and in fact there probably had been more callers because the machine's memory was full. It took me an hour dealing with them all. Most of the callers were in connection with the RWA accident and were still from the media, TV, newspapers, and magazines wanting interviews or articles. Articles I liked writing, but they always took me a lot longer to do than the editors expected and were willing to pay for.

I got myself a sandwich and started to sort out my office. The papers on the RWA accident needed filing and I had to start getting myself organised for the WAA investigation. I decided to call Kim Petersen in the South Eastern Region of the Federal Aviation Agency in Miami. We had met at one of the Society of Automotive Engineers S7 Flight Deck Committee meetings in Washington DC and I always kept a note of all attendees.

"Kim, Peter Talbert here. How are things with you?"

"Hello stranger. I've been reading all about you and the RWA accident inquiry. Congratulations. It seems you did a first class job. How can I help you? I take it you didn't call me just to have a chat."

"Quite right. It's about the loss of the aircraft on a cargo flight from St. Antony to Bermuda last Friday."

"You mean the European Aerospace 412? That's a strange business. The aircraft seems to have disappeared in a tropical storm yet its positions relayed via the satellite showed that it was near Bermuda. Weird. The papers have been full of it over here for the last few days. You can imagine, another modern day Bermuda Triangle mystery. Every expert for miles around has been interviewed. They must have made a fortune. Would you believe, they even had the head of the National Transportation Safety Board on the Larry King Live show even though the aircraft was not on the US register. They also had someone from your Air Accident Investigation Branch; they are doing the investigation, I believe. Anyway why are you interested?"

"Well, Frank Westbourne the managing director of the airline has asked me to help him to look after their interests during the investigation. I'm going to fly out on Wednesday but I thought it might be useful to call in at New York Center on the way out just to talk to the Oceanic controllers and hear their story. However, I don't know anyone there, so I'm asking for your help."

"I'll see what I can do. I know you realise that though the Air Traffic Centers are part of the Federal Aviation Agency, they're really a different firm. It's the same situation as you used to have in the UK when your National Air Traffic Services was part of the Civil Aviation Agency but were completely separate from your Safety Regulation Group. Of course you people have now, very sensibly, made NATS a separate entity though I'm not sure whether letting EASA, instead of SRG, certificate your new aircraft is such a good idea.

"Anyway I need to call a few people and find out who you need to talk to. Give me your phone number and email address and I'll try to get something to you before the end of our working day over here. I expect you want to be making some airline reservations."

"Absolutely right. By the way you said just now that the aircraft was lost in a tropical storm. Is that confirmed or just conjecture?"

"Just an educated guess Peter. We think he must have gone off on the wrong heading. Maybe he put the wrong waypoints in to the Flight Management Systems. Certainly from the weather he reported he must have been in Angela, there were no other storms about."

"Well I suppose you're right but I'm not convinced it was an elementary mistake. It's not possible to go 25° off course without noticing, particularly as the aircraft was giving position reports by satellite to New York Oceanic using ADS. Anyway thanks so much Kim. I'll wait to hear from you."

The phone rang the moment we had finished. It was Mandy.

"I'm just leaving the office. How are things with you? I gather you've got a secretarial agency."

"Yes. Thanks to Mike I managed to get organised quite quickly though I suppose I should have got you to go through the agreement before signing."

"Possibly, Peter. Luckily these agreements are pretty standard so it should be alright. If the people and the office looked normal with plenty of people about, the chances are that you are not going to be ripped off. Did you talk to Bob Furness? How was he?"

"He was very fair and very helpful. I think he told me all he knew."

"Did you talk to the insurers?"

"Yes. That worked out quite well though, of course, the accident is a complete mystery. He invited me round for a chat. Hull Claims feels that the pilots should have spotted that something was going wrong and that it was bad training, bearing in mind that they had a pilot error accident in St. Antony not very long back. They are not about to pay out in a hurry. Their guy John Southern is going to New York to-night and will be in St. Antony to-morrow."

"What are you going to do? Shouldn't you be there before him?"

"Yes you're right. But it's impossible as you know." She had a good point but there was nothing I could do about it. I would be able to look at the documents and training later in the week. "Anyway, I'm trying to visit the FAA ATC Oceanic Control Center in New York on the way out to hear their side of the story. I want to see the whole flight if they have the records. It seems so strange. Southern has too narrow a focus."

"Well you can explain it to me when we meet. When is that going to be, my darling?"

"I'm not sure. I'm trying to go on Wednesday but I can't make any reservations until I hear from my man in Miami. I certainly won't go before then. What are you doing to-morrow night?" There was a pause. "Surely you're diary's not that full?"

"Well I'm going out to dinner in London, possibly going to see a show, with a very handsome man and if he behaves himself, and especially if he doesn't, I might agree to stay the night with him."

"That's a shame because I was going to suggest an early dinner at Rules and then go and see the latest Lloyd Webber musical. I'll just have to find someone else."

Rules in Maiden Lane was one of my favourite restaurants, convenient for the London theatres, and was rapidly becoming one of Mandy's favourites as well.

"Well, if you were to press me I might be tempted and forego going out with the handsome man."

"I don't want to deprive you of your romantic evening."

"You've talked me into it. But it is going to be tight. What time do we have to be at Rules for their special deal?"

"We have to order by six o'clock. If you tell me what you are going to have right now, I can order for you if you're late."

"You can make the decisions for me, haddock soufflé and rack of lamb well cooked."

"That's really strange. That's just what I was going to order for you."

"You can always read my mind if I want you to." She came back to earth. "What are you going to do to-morrow?"

"I'm not sure. Hopefully I will be able to sort out my flights in the afternoon. I'll catch up with some reports I have to write and possibly find time for some reading.. There's a pile of periodicals two feet high which I must look at."

"Alright my love. I'll see you to-morrow. Bye."

It was only half past seven. I called the booking agency straightaway and booked a box. I had never done that before but then I had never had so much money in my bank account. I knew I needed to get some advice fairly soon on what to do with it. I called Rules and made a reservation. It was touch and go apparently, but they fitted us in. I did a bit of filing and then took some magazines into the front room to make a start with the reading. After about an hour Kim Petersen came on the line.

"Peter, I've made some progress. You need to ring the supervisor at New York Center and explain what you want. New York Oceanic is co-located with New York Center at Ronkonkoma on Long Island. Oceanic have got a room on the side of the main building apparently. I've had a word with him and told him a little about you. His name is Jack Maynes. There shouldn't be too much of a problem getting what you want as they made up a special tape from their records immediately after the accident occurred. Jack just needs to be assured that you have a genuine need to look at the data."

Kim gave me Jack Maynes telephone number. I thanked him and then called the number. Jack Maynes answered the phone himself and I introduced myself.

"Well Peter, Kim Petersen told me about you but I'm not quite clear why you are so interested."

"I've been retained by West Atlantic Airways to help them find the cause of the loss of their European Aerospace 412, tail number VP-WAL. There is a problem over the insurance and they want to do everything they can to find out what went wrong. As you will appreciate, the accident seems remarkable to say the least and I would find it very helpful before going to St. Antony to see the aircraft's track according to the ADS reports."

"Fine Peter, I now know exactly what you want. Kim tells me you are planning on travelling Wednesday. Do you want to come in when you arrive or the following morning?"

"Well I would like to try to catch up with what is going on as soon as possible. Could I come in about 5 o'clock? Where exactly are you located? Will it take a long time to get there?"

"You know Peter, the traffic about then is horrendous. By the time you have got through immigration, collected your bags, been taken by bus to the rental compound, signed up for a rental car, found it, left the car park and got lost a couple of times, you are going to hit the rush hour traffic. I think you should plan on staying the night somewhere near our Center and come out at 8 o'clock in the morning." There was a pause. "Hey, I tell you what I'll do. I'll book you in at the Embassy Apartments near our place and meet you there at about 6.30 and we can go out for a meal. You should make 6.30 alright. Give me your email address and I'll confirm the reservation and location of the hotel. In case there is a problem I'll give you my home and mobile numbers and also my email address."

We exchanged details and I called British Airways. I booked on the flight that left 11 o'clock getting in to New York at 1 o'clock in the afternoon. The following day, Thursday, there was a non-stop British West Indian Airline flight out of New York in the afternoon at 2.15 scheduled to arrive in St. Antony that evening at 6.15 and I settled for that. I called Frank Westbourne and told him what I was doing and gave him my ETA.

"I'll make your hotel reservations and confirm them to you by email. I'll meet you off the plane and take you to the hotel. You can decide later whether you are brave enough to drive yourself in St. Antony. By the way there's still no news of any wreckage. I'd have thought we would have had some by now. Do you think you'll learn anything in New York?"

"I just don't know but it's something that has to be done. Are the AAIB planning to visit New York to have a look, do you know Frank?"

"I'm not sure. Shall I ask them?"

"No, leave it for a bit. This guy has agreed to show me everything. If AAIB want to join in it may suddenly get very formal. Looking forward to seeing you then on Thursday evening."

There was not much more I could do. Luckily I remembered that I had agreed with Steve Watson of United to do some training in Denver on the Independant 798. He was in his office when I called him and I explained the situation; we agreed that I would be with him the following Friday. I reckoned that by then I would be well and truly started in St. Antony and I could return there after I had been to United. I finished tidying up my room, watched the 10.30 news on Channel 2 and went to bed. I thought of Mandy, presumably in bed in Bournemouth, of Liz, the girl in Australia who helped me solve the 798 accident and Diana, somewhere in the States. Life was always full of choices and, for better or for worse, we were always responsible for the logical consequences of the choices we made.

***

Tuesday morning was a fine clear day and about 15°C, a wonderful late spring day. Dora came on Tuesdays and Wednesdays, and she was full of the Inquiry and the part I had played. She was a regular at the Fox and Hounds near where she lived in Surbiton and there was clearly a flourishing debating society there. Dora at the moment must be taking a leading part as a vicarious reporter of front page news. I tried to stop her conversation and get her working but it wasn't easy and took the best part of twenty minutes. I didn't want to upset her since she did such a super job when I wasn't there.

I went to the shops briefly and bought a few things for Mandy's breakfast the following morning. I called Mike to find out where to get some financial advice but his secretary told me he had had to go out to the airport and would not be in until the afternoon. I got out the recent issues of Flight and Aviation Week. The 412 accident had happened after the magazines had gone to press but there was plenty about the RWA Accident Inquiry final report. My name appeared in the headlines together with some old photos.

I got out the papers that might be needed in St. Antony. There was an article about the electronics on the European Aerospace 412 which I wanted to re-read in detail on the flight out to New York. It was a very modern design but not in anyway unusual. The Flight Management System used twin Flight Management Computers for controlling the auto-pilot and the pilots' displays using the information supplied by triple inertial laser platforms and two satellite receivers, one for the United States Global Positioning System, GPS, and one for the European satellite system, Galileo European Satellite System, GESS. The FMS had the necessary software to enable automatic satellite position reporting. Typically European in design as well as in name, it had side stick controllers for the pilots but, unlike Airbus aircraft, the throttles moved under auto-throttle control, which most Airbus engineers privately admitted was much better and safer than having them fixed when the automatics changed the engine settings.

The day seemed to race by writing reports, reading and tidying up; Mandy was going to be very pleased with my office. By the time I had finished it was time to go and meet her. Everything was put away with no papers lying about. In addition I had got all my clothes ready for my trip. It would be hot in St. Antony, cold in Denver, temperate in New York, and wet in Bermuda. This meant that unfortunately it was going to be necessary to take a larger case than I really wanted, to be able to accommodate all the clothes I needed for the different weather conditions.

I decided to leave the car in the road near Kingston station and was soon at Waterloo. There was enough time to take a cab to Foyles in Charing Cross Road and look at the books about the Bermuda Triangle. They all looked pretty specious to me but I managed to find one that brought some critical analysis to the proceedings. I still had enough time to walk to Rules though I was glad of my coat and gloves. As I went down Long Acre I spotted Stanfords, the map people, and on impulse went in to see if they had the topographical charts I wanted. Ten minutes later I left with the ten ONC charts I needed and a receipt for nearly £100 to show to Frank. I used my mobile and left a message at my office that I had got the maps. It was twenty minutes to six and I went straight to the table. I chose a good bottle of Australian Chardonnay and ordered our meal. Mandy appeared in a warm looking royal blue jersey dress just before six. She had been working hard and started to relax. The meal was excellent and timed to perfection.

Our coats were produced as if by magic and we walked to the theatre, arriving with fifteen minutes to spare, time enough to check in our coats, my maps and Mandy's overnight bag in the cloakroom. She nearly took-off when she realised that we were going to be in a private box by ourselves. It didn't do any harm either when she saw the champagne on ice in its stand with two glasses on a table, and a spray of red roses on one of the seats. She made it very plain throughout the evening that she liked being spoilt. I clearly had got something right. The musical was super and we left to go home on an emotional and sexual high. We got a cab to the station and I mentally congratulated myself on having decided to use the car at the other end and not walk. Mandy made driving even harder by doing things which I rather liked but I wasn't sure her mother would approve of. We managed to get home and, after a very short discussion, decided that we would retire to bed. Later, as I was lying next to her and starting to go to sleep Mandy whispered my name.

"When am I going to see you again?"

"When you turn the light on. We've got the whole night ahead of us."

"Only for sleeping. You're not much company now that you've had your way with me."

"I didn't notice you holding back."

"Nice men don't mention these things." She wriggled next to me and I shelved my sleeping plans for a few seconds.

"Peter, you never answered my question, when do I see you next?"

"Well I suppose I could be back at the end of next week but the whole thing is very difficult to call. I can't contemplate coming home until I've got some idea of what happened. The moment there is any glimmer of light I'll call you."

All was quiet for a few seconds.

"Alright, you win, we'd better get some sleep. I've got to work in the morning instead of lounging in luxury in an aircraft being waited on by glamorous stewardesses."

"I always get the stewards."

"Don't give me that. I remember that girl who drooled over you all the way back from Seattle."

That was the problem with lawyers, they had such good memories.

CHAPTER 2

'From a small boat that row'd along
The listening winds received this song'

The alarm went off at 6.15. I was down first and we had a light breakfast of orange juice, toast and coffee and then I took Mandy to the station.

"I'll keep in touch, darling. Look after yourself."

"I don't think I want to look after myself any more. I'm counting on some handsome and thoughtful man doing that."

"Not him again. You'll have to put up with me."

"We'll see. Don't bet on it. You had better hurry back or there may be somebody else."

I held her for a long moment and then she backed away, took her case from me and I watched her going speedily into the station. Back home I tidied up, finished packing my bag, drove to the airport and to the valet parking at terminal 5. British Airways had the tickets waiting for me at the desk and I chose an aisle seat. I bought the FT, the Telegraph and the latest best seller, then went through into the executive club lounge. I poured myself some coffee but only just managed to drink it as the man at the check in desk told me that the flight was about to be called. As usual the departure gate was at the opposite end of the terminal from the lounge and it took a bad ten minutes to get there. We loaded quickly and I put all the periodicals and papers I needed to read in the pocket in front of me. The aircraft was a Boeing 747-400 and was quite full in business class so once more British Airways would be making a lot of money, since there was still no real competition on the New York route. However, for a change there was no-one in the seat next to me so I could put my immediate requirements on the empty seat.

We left the ramp spot on time though it took another fifteen minutes threading our way along the taxi tracks and avoiding other aircraft before we got airborne. The captain announced that the flight time would be seven hours ten minutes and that we should be arriving on schedule. I got my newspapers out and spotted the word Bermuda as I was going through the FT. Normally it would not have registered beyond my subconscious but the human brain is remarkable and my peripheral vision had clearly been alerted to add Bermuda and St. Antony to my warning systems. The article was very relevant as it was about the Paragon Corporation, registered in Bermuda. Apparently there had been a lot of activity with the shares in the stock markets. For some reason best known to the stock market, the loss of the paintings on the way to Bermuda had made investors even more nervous. Jimmy Morrison was mentioned and it seemed as if he had been buying shares as fast as some shareholders had been unloading their holdings. I tore the article out and put it in my bag as a matter of routine.

The Telegraph mentioned the loss of the 412 and discussed the possible causes of the accident from pilot error to faulty design with a specific mention of the optic fibre signalling system to the flying controls. The fact that AAIB had been asked to help also got a mention. I put the article with the Paragon cutting.

We went through the ritual of drinks and lunch which I always found rather tedious. However, I passed the time skimming through the book on the Bermuda Triangle that I had bought. Though I regarded some of it as pure bunkum, like being captured by aliens, I was taken with the frequently repeated message that no traces were ever found of the aircraft or ships that had disappeared. I put the book down as I felt that I needed to try to observe the operation of the current satellite reporting system, Automatic Dependent Surveillance or ADS as it was known by the world's aerospace community. The aircraft was steady at its cruising altitude and the work load on the crew would have subsided so I asked the steward to take my card up to the Captain, though I knew, from security considerations, that it was most unlikely that I would be allowed in. To my surprise the steward was back almost straightaway accompanied by a first Officer who introduced himself.

"Hi, Peter." He had obviously been looking at my card. "I'm Jim Sanderson. I'm deadheading to New York. You were involved with the Royal World Airways accident, weren't you?" I nodded. "Sorry we can't get you onto the Flight Deck but, as I'm sure you know, it's not allowed these days."

"Yes Jim, I did know though I thought I would just check nothing had changed. I'm off to St. Antony to see West Atlantic Airways about that European Aerospace 412 they lost."

"So you're involved with that case? It's a strange business. I gather the ADS plot showed that the aircraft got to about 100 miles short of Bermuda before it disappeared."

I moved over and Jim sat down.

"Yes, that's what I understand. That's why I'm on this flight instead of going straight to St. Antony. I'm visiting New York Oceanic to look at the plot history before going on to St. Antony."

Sanderson nodded approvingly.

"That seems a really smart idea."

"ADS wasn't around when I was flying so if I had been able to go onto the flight deck it would have been a good opportunity to see the installation actually working rather than sitting in a simulator."

"Well on this aircraft and a lot of the older Boeing 747s the ADS system was retrofitted when the passenger skyphone telephone system and the internet connection were installed. Two satellite transmitter receiver antennas were fitted on the top of the fuselage and in fact the ADS installation was a very small part of the hardware modification. The twin flight management computers had the software changed so that the aircraft's position plus it's altitude, the next waypoint, and other data is made available for the aircraft's satellite VHF transmitters and, incidentally, for the transponder to transmit whenever it is interrogated. The satellite data is sent to the nearest INMARSAT geostationary satellite which, in turn, then transmits the data into the Air Traffic Control communication network via a suitable satellite ground station. The result is that the controller sees the aircraft on his display, which looks very like a conventional secondary radar plot with an annotated box next to each aircraft showing call sign, aircraft altitude, speed, heading and next waypoint. However, obviously the data is not bang up to date due to delays in the communication system, quite apart from the fact that the transmissions are not continuous."

"Does the pilot have any control over what is transmitted, Jim?"

"A little but not much. The way it works is that a position report is sent once every 10 minutes, or maybe 5 minutes, the frequency being controlled by the ATC Center. However, if there is some sort of emergency or an air traffic problem then the air traffic controller or the pilots can select a higher reporting speed. There is a switch for this on the satellite control box which also enables the aircraft to send a test transmission. There are probably some additional refinements on controlling the reporting speed by selecting the correct pages on the Control and Display Unit but to be honest I'm not sure of the exact details. As you are particularly aware with your job, there are far too many pages on the Control and Display Unit which don't affect the safety of flight. Our trainers warn the pilots not to spend too much time looking at these non-essential pages and concentrate instead on flying the aircraft."

"I agree. The ADS should be transparent to the users, though I suppose it needs checking occasionally."

"Not really. The equipment is very reliable and Air Traffic tell us soon enough if it doesn't work."

I thought about West Atlantic Airways and their European 412. The ADS was so simple that what had happened to the aircraft didn't make sense.

The Final Flight

"The WAA aircraft must have been approaching Bermuda. Why couldn't the pilots contact Air Traffic? The thing's a complete mystery. How could anything have gone wrong?"

"Don't ask me Peter. That's what you have to discover." He paused and then smiled at me. "Meanwhile I think I'll try to avoid flying to Miami on southerly tracks passing over Bermuda. There may be some truth about flying in the Bermuda Triangle after all."

"I know you don't really believe that rubbish. The real danger in the area comes in the tropical season from the weather, not from some indeterminate being with a voracious appetite for unwary travellers. Mind you, what a storm as active as Angela was doing as early as May we shall never know. I hope Global Warming is not making this sort of thing a pattern for the future."

"Well the weather certainly seems to have caught that European 412 one way or another. It really was rotten luck."

We chatted about other things and then Jim left to go back on the flight deck. I read a bit and then dozed for the next few hours. Looking out of the window I saw that we were flying down Long Island and then, just for a moment, I saw New York skyscrapers on the horizon as we approached the airport and gradually got lower. I heard the flaps going down followed by the gear as we crossed the coast and started the final approach. We touched down smoothly and the aircraft slowed down quickly as reverse thrust was applied. For once we were lucky and we exited just by the end of the passenger terminal area and were soon on our stand. I disembarked just after the first class passengers. It was the normal, seemingly endless walk to immigration and my bag with its computer seemed to get heavier all the time. The air conditioning was a bit too warm for my taste and I felt rather uncomfortable by the time I got to the hall, having overtaken most of the first class passengers. There was barely any wait for the baggage and I was through immigration and customs very quickly. That was one nice thing about travelling with British Airways, it had its own terminal at Kennedy, not like some places where the immigration lines could take a very long time.

I went outside and had a longer wait than usual for the Avis bus which took renters to the rental car parking area. In the office there was the normal line to get to the agents renting the cars. I had a discussion with the lady who served me about the punitive cost of insuring the car and made my normal note to myself, which I always forgot to action when I got home, to find out how much of the insurance price is really agent's commission. It was a great relief to drive out of the parking lot and get onto the highway. The traffic was every bit as heavy as Jack Maynes had forecast and it was clearly a good decision to meet for dinner rather than go straight to the office. Everybody seemed to be going to

New York City on 678 and things were no better when I turned east on 495 since every truck and car for miles around seemed to be going up Long Island. As usual, the road was being fixed and it took me about an hour and three quarters to do the fifty miles to Ronkonkoma and the freeway exit for the motel. I finally got to the Embassy Apartments and checked in.

There was no particular hurry so long as I kept moving. I unpacked my clothes and had a shower, putting on a clean shirt and decided to wear the trousers and blazer I had worn travelling out. I hoped that we weren't going to some up-market restaurant. There was a safe in the room and I locked some of my money and valuables away. Even with a safe I never liked to put all my eggs in one basket. I switched on my computer and saw that there was a wireless connection to the internet. I selected Skype, punched in the numbers, and called Frank.

"Frank. I'm in New York. Any news?"

"Not really. The Royal Navy frigate is on station and has started searching for the aircraft's accident recorders. We've still got no wreckage. It's bound to appear soon. I suppose the real problem is that we're not certain they're looking in the right place. Anyway I'll tell you all about it when you get in."

"Good, let's hope they can find the recorders. I'm going out now with the FAA man and look forward to seeing you to-morrow evening at 6.15 off the BWIA flight."

The phone rang the moment I replaced the receiver.

"Peter, it's Jack Maynes here. I'm down in the lobby."

"Fine. I'll be right down."

Jack was about the same age as I was, mid-thirties, thin and about 6ft. 1in. He looked as if he might have been an athlete of some type at college. He had to be a high flyer to be in charge of the New York Center at his tender age. We introduced ourselves and he led the way out to his blue Taurus.

"I've made a reservation at The Green Orange. It's nothing special but I see you guessed correctly that they like their diners to wear jackets. They serve most things and the tables aren't too close together."

"That's fine by me, Jack. I'd meant to ask you where we were going."

We went on to the freeway for two exits and then turned inland somewhere. Jack turned off up a side road for about 50 yards and pulled in to the parking lot. There were a lot of cars there already which I always felt was a good sign providing one had a reservation. The girl who clearly was running the front of house welcomed Jack like a long lost friend and showed us to a table overlooking a large lake, the surface of which looked quite rough from the north westerly wind. She gave us the menus and waited for us to order our drinks; Jack ordered a screwdriver and I opted for scotch and water.

"Well, Peter. Are you going to be the guy who really solves the mystery of the Bermuda Triangle?"

"Jack, believe me I'd barely heard of the Bermuda Triangle until the other day. I have to say it sounds like complete garbage. There's always a logical explanation for mysteries and I'm sure that the disappearance of all these ships and aircraft in the area could have been explained if people had put their minds to it. I read a book on the way over which claims to be one of the more authoritative ones on the subject and it seems to me that, in many cases, the owners of the boat or aircraft quite clearly didn't want the truth to come out. In other words they had a vested interest; if 'their ship didn't come in' they could collect the insurance, like the Marie Celeste I reckon."

"Then you clearly don't vote with Hamlet, Peter?"

"What do you mean?"

"There are more things under heaven and earth than are dreamed of in your philosophy, Horatio."

"Jack, you're not serious are you? You don't really believe all the twaddle about the Triangle, do you?"

"It's all right, Peter, I'm just joking. But you know sometimes in the dark watches of the night I wonder whether it's worth contemplating for a moment if everything is ordered the way we have been taught."

"Yes, I do know what you mean. When I'm feeling too cocksure about something I try to remember Cromwell's advice to the General Assembly of the Church of Scotland, 'I beseech you, in the bowels of Christ, think it possible you may be mistaken'. Nevertheless, I normally work on the basis of his command to his troops, 'trust in God but keep your powder dry.' "

Luckily the girl returned with our drinks at that moment. We were drifting away from reality and common sense to an area where there were no rules and the imagination was in charge. I decided to bring the conversation back to reality, grabbed the menu and ordered grilled salmon. Jack went for a fillet steak and we both had a salad instead of french fries. By now Jack had obviously realised that my view on life was pragmatic rather than philosophical and changed gear. We raised our glasses.

"Cheers. I'm glad you called in here, Peter. This loss of the West Atlantic Airways European Aerospace 412 is really very strange. It's a case of now you see it, now you don't. If this thing had happened twenty or even ten years ago before ADS was available, everybody would have said that the aircraft had headed off in the wrong direction, got into a severe storm, lost control and perished. What's wrong with that explanation to-day?"

"You know perfectly well the problem, Jack. Your people say that the ADS showed the aircraft was approaching Bermuda and it's difficult therefore to believe that this was not the case. I've never heard of an ADS giving the wrong position. The data from each flight management computer on the aircraft is checked with the other one and if there is no discrepancy the position is put in to the buffer and then transmitted to you people. I'm looking forward to hearing the tape of the satellite communications between your controller and the crew. Surely there must be something we can learn from that?"

"Yes, you need to listen to the tape. The crew were getting really worried towards the end. The weather they were flying in was clearly very unnerving. If you would like I can get you a complete copy of the satellite communication tape to take away. You're obviously aware that normally we only have the communication for our sector, New York Oceanic. However, I got San Juan to send us their tape and we have put the two parts together so that you can play the whole flight at your leisure. You can have a transcript as well with the time of each transmission. In fact because the radios were so clear, unusually there was no problem at all producing the transcript. I have to say the hairs rose on the back of my neck when I listened to the actual conversations. Knowing what we do, we can appreciate the whole terrible situation."

"What about the ADS? Nothing unusual at all?"

"Nothing. In this case we received all the ADS reports from the aircraft from the moment it left St. Antony though, of course, at the time we only showed the positions on our screen as the aircraft approached our sector north of 23° 30'N. Its track was a very good straight line from St. Antony until it approached Bermuda. I'll be able to let you have a picture with the whole track very accurately plotted. The position was sent every 10 minutes increasing to every 5 minutes in New York airspace after PISAX. When the aircraft reported that it was in difficulties the pilot apparently switched the ADS to emergency mode as the reports came in every 90 seconds or so. We've put all the reporting points on a chart so that you can see the aircraft plots. You'll notice that when the aircraft was about 280 miles from Bermuda, right on the planned track, the plot started to weave on either side of the line. The aircraft was apparently negotiating its way through thunder clouds which therefore explains why the plot is a bit sinusoidal but nothing very unusual, no large deviations from the flight plan."

"Well, I guess I'll have to wait until to-morrow. By the way the airline boss, Frank Westbourne, tells me that the underwater search has started. We need to find the recorders as soon as possible."

"Surely they won't find anything that deep will they?"

"Well, remember the recorders have sonar beacons which transmit for about a month. It still makes finding the recorder very difficult apparently and, of course, it's important to search quickly before the battery of the beacon runs down. Still they found bits of the DC9 in the Mediterranean some years ago in water almost as deep. It can be done but it takes a long time. It's just got to be found in this case. It would be terrible for all sorts of reasons for the aircraft to disappear without trace. That's reserved for real Bermuda Triangle aircraft."

We stopped talking about Alpha Lima, as it was colloquially called after the phonetic alphabet, and drifted on to the Federal Aviation Agency, its organisation and the way the Air Traffic Service was structured within the FAA. There was pressure to get air traffic as a separate agency from Government, but it was not easy to arrange because of the need for continual injections of large capital sums to keep the service abreast with modern technology. Technically, there was a drive to get all aircraft reporting their positions automatically on secondary radar to the air traffic system, so that a lot of the expensive ground equipment could be decommissioned. I got the impression that the United States Department of Transport kept a close day to day control on the FAA. In the UK the National Air Traffic Service, NATS, had been separated from the CAA, which now was its safety regulator. Of course how much longer NATS would be allowed to control the upper airspace in the UK was clearly debatable due to the overriding and remorseless clutch of the European Commission, sucking the responsibility for everything, including the safety of aircraft, from UK to Brussels. The Commission clearly envisaged the whole of European Airspace under one air traffic system, though the issue of the control of military aircraft in national airspaces was clearly controversial.

Jack had been at the New York Center for nearly two years and thought that he might have to go to Washington, DC fairly soon but so far he had managed to escape. A high flier like Jack had to be able to show that he had had an administrative tour in Washington as well as field experience if he was to reach the top. The meal arrived and we spent a very pleasant evening together. He got me back to the hotel by 9 o'clock. which was just as well as it was 2 o'clock in the morning UK time and I was beginning to show a lack of concentration, finding it very difficult not to drop off to sleep. I turned in straightaway without watching Larry King on CNN, unusual for me when I am in the USA.

In the morning I went down for a swim in the indoor pool as it got light at 7.15. The temperature of the pool was 79°F and it was quite invigorating. I could never make up my mind whether I really enjoyed an early morning swim in an indoor pool but I always enjoyed the event in retrospect and it had to be really good for the muscles. I packed my things, loaded the car and checked out, then sat in the lobby, drank some complimentary coffee and read USA to-day. In the business section I noticed a reference to the Paragon Corporation again. A spokesman had said that the company was doing well and that there was absolutely no reason for shareholders to dump stock. However, the stock had dropped from 32¼ to 20¾ in the last five days. I cut the article out and put it in my bag with the others.

Jack arrived promptly at 8 o'clock and I followed him in my car to the Center. It was a purpose built, square looking block but surprisingly there were no dishes or antennae close by. Presumably the radar sites were some way away and all the information was sent digitally by land lines. The only clue as to the nature of the building was a large sign saying Federal Aviation Administration. I parked in the visitors' parking lot and caught up with Jack who, naturally enough, was parked in pole position by the entrance. We went in and Jack had already arranged for my pass to be made out. I showed my passport, signed the pass, put my copy in a plastic folder, clipped it to my jacket and followed Jack to his office near the front overlooking the parking lot. We got ourselves some coffee.

"Peter, I've arranged for you to go into a small meeting room and hear the tape. When you've had enough of that come back here and we'll run the plot."

Jack asked his secretary to get Francis Devere, head of the Oceanic Center, to come in. He obviously had been waiting for the call as he seemed to come in instantaneously. We introduced ourselves and went to the assigned meeting room.

"How do you want to do this, Peter? If we play the tape in real time it's going to take about one and three quarter hours. As Jack probably told you we've put the San Juan tape in front of our tape so it's all one tape. Then we made a sub-tape which only has the aircraft's transmissions and the Center's replies. I've set this abbreviated tape up so that it goes in bursts, waiting for you to start each batch of exchanges. The tape we will give you will have the complete recording in real-time but there is no point in your wasting your time to-day unless you want to."

I concurred with his plan and we settled down. I got my paper notebook out and punched the start button.

'San Juan Oceanic, this is Victor Papa Whisky Alpha Lima, request clearance from Nelson to Bermuda.'

'Victor Papa Whisky Alpha Lima, this is San Juan. You are cleared as filed, upper amber 632 to Bermuda. Initial clearance Flight Level 100, expect 350 en route.'

The Final Flight

The tape stopped. Obviously the aircraft was taxiing out and taking off. I pressed the start button again.

'San Juan, this is Alpha Lima. Are you receiving our ADS?'

'Alpha Lima, this is San Juan Oceanic. We can see you on the ground at Nelson.'

'San Juan, thank you for check.'

Again the tape stopped, I was getting the feel of the situation now and carried on.

'San Juan, this is Alpha Lima. Airborne from Nelson, on course Bermuda, climbing to Flight Level 100 requesting 350. Please confirm when you are receiving valid ADS data.'

'Alpha Lima this is San Juan. Cleared to 350, advise reaching, Will confirm ADS after next report.'

I paused and asked Francis how would I know the real timings of these transmissions.

"The transcript we've got for you has the time to the nearest tenth of a second against the transmissions that you are listening to. You shouldn't have any problem."

I carried on, fascinated by the conversation, transported in my mind to 35,000 ft. en-route to Bermuda.

'San Juan, Alpha Lima. Level 350.'

'Thank you Alpha Lima. We are receiving your ADS.'

Another pause.

'San Juan Oceanic, this is Alpha Lima, we are showing our position at PISAX, request permission to transfer to New York.'

'Alpha Lima, this San Juan, cleared to call New York Oceanic. Maintain 350.'

A pause

'New York Oceanic, this is Victor Papa Whisky Alpha Lima en route Nelson to Bermuda, position PISAX flight level 350.'

'Alpha Lima, this is New York we see your ADS, check at LOPPS.'

This time there was some concern in the pilot's voice.

'New York Oceanic this is Alpha Lima. We are getting a lot of weather ahead of us. Can you check with met on the latest forecast? We were expecting high cloud and no weather on the route to Bermuda.'

'Copied Alpha Lima. Stand-by.'

Another pause. I was beginning to feel the tension.

'Alpha Lima this is New York. We've checked with the forecaster and your weather en route is fine. There is severe weather in the tropical storm but that is well off to your right.'

'New York, Alpha Lima. Copied your message but weather around us and ahead is very stormy and turbulent. Out'

I went for the next exchange.

'New York Oceanic, this is Alpha Lima. We are in heavy weather with lots of lightning and severe turbulence. We should be 120 miles from Bermuda but we cannot raise them on the VHF and we cannot see Bermuda on our weather radar or receive their radio beacons. Will you please contact Bermuda and see if they can see us on their radar?'

'OK Alpha Lima. According to us you are right on track. Do you want descent clearance?'

'Not for the moment. We must get contact with Bermuda first.'

'Alpha Lima, this is Oceanic. Advise when you have contacted Bermuda Approach on 119.1'

"Francis did you notice? That was a different voice. Presumably the Captain and not the first officer. He sounded very worried."

"Yes Peter. It makes me nervous just sitting here."

'New York, this is Alpha Lima. Situation is getting very difficult. We are having to make quite large changes of course, to avoid the worst cells. We are still unable to make contact with Bermuda. The turbulence is getting almost uncontrollable.'

'Alpha Lima, this is New York. Bermuda Radar advise that they cannot see you on their Radar. We see you 100 miles south of Bermuda on ADS.'

I pressed again but nothing happened.

"Francis, the tape's stuck."

"'fraid not Peter. That's all there is."

We looked at each other. There wasn't anything to say. I was horrified. To read about it is one thing, to hear it is something else. No wonder Jack had said what he did at dinner last night. He had heard the tape and felt concerned. There was no point in hearing the tape again. The satellite communication was crystal clear, every word understandable. I went back to Jack feeling rather depressed. We waited outside for a moment until he came off the phone.

"Thank you for letting me hear the tape Jack. I have to tell you I found it very disturbing. I have a favour to ask you."

"Go ahead."

"Could you make me a tape without any gaps, rather like the one I've just listened to? It would save me so much time when I replay it. However, I'd still like the full tape."

"Sure, Peter. I'll get someone on to it while you look at the plot. Francis take Peter to the plot simulator now and let him see the flight."

We went up the elevator to the first floor and along to another conference room.

"Peter, as you know New York Oceanic is responsible for a huge chunk of the western Atlantic. We divide this area into sectors and each sector is supervised by a controller. When ADS was introduced a year or so ago with satellite communication, we introduced large flat panel screens for each sector but with displays very similar to the old radar displays. The sector you're interested in covers Bermuda to the north, routes to the Caribbean in the south and westward to Nassau and Miami. It's obviously a very small scale but then there is not too much traffic. At any time the controller can expand an area as a window and see the ADS plots and, therefore, the aircraft flight information, in more detail. Remember the plots include replies from normal secondary radar which are in real time as well as the ADS C satellite returns; however in the middle of the Atlantic, of course, there will only be satellite plots.

"We record all the plots on a tape so that we can replay the total scene just the way the controller saw it. We save the last twenty four hours on tape and then overwrite the tape unless something happens and the history is required, as in the case of Alpha Lima. We can replay the whole history in real time or speed it up to a maximum of ten times real time."

I looked at the very large screen in the simulator to get familiar with the display.

"Is this the same size display as the controllers have? The screen seems huge compared with the old radar ones."

"Oh yes. We've been using these large screens for all controller displays for some time now, secondary radar as well as ADS."

I could see that lines representing the airways going down to Antigua, Nassau, Miami and New York were displayed; in addition, the Caribbean islands including St. Antony were shown on the screen if the southern area was chosen. What the controller saw at any one time clearly depended on the scale selected. With the advent of ADS reporting as well as secondary radar, it was much easier for aircraft to fly direct to their destinations and they did not have to follow airways so slavishly as in the past, but it still helped the controller to have the airways marked, particularly as quite a few of the older aircraft were still not ADS equipped. The latitude/longitude grid was also on the screen with reference numbers to help the controller. The computer which stored all the aircraft flight plans and computed the clearances also received the ADS positions which enabled conflict alerts to be computed and warnings given to the controllers, not only between the standard secondary radar equipped aircraft, but also between these aircraft and the ADS equipped aircraft. The ADS aircraft call sign on the screen occulted and there was an aural warning if the computer calculated that there was the possibility of a collision. It was an impressive system and in my view the sooner ADS was made mandatory for all aircraft flying over the Atlantic the better.

Francis started the tape. He showed me how to zoom and enlarge the display area, either for a reporting point like PISAX or for the area round a particular aircraft. I selected the first position report of VP-WAL which was a few miles north of St. Antony and I could see the box with the aircraft's associated details, latitude, longitude, actual altitude, selected heading and cleared altitude. Francis showed me how I could select other data from a menu if I needed to, such as the next waypoint where the aircraft was going. The tape was running slowly and at first nothing seemed to happen until a new reported position for VP-WAL suddenly appeared on the screen, which happened every 10 minutes in real time, and the previous position disappeared. Each position showed the aircraft to be on A632. After PISAX the reporting rate increased to every 5 minutes and all the positions showed A632 moving steadily towards the next reporting point at LOPPS. Once I had got my eye in I started to speed the tape up so that the zoomed window for the aircraft slowly moved north.

In truth, at first there was very little to see. The aircraft was flying steadily at Flight Level 350. I noticed blips from other aircraft flying in the area, one or two going into Bermuda. The ADS blip from Alpha Lima proceeded steadily towards Bermuda. At about 280 miles to go the position reports started to weave on either side of the airway joining St. Antony and Bermuda, just as Jack had said, presumably due to the crew trying to avoid the storms. The reporting rate suddenly increased to one every 90 seconds and the deviations from the airway increased, presumably as the storms were getting worse. At LOPPS the aircraft turned left 16° to fly directly towards Bermuda and then suddenly there no more blips at about 100 miles from Bermuda so that all that was left on the screen was an aircraft leaving Bermuda climbing to Flight Level 330. I looked at Francis and he shook his head.

"That's it. The blips stopped at about the same time as communication was lost."

"What can you let me take away?"

"We've printed out all the data from the position reports. The total duration from St. Antony until the aircraft disappeared was about 1 hour 50 minutes with us and the total number of position reports was 33 from leaving St. Antony. I think Jack has already told you that we've made a plot of all the position reports so that the aircraft's track can be followed very clearly. We also printed all the reports using an eight point font and we managed to get it all on one landscape legal page. It's in Jack's office."

We went back to Jack and again we waited for him to finish talking on the telephone.

"Thank you so much for taking so much trouble, Jack. You've shown me exactly what I wanted to see. To be honest with you it hasn't helped much, but at least we have it all."

"No problem. We are only too happy to help. By the way we've got that extra tape you asked for of the voice communications with the blank bits removed. You do want the real time tape?"

"I may as well take it with me, thank you, even though the other is much more practical to use."

"Peter, have you got time to stay for lunch?"

"No Jack, thank you for the kind thought. I must be on my way to the airport. The flight leaves at 2.15 and the traffic is always unpredictable on the freeway."

"You're right there. On your way then. If you need anything else don't hesitate to call us."

I shook hands with Jack and Francis came with me to see me out. I handed my badge in and went to the car as quickly as I could as I did not have much time if the trip going back was to take as long as it did coming out. I had hoped to do something about the 'Diana' telephone call but there just wasn't enough time. Perhaps I could go home when the investigation was finished via New York and try to do a proper search then. The traffic was still pounding the freeway, the trucks ceaselessly roaring their way up and down Long Island and the East Coast to destinations that were known only to the local inhabitants and the shippers. Luckily the traffic seemed to be moving more easily, probably because it wasn't the rush hour with everyone going home. My car added its insignificant drop to the torrent on 495 going west and I managed to negotiate the interchange once again and emerge triumphantly at the New York International car rental return. I fought my way to the BWIA check-in carrying both my bags. My aisle business seat had been pre-assigned and I went to the departure gate. We got off on time and I was very glad to see New York disappear below and behind me.

***

Four hours later we touched down in St. Antony and it was like a different world. For some reason we had to walk down some steps which had been brought up to the aircraft and across the tarmac for about twenty yards to get into the terminal instead of walking straight in from one of the moving fingers. It was getting dark and the stars were coming out. It was just past full moon and I could see the moon rising in the east. There was a light north easterly wind and the temperature was 78°F. It was difficult to imagine a more perfect setting as the palm trees waved gently in the breeze. Holidays on the beach were not my scene but I wondered if perhaps St. Antony might be different. For a moment I pictured the beaches with the white sands and then quickly remembered the purpose of my visit.

Our bags were already being taken off as we entered the international arrivals. I had imagined that passport examination would be a formality but every visitor seemed to be being questioned and there was a long line in front of me. My turn finally came and I needed to explain the reason for my visit. My inquisitor seemed a nice guy, asked me where I was staying. Frank had told me that he had put me up near the airport at the New Anchorage so I gave that as my address. My passport was stamped and I went through to the customs area. The bags were nowhere to be seen and we had to hang around for about fifteen minutes before they arrived. It was not my day as my bags came towards the end, all priority handling for first and business class passengers seemingly forgotten. I had to go through an inquisition from the customs and to my surprise I had to open my large bag. Finally my form was stamped and I escaped into the terminal.

I looked around and saw Frank. He was very thin, about my height just under six foot, fifty years old or so, the hair he had left was going grey but his small moustache was slightly darker. I knew it was Frank because he seemed to be the only guy not on holiday. He was wearing a white long sleeved shirt and a tie. We smiled at each other and introduced ourselves.

"Here, let me take a bag. It's not worth getting a porter as my parking slot is very close to the terminal."

We went outside to the tropical night, the lights shining down from the terminal roof. The insects were everywhere but somehow it didn't seem to matter with the moon, the stars and the ever present breeze. Frank's reserved parking was right by the entrance to the parking lot only ten yards from the building. I put my bags into the back of his Toyota compact.

"How was the flight?"

"Pretty average. We got here."

"Bad as that?"

"Not really. The flight was fine but I've given up collecting flight time at the back of an aircraft. I didn't mind flying in the planes when I was an airline captain with Britannia, sitting in the left hand seat making it all happen but being a passenger is so boring. Still it's marvellous to be here. What a paradise, though it doesn't seem to have penetrated the immigration hall yet."

"You noticed already? It's a zoo. You should see it when a Virgin 380 comes in at the week-end. The government out here is trying to improve matters but it takes a long time. However, they've done a super job on the hangars and taxiways. Having to rebuild after those big hurricanes hit us some years ago was a blessing in disguise." Frank paused and looked at me. "How long are they going to allow you to stay?"

"What do you mean? Is there any restriction?"

I got my passport out and to my amazement I had been given only four days and I was planning to stay for a week before I left to go to Denver.

"That's crazy, Frank. The guy has put four days. I'll barely have had time to have a shower by then."

"The same thing happened to Charlie Simpson the insurance investigator from New York. We managed to get the permit extended for a few days but they weren't too keen. We had to leave the passport and collect it the following day."

Frank backed the car out from his slot and I realised that St. Antony roads were definitely not like the freeways in New York. We managed forty miles an hour through the bends and the potholes on the way to the hotel. We saw only a few cars and one truck on the way and most of them seemed to be of a much earlier generation than the ones I had just left in New York. Not surprisingly, it was obviously impossible to have an island paradise complete with every modern convenience.

The tourist industry was changing the world or was it the airline industry? Whichever was doing it, it certainly wasn't for the better but it did keep the world's burgeoning population employed. The facts seemed to be that when somebody found a secluded spot on the earth, a paradise, a pearl, somebody else immediately built a 10,000 ft. runway and fifteen hotels so everybody in the world could share the experience, killing the very thing that they all came for. There was no solution. I pulled myself together and tried to concentrate.

"What's new?"

"Nothing I'm afraid. John Southern has been through and grilled Ron Gibbons about why the aircraft went in the wrong direction. Ron's very upset because, as he will tell you, all the crews are trained by Airline Training in Miami. We don't know that the crew did fly in the wrong direction since the ADS said the aircraft was exactly on track but John is blaming the crew. That's why we need your help, Peter, to bring some sanity back to the proceedings."

"Is John coming back?"

"Yes, in about ten days. He has other work to do in the States and Central America and then he plans to go home from here, so hopefully you will see him then."

We reached the hotel down a narrow well surfaced lane and parked at the front. Frank waved the porter away and we went in to the air conditioned lobby. It seemed a shame to have to air condition the tropical night but the hotel had to cater for three hundred people who did not want to share their rooms with the abundance of small animals that flourished in the tropical climate. A smart local girl checked me in and I left my big bag near reception.

"Do you want to drink inside, Peter, or sit on the beach?"

We went outside a few steps to look and we were indeed on the beach. We stayed there. There was a circular hut, roofed with wooden shingles, surrounded by a few chairs and tables. Bruce, the barman, looked at me and then smiled at Frank.

"Scotch and soda Mr. Westbourne? How about you Sir?"

"It's my first night. A rum punch has to be the right thing."

We sat down, looking at the beach with the large modern swimming pool I had noticed behind us. There were only two other drinkers, possibly a couple on their honeymoon. During the day this bar would be doing a roaring trade. Now the holiday makers would be having their meals in the dining room with its air conditioned splendour. The beach was deserted and the waves almost non-existent, sheltered as the shore was from the prevailing easterly winds. It probably took a hurricane to get much in the way of surf. I was already convinced that if I could find a small hotel, St. Antony would be where I would spend my next honeymoon. The drinks arrived and I tried mine. The rum punch must have had ten thousand calories and enough alcohol to take me straight over the limit.

"Well, what do you think, Peter? Where did it all go wrong?"

"Frank, as far as I'm concerned it's early days. Certainly it looks as if either the met was wrong or the aircraft went off on the wrong course. I find it difficult to believe either premise but on balance I favour the wrong heading. If I had to put my money down now I would say that the aircraft got involved with the tropical storm, lost control and dived into the sea. If they had decided to ditch before they ran out of fuel they would have carried on talking to New York."

"Perhaps their satellite radio failed Peter. You know they could probably have flown for another four hours, if they didn't lose control. They took off with full fuel."

I looked at him in disbelief.

"Why on earth did they do that? They should have only needed four hours fuel total even if they took on some extra reserve."

"The tanks were filled with fuel by mistake and though Bill Hudson, the pilot, tried to get it defuelled, the fuel people said they had no empty tankers. He checked the loading with Marion the dispatcher and, as the take-off weight was within limits though only just, he reluctantly agreed to take the extra fuel along for the ride."

The Final Flight

"Well Frank, that seems to confirm my feeling that the aircraft just dived into the sea. If it had enough fuel to get back and the Captain was worried about the weather, the fact that nobody could see him and that he couldn't talk to Bermuda, he would have turned round."

"I suppose you're right. Possibly the weather was so bad that the aircraft was damaged and they lost control. You know I've always been worried about the effect of lightning strikes on these modern aircraft using a lot of carbon fibre in the structure and fibre optic cable in the fly-by-wire and power-by-wire systems. I like aluminium and old fashioned connecting rods."

"Perhaps, Frank, but it's only possible to have competitive and efficient aircraft these days using the latest technology. The manufacturers really do a first class job making sure the design is safe and, of course, they're checked by the government safety regulators like the European Aviation Safety Agency in this case. However, unexpected design faults can and do occur very occasionally and maybe this accident is going to be due to one of these rare mistakes. Certainly the fact that communication was lost and that the ADS position reports stopped seems absolutely crucial."

"I'll tell you frankly Peter, I've got to be able to convince the insurers that it was an accident that could not be avoided or they will not pay up and we may be out of business. All our efforts to grow the airline, which up to now have been going so well, will be completely negated. The insurers might 'buy' a break up but according to the met there was no bad weather on track between St. Antony and Bermuda."

"Look Frank, I know the weather was overcast but the crew would have noticed they were going the wrong way, if that's what happened. They had a stand-by compass and, in addition, they would have noticed the direction they were going as they left St. Antony from the radio beacons and radar. You've engaged me to help and the first thing I've got to do is to explain the apparent discrepancy between the ADS track and the apparent track of Alpha Lima to the north east. However it's all going to take time. My advice to you has to be not to hold your breath for the insurance money. Can you manage with an aircraft short?"

Frank nodded glumly and drained his glass. The moon appeared over the buildings and some people emerged from the hotel and walked along the beach. Frank sensed that I had had enough for the day and took his leave. We agreed that he would pick me up at 8.30 in the morning on his way to the airfield. We went back in to the hotel and after he had gone out to his car I took my bag to the upper floor and along to my room. It occurred to me that that was one good thing about the hotel, it only had two floors so elevators weren't normally necessary though I noticed there was a freight elevator which apparently could be used for wheel chairs.

74

The room was a standard hotel room. I had seen hundreds like it all round the world. Two double beds, a bathroom, TV, fridge and a telephone. What more could a holiday maker want? I turned the TV on while I unpacked. There was the normal assortment of US channels, CNN, CBS, NBC, and the rest plus the Weather Channel, very important out here with the hurricane breeding grounds only a thousand miles or so to the east. I went to bed, exhausted. I hadn't acclimatized yet to the time change, though here in St. Antony it was only four hours from home.

***

I woke up at 6.30 and didn't move for a bit, for me a rare luxury. It was starting to get light and I looked out of my window at the swimming pool just below. It was clearly being kept in tip-top condition in spite of the inevitable deteriorating effect of the climate. The hotel must have been five years old so the pool builders and hotel managers were doing well. In spite of the fact that it was barely light I could see a girl swimming up and down the middle of the pool like the Olympics had come to St. Antony. She moved effortlessly using the crawl, a lovely mover in every way. I could see a pool attendant so I went downstairs and collected a towel. The girl was still there but she must have seen me, as she moved over and continued swimming keeping to one side of the pool. I decided, looking at the length of the pool, that I'd be lucky to do ten lengths in my condition and dived in from the deep end. Half way through I noticed I had the pool to myself and just caught a glimpse of the girl's back disappearing into one of the bedrooms opening onto the pool area as I reached the shallow end and turned round.

I gave up after eight lengths. The pool was longer than I had thought and I didn't want to run out of time and energy before Frank arrived. Before going down to the coffee shop I put the things I wanted into my document case ready to leave after breakfast. Downstairs there appeared to be a choice of breakfast location, air conditioned comfort or just outside the dining room with a view of the pool. I chose to go outside and realised that I was quite hungry as I hadn't eaten the night before except on the BWIA plane. There were a few other breakfasters, mostly vacationers I guessed but one or two were not. There was a man in very smart looking suit at the table next to me drinking coffee. He was swarthy, maybe of Italian extraction looking as if he was in the wrong place. There was also a business like looking lady with dark glasses, blue baggy trousers and a formal shirt, tucked away in the corner surrounded by the New York Times. Finally, there was a tall man, definitely going bald, definitely overweight wearing a white short sleeve shirt and white bermuda shorts. My heart sank as I recognised him straightaway. I wanted to turn away pretending I hadn't see him but there was no escape. He smiled a warm welcome and boomed out across the breakfast area.

"Hi, Peter. You didn't waste much time getting out here? Who's paying you?"

I tried not to look as if Brian Matthews, itinerant journalist of the Daily Mail, was the last person I wanted to meet but I don't think I succeeded. Not that Brian would care, he had a skin as thick as a rhinoceros. He was a first class gatherer of news but not so good at writing the stories up. Brian did not really know me at all but he had seen me in action in court on the RWA investigation and I suppose for someone like him, that was good enough.

"Come and join me."

There was no obvious escape from his entreaties. Reluctantly I went over to his table and the waiter immediately laid another place. I ordered papaya, scrambled eggs and coffee. Brian had finished but he clearly had no intention of leaving.

"This accident to Alpha Lima is amazing. Are you helping AAIB?"

I shook my head and tried to read the local paper, the St. Antony Times, which had been stuffed under my door but it was no use.

"I know, Westbourne must have called you. He's in some trouble with the insurers, isn't he?"

"Mr Matthews, I am here to help West Atlantic Airways if I can. However, I only arrived late last night and I am sure you're much better briefed than I am."

I tried to bury my head in the paper. It was rather insubstantial with more local advertising than news but it was better than nothing and gave an indication of local matters of moment. The accident was still news and mention was made of an underwater search for the aircraft. The writer, Cindy Smart, assumed that the aircraft had broken up in the air some way to the east of Bermuda and I found it difficult to quarrel with her analysis. The papaya was perfect, ten out of ten. I always thought it sad that papaya didn't travel well to the UK, or maybe the climate didn't agree with it. Fresh, with a squeeze of lime it was a meal fit for a king, if that was still the politically correct thing to say.

"I think the aircraft must have got involved with Angela, don't you?" Brian was droning on as I tried to eat. "The pilots almost certainly lost control."

"Mr Matthews, I have no intention of speculating and I would give you the same advice. The sooner we have the crash recorders the better."

I returned to the eggs which were not up to the same standard as mine but no-one could cook scrambled eggs the way I could, at least that was what Mandy always said but I half suspected that that was because she didn't want to cook them herself. I thankfully left most of the coffee, to which in a competition I would have awarded a mark of just one for effort, and escaped from Brian to go up to my room. I was down again just in time to see Frank driving up and got straight into the car. We exchanged pleasantries and were soon at his office in the terminal.

"What do you want to do to-day, Peter?"

"I thought I should start by visiting your maintenance shop and meeting your chief engineer. Then I would like to talk to the AAIB people."

"Fine. Mick Flanagan runs our engineering and he'll be over on the other side of the field checking last night's routine maintenance. By the way, I'm having trouble finding room for everybody in the hangar. European Aerospace, the 412 manufacturer, have three engineers out here and the European Aviation Safety Agency certification people also have two people so we're not short of help. That's one of the reasons I want you out here. I want to know what's going on. Hope you don't mind sharing an office with the Westfield investigator, Charlie Simpson. Anyway, first of all give me your passport and we'll try to get a few days added on. Have some coffee while I try and find Mick."

"That sounds a really good idea. The coffee in the hotel was indescribable. Instant coffee at its worst. It wasn't made any better by meeting the Daily Mail reporter. Has he been worrying you?"

"I'm sorry. I should have warned you. He flew in from London yesterday. He came straight here and started asking me all sorts of questions. I referred him to the AAIB people and the European Aerospace team."

"I'd like to think he's on a tight budget and has to go home in a day or so but I suspect that he'll stay on for days until something better turns up."

Susan Brown, Frank's secretary, a middle aged local girl brought the coffee and this time I gave it nine out of ten. I noticed that Frank had given Susan my passport. She obviously was the one who knew how to get things done without making waves. She had been Frank's secretary since the airline had started and was clearly indispensable. I discovered that her husband was a solicitor in Cape Harbour and they had three children, the oldest just going to college and hoping to go to a university in the USA if it could be arranged. Frank reappeared with Mick Flanagan, a short tough looking guy, presumably of Irish descent.

"Sorry I wasn't here to meet you. I needed to check all the overnight maintenance this morning. It's not like a long haul airline. We utilise the aircraft as much as we can during the day and look after them overnight if they're stopping here. Let me show you what we've got."

We left the terminal building and drove over to the other side of the airfield just outside the perimeter fencing, passing several almost identical hangars on the way, spaced well apart, all with gates onto the taxiway. I could see a collection of general and business aircraft as we drove round.

"That's the fixed base operation on our left. The LIAT hangar is next and then ours."

"What's the first one, Mick. There's no name on the building."

"That's the Paragon Corporation. You've heard of them?"

I nodded.

"But not until the other day when your 412 crashed."

"Well, their flight operations headquarters is based here and they fly all over South America, the Caribbean and the Bahamas, not to mention Bermuda and Florida where Jimmy Morrison has houses. They have a whole range of aircraft from Beechcraft to high performance jets like the Gulfstream 3 and G4. They seems to operate 24 hours a day, goodness knows why."

"What do they do?"

"I've no idea. The aircraft seem to be used for carrying executives round the place. Did you see they are in some sort of financial trouble?"

"Yes, I read about it on the way down."

We left the road and drove through some gates up to the office at the side of the hangar. It looked a really good building, almost too large for the local airline. Mick saw me staring at it.

"It's not our building, Peter. We are renting it from the airport. It's a good deal, both for them and for us. Without the hangar it would have been difficult to have persuaded Frank to move the airline from Antigua. We'd had old Avro 748's for years and there was a strong demand for new equipment both from the tourists and from the business community which had to fly up and down the islands. LIAT also left Antigua to come here when the hangars were finished."

We went inside to Mick's office and I was grateful for the air conditioning. The weather was fine for vacationing but not too good for work.

"What would you like to see, Peter?"

"Can we walk round inside and outside the building so I can get a flavour of what you do? Then sometime I need to see Ron Gibbons and see how the pilot training is done."

"Fine. Let's go straight outside and look at the ramp and then we can tour inside."

The ramp was getting hot by this time but the breeze was blowing making life bearable. There was a 737 outside with some panels open and that was all. Inside, the hangar was large and empty. It was clearly possible to get at least two aircraft, a lot larger than the 412, in tandem in the hangar. I guessed the St. Antony builders, probably with Government money, hoped that the local airline would develop or that they could rent

78

the buildings to larger airlines. I must have shown some astonishment on my face which he clearly thought was due to the lack of activity but in reality was due to the size and high standard of the hangars.

"Peter, we're running an airline. Maintenance is expensive and we try to avoid doing it during the day. To-night things will be very different. There will be two aircraft inside on progressive maintenance and the rest of the fleet will be serviced on the ramp. All the aircraft on our ramp or in the hangar will be towed over to the terminal at about 6.30 in the morning. On Saturday night we try to cut out the progressive maintenance and just do routine servicing to give people some time off. We can do most maintenance tasks ourselves if we have to, including painting an aircraft, thanks to those internal doors. Let me show you some of the facilities."

We went round the various bays all round the side of the hangar. Some, like the tyre and wheel bays, were outside my experience. We went into the avionics lab and the radio repair shop, both of which seemed to be very well equipped. I noticed that the engineers in these labs were all white Caucasian, unlike in the tyre bay. There was no disguising the fact that the education and training required were much higher for these high tech. areas. It was much harder for the people born on the islands to get to the standard needed and, of course, this understandably made the indigenous population resentful, since the wages for an avionics or radio engineer were much higher than for a mechanic working on the wheels.

"Would you like some coffee? We've got a small dining area in the corner of the hangar."

It was an air conditioned area, with vending machines, microwaves and all the things that employers supply these days for their employees. We got some coffee.

"Mick. Those two guys that went out as we came in. I'm sure I've seen one of them before somewhere."

"They're our avionic experts Peter, Tom Mullard and Paul Thomas. Which one do you mean?"

"The short fat one with very thick glasses."

"That's Tom Mullard, he's fairly new. Paul is the supervisor and has been with us three years. The turnover of people is very high in all departments. They come out here entranced with the climate but soon get fed up, especially if they have young children to educate. You know that's not all bad news for us since, when we get new aircraft and equipment, we need to send the old engineers to be trained whereas new recruits may already have completed the necessary courses."

We had finished our coffee.

"Are you ready to go to the AAIB office now?"

"Look I don't want to take any more of your time, Mick."

"You won't. I lent them an upstairs office in this building. I'll show you where to go and then you can come back to my office and we can go over to see Frank."

We went up to the higher level and walked along a corridor, which was actually inside the hangar, to the AAIB office. As we went round the side of the building we could look down to the hangar floor. As we reached the end of the corridor I could see past the central folding doors through the main doors on to the airfield beyond. Mick opened the last door in the corridor and there were three people in the office, two men who I guessed were the AAIB men, Jack Wellings and Brian Fletcher, and the lady who had been having breakfast at the hotel. Mick did the introductions, though he threw me for a moment until I realised that the breakfast lady and Charlie Simpson were one and the same person. The lady, perhaps on closer examination, girl, depending on where one was sitting, turned out to be the insurance assessor for the paintings. She looked every inch a professional though it was difficult to look her in the eye because of the dark glasses she was wearing, possibly the type that changed colour with the amount of daylight but it wasn't that bright in the office. Jack Wellings looked at me.

"Peter, you seem to be going out of the frying pan into the fire. Weren't you giving evidence at the RWA Inquiry some weeks ago?"

"Yes. Frank called for help on Sunday and I couldn't say no as I needed the work. You came out on Sunday, didn't you?"

"Yes, that's right. We saw the Minister of Transport, for whom we're working, on Monday. We're going through all the paperwork at the moment but what we really need is to find the aircraft or at the very least the recorders. There are no clues at all apart from the mysterious disparity between the ADS position reports and the real position of the aircraft."

"How do you know there's a disparity?"

Jack hesitated and flushed slightly.

"Well we don't know for sure of course, but it certainly seems like it judging by the pilots' conversations."

"Did you tell Brian Matthews that?"

"Oh, you've met him already." I nodded. "No, I certainly didn't but I'm pretty certain that's what he's going to say."

"What were you doing in New York, Mr Talbert?"

The voice came from behind. I was soon to learn that Charlie came straight to the point. Her accent sounded to me like Harvard, certainly educated Boston, but I was no expert.

"Trying to do the same thing as you, Ms. Simpson. Establishing what happened to Alpha Lima. My interest is a technical one to establish the facts and prevent a similar event happening again. I guess all you want is to get the paintings back."

Perhaps I should have been more tactful but I had decided that Charlie would take a mile if anybody gave her an inch. You don't get to being an insurance assessor for the world's most valuable paintings without having some hidden attributes, as distinct from virtues. It wasn't her dress sense so it had to be something else. I sensed an unfriendly gaze in my back as I turned again to Jack Wellings.

"Anyway, there's not much doubt that the aircraft crashed or ditched somewhere east of Bermuda though why it was there and what made it crash is beyond me."

Brian Fletcher joined in.

"Jack, how could it possibly crash to the east of Bermuda? You know perfectly well the ADS plots showed that it stopped transmitting 100 miles south of the island."

"I know, I know." Jack sounded very frustrated. They had probably been through this conversation before. "But the crew spoke of lightning and thunderstorms and if you believe the weather people the only weather like that was several hundred miles to the east of Bermuda. I'm wondering if it could be an aircraft design fault. Something wrong with the flying controls for example. The manufacturers and the airworthiness people out here won't countenance it but the system is relatively new and something very strange went wrong."

"Frank tells me that the frigate has gone out to search for the accident data recorders."

"Yes, that's right Peter. In addition, World Underwater Surveys recommended we get a specialist ship in position. The Atlantic weather of course makes things difficult but they felt that, because St. Georges Harbour at the east end of Bermuda is relatively close to the search area, it would be feasible for the search vessel to go to St. Georges if bad weather was forecast. Luckily, Oceanic Engineering in Virginia had a vessel with an ROV and lifting gear immediately available and Bob Furness accepted their quotation to do the job. They should be in the search area by Saturday and hope to start searching Sunday. Fortuitously, there was a towfish available as well so the ship is going to take it along to be ready if the hydrophone search fails. Initially, the ship will provide a second sonar beacon search capability to back up the frigate. As you know, by now time is of the essence before the beacon stops."

"Where will they search, Jack."

"That will depend I suppose on how well the frigate's done. We spent a lot of time trying to decide the optimum place to start and we felt that 31°N 60°W was probably best. We decided to let the Navy coordinate the search. I may visit them in a few days but the World Underwater Surveys man is there and I'm happy to leave it to them to decide, anyway for the moment. I know Brian here doesn't like my saying this but the crew clearly went the wrong way for some reason that we have to discover. They flew into Angela and then seem to have lost control. We must find out if we can whether it was a design fault or not."

I glanced at Charlie but she didn't say a word. I wondered how long she had been out in St. Antony. Whatever she thought, it was not for the public record. I decided to visit the European Aerospace people and the EASA certification engineers next. They were in a very small office next to the AAIB and looked fairly uncomfortable. I introduced myself and it seemed to me was met with some suspicion, at least by the European Aerospace engineer resident in Hamburg, Robin Trethowen, the senior member of the aircraft team in St. Antony..

"Peter, this investigation shouldn't take too long. We've been out here four days now and things seem fairly static. You won't like my saying so but at this stage it looks like a clear cut case of pilot error. The crew clearly went off on the wrong course, didn't notice and lost control of the aircraft. That's the problem with these small airlines. The only problem for us as a manufacturer is that at the moment we can't find the aircraft. The search airplanes haven't found anything yet. Hopefully, the search vessel will manage to locate the accident recorders and possibly some bits. Until they do there's not much more that we can hope to discover."

"Well, I understand your position about blaming the pilots, Robin, but as far as I'm concerned I'm not convinced. For a start how do you explain the ADS reports? For another thing, though I haven't spoken to Ron Gibbons yet, I understand the crews were all trained by Airline Training in Miami. Doesn't that ensure a good standard?"

I saw one of the others in the room nodding agreement, but Robin had made his mind up.

"Those training organisations always say the pilots were good and they wouldn't make any mistakes. If they didn't they wouldn't get the business."

There was clearly no way I was going to change Robin's mind and I decided to approach the guy who had nodded his head at some other time when Robin wasn't present. Manufacturers always tended to blame the pilots when something had happened to their aircraft which they didn't like, but normally only when the facts were fairly clear cut and this was certainly not the case here. I tried another tack.

"Surely we need to find the accident data recorders in order to be certain there wasn't a design fault. Isn't the fibre optic cabling new on the 412?"

"Sure but that's not a big deal and the system has been cleared by EASA." He nodded towards a couple at the back of the room who were keeping very quiet and must be members of the EASA certification team.

Understandably, they seemed to be trying to dissociate themselves from Robin. "However, of course it would be nice to get the recorders and exonerate the design," 'and blame the pilots' was clearly implied but unspoken. "There's not much more we can do to-day here. I don't know about you but I'm going back to the hotel to send some messages."

Looking at his sun tan, he might just as well have added 'and to swim in the pool' but I didn't think it would be particularly helpful to add to his sentence.

"Where are you staying?"

"We're in the Curtain Bluff. Where are you?"

"At the New Anchorage."

"We started there but we wanted something more comfortable. See you to-morrow."

The three of them packed up their bags and departed for their hotel which seemed to me to be a very long way away from the airfield and not ideal for the job they had come to do. However that was up to them. They could be right about not have anything to contribute but I was not convinced that any of us knew the answer at this stage. In my experience, their attitude was most unusual but perhaps the surroundings were getting to them, certainly to Robin. One of the two EASA engineers came over to me after the others had left.

"I'm Simon Stevens and this is Gunter Schmidt, who was responsible for the certification of the controls. My speciality is engines and their control systems." He paused trying to choose his words carefully. "Robin seems a bit protective of the aircraft. We've got completely open minds on what happened. The only thing we agree on is that we need the flight data recorders."

I expressed my complete agreement and after chatting with them about the inexplicability of what had happened I decided to go back to Frank. I managed to retrace my steps down to the hangar floor and find my way towards Mick's office. He saw me and we went out to the parking lot. Charlie appeared from nowhere.

"It's all too convenient, losing the paintings like that," was her thought for the day and swept past. I wasn't about to admit it but I could see what she meant. It certainly looked as if someone was trying to get the insurance money, but that didn't make sense in this case since the paintings were on board. She got into what was clearly a rental car, judging by its extreme youth and discreet fender sticker. The car took off like it was an aeroplane that was late for an appointment, squealing as it made the turn for the perimeter road. Mick shrugged his shoulders as we left and drove steadily back to the terminal.

The Final Flight

"I'd be unhappy as well if I were in her position but I don't see how the insurance company can wriggle out of this one. Goodness knows what the paintings were insured for."

CHAPTER 3

'What should we do but sing His praise
That led us through the watery maze'

Frank got up as Susan showed Mick and myself into his office.

"How about going to the Pub overlooking Seaward Harbour for something to eat, it's not far and won't take too long."

We went to Frank's car and he drove us over to the Pub. It wasn't exactly like an English pub as there was no draught beer but the owner's heart was in the right place. We ordered our drinks and food and sat down in the shade looking down over the bay. What a place to work, though everybody kept on telling me you soon got used to the weather and the view and started to complain about all the things that were not there.

"Did you learn anything new to-day, Peter?"

"Not really, except that the insurance investigator has her own ideas about everything."

"You noticed that? I thought it was just me."

"Jack Wellings believes the aircraft crashed or ditched in the tropical storm well to the east of Bermuda and that's where the main search is taking place, above and below the water. Brian Fletcher says it must have gone in south of Bermuda because that's what the ADS says. Charlie says 'it's all too convenient' whatever that's supposed to mean. The manufacturers predictably believe it's not their problem and would like to blame the pilots. Well, maybe it's just Robin who takes that view. The EASA certification engineers are waiting for the flight data recorders. I want to talk to your avionic experts as soon as possible and I need to talk to the met forecasters sometime."

"Well, Mick will take you back after lunch to the hangar and you can call Miami or Bermuda anytime for the met people."

We left the Pub and returned to the terminal and Frank's office. Susan had obviously been looking out for us as she came outside and waved us all in. As we went into Frank's office Susan whispered to him and I saw her give him my passport.

"Well here's your passport, Peter. Susan said they were very reluctant to extend the permit, as if the guy on duty who she spoke to was under some special orders. Susan explained you were leaving Thursday anyway and so they gave you the extra days." He turned to Mick. "Susan says the Daily Mail man is after you."

Mick grimaced. I looked in my passport and saw the initialled alteration and put it away in my bag.

Mick drove me back to the hangar. I watched a Gulfstream 3 with Paragon Corporation painted large on its fuselage land and taxi to the Paragon ramp. The gates opened and closed to receive the plane.

"The security seems very high for all these hangars, Mick. Paragon has even got gates from the road as well."

"They want to make sure that no local people, or animals for that matter, can damage anything. They had some bad experiences from aircraft hitting cattle some years ago and that's why these private and general aviation facilities, as well as the airline servicing ramps, now all have the gates and fences."

I left Mick in his office and went in to the avionics lab. Paul Thomas, who Mick had pointed out to me earlier, came over when he saw me come in.

"You're Peter Talbert aren't you?" I nodded. "You're helping Frank. I knew you'd be coming over. What can I do for you, Peter?"

"Paul, I'm obviously amazed by the fact that Alpha Lima seems to have crashed to the east of Bermuda in that tropical storm Angela while the ADS reports say that the aircraft was 100 miles south of Bermuda. Have you any ideas how that could happen?"

"Not really. To be truthful I think it's impossible. The weather people must have got it all wrong and Angela had it in for Alpha Lima. You see Peter, the pilots must have been able to see where they were on their Navigation Displays, south of Bermuda. In my view they should have let down and all would have been well."

"You don't think there could be something wrong with the aircraft?"

"Well it's always possible. Robin Trethowen, the senior guy, won't hear of it but I think the others have a more open mind."

"Do you look after the flight control computers as well as the flight management ones?"

"Absolutely. All the computers are under my control and there are a lot of them. That's why we have so many test rigs. In fact, with the 412 we had to invest in even more gear so that we could check the new fibre optic cabling. Tom went away on a course to Thales in France. It's a great system."

There really was not much more that could be said. Everything seemed to be very well organised. Paul showed me round the lab. As far as I could see it was equipped to the very latest standards. I noticed not only did they have a data loader for transferring the monthly navigational updates to the flight management computers in the aircraft as would be expected, but in addition their computer in the lab was connected to a network, presumably giving internet connection. Clearly they could get their software and database updates direct from Honeywell. In addition, I noticed that there was a dial up modem as well which seemed a bit of an overkill, but perhaps the network and internet access was a recent addition. Next door was the radio lab and Chuck Curtis, the supervisor came to meet me. He showed me round his facilities. Again the lab was well equipped. They could set up the satellite communication sets as well as the normal communication equipment.

"How does the ADS setup work on the 412, Chuck?"

"Very simple. The software in the flight management system continuously puts all the agreed data to be transmitted into so called buffer stores. The data is actually only transmitted periodically to the satellites because every time the data is sent, INMARSAT and the other providers on the network make a charge. In addition, the communication system would get overloaded if the reporting rate was too high. As it is there can be quite a delay between the report leaving the aircraft and it appearing on the controller's screen. The air traffic controllers don't need a continuous update since the separation distances and altitudes are quite large over the Oceans. Here in the lab we do a routine check on the total system whenever a unit is reported defective or whenever the maintenance schedule calls for the check. When we send test data, which has a special identification of course, to San Juan Oceanic they automatically send a confirmatory message back which we can view on a page of the flight management display."

"Have you any theories on the accident to Alpha Lima, Chuck?"

"Not really except that I wonder if somehow the software in the flight management system was faulty. Not that that would explain the accident unless they flew into Angela."

"But apart from anything else, the stand-by heading would not have agreed with the main heading on the navigation display, allowing for the 10° magnetic variation. The pilots would have noticed."

"You would have thought so but maybe they didn't. Remember the stand-by compass is tucked away out of sight unless they pull the tray down, Peter."

I went back to Mick. He looked uncomfortable and then I saw the reason. Brian Matthews was sitting in his office. Mick tried to introduce us but gave up when it was clear that we had met.

"Excuse me for interrupting, Mick, can someone take me over to the other side of the airfield."

Mick leapt to his feet and made excuses to Brian, obviously glad to have a reason to escape. We went out to his car.

"Thank goodness you arrived. He was trying to get me to make all sorts of judgements on what happened. I needed to see Frank anyway. Where are you going? Still Air Traffic?"

I nodded. He rang the Tower as we drove across the airfield and told them that I was coming over. He dropped me at the Tower door where there was a keypad and a button next to a loudspeaker to gain admittance. I pressed it and after suitable interrogation was asked to go up. I climbed up two flights of stairs and arrived in the local control room. Tim Hardcastle, the senior air traffic controller happened to be on duty and we introduced ourselves.

"How are you getting on, Peter? It's a strange business. I gather you were in New York Center yesterday talking to Jack Maynes."

We chatted about the accident but there was no point in going through the whole thing. He knew it as well as anybody. I looked out of the windows. There was an unobstructed view of the ramp, the new taxiways and most of the runway from the start of Runway 25 down to very nearly the other end at the start of Runway 07.

"You saw Alpha Lima take-off? Anything strange?"

"No, Peter, I didn't see it take-off. That was before I came on duty at 8 o'clock. It had been gone about an hour and a half by then. I did ask the controller who was on duty and all he said was that it seemed quite a long take-off. The 412s normally get airborne pretty quickly. It must have been heavy."

"What happened then?"

"Apparently nothing unusual. He turned right on course but my man lost him visually in cloud before he was settled on the heading for Bermuda. You remember the weather was very strange as a result of Angela."

'Tower this is Paragon 31, permission to taxi from our hangar to 25 for departure to Barbados.'

Tim concentrated on the aircraft calling for taxi clearance. He cleared Paragon 31 to the holding point of 07 and checked on the phone with San Juan that the aircraft had its clearance and was clear to join the airway. I looked around for a plane on the ramp and then realised that it was down at the far end where the visibility from the tower was poor. The tower would have needed to be a lot taller to see the taxiway by the Paragon hangar. Tim cleared Paragon 31 on to the runway to backtrack to the other end of the runway as there were no other aircraft about. We saw it was a Raytheon 125 emerging from the far end of 07 and taxiing slowly along the runway. At the 25 end it turned round and Tim cleared it for take-off. It accelerated quickly, climbed effortlessly from the runway and then turned left towards Barbados.

Tim made the necessary notes in the log and turned towards me.

"Tim, did anybody watch him depart on the radar?"

"I believe so but I can't answer that question myself. The radar room is on the floor below and Chris Mattinson was on duty. He's off duty at the moment. Shall I get him to call you sometime?"

"Yes please, that would be very helpful. I'm staying in the New Anchorage. Anyway, Frank will always know where to find me during the day. By the way, do you keep records of communication and radar plots?"

"Yes to the first and no to the second. We record the normal VHF communication but we wipe the tape after one week if nothing goes wrong. We keep the emergency communication for four weeks. In this case we obviously didn't wipe the tape but kept it and started a new one. However I'm afraid we don't record radar displays. We'd like to but the equipment costs money and we're not anticipating getting the recorder until next year. To be blunt, this accident will probably ensure that it will be in the next budget."

"Presumably you keep a log on movements?"

"You bet we do. We're not mechanised with computers like larger airports so the log is very simple to look at. Of course we can't search it with a computer but that doesn't worry us. Would you like to see the log?"

"That would be good."

Tim had the log in front of him and he turned back the pages. While we were talking aircraft were taking off and landing but another local controller had arrived and was managing it all. Tim showed me the entry for the last take-off of VP-WAL. It had been logged at 22.31Z, 6.31 in the evening local time. I glanced at the entries around that time. The large aircraft were departing for Europe and there was the local airline traffic of LIAT and West Atlantic. There were a few BWIA entries flying between the larger entries. There were also a few private and business aircraft.

"Could I have a copy of the log from 2100Z?"

"No problem at all. I'll send it to Frank for to-morrow morning. Anything else you need?"

"May I look at the radar room?"

"Sure. I'll take you down.'

We went down one flight and into a partially darkened room. I didn't interrupt the controller but looked at the display. It was a secondary radar display so that the aircraft's transponder sent details of its height and other data every time the ground radar requested the information. The name 'secondary radar' was in reality a bit of a misnomer since it was actually the primary way for controllers to see the aircraft. However, the radar was so called because it came many years after the original radar system which illuminated all aircraft with the rotating radar transmitter and looked at all the radar reflections which were sent back. With secondary radar, only the aircraft fitted with transponders replied and were shown on the screen. The controller was able to give each aircraft a code to transmit when it was illuminated by the radar and this code was immediately equated to the aircraft's call sign. The call sign, height and other data was displayed on the screen and this made it easy for the controller to recognise which aircraft was which and where they were all going. It was a very good system.

"Tim, do you still have primary radar?"

"Sure. But we only use it in an emergency. Even the smallest puddle jumper now has a transponder so we can see it. We haven't used primary radar for controlling aircraft for years but we check it on a routine basis and, of course, use it if there is a problem."

I'd seen all I could usefully see at the moment. I asked him if he could get me a copy of the VHF tape and took my leave. I walked back to Frank's office. Charlie was in there and Frank looked a bit frustrated. My arrival was obviously a godsend.

"How are you doing, Peter?"

"I'm working at the problem Frank. Could you ask Ron Gibbons if I could see him to-morrow morning, even though it's Saturday?"

Frank made a note and looked at Charlie.

"Ms. Simpson is convinced that the aircraft did not dive in from 35,000 ft. She thinks that it was ditched close to the east end of the island and the paintings were taken off by boat. She's going to start a sea search to find the wreck. She's off to Bermuda to-morrow to see Jimmy Morrison."

A hundred questions flooded through my mind but I resisted the temptation to say anything. I wondered how much Charlie knew about aviation. She obviously knew a lot about paintings and the fallibility of human nature. I looked at her.

"You think it's a case of barratry, Ms. Simpson?"

In spite of her dark glasses it was clear she didn't expect other people not in her business to know about insurance swindles.

"Since you ask, Mr Talbert, I most certainly do. The whole thing stinks of an insurance swindle. A very clever one. But a swindle to get the insurers to pay for a contrived loss. As you said so succinctly, barratry."

"Has Morrison filed a claim?"

She looked at me, or I think she did, behind those dark glasses. "That's a very interesting question, Mr. Talbert. No, on the contrary he has asked for our help because he treasures the paintings and would love to have them back. He believes that the aircraft has dived in to the sea to the east of Bermuda, out of control, but he will do anything he can to help. I've just been talking to him and he is going to organise a search off the coast in case the aircraft was ditched."

"Surely that's going to be a bit difficult? The visibility of the water can't be that good this time of year."

"We've thought of that." I liked the use of the word we. "Mr. Morrison is getting hold of an aircraft fitted with a device that can detect metal in the water."

"That's very interesting, Ms. Simpson. I thought only the military had aircraft fitted with magnetic anomaly detectors, MADs I believe they are called."

"Well apparently that's where you've been misinformed, Mr Talbert. Mr. Morrison tells me that some civil prospecting firms have fitted those things to small airplanes and he hopes to have one in position by to-morrow."

"Is the magnetic presence of an aircraft sufficient to trigger an airborne magnetic anomaly detector, particularly if the aircraft is quite deep?"

Charlie looked at me and hesitated as I watched her very carefully.

"I cannot answer that question, Mr. Talbert, because I just don't know."

She went up in my estimation. At least she didn't try to bullshit.

"Nor do I Ms. Simpson but I feel it is very important that we find out, because it may be that more sophisticated tools are required. As you may know, the search at the moment is being concentrated on finding the accident data recorders. That needs to be done as a matter of urgency before their batteries run down and their sonar beacon stops transmitting. However, since the aircraft has not yet been found and if you're convinced that it's in shallow water then there may be better ways of searching than using a MAD. The UK Air Accident Investigation Branch has a search manager, a member of World Underwater Surveys Ltd., working in the Royal Navy search coordination centre in Bermuda and perhaps you should speak to him to advise you. Possibly the same system could be used in shallow water as in deep water, that is a listening hydrophone is towed behind a boat to locate the beacon. Perhaps the Nimrods should drop some passive beacons in the most likely area for the aircraft to have crashed. Alternatively, perhaps sidescan sonar can be used. That is what Oceanic Engineering are going to provide as a backup to the hydrophone in the deep water search if neither recorder is found in the next week or so."

"How does that work, Mr. Talbert?"

"A device, commonly called a towfish for obvious reasons, is dragged through the water at about 2 to 3 knots and transmits a sonar pattern on either side to a distance of about 500m. The returns from the bottom are shown on a trace recorder so that any unusual objects can be spotted. Obviously, the bigger the object on the bottom, the more clearly it can be seen. As you can appreciate, the search area covered in 24 hours is quite small. One of the difficulties is that when the boat has to turn through 180° the towfish swings out sideways, so it takes a very large turn indeed to bring the towfish back onto the adjacent desired track, 1,000m parallel with and next to the previous track. All in all, a rough guide is that in one period of 24 hours the towfish will have travelled 50 nautical miles along the desired search track and, since 1,000m is about .5 of a nautical mile the area covered per day will be 25 square miles which is a drop in the bucket of the Atlantic Ocean. Let me emphasise that it is much better if the sonar beacons on the accident recorders are still working since by using a hydrophone, the search tracks can be further apart. However, the hydrophone tow still has to be very slow, so the area that can be searched by one hydrophone in four weeks, the life of the sonar battery, is comparatively small."

Frank considered what I had just explained.

"It doesn't sound too slow, Peter."

"It is really, Frank, because one never knows accurately where to start searching, certainly in this case, and one is always at the mercy of the weather so that the ship will have to wind in the hydrophone or the towfish and head for St. Georges if bad weather is forecast. It could take a very long time indeed to reach the wreckage and, therefore, being realistic, there is a very good chance that the wreckage will never be found. There's another point as well. Every response that looks possible has to be investigated by launching a remote observation vehicle carrying a grab to bring pieces to the surface. That requires extremely accurate navigation to find the object spotted by the sonar and can waste a lot of time as well as money."

"The towfish doesn't sound a very suitable device for shallow water where Alpha Lima has been ditched, Mr. Talbert, the hydrophone sounds much better."

"Ms. Simpson, please, surely you're jumping the gun? The jury has not even been convened, let alone heard the evidence on where Alpha Lima hit the water. However you're right in one way. In shallow water a towfish is probably not the best solution but the hydrophone might be quite good because the lateral audible range of the sonar beacon will be much greater. That's why it is so necessary to get the searching under way as quickly as possible while the sonar battery is still good. If your Mr. Morrison truly wants to help and is not just pretending, I suggest you talk to the World Underwater Surveys man and get some expert advice on the best way to search in shallow water."

"Well I really do think we need to try searching in shallow water. As far as I'm concerned the disappearance seems very suspicious."

"Ms. Simpson, I have three comments about that. Firstly, if you believe this is truly a scam, an accident to secure the insurance money, then surely it follows that the paintings were probably never loaded in the first place. That way the perpetrators of the crime can get the insurance money and can also sell the paintings on the black market. In fact they may have been sold already. If that is your scenario, then the loss of the aircraft would be a clear cut case of murder and the instigator is almost certainly your Mr. Morrison since he is the only one to get the insurance money."

I could see Charlie wanted to interrupt but I put my hand up.

"Please let me finish. My second comment relates to Bermuda itself. It is a remarkable island. If it were a mountain it would be almost the eighth wonder of the world, rising ten thousand feet from the ocean floor in six miles with no other 'hills' near it. My guess, and as I said it is only a guess, is that since the aircraft with a magnetic anomaly detector can only be effective in relatively shallow water, it will only be of use in the case of Bermuda up to 10 miles to the north of St. David's Head at the east end of the island and up to no more than five miles to the east of St. David's Head. In a way that's good news since the airborne search will either be successful quickly or not at all. Mind you apart from the engines there is so little ferrous metal to attract the detector that I can't believe that a MAD is the way to search."

"Well I can see nothing wrong in Jimmy Morrison having a try, can you Mr. Talbert?"

"No, Ms. Simpson, as long as one realises the limitations of the search vehicle and the true objectives of the person organising the search. We must find the aircraft wherever it is and we must be prepared to extend the search. Please speak to World Underwater Surveys, they are the experts in these matters not me, not you and certainly not your Mr. Morrison."

"Mr. Talbert, he is not my Mr. Morrison. I barely know him but he seems to want to help get his paintings back and so does my firm. By the way you are wrong in saying that if the paintings were never loaded Mr. Morrison had to be in on the scam. He would still get the insurance money and the person who didn't load the paintings would have them to sell."

I nodded indicating that she had a good point. I waited to make certain Charlie was listening to me.

"My third and main comment, Ms. Simpson, is that it is just not feasible for a controlled ditching to have taken place for all sorts of reasons, like it was dark to name just one. However, as we haven't found the aircraft I agree with your suggestion. We might as well try to eliminate its being in shallow water."

I should have kept my mouth shut then but I didn't. Maybe it was the male in me determined not to be outdone by this confident, if not over confident, female insurance investigator.

"Perhaps Mr. Morrison is very keen to be seen to help because the sooner it can be established that the aircraft has crashed in the sea, out of control, the sooner you will pay him."

"Don't you think that that is a rather uncharitable remark, Mr. Talbert?"

"Possibly Ms. Simpson, but Jimmy Morrison didn't get to where he is to-day by being Mr. Nice Guy. It must be great to be a billionaire and be able to do these things."

"Well he may not be a billionaire much longer. Have you been reading about the Paragon Corporation in the press? The stock is falling fast because there is a rumour that Paragon is involved with drug trafficking on the side and Mr. Morrison owns most of the stock."

"All the more reason why he wants a quick settlement. As I said, I don't vote on ditching. If I were in your position, Ms. Simpson, and believed that the accident was deliberate, probably due to a bomb, I'd be talking to the chief of police here in St. Antony and looking for the paintings on the island. Mind you, I can't see how they had time to switch the crates containing the paintings to dummy ones, certainly not with your guards, the customs and the shipping agents in position. Perhaps on second thoughts you should be searching in London."

"And also wherever the ship stopped on the way out here, Mr. Talbert. Did you appreciate that the paintings came out by boat?"

"No I didn't. I find that very interesting. Doesn't that mean there would have been a lot more opportunity to pinch the paintings?"

"Yes, but of course we had a couple of guards keeping an eye on things."

"That's alright if you can trust the guards, but the paintings were so valuable somebody might have been tempted to bribe a guard or two."

"Mr Talbert, you don't seem to trust anyone."

"You know better than I do, Ms. Simpson, that there are some very nasty people in this World."

I considered telling her to be careful and not to fly in an aircraft provided by Morrison since he probably had an aversion to all investigators, even female ones, but I decided she might think I was being pushy. Anyway it was time to get back to the hotel and I asked Frank for a lift. In spite of my slightly provocative remarks Charlie volunteered to take me and I accepted with some apprehension. Her driving had looked stimulating from the outside and I wasn't sure I was ready for the inside experience.

"The papers will be in by now, Ms. Simpson. I'd like to get some from the terminal before we leave."

"Fine. I'll pick you up at the front." She didn't look as if she expected any comment and so I didn't make one. I went to the shops and found an FT and a Wall Street Journal. I stayed inside the terminal until I saw Charlie approaching. Despite my misgivings the drive back was uneventful. Perhaps her afternoon driving performance leaving the WAA hangar was a mixture of showwomanship combined with frustration with all the men from AAIB, the manufacturer, the European Aviation Safety Agency, and yet another expert interfering, all of whom, for different reasons, had understandably decided that the aircraft was sunk in the deep either east or south of Bermuda. Certainly life was not going to be smooth working with Charlie, but work with her was something I certainly had to do.

I got my things out of the back of the car and noticed that Charlie had already bought her copy of the FT and Wall Street Journal. I held the hotel door open for her as she swept in to the lobby and we got our keys. Her room was on the ground level. As she reached the far side of the lobby at the entrance to her corridor I saw a somewhat thin, shortish man wearing a long sleeved shirt and tie, who I did not recognise, go up to her and introduce himself. She turned back and they sat down together in the lobby.

It was a relief to feel the air conditioning in my room when I got upstairs. Apart from anything else it stopped everything getting that slightly damp feeling which is a feature of being exposed to the warm moist climate. There was a message to call Cindy Smart on a local number. The name sounded familiar and then I remembered she had written the article about the European Aerospace 412 in the local paper this morning. I knew that Alpha Lima's disappearance was very newsworthy with the Bermuda Triangle connotation but I hadn't realised the obvious, that I would be chased by the media. I didn't have long to wait. The phone rang.

"Cindy Adams here of the Announcer." She sounded like a local girl. "I gather you're in St. Antony to help West Atlantic Airways." I didn't say anything. "Are you still there?" I grunted. "I'd very much like to meet and have a chat."

"Well Ms. Adams, I only arrived last night and there's very little to add to your article in the paper to-day. What we need is to find the crash recorders. Without them we're all speculating."

"It would still be nice to meet."

"Alright. I'll call you to-morrow on this number when I've sorted my commitments out."

"Fine. Just leave a message if I'm out."

The Final Flight

I took out the newspapers that I had got from the airport terminal and started reading. Paragon Corporation stock was down to 8½ as investors panicked. I wondered how much stock Morrison had managed to unload. Perhaps Charlie was right and his billionaire status was going to disappear, in which case he would be desperate for the insurance money. However, in my experience it was never the big guys that got hurt and Morrison was clearly a survivor.

***

It was going to be another marvellous day. I looked out of my window. It was just getting light and the girl I had seen yesterday was trying to set another Olympic Record. By the time I got to the pool the sun was shining and I had the pool to myself. I managed ten lengths after a struggle and returned to my room. It was Saturday I reminded myself and tried calling Mandy in Bournemouth but she was out. I left my hotel details on the answering machine but it was going to be difficult to communicate since by the time I got home Mandy would be asleep. To my surprise there was more success with my new secretarial agency. There was a duty operator who put me through a very searching proof of identification routine after I explained who I was. Jill, who seemed to be looking after me, anyway for the moment, had left a long list of messages to be passed on if I called. I stopped the operator from going on.

"Shall I fax them to you?"

For some reason I didn't fancy the faxes appearing in the offices downstairs, specially as I had no idea of the content.

"No, thank you. Can you make them into a big file and attach it to an email? I'll log on to-night and take it off my mail box. I'm not sure of the security in the hotel fax room here. Did Jill say if there was any regular mail?"

"Yes, she said they were mostly routine but there were one or two letters you might want to read."

"Fine. Ask her to scan the important ones and email them to me. I'll call her Monday after I've checked my email."

How wonderful it was to have such first class support, and on a Saturday. Unfortunately the mobile phone networks hadn't got their 3G/GPRS support going yet and neither had the hotel got internet support which I found disappointing since it would have made things so much easier using either my phone or laptop, but luckily it did not matter. America OnLine had bought out Compuserve quite a few years ago and it was a really useful back up organisation for world travellers, since by using a dial up modem it made email available in almost every country in the world. It was ideal for small companies like Drake Williams. America

On Line seemed to have worldwide local telephone numbers which meant that I was never out of touch with my mail.

At breakfast by the pool there were a few people sitting outside. When I had got in the previous evening I had asked the desk to organise me a rental car and had called Frank at home to let him know, so that he would no longer have to act as my chauffeur. Charlie might have helped but she'd had to leave early to catch her flight to Bermuda and anyway the last thing I needed was to have to rely on her for transport. The rental car finally arrived twenty minutes after my requested time of 8 o'clock sharp and we did the formalities. With some trepidation about the St. Antony roads, I launched myself forth to the airport.

Frank was already in his office, even though it was Saturday, and we discussed what was happening in relation to investigating the crash. For me it was very clear what I had to do. My expertise was electronics and crew procedures. All I needed to do was to concentrate on these areas. I had to find out why the aircraft was in the wrong place. It was not my task to search the sea bottom and try to find the crash recorders. Frank's life was much harder, he had to run an airline and keep it solvent, with the new extra task of keeping the investigation moving to try to get the insurance money. We discussed Charlie's ditching theory. It seemed pretty unlikely. Either Bill Hudson and Jim French had to be in on the plot or the guards must have forced them to co-operate. Either way, carrying out a successful ditching was very chancy and to get valuable paintings out from the aircraft seemed even more unlikely. They would be inundated with sea water. I made a note to ask Charlie how the paintings were packed and whether they were in some sort of waterproof containers.

The telephone rang. Frank picked up the receiver and listened intently.

"When will the wreckage and the body be in Bermuda?" I couldn't hear the reply. Frank carried on listening. "You say the body has a beard. Then I can't help you with identification. It would be one of the guards. Let me think about it and I'll come back to you. Bye."

Frank turned to me.

"As you've probably gathered they've found some wreckage and a body. One of the planes spotted it first thing this morning and a high speed launch is on its way out now to bring in the wreckage. They've winched the body into a helicopter and it's on its way to the mortuary right now."

"Where did they find it Frank?"

"About 50 miles south east of St. David's Head spread over a fairly wide area. Apparently in the wreckage there were a couple of dinghies and some life jackets. I said I'd send some people up to look at the stuff.

The Final Flight

They can catch our afternoon flight to Bermuda and look at it this evening. I'll ask Mick to go and I'll talk to Jack Wellings, he'll probably want to be there. I'd better ask the European Aerospace people as well."

On thinking some more about things I decided that perhaps I should visit Bermuda since that seemed to be where the action was. However, a moment later I realised that I would not be keeping to my plan of confining myself to the electronics and the cockpit/crew interface if I went to look at the wreckage. I decided to give my Bermuda visit a coat of observation.

Ron Gibbons, WAA's chief pilot, had his office near the airline operations room. The whole area was really a warren of offices. It had grown like topsy and the airport authority really needed to build an operations block for the airlines, freight forwarders etc. They had probably run out of money after they had finished the new terminal. I found the office eventually and even though it was Saturday his secretary was obviously expecting me and she showed me in to Ron. As he got up to greet me I could see he was a good six foot tall, lean and looked very fit. I guessed his age as on the right side of fifty. He had clearly been in the Tropics for a long time. He was wearing his uniform but his jacket must have been hanging in the small closet behind him. I sat down and looked out onto the ramp. It may not have been the best office in the world but Ron could certainly see what was happening to his aircraft. As Ron poured some coffee from a jug at the side of the room he started to talk. He was obviously glad to share his worries.

"Am I glad to see you. If you don't mind my saying so, it was a smart move by Frank to get you to come over. What do you need from me, Peter?" He clearly didn't expect an immediate answer. "Obviously we're all very worried about losing Alpha Lima for many different reasons. I'm very concerned because my job must be on the line; the insurers are saying it is the second case of pilot error in a very short time span. I expect you know that John Southern of Hull Claims came in on Wednesday and said that the crew should have realised that something was wrong and done something about it, though how he can possibly say that I really don't know."

I decided to interrupt the flow and try to put some order into our discussion.

"Why don't we start on that subject, Ron, since we can't put the clock back and it looks as if crew training and the way you keep a check on your crews is going to be crucial from an insurance and financial viewpoint. How do you do your crew training?"

"Well, we can't afford a full blown flight simulator here so what we do is get the initial training done at the manufacturer's training base at Hamburg and then, when that is complete, the first competency check and

98

all routine checks are carried out at the Airline Training Center in Miami. Their 412 simulator is approved for all regular checks, proficiency and route, so we don't waste crew hours on the aircraft. It's very cost effective and ensures a consistent and high standard for all the pilots."

Certainly as Ron explained, it seemed a good way for a small airline to get vital training carried out. Only the big airlines could afford their own simulators and keep them busy enough to justify the enormously high capital cost, not to mention the running cost of maintenance and training captains.

"What did John Southern say when you explained all this to him?"

"He agreed Airline Training had a good reputation but he'd heard that some airlines wouldn't allow Airline Training enough simulator hours. What was our policy? He asked to see all my records."

"Was he satisfied?"

"No. I told him that as far as we were concerned we trusted Airline Training completely and let them advise us on how many hours a pilot required. I explained that they always called me if there was a problem. Southern looked at all the route checks and, of course, concentrated on the records of Bill Hudson and Jim French. He tried to pick holes in the records but he didn't get anywhere. Not very surprising really, since if I'd had to pick a really good crew from all my pilots I would have chosen those two. Even Southern could see that Bill was very experienced on the type as well as having flown in the area for many years and that Jim, though he hadn't been with us very long, was an extremely good and experienced pilot. Southern's problem was that his firm sent him out to find out why they shouldn't pay out and the only excuse they have for not paying is if they can show it was pilot error."

"Well Ron, something pretty serious went wrong with the systems or the weather and so the insurers are not going to roll over and sign a cheque until they know what really happened. You can't blame them for that. The way you do your training is clearly very important. What do you think might have happened? Do you have any ideas?"

It was always interesting to ask that question since it gave me an insight into the person answering the question and, who knows, it might even help solve the mystery.

"Well I don't subscribe to that crack pot ditching idea of the investigator whose firm insured the pictures. She may be good at judging paintings but she has clearly never seen the Atlantic breaking over the eastern end of Bermuda when there's a tropical storm a few miles away. If I'd wanted to get the paintings out of the aircraft and I was that close to Bermuda I'd have turned off all my lights and landed at the airport. They don't man the radar all the time if no traffic's expected. It's not like it used to be when the US Department of Defense were operating the airport under the name of Kindley Field. The chances are that no-one would have seen them if they'd landed. Have you checked that?"

I shook my head and made a note to talk to the air traffic people in the tower at Bermuda airport, not that they were likely to go along with Ron's suggestion.

"But Ron, someone would have seen the aircraft in the morning."

"Well it was only an idea, Peter. Perhaps the aircraft took straight off again if it had enough fuel; I don't know, but ditching and getting the paintings out just isn't on, not near Bermuda. If the aircraft went into the sea it would break up and that seems to be confirmed by the fact that I now understand that they've found some wreckage and a body which must have been one of the passengers and not the pilots since it had a beard. I don't like to think of the idea but I wondered if there was actually something wrong with the aircraft."

"How do you mean?"

"Well the flight control computers giving the wrong signal or something like that. You see the ADS and the satellite radio failed at almost the same time, it was all so sudden. You know all we've got between us and the control surfaces is that new fibre optic cable system?"

"But that should make things better."

"Only if it works. Things don't always go as planned."

I let that go and Ron carried on.

"Perhaps somebody put a bomb on the aircraft to get the insurance money."

I explained that that would only make sense if the paintings hadn't been on board. However, I was beginning to feel that there might be some merit in going to Bermuda. The action was all there and here in St. Antony I was just one of the holiday makers. It had been my intention to change my airline booking to call in to Bermuda on the way to Denver and United. Now I decided that I had better pay a visit to Bermuda to-morrow, even if it was a Sunday. Another job I realised I had to do was get a detailed briefing on the 412's flight management system and I needed to do that at the manufacturers. I decided I'd spend Sunday at Bermuda, Monday in St. Antony, travel to Phoenix on Tuesday for an FMS briefing on the Wednesday with Honeywell, then Thursday en route to Denver and then start as planned with United on Friday.

"You say that Bill Hudson was a good pilot, and Jim French for that matter."

Ron interrupted.

"They really were both excellent, Jim in particular, though of course he wasn't a Captain. I can show you the scores for all the checks they've been having with Airline Training."

"But you know there's more to it than that. It's very difficult to judge how people will behave in an emergency, even with a flight simulator since the pilots are expecting an emergency."

"Bill was tough. A tropical storm wouldn't upset him."

"How about a gun? The guard forcing him to ditch. Would that upset him?"

Ron looked at me and I could see him trying to work it all out. It was a far cry from electronics.

"He wouldn't do anything stupid. He'd probably do what he was told but he certainly wouldn't want to ditch in the Atlantic swells. But anyway a gun won't wash, Peter. Remember, everything stopped just south of Bermuda. The most likely thing is a loss of control for some reason. I think I'm forced to vote with AAIB and the others."

There was a knock at the door and a thick set man came in wearing an airline captain's uniform which I didn't recognise. It reminded me, somewhat unkindly, of Mickey Mouse airlines. He obviously knew Ron very well and Ron introduced us.

"Peter, meet Greg Fairclough, head of Operations for the Paragon Corporation. He runs a bigger fleet of aircraft than we do."

Greg smiled.

"I'm not sure about that but we do have quite a few different planes. You're out here because of the accident to Alpha Lima, I understand. That's a terrible loss. I knew Bill Hudson well and, of course, Jim used to work for me."

"Do you have any theories, Greg?"

Ron interrupted.

"Peter wondered if one of the two guards had held a gun to Bill to make him ditch the aircraft."

Greg looked slightly surprised.

"It's a theory but it sounds pretty unlikely to me. Apart from anything else ditching on the Atlantic, even in sheltered water in smooth weather, is a very chancy business and the swell from Angela would have made it hazardous in the extreme. Anyway, there were only four people on board, weren't there, and the guards came from Westfield Insurance. It's much more probable that they flew into that tropical storm Angela, but why they lost control I don't understand. It sounds like a classic jet upset to me, the aircraft got some bank on above the permitted speed and the controls became ineffective. Of course the 412 has some pretty advanced flight features, I believe. Maybe they don't work as well as they should. God forbid it's not that, as it will affect all 412s and we don't need that."

"Why? Do you have any 412s, Greg?"

"No, Peter, but apart from anything else it would upset the airline schedules."

"Well let's hope we can find the aircraft because if it is a technical problem we must find the cause. Finding the recorders or the wreckage on the sea floor would be a great step forward. The problem is that though the hydrophones and sidescan sonar can find wreckage even at great depths, the area to be searched is so large that the chances of finding even one of the recorders or any significant small bits must be very small."

Greg looked at me carefully as if deciding whether he should continue.

"Peter, have you thought it might be a bomb?"

"That's what Ron wondered. But why, Greg? Only your boss Jimmy Morrison would gain in that situation since he would presumably get the insurance money for the paintings, but it would only make sense if the real paintings were not on the aircraft at all. Presumably there's no suggestion that the paintings were switched as they came out of customs?"

"I've no idea. I certainly didn't watch the loading myself."

"But the flight was for you?"

"Yes. But it's not my job to supervise to that detail. Anyway, surely there wouldn't have been time and my information is that the Westfield guards and customs were there. If the paintings weren't on board then they must have been switched on the ship or they were never loaded in London."

"Yes Greg, I did hear that for some reason the paintings came by ship and not flown in."

"Apparently the shipping agents in London were offered a very good deal by one of the cruise liners to take them to St. Antony and then fly them to Bermuda using BWIA. I tried to persuade Jimmy not to use a ship but he wasn't prepared to argue with the shippers and anyway the insurance company favoured the idea of using a boat. The moment that happened there was enough time for some firm in Texas to bring a court action here, claiming Jimmy owed them money and stop the paintings going to Bermuda."

There was a pause and I went back to a point that interested me.

"Greg, you mentioned you had a lot of aircraft. What have you got?"

"Well we've got two Gulfstream 3s and a Gulfstream 4 plus a variety of Beechcraft and Cessnas. Also a Raytheon 125-1000. We've got fifteen pilots at the moment which keeps me busy. People are very time consuming."

"Are they all qualified on all the types?"

"Not quite. Of course they all want to fly the G3s and the G4 but we have to restrict Captaincy to our more senior and experienced pilots. Still all the pilots have to know about the large planes since they have to act as first officers."

"It sounds a very interesting job. If I may ask without being nosy, why do you need so many aircraft?"

"Well Peter, Paragon deals with commodities, sugar, rice, potatoes, oil, anything we can buy and sell. It's a very tough market and we get the business by having a very fast response time. We can't do it over the phone since we need to see what is being sold and we are flying people the whole time into and out of South and Central America. You name the country, we've been there. And we have to go into some pretty uninviting strips sometimes, so we fly the aircraft right to the limit of their runway capability. It's very demanding flying as well as being very interesting."

"Where do you get your pilots from, Greg?"

"Everywhere. Our aircraft are all registered here and the St. Antony Government recognises most bona fide pilot licences so we can recruit where we like. To be honest, that keeps our costs down since we are not competing with US or European airline salaries. I've got pilots from Brazil, the States, UK, Colombia, Mexico to name but a few. Somehow they fit in well together and morale is high. Of course we're always flying backwards and forwards to New York where our headquarters are, to Bermuda and to Sarasota in Florida because that's where Jimmy Morrison, my boss and the head of the Corporation lives. He also has a pad in London and, of course, the G4 can go non-stop which he and Samantha like."

Greg stopped and turned to Ron.

"I really came in because the FAA Maps and Charts Office have had a problem delivering some topographical maps I asked for, covering Colombia and Venezuela. Could I look at them in your ops. room?"

"You can borrow what you want, Greg. I'm pretty certain we've got some spares and you can let me have them back when yours come in."

Greg Fairclough went off to the WAA operations room.

"He's a very capable operator, Peter. I wouldn't like his job though. He rarely knows from one day to the next what his programme is going to be. As for being one of his pilots, I wouldn't like that either. You don't get any home life. I reckon it's a job for bachelors. Mind you, Greg's son by his first marriage is married and flies for Paragon but he lives in Bermuda. Still Greg manages alright. He plays a great game of golf. His handicap is allegedly 12 but he normally runs rings round me. I think he should be playing off 6. Still I thrashed him yesterday. I think he was thinking about his new girl friend who lives near Frank."

I decided to stop questioning Ron at that moment and wait until my return from Denver before continuing. When I reached Frank's office I asked Susan if she could fix me a trip to Bermuda for the following morning getting back the same night. She undertook to change my ticket to Denver and reserve a flight to Phoenix arriving late Tuesday night. I told her I would fix the Phoenix hotel.

"Am I going to have trouble getting back in again from Bermuda, Susan?"

"No I don't think so. I'll mention it to the immigration chief. Charlie's on the same flight as the one I'm trying to get you on so I can do both of you together."

"Why are they giving us such a hard time?"

I asked Susan rather than Frank because I suspected in this respect, being a true local, she knew more than he did.

"That's because you're both trying to find out what happened and the customs are afraid that they may be criticised, so they are trying to get the immigration officials to make you uncomfortable and get you to leave. St. Antony is not like Bermuda any more. It's still in the Commonwealth but not a colony and some hotheads are determined to make this quite clear. I think you're suffering because someone is getting at the junior officials."

She was probably quite right about our immigration problems being a local problem within the department and not government policy. After all, St. Antony still used a lot of the UK systems and firms like International Air Radio to do the local air traffic and AAIB for accident investigation. They also used the European Aviation Safety Agency to do the certification and some parts of the safety regulation.

Susan showed me in to Frank who was still trying to run the airline in spite of all the interruptions. I told him my plans.

"Put him first class, Susan, if there's a problem. That's what we had to do with Charlie. Don't worry Peter, it won't cost us anything except the extra fuel required to carry your weight backwards and forwards to Bermuda."

He could see I was concerned.

"But you will lose revenue?"

"I wish you were right. We still have four first class seats and we never seem to fill them all, certainly not on Sundays. I really should get them removed. It would save a cabin attendant and give us at least six extra tourist seats, possibly twelve. First class seats have a very good revenue yield but if there are no first class passengers then it is better to have the extra seats in the back, even if the return is much lower. We do pretty well for numbers in the cabin and on occasions we could use the extra seats."

"Don't Jimmy Morrison and his people commute down here and use the first class seating? The Paragon Corporation has a facility here doesn't it?"

"You have to be joking. They have their own Gulfstreams, two 3s and a 4. They never fly with us."

Susan appeared and said my seats were confirmed, sitting next to Charlie on the way back. I noticed they all called her Charlie behind her back but seemed to favour nothing or Ms. Simpson when she was there. Ms. Simpson had the same effect on me.

"Frank, do you know any people in Bermuda?"

"Well, there's my head of station, Phil Mancuso. He looks after the whole WAA operation there. Maintenance, reservations, crew scheduling etc., the lot. I'll get him to help you. What do you need?"

"I need to look at the wreckage, the body, talk to the guy who did the post mortem, go to the Royal Navy search co-ordination center, talk to the World Underwater Surveys guy and I'd better talk to Air Traffic."

Frank looked at me thoughtfully.

"I know Frank. It's a far cry from avionics but it's the way I'm made. I want to know everything so that I can spot if anything unusual is going on. If you would rather I didn't get involved I'd quite understand."

"No, somebody's got to look after WAA's interests and I can't think of anyone better, Peter."

"Thanks for that. Is Sunday going to be a problem?"

"Not really, they'll still be dealing with the problems of the wreckage. Anyway I'll get Phil to warn people you're coming. Say that list again slowly, Peter."

He wrote an email and gave it to Susan. "Phil is so busy I'm very lucky if I can get hold of him straightaway. Apparently he can read email when he's got time on some portable device he's got. Of course to-day he's got Charlie to look after as well as his normal work."

"I thought she was hobnobbing with the great Jimmy Morrison sweeping the seven seas."

Frank smiled at me. "You don't have to be quite so sarcastic, Peter. She may not have got the right technical solution for searching for the aircraft but there's something in what she says."

"About being too convenient? I'm not sure she's right. After all from Jimmy's point of view the paintings were his already so unless he needed the money quickly the accident wasn't too convenient, quite the reverse. Anyway he would know that Charlie's firm would not pay him the insurance money in a hurry. Of course, if the paintings were forgeries or weren't on the aircraft then it would be a different story, since the paintings could be sold to unscrupulous collectors and Jimmy would get both the sale money and, eventually, the insurance money as well. Luckily, the Westfield guards ensured that what was in the crates in customs got loaded on to the aircraft. Anyway Frank, if Charlie's right then it wasn't a very good plan by the swindlers. You should hear what

Ron thinks of ditching in the Atlantic. He reckons they would have been better off landing at Bermuda and taking straight off again."

"Peter, have you checked with Bermuda Tower? Perhaps they ditched in Murray's anchorage or even the other end of the island to get in the lee of the swell."

"But the wreckage that's been found?"

"Well, if it was a scam they would put the wreckage where we would expect it to be, wouldn't they?"

He had a point there. Perhaps I was being too hasty. If the explanation of what had happened was easy, we would all know the answer by now. I'd better check if it was possible to land the aircraft at night in Bermuda.

"If something like that happened, Frank, then Bill was either part of the plan or under duress."

"Peter, did you know that Bill saw Jimmy Morrison about a month ago? The alleged reason was that he was delivering an important letter and Jimmy wanted it done personally."

"No I didn't. I never met Bill. Surely you don't think he would have done anything like that? Ron certainly doesn't."

"I just don't know. Some people say that everyone has a price. I don't know if I have one, Peter, but if I have, it would be pretty high."

"And for me, Frank."

"And for Bill?" He saw me looking troubled and added sympathetically, "It's so difficult to be sure. Let's go and have a sandwich, you look as if you need it after what I've just said. By the way, Susan asked me to give you this tape from Tim Hardcastle."

We went to the Pub again. It was clearly Frank's lunch room. I was busy thinking I needed to check with Charlie about how reliable the Westfield guards were and whether the area of search shouldn't be extended to the other end of the island. I added the points to my list that I clearly needed to raise with Charlie when I saw her next.

"Peter, on Monday night Pamela and I would like to entertain you and Charlie at home. Is that OK or have you got something else fixed up for Monday?"

Frank brought me back from my mental notebook.

"Thank you very much. I'd love to come." I smiled. "I'll put off my visit to see the night life of Cape Harbour until I get back from Denver. Where do you live?"

"I'll show you when we get back to the office if you bring your rental map in from your car. I've already shown Charlie. Presumably you'll share?"

"I never try and second guess the inestimable Ms. Simpson. She may have to do some work on the way home."

"You're at it again, Peter. I think you think Charlie is too smart for her own good and not as smart as she thinks she is."

I grinned. "That's just the way I would have put it if I'd been as smart as you."

Frank was right of course. Charlie was obviously a first class operator, but I had not yet decided how good she really was. Mind you, what the devil I was doing straying outside my knowledge base I wasn't sure. My job was to find out about electronics and software, I kept telling myself, but I wasn't having much success. Back at the office Frank marked my map and wrote the final instructions to locate his house after leaving the official roads. It was near Paradise Harbour which meant quite a long drive.

I needed to call Honeywell to arrange my visit to discuss some of the finer points of the Flight Management System. Luckily, I had met Max Postwick, one of their experts, at an S7 committee meeting, and I decided I had better call him when I got back to the hotel. I said goodbye to Frank and drove off to the hotel, parked the car and went up to my room. I looked round. The room had been disturbed by some one other than the cleaner. The magazines and other unimportant papers were no longer in the same order as I had left them. Luckily I had my computer and everything else of importance with me except my money and passport. I opened the safe where I had left them. They were there but I was fairly sure they had been looked at. I clearly needed to be very careful.

Cindy Smart answered the phone immediately when I called her. She said she would be at the hotel in about an hour. I got out the S7 committee's listings to get Max's home address.

"Excuse me calling you on a Saturday, Max, but I'm working in St. Antony."

"No problem, Peter. I like talking to the famous. You've really been in the news. Are you going to be able to make the next S7 committee meeting in Seattle?"

"I hope so though my business seems to be changing direction. Instead of doing just training I'm being retained to look after insurance issues related to accidents."

Max laughed.

"I have to tell you, my son, that there's a lot more money in doing that than there is training the hoi polloi."

I thought of the cheque I had received from Mike Mansell for the RWA accident and could see that there was a lot in what he said.

"Max. I'm going to send you an email. What is your email address and will you be able to reply by Monday? You can use my normal email address even though I may have to use America OnLine for my reply."

We exchanged email addresses. I had intended to tell Max what I wanted over the phone but I realised now that my phone might be bugged. If this accident was an insurance swindle then the money involved was huge and I was just a tiny pawn of no account. I switched on my computer and wrote a letter to Max and attached it to an email letter for his email address. I connected up to the telephone system and dialled America OnLine. The email letter was gone in no time flat and my email from Jill was delivered to me, though it took a bit longer copying down the attachments.

I called Steve Watson of United and told him that I would now be coming from Phoenix on the Thursday night and at the same time asked him to confirm his email address.

There was nothing really desperate in Jill's email but it all needed dealing with. I started answering my messages, attaching the files to my email so that Jill could word process them. My phone rang, Cindy Smart was in the lobby.

As I had guessed, Ms. Smith was a local girl but very much of the modern generation. She was dressed in a very smart pair of shorts with a contrasting but matching top which didn't do any harm to her figure. She was probably twenty five years of age and knew she looked good. We introduced ourselves and then she suggested that we went outside under a parasol. As we left the lobby she called a waiter over, asked me what I wanted to drink, ordered two iced teas, and then followed me out.

"Mr. Talbert, it is good of you to let me interview you. I know you must be very busy."

"I didn't know this was going to be an interview. I thought we were just going to have an unattributable chat."

"Whatever you like. I'd prefer an interview but it's up to you."

She smiled, slightly mischievously, and I realised she was obviously a great asset to the Announcer.

"You know it might be better for both of us if we just talked. Otherwise I won't feel like saying anything."

She agreed and we discussed the loss of Alpha Lima and everything that had happened so far. She knew about the wreckage and was thinking of going to Bermuda, since finding the crash recorders was clearly key. It didn't seem necessary to comment about my trip. She closed her notebook and we shook hands.

"I'll be in touch again Mr. Talbert, perhaps for an interview next time. Our readers are always interested in visits by celebrities," I started to shake my head, "and they've all read about you and the London Airport accident."

After she left I decided to snatch a quick sandwich. The coffee shop had emptied as the holiday makers who were on a bed and breakfast tariff had finished eating. I had a club sandwich. There was no-one I recognised in the place which pleased me. Undoubtedly, the searching of my room had unsettled me. The keys were of the plastic magnetised card type, each key programmed for the guest. I went to see the manager and told him what had happened. He protested it could not possibly have happened but he didn't look too surprised. Whether he was in on it and made money on the side I could only guess. I asked for a new key to be programmed for my room but I knew I was wasting my time since there were master keys which could open every room in the hotel. I supposed it was the safe being opened that really concerned me. Again the safe was of the programmable type in which the user chose the password and again I was fairly certain that there was one password which would open all the safes so that, not unreasonably, the safe of a guest who forgot the password could be opened. I hated to think how many people in St. Antony knew the master password of the safes.

I went back to my room and finished composing my mail to Jill and finally sent the lot off. It was a great system though not all that secure. I wished I had arranged a digital signature and encryption for the email before I left.

***

I got up at seven and looked out for the Olympic swimmer. She was nowhere to be seen. I decided she must either have finished early or she was fallible after all and had overslept. After a quick swim I got dressed and left for the airport. There was no point in having breakfast since there would be a first class breakfast on the way to Bermuda. I had everything with me in my flight bag. The safe was now empty and I placed a tiny piece of matchstick inconspicuously inside which was bound to be knocked over if the safe was opened. There was no point in doing anything to the papers I had left since the cleaning lady might move them, though not of course change the order as had happened yesterday. I got my boarding pass and waited in the first class lounge which turned out to be more like a large cupboard. I drank some coffee and a ground hostess appeared and asked me to go to the plane.

There was a line going through passport control. I noticed with some amusement that Cindy Smart had decided to go to Bermuda as well. When I reached the front of the line I showed my passport but this time the immigration officer wrote down my name. For some reason I was a marked man.

I was glad to see that the plane was nearly full though I was the only person in the first class cabin as Frank had foretold. There was one very smart local girl to look after me and I was spoilt all the way. I felt I had to eat a cooked breakfast so as not to disappoint her. Half way through though Ron Gibbons appeared.

"I heard you were on board. I didn't come back earlier so you could enjoy your breakfast. I'm having my weekly flight. I prefer to take this one as it is a straight out and back. I can be back in my office by 3.45 in the afternoon, not that I will to-day as it's Sunday. If I take a plane and go down the islands it takes all day. I don't get a chance to do much flying these days with all the paperwork and the personnel problems. You've no idea."

I had but there was no point in saying so. Ron had all the local employment politics to deal with and it wasn't easy.

"Would you like to sit in the jump seat for landing?"

"Is that allowed? I thought no one other than flight crew were allowed on to the flight deck these days."

"At the moment the captain is allowed to ask first class passengers at his discretion, but I suspect we may not be for much longer."

I would have been quite happy to remain where I was but it would have been churlish to refuse. I arrived as Ron was signing off from talking to New York Oceanic using the satellite system and was just opening up with Bermuda Approach on the normal VHF frequency. There was no need to wear a headset as the crew were clearly going to use the cockpit speakers right down to landing which surprised me a little. Perhaps WAA didn't insist on wearing headsets when landing and taking-off.

"Alpha Juliet, this is Bermuda. Squawk 1201 and press ident."

"Alpha Juliet."

Ron selected 1201 on the secondary radar transponder, switched the transponder to transmit and pressed the ident button.

"Alpha Juliet, we see your squawk. You may descend to 150 when ready. Advise leaving 350."

The aircraft descended slowly under auto-pilot control, signalled from the flight management system. The flight deck was superb with an unobstructed view of the displays because of the 412's side stick controllers like the Airbus aircraft, instead of the conventional yokes that pilots formerly used to fly the aircraft. I could see Bermuda clearly on the navigation display and also on the weather radar. As we closed in there were some blips of the other aircraft on the Traffic Collision and Alerting System, now mandatory equipment for all aircraft flying in controlled airspace as a second line of defence against mistakes by air traffic controllers. I noticed that the pilots were not checking the Bermuda VOR beacon; possibly they thought it seemed superfluous with all the other aids available. It took me some time to discover where the stand-by compass was but I finally remembered what Chuck Curtis had told me. The compass was stowed away into the bottom of the overhead roof panels as Airbus had done with their A320 aircraft. In my view it was a bad thing to do since the crew never bothered to check the stand-by but relied exclusively on the digital computers and the laser gyros. The Boeing airplanes kept the stand-by compass in view all the time which was good airmanship in my opinion. I thought of poor Bill faced with the emergency two weeks ago and then I thought of Frank's story of Bill's visit to Jimmy Morrison. What a tangled web to untangle. And a dangerous one I was beginning to realise.

Ron disconnected the auto-pilot at 3,000 ft. and flew the aircraft down to touch-down. He felt he needed the flying practice rather than letting the auto-pilot do all the work including the landing. He made a good landing and I left the flight deck as we taxied in. I was first to leave the aircraft and was through the Bermudan immigration and customs barely pausing in my stride. Phil Mancuso was there to meet me with a great smile on his large face, attached to a very large body. His WAA uniform must have cost at least twice as much as my cabin attendant's on this morning's flight from St. Antony.

"Glad to see you Mr. Talbert. Where would you like to go first?"

"Wherever you've planned Phil. Please call me Peter."

"OK. Peter. Let's go to the mortuary. The doctor's there who did the post-mortem last night."

We drove down to Hamilton. The mortuary was conveniently placed between the hospital and the police station. Dr. Fred Baxter met us and we went to his office.

"What's the position on the body, Dr. Baxter?"

"Well Mr. Talbert, I've examined it and death was clearly from drowning. I'm no expert in these matters but it is likely that hypothermia would have occurred very quickly and that tends to make the victim breath in rapidly and take in water unless the head is well clear of the surface and sea conditions are smooth."

I thought about that for a moment.

"Was the body wearing a life jacket?"

"Yes. But it was only partially inflated. It wouldn't have helped much in the sea conditions, I suspect. Death would have occurred from hypothermia even if he hadn't drowned."

"Doesn't that suggest the aircraft was under some sort of control when it hit the water? If the aircraft had dived in from a great height wouldn't the death have been from crushing? The body would have been dead before entering the water. Certainly no breathing would have taken place."

"Yes, I think you are right but as I said I'm no expert in these matters. Jack Wellings, the AAIB inspector in St. Antony, made the very same point to me this morning. I'm glad to say that there is a real expert arriving from London this afternoon to give me his opinion. All I can tell you is that death was not from physical damage though incidentally there was a mark on the back of the head and scratches and scars on the body."

"Surely that is what one would expect in this sort of accident"

"Yes, of course."

"Do you know if the body has been identified?"

"I don't believe so but you will have to talk to the chief of police. Do you want to see the body?" The true answer would have been no, but I felt I ought to look at it. Baxter took me along the corridor to the room where the body was lying. I looked at it and I was nearly sick. This sort of thing was right outside my experience. The body had been in the water some time. I guessed that the face would probably be recognisable but it wouldn't be easy in my opinion, particularly with the beard. Still there was always examination of teeth and similar things which might help in identification. I left hurriedly. Baxter gave me his number so I could call him from St. Antony.

As we got into the car I asked Phil if I could talk to the person in the police who was in charge of the identification. He suggested that there would be no problem at all as the police were currently looking after the wreckage. We got out at the block next to the police station where it had been stored. The guards let us in by prior arrangement and I inspected the wreckage. Mick and Jack Wellings were still there together with the friendly looking guy from European Aerospace who had smiled while Robin was shooting his mouth off the other day in the hangar. We introduced ourselves, his name was Martin Frost and he specialised in flight control systems.

The two prime items in the wreckage were the aircraft dinghies. There could be no doubt where they had come from because they both had VP-WAL painted on the fabric. The dinghies were almost fully inflated but looked as if they had been damaged on leaving their stowages in the aircraft. There were torn attachments and other marks on the dinghies. It looked as if it was just pure luck that the actual fabric had not been punctured. There were three partially inflated life jackets, various bottles of drinks, some broken panels and quite a few cushions of various types.

"What do you make of all that, Mick?"

"Well it's all from Alpha Lima. I'm not clear what's happened to the other two dinghies and how there are some partially inflated life jackets but I suppose all sorts of queer things can happen when an out of control aircraft hits the water."

Jack Wellings came over with Martin Frost and joined us.

"Let's hope we get some more wreckage soon. I'm not sure what to do about Oceanic Engineering and the hydrophone search which they've just started. The frigate started at the position I mentioned to you the other day and Oceanic Engineering has been helping search that area. However, the position of this wreckage suggests that the aircraft may have crashed rather closer to the island than we thought."

"Why don't you talk to World Underwater Surveys. They are very experienced in these matters and they're your search managers anyway. In fact I was planning to call in there after I've spoken to the Chief of Police in about an hour." I looked at Phil who nodded to the time scale.

"Good idea, Peter."

When we left, Phil took me to the office of the chief of police. He obviously knew Phil well and came out of his office to invite us in. I asked about the identification.

"No we haven't had the body identified yet. We know that if it came from the aircraft, it must have been one of the guards, because the two pilots didn't have beards. There's a supervisor from Westfield insurance due in the next hour or so flying in from Miami so we should know the name of the body quite soon. Would you like us to let you know?"

"Well it would be very helpful. In fact Charlie Simpson, who is an insurance investigator for Westfield, is here on the island and is flying back with me to St. Antony late this afternoon. I think she may be with Jimmy Morrison at the moment. Anyway his office will know where she is. Perhaps you could let her know."

There was nothing more to say and Phil took me to Hamilton where the Navy had set up the search coordination centre. There was a Lieutenant in the main room who came up to us as we went in.

"I'm David Roberts. Phil told me you were coming in to-day."

"How are things going? Any luck finding the recorders or with getting more wreckage?"

"I'm afraid not. Let me show you what the search situation is." We went over to the walls of the operations room. "Here is a chart of the whole of the area around Bermuda but that of course does not show the search area. The normal admiralty charts of the Atlantic are far too small a scale for our purposes since the search tracks of the boats have to be so close to make sure we don't miss anything. Consequently, we've drawn up these special charts ourselves which go out to about 300 miles east of Bermuda"

The charts were fixed all round the walls and covered the whole of the area being searched extending south east from St. David's Head to 59°W and 30°N. Parallel tracks had been drawn starting at Jack Welling's recommended start point of 31°N 60°W.

"As you can see Peter, we've marked the areas in red that have been searched using a hydrophone listening for the accident data recorders' sonar beacons. I've used a different colour for the Oceanic Engineering ship which, is of course, supplementing HMS Broadside."

It was all too clear how slowly the search was going in relation to the area to be searched.

"It seems a slow business David, even though the ships are working 24 hours a day. What's the significance of the position of the wreckage in relation to the area you're currently searching?"

"We've been just been discussing that very point. Have you met Philip Smith of World Underwater Surveys? He's advising us in this matter."

Philip had appeared from the back room where he had been on the telephone.

"Bob Furness has just been on the phone checking up on how we're doing. We've marked the wreckage position on the chart here and you can see that wreckage was found much closer to the island than the area we've been searching and we've got to make a decision what to do. We've been working out the effect of the wind over the eight days since the disappearance of the aircraft and strangely enough the total effect seems to balance out which probably accounts for the reason why the wreckage is comparatively close together. My recommendation to Bob which he has accepted is to bring the Oceanic Engineering boat in and start searching in the area of the wreckage and to leave Broadside searching where it is now." Philip turned to David. "If that's OK with you I'm going to call *Ocean Searcher* now."

"Yes, that's fine." He thought for a moment. "How about getting a Nimrod to drop a hydrophone in the area. It's a long shot but it will save a lot of time if it works."

"First class idea. Can you contact the Nimrods?"

"It would be better if Bob did it, Philip."

Philip nodded and disappeared into what was effectively the communications room of the search centre. He reappeared in a few minutes.

"Well that's done. They are going to start winding in the hydrophone and start searching closer in. Bob's also going to try to get a Nimrod to drop a listening device. By the way, Paragon Operations have been on the phone and want to help searching in-shore. Apparently someone's got a theory that the plane actually ditched in shallow water. I told them as politely as I could to forget it but Jimmy Morrison is putting pressure on his people to rent a boat and start. It so happens that I brought out an AAIB's hydrophone kit and Bob has said that we can lend it to them. They are going to be ready to-morrow and they've asked me to give them a position to start. Even though I think they're wasting their time and money I still feel we should coordinate their searching and Paragon thought that was very sensible."

There was nothing I could contribute to the problem so I made my farewells and I asked Phil to take me to the control tower at the airport. We drove quickly from Hamilton along the north coast looking out at the shallow flats and then the Murray anchorage. The weather was quite mild with odd showers of rain.

"Phil, I've taken quite enough of your time, particularly on a week-end. When I've finished here I'll go to the terminal and wait for the flight. What time do I have to check in?"

"The flight leaves at 6.30 and gets in at 9 o'clock. You're first class so you can leave checking in until the last moment. At the moment only you and Ms. Simpson are in the first class cabin."

"If I don't see you before I leave, thanks for everything."

I went into the tower and there was a guard on duty. I asked to speak to the chief controller and the guard made a phone call. James Donald appeared and we exchanged our visiting cards. He invited me into his office.

"Well how can I help you, Peter? I guess it's about the loss of VP-WAL."

"Yes, James. It certainly is a strange business. Do you have any views?"

"Well it really is nothing to do with us because it never entered our airspace. It's true the flight plan had the aircraft landing at Bermuda but in the event we never had contact with it. We are convinced that the aircraft was way out to the south east of Bermuda and got into difficulties in the tropical storm. You people have got to find out what was wrong with the aircraft systems that caused it be in the wrong place."

"What did you do when New York told you that the aircraft had 'entered' your airspace?"

"We called the aircraft on a variety of frequencies without any success. We used both primary and secondary radar to search for it and completely failed. When New York told us that the ADS had stopped and also the satellite communication, we started the emergency procedures."

"Did any other aircraft hear Alpha Lima calling?"

"No. We did ask aircraft that we were working on VHF at the time to listen out on 121.5 MHz, the international emergency frequency, as well as the normal frequencies but we had no reports of any contact."

"Is it possible to see your log so that I can see where all the aircraft were at the time?"

"Sure. We're all computerised now so what we do is to call out for a print out of all movements between set times when we need it which, let's face it, is very rarely. Are you interested in ground movements."

"I don't think so. At any rate for the moment can I just have a print out of all communications excluding the ground frequency 121.9 MHz."

"Fine. Let me show you the print out we did make of that night. It's up in the tower. I'll organise a print out for you to take with you."

We went up to the tower and James showed me the log which was a continuous dump from a line printer. I looked at the log. There were only a relatively few flights covering the period. The British Airways flight for London left at 7.30 and flew in a northerly direction away from Bermuda and Angela. There was also a German package holiday flight that left at 7.45 on a similar route. There were no in-bounds from the east. There were two flights from New York, a US Airways MD-95 which arrived at 9 p.m. and a United flight at 9.10 p.m. The last flight on his list was Paragon 56, a Paragon Gulfstream G3 going to St. Antony.

"So you'll let me have a copy of this print out?"

"You bet."

"There's something else I wanted to ask you James. If you have no traffic in the middle of the night what do you do?"

"We bed down and go to sleep with an alarm next to our ears if anybody calls on the radio or the telephone. Why do you ask?"

"Well on the fateful night when Alpha Lima was lost, did you have any traffic that night? Were you on duty, by any chance?"

"Yes as it happens I was. In fact we had no more traffic that night and normally we would have gone to sleep. But not that night. Remember we had a full emergency on, looking for the aircraft. The US Navy were organising a search first thing in the morning and the Bermudan Government duty officer was on the phone to me, to the St. Antony Government and the UK trying to organise Nimrod maritime search aircraft. If you were wondering whether Alpha Lima could have landed here unannounced while the tower was closed for the night," he looked at me and I nodded "I think it almost impossible. I suspect that under normal circumstances a light aircraft might be able to land at night without being caught but it would be very chancy. Anyway on the night in question, no chance. The aircraft wasn't on the ground in the morning and it definitely would have been heard taking off. By the way what time is your flight so I can get you the log?"

We sorted the details out and he promised to send the copy to the first class check-in desk in time for my departure. I looked outside the control room windows at the airport. I saw a hangar with Paragon Corporation painted on it, where there were one or two aircraft.

"James, do they do a lot of flying?"

"Yes they do. They seem to fly to most of the Caribbean Islands, to the Bahamas and of course, to the States. They have two top of the range Gulfstream 3s and a Gulfstream 4 which have an enormous range."

"Do you have any other private operators?"

"Yes, there are one or two but not on the scale of Jimmy Morrison and his corporation."

"Has he slowed the flights down since the stock market problems?"

"Not at all. If anything they've speeded up. They do a lot of night flying. It gives our night watch something to do. Funnily enough, Tim Hardcastle in St. Antony said the same thing."

"Surely all the night flights don't go just to St. Antony?"

"Oh no! I just happened to be talking to him the other day discussing Alpha Lima. The aircraft go to Nassau, Barbados and a lot of the other islands."

He left to get the pages of the log printed and I went to the terminal. There was quite a lot of activity as the flights from Europe were arriving. I checked in, changed my pre-assigned seat so that I was not sitting next to Charlie and wandered round the shops. There was plenty of time. Like most airport shopping areas it was inadvisable to buy anything as the goods they were selling were more expensive than in the towns; it always amazed me how the shops managed to survive bearing in mind the high cost of the airport ground rent. While I was in the news stand buying the papers that had just arrived from the UK, I saw Tom Mullard, the WAA avionics mechanic but I judged he hadn't seen me. We had definitely met or I had seen him somewhere, sometime but I couldn't remember for the life of me where it was. He bought some newspapers and left the terminal. As he left I saw Charlie arrive with a short thin man wearing a smart suit. I recognised him from photographs as Jimmy Morrison. They were obviously making farewells. They shook hands and Morrison left. Charlie was carrying a brief case and went to the check-in desk. When she had finished she wandered over towards the news stand.

She looked slightly smarter than in St. Antony with a light brown blouse and a matching pair of trousers. She saw me and came over and smiled. As usual she was wearing her dark glasses but, unusually for her, but very understandably, she volunteered some information.

"Mr. Talbert, did you hear that the body has been identified by one of our supervisors? The guard's name was Roger O'Sullivan and he was the best guard in our employment by far. He'd been with us a long time and as it happens I knew him quite well from a loss we had in Germany. He was chosen to go to St. Antony to supervise the transfer of the Morrison paintings from the custom sheds to the aircraft and then to supervise the transfer from the aircraft to Jimmy Morrison's house. His death is very sad for us. People like him are very hard to find. Completely straight and full of constructive ideas."

"I'm so sorry Ms. Simpson. Was he married?"

"Yes he was, with two young children. It's terrible for them and their mother and so difficult to explain. We will look after them financially of course, but that doesn't help much."

"Ms. Simpson, what puzzles me about all this is that your firm allowed all the paintings to go in one aircraft. I would have thought your rules would have stopped that happening. Like our rules with the Royal Family."

Charlie looked at me as if she saw something she hadn't seen before.

"Mr. Talbert. I'm ashamed to say you are absolutely right. Our rules did forbid it. But Morrison wanted the paintings in a hurry for some special exhibition and talked my firm in to agreeing to put all paintings in one aircraft. I pleaded with my boss not to allow it and she agreed with me but we were overruled by our Chief Executive. Apparently Morrison agreed to pay an extra premium. Not sure you can do that with the Royal Family."

There wasn't much more I could say. I did wonder if she knew about the mark on the back of the neck and the scars and scratches but I decided to wait until the morning before mentioning it, by which time I should have spoken to the UK expert who was due to examine the body to-day.

"Did you know the other guard?"

"Claudio Fernandez. No he was fairly new. Apparently he was a good guy of Spanish extraction, Columbian I think."

She hesitated and then clearly she decided to continue.

"To be honest with you, Mr. Talbert I'm a bit worried about the body because it had had a knock on the back of the neck. I don't know if it's significant. I expect you were aware of that." I nodded. I should have realised that nothing was missed by Ms. Simpson. "If the aircraft did not break up in the air but perhaps was under some sort of control when it hit the water then there would be marks on the body?"

I nodded and decided to try another tack.

"Ms. Simpson, why don't we give up the Simpson/Talbert routine and use our first names? We are going to see a lot more of each other while we are trying to solve the reason for this accident."

"Mr. Talbert, I like to keep business relationships on a formal footing." She paused and looked at me carefully through her dark glasses, possibly trying to decide what to say. "Furthermore Mr. Talbert, I'm not sure I want you to see a lot more of me. We will just have to see what develops." She smiled and I realised that I would have to be very careful. "And another thing, I'm not convinced it was an accident, it looks more like a very carefully premeditated crime."

She turned away to buy some papers leaving me to consider her last remark. I examined her back view as she looked at the books and papers and paradoxically came to the conclusion that if she had some smart

118

clothes on it might not be such a hardship after all to see some more of her. Suddenly I realised that she knew that very well. She chose the Sunday Times which had just arrived from London which suited me as I had settled for the week-end FT and the week-end edition of USA Today.

"I saw you hadn't bought the Times, Mr. Talbert. Perhaps I could look at your FT, I stupidly left mine in the hotel. Shall we go to the first class lounge?"

"Good idea. I didn't know they had one."

She led the way through an inconspicuous door which led upstairs to several small rooms overlooking the ramp. We found the right one and helped ourselves to coffee.

"You have an advantage over me, Ms. Simpson. Everybody behind your back calls you Charlie; is that how you like to be addressed when you are talking on an informal basis to your acquaintances?"

"I like to be called Ms. Simpson by my acquaintances, Mr. Talbert but it is true that my friends call me Charlie."

"But Ms. Simpson, Charlie is usually reserved for a man and, if I may say so, in your case there has clearly been an exception."

"My English mother christened me Charlotte and somehow that didn't seem to suit me." I definitely couldn't help agreeing with that. "At school very early on everybody started calling me Charlie and it caught on. Even my parents decided to change." She paused. "As for your views on my sex, Mr. Talbert, if I may give you some professional advice, never accept things at their face value. In my business things are often not what they seem."

It was a good piece of advice but there didn't seem much chance of her letting me check things out.

"You've obviously had a lot more experience in these matters than I have, Ms. Simpson."

I grinned and was pleased to get an answering grin in return. We decided to read the papers until our flight was called.

"What on earth is happening to the Paragon Corporation, Ms. Simpson? Their share price seems to get lower and lower, it's down to 7."

"Very good question. Paragon has a lot of stock in Central and South American countries and there are rumours running around that the stock is vastly overvalued. The company buys and sells commodities. The word drugs has now been mentioned and everybody is taking fright. Furthermore, people had noticed that Morrison had been unloading some of his shares so that he only owned 33% instead of nearly half. Incidentally, it is now being said that he is buying some of the shares back to stop the rot."

"That's what I read. But why did people buy the shares in the first place?"

"Well the prospectus was very good and they have been paying very high dividends. In fact they still are. The company has just declared very good profits and increased the dividend by nearly 40% but people are still very nervous."

"Shouldn't someone be investigating what is the truth of the matter?"

"Actually that's not nearly as easy as it sounds with a multinational organisation quoted in Tokyo, Frankfurt and London as well as New York. However, the investigative journalists are doing all they can, not to mention the brokers, so we should be hearing what's going on fairly soon."

A ground hostess appeared to tell us that our flight was being called and we could board when we liked. Charlie helped herself to another cup of coffee.

"How did you get on to-day, Mr. Talbert?" I sensed that this was going to be an investigation, not a conversation.

"Quite well, thank you. How have you been doing since I saw you last, Ms. Simpson?"

"You sound like a politician, ducking my question and asking another. However, to show willing I'm prepared to pool some information and ideas. Of course your question is a very comprehensive one which I'm not yet ready to answer in detail. As I am sure you noticed at the airport I have been talking to Jimmy Morrison. Yesterday he brought in the aircraft fitted with the Magnetic Anomaly Detector that we discussed," I noticed she had confidently added the words to her vocabulary since Friday, "a Norman Trislander, and it has been sweeping the east of Bermuda without I'm afraid much success. He feels that the aircraft just dived straight into the water out east of Bermuda somewhere and now, because of the wreckage, it may be closer to the shore than we think. What he wants is the whole thing settled so that we pay him the insurance money as quickly as possibly. Hence the Trislander aircraft. You won't be surprised to hear that Morrison doesn't admit to arranging a ditching and off-loading the paintings."

"You couldn't very well ask him if the pictures were really loaded, I suppose?"

Charlie looked at me.

"You have to be joking. Of course I asked him. He said he didn't like the implication and of course they were on board.

"I discussed with him your idea of a hydrophone and he saw straight-away the advantage of such a device and the need to act quickly. In fact he spoke to someone from World Underwater Surveys as you suggested and he is arranging a boat."

"Yes Ms. Simpson, I had heard that. I was in the Navy control room earlier this afternoon." I looked at her dark glasses. "You know when we discussed ditching the other day I was very dismissive. Would you like me to tell you why?" Charlie nodded. "Ditching any aircraft is a very dangerous thing to do but to ditch a modern jet aircraft safely is virtually impossible, especially an aircraft like the 412 with underslung engines. The moment the engines touch the water the drag would make the nose of the aircraft dig in and it would dive straight down. Alternatively, one engine would touch before the other because of the waves and the aircraft would be slewed sideways, then the opposite wing would dig in and the aircraft would break up. If I'd been going to do it, and I would have had to be drunk to agree, I would have insisted on having a fortune paid in advance to a Swiss bank account and I would have given my girl friend the number. Then I would only have agreed to do it in daylight, I would have chosen a very sheltered stretch of water, not a place exposed to the full force of the Atlantic and the touch down would have to have been very slow with the nose of the aircraft well up so it touched smoothly down, tail touching at the same time as the engines, and the aircraft would probably still have broken up and sunk in the water almost immediately."

"You're the expert." She looked at me quizzically. "I suppose Morrison could be deliberately looking in the wrong area. I'd better check on that."

"There is another point that may be relevant. Are you certain that your guards were working for you and hadn't been got at? If the guards had switched allegiance and were working for Jimmy then it is much more likely that the paintings may still be in St. Antony, even as we speak, or worse, on their way to places unknown."

Charlie looked uncomfortable.

"Mr. Talbert you have touched on an important point. However, as we know, the guard Roger O'Sullivan was a very reliable man. In my opinion he was incorruptible. I wish Roger was still alive but now it is confirmed he was on the aircraft I am convinced that the paintings were on board."

I could see why she placed a lot of reliance on Roger O'Sullivan and I only hoped she had considered all the alternatives. I decided to keep my own counsel as she clearly didn't feel the need for my advice. Charlie carried on.

"You know that Bill Hudson, the Captain, had been to see Morrison a few weeks earlier?"

"Yes, I discovered that from Frank. By the way don't you think it's time to go, WAA won't lose revenue if they leave us behind. I don't know about you but I don't want to stay here to-night."

Charlie put her coffee down as the hostess reappeared to chase us through immigration into the plane. She gave me a thick envelope from James Donald which turned out to be the air traffic print out he'd promised me. They closed the door as we boarded and the engines started straight-away. That was the way I liked to board an aircraft but I seldom had the opportunity since one had to be a first class passenger with good nerves. Perhaps Charlie was an expert on both counts. We went to our seats. I was in the aisle and Charlie was sitting next to me. She clearly wanted to talk.

"That's strange, Ms. Simpson, there must be some mistake. I moved my seat so as not to crowd you."

She smiled at me through her dark glasses. "I know." I got up to move.

"Why not join me for dinner and drinks and then give yourself some more room later?"

Maybe she hadn't yet discovered to her satisfaction what I'd been up to and I guessed she wasn't going to arrive in St. Antony without knowing. We taxied out and took-off almost immediately, turning south to pick up the track. Charlie ordered a spritzer specifying Chardonnay and I settled for scotch and water.

"Now Mr. Talbert, it's your turn."

"Well, I wanted to check on the body and the post-mortem. As you discovered, Dr. Baxter is a very good man but not an expert on air disasters. That's why he wired for an expert from the UK who, even as we drink, is probably examining the body."

Charlie nodded.

"You're worried because the death was from drowning and not impact, aren't you Peter? It doesn't agree with your loss of control theory and diving into the sea?" She had inadvertently slipped into using my name. Perhaps she was human after all.

"Yes I am, Charlie. It suggests the aircraft was ditched but as you know I don't believe in the ditching theory. However, the body was wearing a life jacket which would support a premeditated ditching. I want to talk to the doctor from the UK to-morrow after he has had a chance to examine the body. I suppose the aircraft might have been spinning when it hit the water so that the body survived the impact and then died in the water."

"Did you do anything else? Inspect the wreckage?"

"Yes I did look at the wreckage. I would have expected the life jackets to have been fully inflated but I suppose they might only have been partially blown up or, more likely, leaking after this length of time. The dinghies looked in very good condition, but they were scuffed in places as one would expect."

"But why are there only two and not four? And when are the other bodies coming ashore?"

There were no definite answers to her questions so I didn't give any. The hostess entrapped us with the trays fitted to the side of our seats and put the meal in front of us. It looked a typical airline meal. We were having filet steak as the main course and we had both chosen medium rare. Charlie ordered another spritzer but I was deliberately only sipping the double scotch that had appeared, very gingerly. Now was not the time to relax and enjoy myself.

"Aren't you enjoying the whisky?" She had noticed.

"It's OK but I didn't want a malt. I would have preferred Bells."

She became very solicitous.

"I'm sure they'll change it."

"Thanks but I'm fine with this."

Charlie decided to return to elucidating how I had spent my day.

"How else did you pass your time?"

"As I told you I went into Hamilton to see the Naval control centre and I spoke to David Roberts as well as Philip Smith of World Underwater Surveys. I must say that I think that David is doing a first class job there coordinating the search but I expect in due course Philip will take over. After leaving them I visited the control tower and asked about the fateful night. I found it very surprising that the other aircraft flying in the area hadn't heard Alpha Lima calling for help. The only explanation is that Alpha Lima was too far to the east and out of range, which tends to support the theory that the aircraft was flying into Angela."

"Or Bill Hudson was in on the scam and didn't answer and was using a different frequency," she added.

Charlie was learning fast. I'm sure she hadn't known about these things before she arrived in St. Antony.

"What happens next, Peter? If we can't find the wreck both your insurance firm and mine are in trouble."

"It's not my insurance firm, Charlie. I'm working for Frank. In fact I've got to be in Denver on Friday for a few days on a previous job I promised to do."

Charlie didn't seem to be too heartbroken at the news.

"But Charlie, you've reminded me of something I kept meaning to ask. How were the paintings wrapped?"

"Well they were first wrapped in acid free tissue paper, then blanket type material and then placed in very thick plastic envelopes with chemical sachets which controlled the humidity. The packing had some of the air extracted so that when the crates were at the aircraft cabin pressure altitude of 8,000 ft. the packages would not explode. The whole packing process was virtually repeated so they were in effect double wrapped. The packages were then surrounded in thick compressed foam so that the paintings were in fact suspended in their crates. Waxed waterproof paper was used on the inside of the crates to guard against rain when the crates were being loaded. That should mean that within reason the paintings will survive being immersed providing no force is placed on them."

"Down to what depth?"

"Can't answer that for sure. 100 ft. would probably be alright, 1,000 ft. would probably not. There was a case of a painting falling into the Hudson river in New York without being damaged, but we don't encourage such happenings."

"How about 5,000 ft. plus in the bottom of the Atlantic?"

"Forget it."

"So if the aircraft is found at the bottom of the Atlantic then you would have to pay up?"

"I suppose so."

"So going back to your earlier comment, finding the aircraft isn't going to help Westfield?"

"Yes, you're right. But finding it will help Hull Claims won't it?"

"Only if they can prove the accident could have been avoided by the pilots taking corrective action. Otherwise they will have to pay up." I paused. "Charlie what are you going to do next?"

She didn't seem to hear my question. My guess was that she would be checking in detail how the paintings arrived in St. Antony, how they were put in customs, how they came out of customs and how they were loaded into the aircraft. Presumably they had had the guards present for every move, apart from when the paintings were in the customs shed with 'bleepers' fitted.

I tried again.

"Charlie, how on earth did you become such an expert on paintings and get such an important job?"

"Well, I studied the humanities in college and fine arts at Yale. I took a masters on the Impressionists."

"But that makes you an egg head. If I may say so you look like an action person, not someone devoted to learning."

"I was quite a gymnast at University. It was something I could do by myself. I'm not a team player," I had noticed but decided to keep quiet, "but I needed the exercise. It was only a matter of time before I decided that I had better learn some martial arts to defend myself. Later, when I was working at Christie's in New York I saw an advertisement in the Wall Street Journal for investigators and the rest as they say is history."

"Have you had anything quite like this one before?"

"No, but I have had some attempted swindles and I can smell one here. How about you?"

"No, Charlie. this is a new experience for me. My expertise is with aircraft electronics and computers, avionics as we call it, and so I'm keen to understand what went wrong technically."

"One of the engineers in the WAA hangar told me that you've just finished doing a first class detective job discovering what happened to that aircraft which crashed at Heathrow."

"I don't know about first class but I did manage to find out how the accident happened. Mind you, that case is going to run and run from an insurance point of view. It's a great shame the various companies concerned can't agree shares and pay the poor dependents. The Warsaw convention is pitifully inadequate and the claimants may have to wait for years. There's just got to be a better system."

"Yes, you're right. Perhaps they should put up the minimum liability to something realistic and pay the money straight-away. That way the dependents could wait in comfort."

"Charlie, tell me about the paintings. Why were they sitting in St. Antony so long? Was there a legal problem and if so, had it just been settled?"

"Very good questions. The situation is that Jimmy lent ten paintings, insured for a total of about $100M, to the Royal Academy in London for an exhibition. A US firm based in Texas got a Judge in St. Antony to hold the paintings because it claimed that they belonged to them as Jimmy had not paid $120M which he owed the Texas firm. The case was being heard in New York and it went on for about six months but then the case was settled. So the Judge in St. Antony released the paintings and, understandably, Jimmy wanted them delivered to Bermuda as quickly as possible. My firm, Westfield Insurance, was keeping the paintings insured and charging Jimmy for the pleasure. We insisted that he ferried the paintings on a regular airline rather than try to cram them into one of his own aircraft."

"Well it all seemed to happen very quickly after the case was settled."

"As I said, Jimmy was pressurising us to agree to the ferry arrangements for the pictures. So the timing of the trip does seem kosher, if that's what was worrying you, Peter."

We had finished our meal and I decided to move to the other side and read the newspapers. The cabin attendant asked me if I wanted to sit in the jump seat for the approach. The crew obviously knew I was on board and after a moment's reflection I realised it could be interesting. I got up, introduced myself and sat in the jump seat. The Navigation Displays showed our projected track to the airport.

"Do you use the VORs much now that you've got the Navigation Displays showing your position all the time?"

"Not much. Some pilots display the bearings on the compass display; the VORs and DMEs are tuned automatically by the FMCs." The Captain turned to me. "Did you know the VOR and the DME have been out of service?" I nodded. "In fact the VOR has only just come back on line."

It was completely dark and I found it difficult to distinguish the runway from all the other lights until we were quite close. The first clue for me was seeing the Precision Visual Approach Indicators telling the pilot when the aircraft was on the correct approach angle. We were on the ILS glide slope and so the PAPIs, as they were called, were showing two white lights and two red lights. We made a good touch down and exited on the high speed turn off towards the ramp. I could see a lot of WAA aircraft being serviced in front of their hangar and there seemed to be some activity at the business aviation hangar and the terminal. There were no lights at the other hangars which surprised me slightly, as both Tim Hardcastle in Air Traffic and Mick Flanagan had led me to expect that the Paragon hangar might be busy.

As Charlie led the exit from the aircraft along the finger into the terminal she looked at me.

"It's a male chauvinist world, Mr. Talbert. I would have liked to have watched the landing. They didn't ask me."

"That's because they know I'm an aviator. I'm sure they will be falling over themselves to have you on the flight deck next time if they know you are interested." She had relapsed into using my family name. Perhaps she thought she'd better keep me at arm's length, hers not mine. There was only one immigration officer on duty because the flight was not full. He looked at Charlie's passport, hesitated, looked at some notes and let her through. When my turn came the same thing happened. I caught Charlie up as we were going towards our cars.

"They seem very suspicious of the two of us in immigration. How are we going to find out what's troubling them?"

"It is curious. It's on my master list of jobs to be done."

We got into our cars but Charlie had disappeared by the time I reached the hotel desk and collected my key. I opened my safe and the piece of wood had moved. The rest of the room looked the way I had left it except that the cleaner had been in. I was pretty certain that my papers had not been examined. As I dropped off to sleep I realised that the crew of VP-WAL would not have been able to check their correct outbound heading against the VOR beacon because it had been out of service. Certainly all the cards had been stacked against them that night. I wondered if the card player was divine or whether it was someone local who'd been dealing from the bottom of the deck.

CHAPTER 4

'Where He the huge sea-monsters wracks,
That lift the deep upon their backs,'

In the morning I woke up at 7 o'clock as usual, shaved and went down to swim. The girl who had been trying to beat the Olympic record was disappearing into her ground floor room wearing a one piece costume that left everything to the imagination. However, there was something familiar about the back view which was not unpleasant in any way. I suddenly realised it was Charlie keeping herself fit. I couldn't believe I had been so slow in recognising her. She had a superb athlete's figure but clearly she didn't intend any of it to show inadvertently. I did my ten lengths and returned upstairs. There was no immediate hurry and I decided to look at my email. Max had replied from Phoenix that he had got permission to talk to me and to call in some more experts if necessary to answer my questions on the flight management system and the data flow to the satellite transmitter. He had booked me into the local Marriott near the plant for Tuesday and Wednesday nights.

I reviewed the situation in the light of day. Charlie might be right. Everything about the accident did seem strange. She clearly sensed a human hand, not the hand of God, but it would have to be a very clever hand and a very ruthless one, to kill four people without compunction just for personal gain. I went down to breakfast and Charlie was there wearing a floppy blouse and Bermuda shorts, neither garment being in my top ten list of nice things to look at, which I realised subconsciously was just as well. I wasn't sure of my reactions if she decided to take trouble with her appearance. Her glasses were impenetrable as she waved me to join her.

"Did you sleep well, Ms. Simpson?"

"That remark is associated with 'Charlie' not 'Ms. Simpson' Peter."

"It was a professional inquiry checking you had not been out snooping round the airfield."

Just for a moment I thought she flushed. Perhaps I had been nearer the truth than I expected with my flippant remark. I studied the menu the waitress had brought me to hide the fact that I had noticed her embarrassment. I ordered Papaya again, orange juice, dry toast and coffee. Charlie was eating special K with a banana on top.

"I gather we've both been invited to have dinner with Frank to-night, Peter. Your car or mine?"

She obviously didn't feel the need to check the airfield again.

"I'd be delighted to escort you, Charlie."

"Good but it'll be a 'take', not an 'escort' which has other connotations."

"I bow to your superior knowledge, though in the British English dictionary you'd be quite safe with an escort."

"Maybe, but I never take risks," a remark which I was beginning to think might not be entirely truthful. We finished sparring and reverted to as normal a conversation as was possible in the circumstances.

I decided to try and be helpful.

"I'm going to ring Baxter to-day to hear what the medical expert thinks. I also want to wander round the avionics lab if I can, when there's no-one there."

"I'm going to try to explore our immigration problem through our consulate, Peter. I sent them a message to expect me."

"Charlie, I've been thinking. Jimmy is clearly incurring a lot of expense apparently searching for Alpha Lima in the shallow water to the east of Bermuda. He's virtually agreed that a magnetic anomaly detector is the not the way to go and is to-day starting to use a hydrophone to find the recorders. It's obviously very important to try to discover whether Jimmy believes the paintings might be there or whether he is doing it just to accelerate the insurance money."

"I'm not sure I follow the point you're making."

"Well, it's important in the total investigation to find out what is Jimmy's real agenda. Does he want the paintings back, does he need the insurance money, has he got the paintings hidden somewhere, has he got the freight? I'm not sure how we do it. However, I believe our only hope of finding the aircraft, wherever it is, is by carrying on what has been started, that is searching using hydrophones, sidescan sonar if we run out of battery life, and having a remote observation vehicle on standby."

"Surely it will be like looking for a needle in a haystack?"

"I'm afraid so, but if they concentrate on looking in the likely areas it may not be so bad."

"Peter, how expensive is the search going to be?"

"Well that's a very good question. It depends how it is costed and who is doing the searching. The hydrophone search is not terribly expensive, especially if military ships and aircraft are used. However, getting the recovery equipment on station and then getting it back to base again will I understand probably cost well over $250,000. The catch phrase for that is apparently 'MobDemob'. The cost per 24 hours on station is around $100,000 a day, though it depends on whether they are just searching with the hydrophone, using the towfish or using the submersible."

"How long will the search aircraft carry on if they can't find anything?"

"Charlie, that is going to be the real problem. My bet is that the UK Government, pressurised by the Treasury, will not have the stomach to carry on the search for too long and the St. Antony Government is even poorer than we are. My feeling is that unless there is a miracle, we've got to assume that the aircraft is not going to be found. I don't suppose the US Government will want to keep on searching? Particularly if the Brits stop."

"No Peter, you suppose correctly." A pause. "What happens if the sonar beacons on the crash recorders are found?"

"My guess is that the UK Government will carry on paying for the MobDemob, for a few days anyway. Who knows perhaps St. Antony might chip in a little as well."

"Well the US Government might try to curry favour with St. Antony and give them a little help, particularly as it is a US firm doing the searching."

"Well, we've got to cover all the options and on balance it is probably sensible to look for the actual aircraft in every way we can if we have located the recorders."

"How about the paintings?"

Understandably, Charlie was only concerned with trying to recover the paintings whereas all I could think about was the cause of the accident.

"A lot will depend on the depth of the aircraft. We need to look at the hull first and see if it is one piece. Of course it may be a complete waste of time looking for the paintings there because they may not be there at all."

"What do you mean by that?"

"Look Charlie. You feel that there's something fishy going on and you may well be right. Perhaps it's not only the customs who want both of us off the island. If that's the case then we've got to assume that there is something to be discovered and that there are people who don't want us to discover it. People incidentally who, if they are prepared to 'blow up' an aircraft and kill four people, won't stand any interference from us. Finding the aircraft will not be a very remunerative goal whether it is lying 'full fathoms five' or more likely at more than five hundred fathoms. It will have been damaged irretrievably." I carried on firmly. "No, what will be worth having will be the paintings, so we've got to assume that a trick has been played in some way so that though the aircraft was lost, the goods were not. The paintings therefore are not down there in the deep. I'm curious, of course, about the freight. We don't know what it was or whether or not it was insured. All we do know is that it was very heavy. The only logical conclusion if the aircraft is down there, is that it was not worth anything and that it could be safely disposed of in the deep. Possibly, like the paintings, the machinery was replaced with lumps of concrete." A thought occurred to me. "Did you ask Morrison what the freight was and why it was on board?"

Charlie thought about that and shamefacedly shook her head.

"Peter, did I tell you that I don't like having my mistakes pointed out to me?"

"No you didn't Charlie, but if it makes you feel better I only just thought of it myself. In fact I can match your oversight. I met Greg Fairclough yesterday and I should have asked him the same question." I pondered for a moment. "My view, Charlie, is that we should search for the paintings on land. I believe we should assume that they were too valuable to go down and take it from there. The crates must have been empty or be filled with forgeries." Charlie wasn't convinced. "Furthermore, I've got to try to find out why the aircraft went the wrong way. I feel that if we could answer that then we would be well on the way to solving the whole problem."

Charlie eyed me reflectively through her glasses, if that was possible.

"Have you ever thought of taking up electronics instead of trying to be a detective?"

"Well as I said yesterday, I believe it is necessary to recheck every movement of the paintings from when they left the Royal Academy to when they were allegedly loaded on the aircraft. Furthermore, we need to think some more about freight. What was it, was it valuable, had it been switched as well as the paintings? What do you think Charlie? Am I talking nonsense?"

"Probably. After all, has it occurred to you that everybody except us would be quite happy with the aircraft diving into the sea, freight, paintings the lot and blaming the weather? The insurers will have to pay up but who cares? Nobody has any sympathy for insurers. All the accident investigators want to do, very understandably, is to find the cause of the crash so that they can be sure that the aircraft was safe as designed and then they'll go home. We seem to be the only ones that believe somebody is playing a three card trick, seemingly oblivious of human life." She stopped for a moment. "Has a guy from Aviation Week been on to you?" I shook my head. "Well he will be for sure. Walter Thompson is his name. He travelled up on the flight I took to Bermuda and presumably is still there. He didn't seem to know much about paintings but he seemed red hot on airplanes."

"You don't surprise me. That will make three reporters to avoid." She raised her eyebrows quizzically and I told her about Brian and Cindy. We agreed that in the circumstances public interest was inevitable and understandable. We separated and I managed to speak to Baxter when I got to my room.

"Mr. Talbert, you had better speak to Dr. Newhouse yourself." He passed me over to the expert.

"Dr. Newhouse, Peter Talbert here. What did you make of the body?"

"There's not much doubt that he died from drowning."

"What about the marks on the neck and body?"

"They must have happened during the crash. As I said, in my opinion death was from drowning accelerated by exposure to the cold waters of the Atlantic. The body had been in the water for about a week."

"Dr. Newhouse, presumably you are satisfied that the state of the body is consistent with dying after the aircraft hit the water?"

"It's very difficult to be certain in these matters. In all the circumstances it is reasonable to assume that death occurred some time after the time of impact but it is impossible to be sure. The body was wearing a life jacket so it would have floated after the crash. I shall be making my report and sending it to the chief of police here, the AAIB inspector at St. Antony, the chief of police in St. Antony and, of course, to London."

He rang off leaving me considering the impact of his remarks. I decided to call Charlie since everybody was going to find out soon enough. She hadn't gone out yet and we met outside her room. She was still wearing her Bermudan shorts. I broke the news to her.

"Peter, I'm sure something fishy is going on, if I may use your phrase. The doctor is saying if I understand you aright that the body did not die when the aircraft hit the water, but drowned after floating in the Atlantic. Bearing in mind that the guard was Roger O'Sullivan, who in my opinion was incorruptible, I suppose the other guard could have knocked him out during the flight and put him in the sea some time after the ditching."

"You're still ditching the aircraft then?" She nodded without smiling. "Perhaps it was just coincidence that the body was found where it was, Charlie. After all the other bodies have not appeared. Maybe the body had nothing to do with the wreckage. Maybe it wasn't Roger O'Sullivan after all. Do you think you should re-check with your man from Miami? Perhaps the doctor was wrong."

We both mused over the news pondering its significance. Charlie said she must go to the consulate. She'd call me when she got back. I called Frank at the office and brought him up to date. He listened but didn't volunteer anything of any import. He said that he would get Mick to meet me at the hanger at 2.30 that afternoon unless there was a problem. I was now at a loose end but before relaxing completely I decided I had better introduce some security into my laptop computer. At the moment anyone could switch it on and read all my files. As usual anything to do with a computer took a lot longer than expected but after spending a lot of time reading the help files I managed to make the data reasonably impenetrable though, given enough time, a determined hacker would always be able to get through. I chose passwords which I would not forget and did not have to write down. I had a sandwich by the pool but there was no sign of Charlie.

At 2.30 I met Mick and we went into the hangar. There were one or two people there but no-one in the avionics lab. I switched on the computer which had the modem attached. There was no password and I looked at the communication package being used. I didn't recognise it. I inspected the dialling directory and there was just one entry which I recognised as a Phoenix number. I was about to shut the computer down but decided instead to look at all the directories to find if email was being used. It wasn't obvious since, though the machine used the standard Windows operating system, the communication icons were not on the desktop. I found there was another standard communication package but there were no numbers in the telephone directory. Finally, I looked at the favourites drop down list on the Microsoft browser but everything looked normal. I went back to Mick's office and he looked up.

"Did you see Tom Mullard? He was going over to the lab. I tried to call you to warn you but I was too late."

"No, I didn't see Tom. Curious. By the way, can I look at the technical log sheets of Alpha Lima to see if there's anything unusual?"

"Not at the moment. They've been locked up by AAIB. However, I did get them to agree to let me have a copy of the sheets for the last ten flights." Mick passed me a folder and I scanned through to see if there was anything that looked strange.

I drove back to the hotel and relaxed on my bed. I called Mandy who had got home.

"At last, my darling. How are you managing without me?"

"Very well thank you though I'm working too hard. I'm at my desk here in the flat reading client's papers. I have to say I'd prefer to be in bed with you, keeping me safe, or something like that. How are you getting on?"

"It's all very strange, Mandy. Nothing adds up and I'm beginning to feel very nervous. I'm off to the States to-morrow and we can have a long conversation then. I'd rather not talk now."

Mandy was nothing if not quick.

"I understand. Call me from Phoenix even if its late or first thing on Wednesday. Glad to hear you're alright, my love."

She rang off and soon afterwards the phone rang again. It was Charlie.

"Home safe and sound. I'll tell you about immigration on the way over to Frank's. What time did you say?"

"I didn't. We need to leave at about 5.30. It's going to take quite a long time to get over there."

"Well let's meet in the bar, Peter, at 5 o'clock. I want to talk to you about searching for the aircraft."

I got dressed informally and suddenly found myself wondering what Charlie would wear. I soon found out. She was still wearing trousers but this time they were very sleek with a smooth V-neck blouse on top buttoned up high to keep her well shaped breasts firmly out of sight. I noticed she had put some perfume on. We went over to the bar in the hotel, sat down, Charlie ordered a diet coke and I had a coffee.

"Peter, when I was in Cape Harbour to-day I spoke to our attaché and we went over to talk to the Minister of Transport. The St. Antony Government really believe in the underwater search. They feel as you know that the aircraft dived into the sea east of Bermuda from 'natural causes' and that it is very important to find the fuselage etc to discover what really happened. Understandably, the St. Antony people don't care about the paintings and the freight. I made my views known about the remarkable coincidence of the aircraft crashing with the paintings on board but no-one seemed to think it was significant. The St. Antony Government is talking to the UK Government in order to ensure that the exploration carries on until the aircraft is found. The Minister made it clear to our attaché that no reasonable financial offer of help would be refused and our man took some notes but I don't expect they're holding their breath, Peter, waiting for our money."

"Excuse me asking, but were Westfield represented when the paintings were sealed? You know I'm not happy about the whereabouts of the genuine paintings."

Charlie grinned.

"You think Morrison wrapped forgeries in the crates?"

"Well it's been done before."

"You're quite right to be concerned. However, I'm fairly relaxed about it because we had Christies supervise the packing before they were shipped. The paintings had been on exhibition in the Royal Academy and they were taken to a place just down the road behind the Burlington Arcade for freighting. They use a firm called Jenkins Packaging who always do a super job. To be honest with you I wish I'd been there but my boss reckoned we could trust Christies and they put on a special seal which only they and we know, so that we can see if the crates or the packages have been opened."

"Well that sounds alright. However I'd like to make my position completely clear. I feel like you that the accident has happened at a very convenient moment for anybody wanting to get the insurance money but at the moment we don't have any other lead. If we can find the wreckage we should be able to determine what happened. If we can't find the wreckage I'm not for one moment suggesting that we should give up and put the loss down to the black hole in the Bermuda Triangle. My game plan is to do some more investigation to find out how the automatic satellite position reporting could have been wrong, because I'm convinced as most of us are that the aircraft, initially anyway, headed towards Angela. On my return, hopefully, I may have something more definite to go on."

We walked over to the car, both carrying bags which we put in the trunk. I opened her door to let her in.

"Why did you bring your bag, Peter?"

"For the same reason I guess as you brought yours. Someone is going through my room and opening the safe."

Charlie didn't look surprised. If her room was being done over she didn't say so. But then she played her cards very close to her chest, which was fine for the cards, but not for the other players. She navigated as I drove. I told her about the visit to the avionic shop and the non-appearance of Tom Mullard.

"You've got to assume that he either went to the rest room or, more likely was watching you, wondering what you were doing. What were you looking for?"

"I just wondered if someone was using the computer to send mail or something to another address or addresses rather than to Honeywell. I found one communication program with a Phoenix dialling directory but by chance I decided to have another look at all the directories and found another communication program but there were no numbers in the directory."

"Isn't that rather unusual? Surely most programs keep the last few numbers dialled?"

I looked at her dark glasses and realised I had missed a bet. I hadn't checked the program thoroughly enough.

"Fifteen all. You're right, I missed a bet. I'll have to go back and have another look."

I didn't fancy going back. For some reason I felt afraid. Where had I seen Mullard? Charlie started talking about her visit to the consulate.

"Apparently the St. Antony Government is very worried about there being after effects of this accident. The Caribbean is used as a staging post for drugs and there are some people in St. Antony who believe that this accident is part of that story. If we uncover what really happened,

134

who knows, some big names here might be affected. The other view is that the loss of the aircraft is just an accident, pure and simple, and they hope that you and I won't make it impure and complicated. However they appreciate they just have to let us get on with it. Meanwhile the customs people are twitching and asking the immigration people to make our lives difficult. What puzzles me is why the Government asked AAIB in to investigate the loss at all if they want it to be a pure and simple accident?"

"They didn't have much alternative, Charlie. St. Antony is a member of ICAO and the rules say that there must be an independent investigation. Not to do so would look like a cover up. I suspect that they thought AAIB wouldn't make too many waves whereas you and I seem to be putting the fear of God in them." I looked at her glasses again, narrowly avoiding a truck coming the other way and added "I can't think why."

We arrived at the Westbourne's without further incident and had a super evening. There were four other guests, Adrian and Sheila Cartwright who ran the hotel at Full Moon Bay, and Greg Fairclough with his new girl friend, Margaret Springfield, who was coincidentally the Westbourne's next door neighbour. She was a glamorous American lady of about forty who apparently had divorced her very wealthy husband and had taken over their holiday home for permanent residence. I was a little surprised that there were no local people since Frank must be an accomplished negotiator and politician to run a St. Antony based airline, but perhaps he had chosen his guests because he knew it would be a good mix and wanted to relax for just a moment from his responsibilities.

The view of the ocean from the house was superb and the weather was pleasantly cool with the wind blowing over us when we went outside to drink it all in. Pamela and Frank were excellent hosts and it was an interesting evening. Charlie and Margaret Springfield got on famously, possibly because they both came from Massachusetts. Inevitably we talked about the accident and the Cartwrights were concerned for Frank and the possibility of not getting the insurance money. Greg seemed upset that the world had lost so many superb and irreplaceable paintings. I saw Margaret thinking about adding to the conversation, looking at Charlie and then deciding to keep quiet. She realised I had been watching her and winked. Frank asked Greg about the Paragon Corporation and what was going on financially. Greg said it was all ridiculous, the company trading position was very sound and someone was trying to make a killing on the share price. However, he gave me the impression that he too was worried. I supposed that if things got tough for Paragon one of the first things to go would be the aircraft and flight operations. Greg also gave me the impression that he quite liked Charlie who to my surprise did not discourage him. I realised that I did not like Greg chatting up Charlie.

Margaret too was keeping a close eye on Greg and, like me, was clearly not too pleased by his interest in Charlie.

The evening raced by. The Cartwrights started the good-byes, followed by Greg Fairclough and Margaret; they had come in Margaret's car even though it was only a few hundred yards away. Frank persuaded Charlie and me to stay for another drink and we both opted for decaffeinated coffee.

"How are things going? Any more ideas?"

Frank looked at both of us and I just shook my head and then wondered if the atmosphere was getting to Charlie as she started mixing her metaphors.

"There's a lot more water to flow under the bridge yet and Jimmy is going to be very lucky indeed if his boat comes in underneath it with any of our money on it."

Frank mentioned he had received the maps and charts I had ordered. I asked him if he would order a few more for me.

We left at about 10 o'clock, neither of us had drunk much and I drove carefully home.

"You didn't ask Greg, then, Peter?"

"No, for some reason I feel the need to be very circumspect in asking that question. The nature of the freight could be a key question and I didn't want to waste it."

We chatted and I was pleased that Ms. Simpson and Mr. Talbert seemed a thing of the past though I was very careful not to show I had noticed.

"Peter, I sometimes think you have a lot of ideas in your head which you are not sharing with anyone. Why did you ask Frank for more maps and charts?"

"As my maths. master used to say Charlie, for the sake of completeness."

"As my last boy friend would have said, screw your maths master. For God's sake Peter, let's share in your ideas."

We proceeded in silence for a moment. I wondered about Charlie's last boy friend and caught myself wondering whether he had screwed Charlie and what it would be like. She certainly was very athletic.

"Anyway, what did you think of Greg, Peter?"

I returned to reality.

"I expect he's an adequate manager here for Jimmy but he didn't strike me as one of the world's leading business men. However, he's not dim by any manner of means. I have a feeling that he and hard work are not close companions."

"You're probably right. English degenerate upper crust. Still he has excellent manners."

136

"I did notice you were impressed. However, if you're trying to start an argument, you haven't succeeded. I don't move in the circles you clearly do and I bow to your superior judgement."

We drove up to the hotel and I released the catch of the trunk. I collected Charlie's bag, opened the car door for her and helped her out. She turned, took her glasses off so I could look at her properly in the eye.

"Thanks for escorting me, Peter," she murmured and went inside carrying her bag, leaving me to smell her perfume.

***

It was yet another marvellous day. I was up later than usual and watched the holiday makers starting to surround the pool. There was no sign of Charlie who had presumably finished her exertions long ago. I wanted to call Mandy but it would have to wait until I was sure my phone wasn't bugged. It wasn't any use sending her an email since that wasn't her favourite means of communication and anyway I was beginning to worry about the fact that I was not encrypting my emails. As I was debating my next move the phone rang.

"Peter, we haven't met yet. My name is Walter Thompson of Av. Week. Can you spare me a moment for a chat?"

"Ms. Simpson, the insurance assessor told me you were here, Walter. Where are you?"

He was in the lobby and I agreed to go straight down. We sat down in the coffee shop and ordered two coffees.

"Ms. Simpson said you were in Bermuda?"

"I was but I came in last night." He looked at me, very carefully. "Peter, you know this accident is unique. It's the first one when an aircraft with ADS has disappeared. Of course it's made even stranger because Bermuda couldn't see or talk to the aircraft. What's your view of the matter?"

"Look Walter, is this conversation off the record?" He nodded. "Well I don't want to be quoted but I find the whole thing inexplicable. How much did Ms. Simpson say?"

"She was very cagey. Obviously her company doesn't want to pay the insurance money so she's very suspicious."

"Well that's what so difficult about investigating this accident. There's no aircraft, no recorders, and no paintings. You know as well as I do that most aircraft accidents are just that, accidents, which happen from a combination of extremely unlikely occurrences and in my view the loss of Alpha Lima was almost certainly an accident. However, the problem with the disappearance of Alpha Lima is that it is just possible that it may not have been an accident and we've had a lot less practice in investigating crimes. Look at the Lockerbie accident to the 747, look how long that investigation took and it took even longer to get the criminals responsible."

"You're right of course. My problem is how to pitch my article for the next issue. I'm very nervous of suggesting it may not be an accident. On the other hand if it is a crime I want to be the first to expose it."

"Well you can't win. My advice is to concentrate on the search for the crash recorders, we're going to need them whatever's happened."

We talked some more and then he left to compose his copy for Aviation Week. I saw Brian Matthews talking to Charlie as I went towards the stairs up to my room and I tried to make myself as inconspicuous as possible. Charlie was looking impatient which didn't surprise me and she didn't look too pleased as she saw me skulking by.

My flight to Phoenix wasn't until 2 o'clock so I decided to do something I had never done before and go on a sight seeing trip round the island. At the airport, Island Flight Inc. had a booth inside the terminal and the next flight was at 10.30 scheduled to take an hour. It seemed a good deal and I paid my $40. The aircraft turned out to be a Cessna 420 with six seats, seven passengers including the co-pilot's seat and the pilot.

"Any of you fly?" asked the middle aged lady who was going to give us our air experience. I admitted that I had done some and she invited me to join her and sit in the right hand seat. I put my bag in a stowage and strapped myself in. It was warm on the flight deck in spite of the cockpit fans, which sounded like angry wasps. Honey, the pilot, her hair bleached almost white by exposure to the sun, called over the loudspeakers for everyone to do up their seat buckles, started the engine, got permission to taxi to Runway Zero Seven, waved the chocks away to a fellow member of the Island Flight enterprise, carried out the check lists, taxied towards the holding point, asked for take-off clearance, entered the runway, opened the throttles and took-off. I came to the conclusion she had done this trip before, which gave me some confidence.

The rush of air from the outside as we picked up speed made life bearable. We were soon looking down at the incomparable beaches below with the sand even whiter than the detergent advertisements. We went clockwise round the islands and Honey kept us fully informed of the things to look at. Below us we could see the occasional ruin, evidence of wars and occupations of the past. We saw the famous beaches and resorts of Atlantic Reef and Full Moon Bay, refurbished after the latest hurricanes. Perhaps Mandy and I would stay there one day.

For me Paradise Harbour was outstanding. I was not a historian but I imagined how the sailors must have felt as they entered this haven set in the middle of the treacherous rocks. From June to October, since civilisation began, successions of storms must have swept the Caribbean but, in this natural harbour, boats had always been able to shelter in relative safety in a similar way to English Harbour in Antigua. In fact, though man had very obviously put his mark on the land since Nelson's day, nothing had altered the cliffs and the sea which roared ceaselessly on the shore. Nelson, if he were to look down to-day, would still see boats sheltering, though they would not be his men of war but sailing yachts and motor cruisers by the score. Honey could see I was very interested in the harbour, as were all the other passengers and she did an extra 360° turn as she filled us full of historical information.

We carried on flying by St. Antony's only high ground, Crazy Peak, reaching alas only to 1,319 ft., not really high enough to catch the tropical rains and fill the reservoirs. The Caribbean islands to the south of St. Antony were better off for rain, but not for beaches. As we turned north we could see Redonda, a lonely rock in the distance on our left and then the capital Cape Harbour went past us on the right. I looked down and could see two cruise ships in the harbour and small boats plying ceaselessly backwards and forwards between them and the town. My watch showed that we had only been 30 minutes but I need not have worried that we were going to be short changed. Honey announced that we were going to Shell Island, about 10 miles north of St. Antony. We flew round the small island but there was not much to see, a settlement at Exeter, a lagoon, a ruined castle and a hotel right at the southern tip. There was a landing strip by the settlement and another one by the hotel. We headed south back to St. Antony and Honey spoke to the tower, reduced altitude, told everyone to strap in, lowered the flaps, then the landing gear, made a smooth landing, got clearance to the gate, turned into the ramp, swung towards the marshaller who had seen us off, and cut the engines so that we glided onto the chocks. Another mission accomplished for Island Flight.

We got out and walked into the air conditioned haven of the terminal. I went to my car and drove back to the hotel and up to my room to prepare for the flight. There was a message telling me there was a fax downstairs. There was very little to do as I had already packed my Denver clothes in the bag I was going to check. At the desk I collected my fax, looked at my bill and agreed to let them debit the credit card imprint they already had. I felt I was being observed and saw Charlie watching me through her glasses.

"Did you enjoy your flight?" was her starter for ten.

"Were you the one I waved at near Long Bay?"

"No. I was the one who watched you from the control tower and you never manage to answer my questions. And Long Bay is a nudist colony."

"That explains it. However, to answer your question, I did enjoy my flight. It was actually super and we even did a side trip to Shell Island. The whole thing was most interesting, it was worth $50."

"But the sign said they were only charging $40." She stopped as she realised she had walked right into it.

"I told you it was good value." She had the grace to smile. I didn't think she was used to having her leg pulled, physically or metaphorically. She rallied immediately.

"I've a bone to pick with you. Why didn't you rescue me from your reporter?"

"He's not my reporter. He's a journalist from the Daily Mail and he was only trying to do his job."

"He seems very sure of himself."

"Actually I think he's very good at finding facts and his argumentative approach was probably to get you to argue." Charlie was clearly reviewing what she said to Brian. "Did he say it was clearly an accident?" She nodded. "And you queried it?"

"Perhaps a little."

Even with her dark glasses she looked slightly concerned. I smiled sympathetically.

"We'd better read the Daily Mail next week." I consulted my watch. "I must be on my way. See you some time soon. Can I contact you at all if I need to?"

"Yes of course, Peter. But you have to do it through my secretary in New York." She got a pen and a business card out of her purse, wrote something down and gave it to me. "You have to give her this password, your date of birth and the expiry date of your passport before she will take any messages."

"But she doesn't know that information."

"Yes she does. It's on your passport." I felt I had missed a move in the game.

"Fifteen thirty."

"Thirty Fifteen"

She smiled. "Peter, how can I contact you?"

I gave her my email address on the back of one of my new cards with my London office number. There didn't seem to be any point in letting her have my transient numbers. Anyway she was so omniscient she probably knew them already. How many people were bugging my phone? The sooner we all had satellite phones the better. I suppose she might be having my room searched or even doing it herself. On balance though I thought it unlikely as she had carried her bag when we went to Frank's. Mind you, she was a professional and it could be a double bluff!

I read my fax. Susan had sent it to me from Frank's office. John Southern of Hull Claims Insurance would be passing back through on his way to the UK on Sunday. It wouldn't worry me as I would be in Denver.

"I suppose you know that John Southern is coming out on Sunday on his way home?" Charlie nodded. There were all sorts of ways she might have known, she could have got a similar fax from Susan, Frank could have called her, her office might have known or she might have just read my fax.

"Hurry back, Peter. I may need you." I think she really meant it.

"That's the nicest thing you've ever said to me. I come expensive though, but you get a special rate."

"I'm not sure I wouldn't prefer to pay the full price and no favours."

We shook hands and I felt it took ten milliseconds longer than she normally permitted. I carried my bags to the car, luckily very close, and drove to the car rental return at the airport. The incoming flight was already unloading as I checked in for Dallas Fort Worth and onwards to Phoenix. The flights met my exacting standards. They were on time, uneventful and, a definite bonus for me but not the airlines, not full. There was a Marriott courtesy coach at Phoenix and I was soon safely ensconced in my air conditioned room. It was too late to call Mandy with the seven hour time change between the UK and Phoenix. If I stayed awake to 11 o'clock it would be alright to call then. Thank goodness there was wifi in the hotel but there was nothing on my email and I passed the time having a late swim in the pool and eating a snack in the coffee shop. I read the FT which I had purchased in Dallas and tried to catch up with the news. In the city columns Paragon got a mention but I noticed that the stock was steady at 7. Maybe the dividend matched the risk.

Masterpiece Theatre on the Public Broadcast Service was showing a new production of Lady Windermere's Fan. It was superbly done but I was not sure the audience in the States would be able to follow the English class system. At 11 o'clock prompt I called Mandy using my credit card. A sleepy voice eventually answered the phone.

"Alright, I know I agreed you could call but I'm still asleep." There was a pause with awakening noises at the other end. I could hear her stretching as she lay back and put the portable phone to her ear. "That's better my darling. Now then you can begin." It sounded a bit like Charlie.

"It's good to hear you, my love. It's also very good to be in Phoenix and not St. Antony. I was beginning to feel most uncomfortable when I left. I was being watched, bugged, searched and encouraged to leave the island. It's really weird."

Mandy sounded concerned.

"It sounds to me as if the aircraft accident was arranged. You had better come straight home. It's almost certainly an insurance swindle, barratry as we say in the trade."

"I'm beginning to think you're right. In fact I used that very word myself."

"Who were you talking to?" She had a sixth sense.

"The Westfield insurance assessor. She's even more suspicious than I am and much more experienced in these matters. She's convinced the paintings are still around somewhere."

"I must hear more about your experienced female insurance agent. Do I need to be concerned?"

"Don't be silly, darling. She wears glasses, ungainly trousers and ugly blouses. But she's smart and nobody is going to get ahead of her if she can possibly prevent it. I think she's the one bugging my phone if not searching my room and my safe. Somebody is for sure. The problem is that if the accident is an insurance swindle I'm definitely expendable. We've already had one body which was the insurance company's best guard who was assigned to look after the paintings. They belonged to a guy called Jimmy Morrison who owns a bundle of stock in the Paragon Corporation which is not the flavour of the month on the world's stock exchanges. He has a home in Bermuda, a home in Florida, something in the UK and fingers in pies all round the Caribbean and South America."

"My poor love. You should come home. It really doesn't sound like a job for you."

"Yes, I think you're right. However, I would like to find out what happened on the aircraft side before stopping, if I could. The automatic position reporting seemed to be transmitting the wrong information and we clearly need to understand how that happened, if not for this aircraft, for all the other aircraft flying around the world."

"Stop being altruistic, my darling. You're not being paid danger money. Leave criminal investigations for someone who is. Why don't you come straight home from Denver?"

"Possibly. But could you do something for me? Could you find out all you can about the Paragon Corporation and Jimmy Morrison. If you can get anything, you can send it over to my office and they can scan the information into files and send them to me. If I'm near a printer I can print the stuff out or at the very least read it on my machine."

"No problem. We have a research agency at the office as I expect your Drake Williams people have. However I'm probably better placed to filter the stuff. But Peter this really isn't up your alley. You're a first class avionics engineer, not a sleuth, and you've led far too sheltered a life for the world of robbery and swindles. A nice guy like you shouldn't be in a place like that. You could get permanently hurt and I don't want that to happen. If you don't behave I'll come out to St. Antony and help you and the insurance lady."

"Done. When can I expect you?"

"That was only a threat, not a promise."

We carried on talking for a bit and then agreed I would call her at the same time the next day. It had been a long day with a four hour time change and I went straight to sleep.

***

When I woke up it was too late for a swim and I grabbed some coffee in the lobby. Max Postwick was at the front at 7.45. He was getting towards retirement but he knew the business like the back of his hand. He had been with Honeywell since the first digital aircraft, the Boeings 757, 767, 777, 787 and the Airbus 310, 300-600, 340, 350 and 380. An expert programmer, turned manager. We drove straight to the plant and parked in his reserved space, not too far from the space reserved for the top brass. I filled in the form and got my accompanied day pass. Max led me to his office at the side of a very large drawing office, except it wasn't a drawing office but a room full of young men and women with computers, filling Honeywell's products with software.

"Well, Peter. You've come a long way to see me. What's the problem and why couldn't we talk on the phone?"

"Max, it's good of you to find time to see me. Are you aware of the accident to the West Atlantic Airways European Aerospace 412? The one that happened twelve days ago flying to Bermuda?"

"Sure. It hit the headlines over here. 'ANOTHER AIRCRAFT LOST IN BERMUDA TRIANGLE', 'THE BERMUDA TRIANGLE STRIKES AGAIN' and lots more. The crew got lost didn't they? They thought they were at Bermuda but they strayed into the first storm of the year, Angela."

"Yes, that's about right. Wasn't your firm asked some questions by our AAIB? Surely it's impossible to get lost with your flight management system, or anybody else's for that matter?"

"Our product support may have been asked some questions but they didn't come my way. Let's do what you like doing and start at the beginning. What's the avionic story?"

"Well the aircraft was cleared to fly direct to Bermuda and the ADS showed it doing just that until it was 100 miles south of Bermuda when the ADS and all communication stopped. Up to that point the crew had been talking to New York Center by satellite and saying that they were approaching weather, and then that they were in the weather with lightning, turbulence and then nothing. The answer to your next question is that Angela was sitting 200 miles due east of Bermuda and it looks as if the aircraft flew into the storm and..."

Max interrupted "...lost control and crashed."

"That's about it. But you need to know that the aircraft was carrying some of the world's most valuable paintings being returned to Jimmy Morrison's place in Bermuda and the paintings were heavily insured."

"No, Peter. I don't need to know that. The insurers do but you and I should only be interested in whether the ADS was correct or not and if not, why it wasn't. I take it that you don't believe the aircraft was where the ADS said it was?"

"No, I don't believe I do. If it had been, the crew would have been talking to Bermuda, the radar on the ground would have seen them, the crew would have seen the island on the aircraft weather radar, etc. etc."

"So we have to ask ourselves how could the position have been wrong."

"And Max, how could the heading have been wrong? Because clearly the crew thought everything was going alright until they realised that something was horribly amiss."

"Right, Peter. Don't let's mess about. It's got to be some form of software malfunction." He considered the situation for a moment before carrying on. "You know my days of software writing are long since past. Though I says it myself, I used to be damn good at it. But some time ago when I came into this office I had to throw away my debugging tools and now I use the telephone instead."

Max dialled a number. "Jessica, would you like to come in for an intellectual discussion on 412 software?"

We didn't have to wait long. A rather intense lady of about thirty two came in wearing a green jumper, striped trousers and a large wedding ring. He introduced me and I gave her my business card, which she read carefully before putting it in her purse. I thought for a moment she looked a little bit apprehensive. Max went on to explain very clearly the reason for my visit; she looked slightly concerned but launched straight into the software considerations.

"Well Max, you two are obviously convinced that the aircraft was not where the ADS said it was because of the weather being experienced by the crew. As you would expect my first reaction is to ask you to double check that, because I'm not convinced that it is possible to be in one place and for the ADS consistently to say the aircraft is somewhere else. Let me try and explain why. If the crew thought they were on the right track but in the wrong position then the electronic display must have been showing an incorrect heading. The heading is derived from the inertial reference systems and sent to the flight management computers and then sent onwards to the navigation display in front of the pilots and, as you know, this display is the key display on which the pilots navigate and check the position of the aircraft. Clearly the software would have to behave in an inexplicable manner without any warning being given to the crew."

Jessica stopped for a moment to let me keep up with my note taking.

"For example, I suppose it is possible to envisage a 30° right error occurring for some reason. But the navigation of the aircraft would go completely wrong and the crew would be bound to notice the aircraft was not following the desired track. You see the auto-pilot would try to steer 30° to starboard of the correct heading and the aircraft would turn but the computer would know the aircraft was not on track immediately and correct to bring the aircraft back on track. It just couldn't work like that. What would have to happen for the ADS reporting to behave as you have described is that the computers would have to be programmed to fly 30° right of the correct track, but the plotted positions would have to appear on the desired track and, of course, it would be those positions that were transmitted by the ADS system."

I joined in.

"Could that happen?"

"No way. You guys need to check what the weather was really like."

I decided I had better press Jessica some more because it was quite clear that this point was crucial. If the aircraft had been really on the correct track we were looking for the crash recorders in the wrong place.

"Jessica I know it shouldn't have happened but are you quite sure it couldn't happen?"

There was a very long pause. She was clearly reviewing the whole situation very carefully before replying.

"I don't see how. There would have to an error in the computer software that looked at all the waypoints, rotated the tracks by 30°, used those new waypoints for steering but used the original waypoints for display then the circumstances you describe could occur.."

I considered her statement for a moment.

"Shouldn't the GPS updates to the flight management computer ensure that the transmitted ADS positions were always correct?"

"In reality yes, though remember the aircraft's position that is transmitted is a mean position, heavily weighted in favour of the GPS positions."

Max joined in. "Jessica, you seem to have the answers off pat."

"Well yes. The British AAIB asked me something similar last week. I was just about to send them a reply. The point is that if the software was faulty the crew would pick it up straightaway. You are the first people to hear it."

It was time for me to ask the key question as far as I was concerned.

"Jessica, are you saying that the whole thing is impossible for the wrong ADS positions to be transmitted or are you saying that it could be done but it would need a computer software modification?"

"Hardly a modification, almost a complete rewrite of the navigation routines."

We went round and round the problem and made no further progress. I got the feeling that Jessica was slightly hesitant towards the end but I didn't say anything. In the end Max released her back to her office and she seemed pleased to be leaving, not altogether surprising since her software was being questioned.

"What do you make of all that, Peter? It all seems incredible to me."

"I really don't know. I think I'll have to go back to the met people to double check the weather situation though I'm sure I will be wasting my time. I have a feeling there is something we have overlooked."

We chatted for some time without making any real progress. It was time for me to leave and Max sensed my impatience.

"Is there anything I can do to help?"

"Well I need to get back to the hotel and catch up with a few things."

Max took me out of the building and I saw Jessica watching me. We got into his car and he drove me back to the Marriott and said good-bye.

"Look after yourself."

I went up to my room, connected with wifi and got my mail from Jill in the London office. Mandy had given her the details on the Paragon Corporation and she'd put them in a different attachment from my mail. I decided to start on Paragon. Up in my room I called Frank. Hopefully they weren't bugging his phone.

"Is there any news, Frank? Has there been any more wreckage?"

"No, nothing to report. Charlie persuaded Morrison to carry on sweeping round Bermuda for the wreckage with the aircraft and the boat but it's a waste of time if you ask me. Charlie has told me about the deep water search going on where the wreckage was found. That sounds much more sensible. How are you getting on?"

"Not very well, Frank. I'm beginning to wonder whether the met information was really correct. Perhaps everything was working correctly and some of Angela's weather was still on the planned track. A software fault seems impossible and anyway such a fault would have been noticed by the pilots straightaway on their navigation displays as they taxied out. The runway on the display would not match the real world. To be honest, Frank. I'm out of ideas. I don't want to waste any more of your money. I'll carry on to United as planned and call in to St. Antony on the way home."

"Peter, I need you more than ever. For a start John Southern will be arriving here to-morrow and I will need your help dealing with him. We need you back, Peter, and to be frank, we need you back as soon as you have finished with Honeywell."

I thought about what Frank was saying. If we believed the aircraft ditched near Bermuda, or anywhere else for that matter, then the crew could well be alive. I decided to call Mandy to get some advice. With the seven hour time difference she was back in her flat.

"You must do whatever you think is right, my love. You must certainly check the weather. Perhaps you should go to Bermuda again and talk to the met people there. But remember whatever you do, someone may be operating a very sophisticated plot which must have taken a lot of money and effort to arrange so you need to be very careful. If you do go back and carry on searching for an explanation, don't keep any hunches you might have to yourself, Peter Talbert. I know you. Don't try and be clever and do the investigation by yourself whatever you do. You are just not equipped for that sort of work. The Westfield insurance lady sounds as if she has had the training, you haven't. Don't be a gentleman and try and help, I need you."

"Thank you for that, my love. My real concern at the moment is for the pilots if they are alive and being held somewhere, though I suspect the stakes are so high that they would be dispensed with, the moment their usefulness was over. I think I'll call Steve Watson at Denver and see if I can't delay or cancel the visit though I do need the money."

"Not as much as you did a few weeks ago, my love. Let me know what's going on. By the way the information you need should be in your mail box."

"Yes, thank you. I've got it already."

We said our farewells and I called United.

"I'm not entirely surprised you called, Peter. I thought you might have difficulty finishing the investigation in time. That accident in Bermuda seems very odd and in my book a little suspicious. Be careful my friend, the stakes may be very high. Call me when you feel you can come and we'll try and sort something out."

It was good to have such an understanding customer. I called Frank and told him of my decision.

"That's great news. I really appreciate it. I'll book you in to-morrow assuming there's a flight. At the New Anchorage again if that's alright with you?"

"I suppose so. The security is not very high but I expect that's true of most hotels. Can you fix a hire car for me? Don't bother to meet me. I'll try and catch an early flight out of here if I can. The four hour time change is a real killer to get into St. Antony at a reasonable time."

I went up to my room and called American. There was a flight leaving at 6.30 in the morning direct to Miami and then BWIA again to

The Final Flight

St. Antony getting in at 6.30 in the evening. I cancelled my flights to United and back to St. Antony and hoped that Susan would be able to organise getting my money refunded or credited for further bookings. I finished my mail and then grabbed a book and went down to the coffee shop for a meal. It didn't take long and I got ready for an early start. But I didn't sleep very well. Jessica clearly was not convinced that there was a mistake in the position reporting and thought the weather was wrong. I wondered if there was something we'd all missed. The whole thing was completely outside my experience. I wondered what I was getting myself into.

CHAPTER 5

'And makes the hollow seas that roar Proclaim the ambergris on shore'

I was at the check-in desk at 5.45 and so were about another hundred people. It was always fascinating wondering where they all came from and where they were going but one thing was always certain, people travelled everywhere in huge numbers, twenty four hours a day. We were off on time and the cabin attendants served a very welcome breakfast. They all looked remarkably cheerful considering the time they must have started. We had a stronger tail wind than the flight schedules allowed for and we landed at my least favourite airport fifteen minutes early. As usual Miami was jumping with people but I threaded my way, more slowly than I wanted, through the fingers and security checks to my gate. Perhaps it was just as well we were ahead of schedule as there wasn't a lot of time for my bag to catch the BWIA flight even though I had managed it. In the event we were a few minutes late off. The strong westerly wind blew down the Caribbean as well as across the southern States and we arrived on time.

My day wasn't over. The immigration officer looked at my passport, checked with her list and started to give me a hard time on the reason for my visit. Why was I coming back? Did I have a work permit? I decided that enough was enough and asked to see her boss. She put her attention light on and a supervisor appeared and took me in to a side office. The man didn't look particularly smart and he started talking in a rather offensive way.

"Mr. Talbert, what brings you back again? We thought you had finished in St. Antony, investigating that aircraft accident. We don't need people like you in St. Antony. We are well able to look after ourselves."

I tried to keep my cool, having an argument was not going to achieve anything.

"I'm afraid I don't understand. The chief executive of West Atlantic Airways has asked me to help him so that his airline does not go bankrupt and so that a lot of people living here do not become unemployed. I've started the job but the aircraft has not been found and the insurers are not going to pay up until the investigation is concluded. The airline is still under threat."

"Mr. Talbert. The loss of that aircraft was an accident and that's all there is to it. If you don't want to get into any trouble you had better leave here."

"Are you threatening me? My passport is in order, no visa is required to visit your country. What is the real reason for discouraging me from visiting your lovely island?"

"Mr. Talbert, anybody can come here on holiday. People who come on business have to justify their reasons for visiting and in your case we don't need you to do our business. Our police, helped for a few days by your country's accident investigators, are well able to settle this matter."

I looked at him and he stared back but finally looked away. He clearly wasn't the head immigration man. I remembered Susan's advice about where the problem was.

"May I speak to the head of the St. Antony immigration department, please?"

"What do you want to speak to him for?"

"I want to find out whether the views you are expressing are the views of the St. Antony government."

"He's not here."

"Look, it's late. Are you going to stamp my passport or are you going to advise the UK consul that you are holding me here."

The supervisor started to look unsure of himself.

"We're not holding you. We are just trying to find out why you keep on returning here."

He took my passport, ungraciously scribbled on it and gave it to back to me. I opened it and saw he had given me two days.

"Thank you but that's not much use to me. Despite what you may think, there is a lot of work to be done. I'll go and see the head of your service to-morrow, Mr. Justice."

I had read the name on his badge. I turned to leave and he grabbed the passport back, altered two days to seven and initialled the change. He didn't look pleased but I was very encouraged. Susan was right. Maybe the trouble I was having was not government policy but someone getting at the supervisors.

By the time I got to the customs area I was alone and my bag must have been going round and round the carousel by itself for at least 30 minutes. The customs man waved me straight through, perhaps the word had got around. There was still someone at the rental car desk and I got fixed up quickly. I left the airport and was soon back at the hotel. The girl at the desk welcomed me as she checked me in.

"Nice to have you back, Mr. Talbert." She looked at the room vacancies. "We'll have to put you in a poolside room, this time."

I nodded assent and hoped Frank could afford it. She gave me back my credit card after she had taken an imprint and I made my way to my room. It was definitely superior to my previous room but I wasn't sure I liked being so close to the pool. It meant keeping my net curtain shut all the time, though it was convenient for swimming in the morning. As I started to unpack there was a peremptory knock on the door. I wasn't altogether surprised to see Charlie outside. We looked at one another and it was quite clear she expected me to let her in. She wandered over to the only comfortable chair and sat down. I noticed she was wearing a blouse and long shorts, but not as bad as some of things she'd been wearing, though she still had the dark glasses in position.

"Did you have a good trip?" I nodded assent. I wasn't sure I welcomed her presence in my room as I tried to unpack. "Well, you'd better tell me what you've been up to since it is a basic rule in my business that keeping things to yourself can be a life shortening experience. What did you find out at Honeywell?"

I had no recollection of mentioning Honeywell, or even Phoenix to Charlie but she seemed to know everything I did. I was glad she had decided to sit on a chair on the far side of the room, that way she wasn't too close.

"Not a lot but perhaps you're right. Maybe I should tell you about my visit. You know my girl friend always tells me I'm not very good at divulging information. And I don't know you at all really."

I got the distinct impression she wasn't too interested in Mandy or what she thought.

"What do I have to do to prove I'm on your side?"

I felt it would be wise to treat the question as a rhetorical one but I wasn't very strong at rhetorical answers.

"Well, my journey was probably a waste of money, Charlie. It seems virtually impossible for the system to transmit incorrect ADS positions. The chief software programmer told me to recheck whether the weather was really what they said it was. If there had been something wrong with the software the pilots would have noticed immediately they got into the airplane."

"You mean there would have been a warning on the displays?"

I looked at her. It was a remarkably shrewd question from someone who nothing about aviation. It confirmed my view that there had to be more to her than met the eye. However I was not sure how much I was going to uncover.

"Not necessarily, but the heading on the displays would not have matched the real world."

"Peter, is it easy for the software to be wrong? Is it ever changed?"

Another very good question.

"No, it is incredibly difficult to answer your first question. For the second, the airline has to change the software every time a new release of the operating system is made but that is done in very closely controlled conditions. The software checks itself as it loads and again when the complete program is loaded. You can do it on the aircraft or in the lab. If it were me I'd do program changes in the lab and then swap the computers over. I must remember to ask Paul Thomas how WAA do it."

"Well Peter, however they do it seems to be irrelevant to our problem since faulty software would be spotted by the pilots."

"That's the way I see it. Tell me, what's been going on while I've been away?"

"Well, Jimmy has had the Islander touring all round Bermuda and his boat is now on the east coast but so far nothing has been found."

"Who's paying for all this, Charlie?"

"Morrison. I took your advice and asked him why he was doing all this."

"You phoned him?" Perhaps I sounded incredulous.

She nodded but didn't look too pleased. My face must have shown I thought that inadvisable; in my view it was always better to look people in the eye and see if they looked back.

"He said he wanted the insurance money quickly, probably because of the price of Paramount stock, and he reckoned the only way he could convince Westfield was either to find the aircraft in shallow water with the paintings on board or convince us that the aircraft was lost in the deep Atlantic. He reckons either way we'll pay up."

"And will you?"

"Don't know. Depends what we find. Anyway we mutually agreed that we had no objection if he carried on with his shallow water investigation supplementing HMS Broadside, the aircraft and the Oceanic Engineering ship searching the deep."

"Have Oceanic Engineering started searching near where the wreckage was found?"

"I don't know for sure but I would have thought so. By the way I asked him about the freight. He said it was machinery for exporting to S.America and that he was repositioning it to Bermuda to keep in a transit shed because St. Antony was becoming too expensive. I asked him who were the insurers and he said he didn't know, he left matters like that to Greg."

There was no point in telling Charlie she should never have asked such critical questions over the telephone. The damage was done, the question was asked. Jimmy would have called Greg straight away, telling him what to say.

There was a long pause which I had no intention of breaking. Charlie realised the ball was in her court.

"You'll be glad to know the Av. Week and Daily Mail reporters have checked out."

"Good. Their reports should be interesting if not informative."

Another long pause. Charlie was clearly not feeling sleepy.

"What are you going to do now?"

"I thought I might unpack and go to bed."

She flushed slightly. Perhaps she knew she had overstayed her welcome.

"Sorry if I've disturbed you." She hadn't and I didn't want her to. "I'll see you in the morning."

She got up and let herself out. I felt relieved to see her go. There was something about her that was definitely attractive in spite of the way she dressed and acted. I didn't want any more complications in this business than there were already.

***

I was awakened by the phone. It was 6.30 a.m. It was Mandy.

"This is your wake up call."

"Yes, darling, for once it really is."

"Well, have you decided what to do? When are you coming home?"

"'No' and 'definitely don't know' I'm afraid. Why don't you come out here?"

"You know I can't. I've got far too much work."

"I suppose so but it's a pity. It's wonderful here if you're not working. Actually I've been considering the situation and I think I'm going back to Bermuda. I want to check the met charts and talk to the experts who were on duty to see if Jessica was right."

"Jessica?" Mandy sounded suspicious. "Not another lady who you're involved with?"

"I'm not involved with any ladies." Mandy's training always ensured she knew how to phrase her questions. "Jessica is the flight management software expert in Honeywell who believes implicitly in the sanctity of her software."

There was a pause.

"That could be misconstrued."

"Not by me. She's a very correct married lady who takes her work very seriously." I changed my tone. "Anyway I want to see how the search is going on. If there's any doubt about the weather they may be searching in the wrong place."

"What's that got to do with you?"

"Mandy, you know when I'm asked to do a job I look at every angle. Apart from anything else it's much quicker in the end."

"Alright, off you go to your island. Don't get involved in any triangles."

She rang off leaving me to ponder on her last remark. Presumably she was worried about my safety but with Mandy one could never be too sure.

I called Frank and asked him if he could organise me another trip to Bermuda. He said he would call me back. Charlie was nowhere to be seen, she had probably finished her swim. Ten lengths later I felt properly stretched and exercised and ready for breakfast. I did not see Charlie when I had finished dressing and was looking for somewhere to eat. She suddenly appeared looking a bit cross.

"Are you ignoring me? I was over there on that table in the corner."

I was just about to reply when the bell boy came round with a message for me to pick up a call. I went in to the telephone cubicle and the hotel put Susan through. I was booked on the 1030. Charlie was still there when I got back.

"My fault, I really didn't see you." She looked as if she wanted a chat but I was getting short of time. "If you'll excuse me, Susan has just booked me on the 1030 to Bermuda so I must fly."

She grimaced and we went down the corridor to our rooms. I decided to keep my room in the hotel and just put a very few things in my travelling bag. I checked the car at the airport and bought yesterday's FT to read in the plane. We left on time and once more I was in the front but this time alone. On arrival I took a cab to the Waterfront at St. Georges where Susan had made a reservation for me. I had made no plans and after unpacking what little clothes I had with me, I wandered down to the coffee shop. To my surprise Greg Fairclough was ordering his lunch. He beckoned me to join him.

"Didn't expect to see you here. What brings you to Bermuda?"

"Well, I want to talk to the met forecasters who were on duty the night Alpha Lima was lost. I've just returned from Honeywell at Phoenix and the software people there are convinced that the ADS positions must have been accurate so I thought I'd look at all the charts. I want to see how the search is going as well."

"The search seems to be going alright but there's no sight or sound of the crash recorders. I brought our G4 in last night and went to the operations room this morning. David Roberts showed me the plots. It's very discouraging."

We ordered our lunch. I too felt rather discouraged. Greg looked at me.

"What do you make of all this, Peter. It's very difficult to know where to search."

"I agree. You know one of the things that puzzles me slightly is the wreckage."

"What's the problem about the wreckage? It's given us very valuable information."

"Yes, it has. But surely, Greg, there should be more wreckage? Where are the other dinghies? Shouldn't there have been more life jackets, more bulkheads?"

Greg thought about what I had just said.

"I don't know, Peter. Weren't most of the seats with their life jackets left behind? Anyway the life jackets don't float."

"But the dinghies? They probably would have inflated automatically."

"You've got a point there."

"And a lot more bric a brac, Greg. There's got to be more to come."

"You may be right. You know the sea is so vast, these things may take a long time to appear."

Greg was right. But I was still a bit surprised at the dearth of wreckage. But then Mandy always did say I was impatient.

"How long are you planning to stay?"

Greg's voice brought me back to the hotel.

"I'm not sure. A couple of nights I expect."

"Why not join me for a meal to-night? Do you like Italian food?" I nodded. "OK, I'll make reservations at La Trattoria. 7 o'clock? We can meet here at 6.30 if that's alright. I've got the use of the Flight Operations van so we won't have to get a cab."

We finished our sandwiches and Greg left the hotel. I phoned air traffic. Luckily James Donald was in and I explained the reason for my visit.

"Come round and I'll take you into the met office."

There was a cab outside and one of the benefits of staying in St. Georges was that it was so close to the airfield. We were there in no time and I walked over to the tower; and after a security check I went up to Donald's office. He questioned me about the progress of my investigation and I brought him up to date. He took me over to the meteorological building next door, introduced me to Guy Wostenholme, the chief forecaster who was about my age, slight and spoke with a mid-Atlantic accent.

"Guy. Peter here wants to talk about the weather at the time of Alpha Lima's accident."

The Final Flight

I started to explain as politely as I could that I was questioning whether the weather en route to Bermuda was really as good as it was said to be in the forecast. Guy interrupted.

"Peter, I've been doing this job for quite a few years now and I know that forecasters cannot win. In spite of all the modern tools we have, it is still very easy to get things wrong. If we forecast bad weather and we get it right nobody loves us, if we forecast bad weather and we get it wrong we are still criticised and, of course, if we forecast good weather and it's bad, then we're really in trouble. Even if we forecast good weather and it's good there are still people who are unhappy.

"Let me take you into the briefing room and I'll show you what we've got for the night in question."

Donald left us and we went across the corridor into what was obviously the place where the pilots got their forecasts. Guy lifted a flap in the counter and we went to a large table in the middle of the room. He brought a box folder over from a large filing cabinet in the corner of the room.

"As I'm sure you realise, you're not the first person to discuss this matter with me. I've had the Director of Civil Aviation here and his staff. I've had the AAIB inspectors up from St. Antony and I've had to answer countless queries over the phone. Let me show you these satellite photos first."

He pulled out a set of incredibly clear photos, all date/time stamped, of the Caribbean with a very large anti-clockwise spiral of white cloud covering part of each print. The position of the centre of the spiral slowly moved from West of St. Antony towards and to the East of Bermuda on each consecutive print. Any possible doubt about the position of Angela was removed because a latitude/ longitude grid overlaid each print. Even to my untutored eye the track of the hurricane was crystal clear.

"What superb pictures. Did you print those here?"

"Yes we did. We're quite proud of them."

"Well I have to say there can't be any doubt about the movement of Angela. However, the radius of the spiral of cloud is very large and covers Bermuda and the track up from St. Antony. In fact I know that there was some lowish cloud at St. Antony when the aircraft took off. How do you know the weather conditions on track were benign?"

"That's a fair question. We based our forecast on many things. Infrared satellite pictures, balloon ascents from Bermuda, weather radar returns from Bermuda, pilot reports and other pieces of data. We were confident that the severe weather from Angela had cleared the normal track leaving only high cirrus and some scattered low level stratus and cumulus which, of course, is what you can see in these last few photographs."

156

"I'd have been a lot happier if I could have seen Bermuda from this picture here, taken at midnight GMT. Then I would know that the weather was clear. It seems to me you can't be absolutely certain."

"Well here's a water vapour infra-red satellite shot and a normal I/R shot. You can see Bermuda here."

"Yes but that's not the same as having no cloud."

"Well I suppose you could be right but there is something else that confirms our opinion of the weather. At 0100Z, an hour after Alpha Lima went missing, there was an aircraft flying from Bermuda to St. Antony and flew right along the expected track. I got air traffic to ask him the weather and he reported only some low level cloud below at 35,000 ft., no turbulence and fine cirrus above."

I didn't want to be convinced by Guy since the accident would have been so much simpler if Alpha Lima had just dived in to the water on track. Jessica said it was impossible to get incorrect ADS reporting. Somebody had to be wrong. I said goodbye and Guy went with me to the door of the building.

"Well if it makes you any happier..." Guy interrupted my train of thought "don't forget Bermuda radar couldn't see Alpha Lima and the weather radar could only see bad weather a long way to the east."

He might be right but if he was it would certainly make the investigation much harder. It was now 5.15 so I went into the terminal, bought the FT, and then caught a cab back to the hotel. There was a message to call Charlie.

"Just checking to see how you are getting on. Not much happening here except my boss is telling me she is expecting results."

"What does that mean, Charlie? You can't very well bring the pictures up from the Ocean bed. Anyway if it comforts you, I'm not getting anywhere. The met data looks pretty convincing that there was no bad weather on track but there was cloud on track, though the forecaster said it was only cirrus." Charlie was obviously not in a hurry and wanted to talk. I had to interrupt. "I must go now, if you'll excuse me, I'm having dinner with Greg."

"With Greg? What's he doing up there?"

"Well he does work up here as well as at St. Antony."

"It's alright for some. I'm stuck in the hotel."

"It's an island paradise, Charlie."

"As they say in England, piss off."

The phone went dead. I changed and put on my blazer. Greg was waiting as I went into the lobby. We got into the van and parked near the restaurant. The menu was as one would expect in an Italian restaurant but the food, when it came, was extremely good. We had a bottle of Chianti and I got Greg to tell me some more about his flight operations.

The Final Flight

"We do an awful lot of business in South America as well as Central America. We've been down to Buenos Aires, Santiago and even as far as Cape Horn on the Chilean side. The guys we take down with us have to look at the food and other stuff being sold and then try to agree a price. It's demanding work. Sometimes the job can be done quickly, if the produce is near the main airfields. Other times they have to go inland and then we try to get permission to fly them into the interior."

"You told me the other day that some of the airfields are pretty grotty?"

"You're right. Some of them really are. Whether we can help depends on the aircraft we're using. If it's a G3 or G4 then obviously there's not much we can do if there is no long airfield close to where we need to go. If we're in the 125 then we can manage quite short paved strips. If the fields are very short and rough then we need our piston engined aircraft. The problem with that is that it takes so long to get anywhere in a piston engined aircraft. Still we normally manage to get the job done one way or another."

"Well it sounds very interesting flying though rather demanding. You need good pilots."

"Yes we do. And it helps if they're of Spanish or Portuguese extraction."

"Do you speak Spanish?"

"Actually I do and it comes in very handy arguing with air traffic and all the officials we come into contact with."

Our meal came to a close and I was ready for bed but Greg clearly wanted to go on drinking somewhere, preferably a night club. I found it difficult to refuse and he headed for Domingos which was on the way home. He was clearly no stranger to the proprietor nor, I suspected, to the scantily clad well proportioned girls who took our orders for drinks. There was a small dance floor and a local pianist who sang as well. After a couple of drinks I made it clear that I was ready to leave and we left for the hotel. Perhaps it was just as well that breathalysers were not in use in Bermuda, I wasn't convinced that Greg would have passed, though to be fair he drove immaculately. I went straight to my room. I was just about to draw the curtains when I saw the van we had been in leaving the parking lot. Greg clearly needed at least another drink, perhaps he needed to see one of the girls in Domingos.

***

I had a leisurely breakfast and then called David Roberts in the operations room. He told me he was out until lunch time so I told him I'd be over after lunch. I wondered how to spend the morning and decided to go for a walk out to St. David's Lighthouse. I took the courtesy van to the airport and walked along St. David's Road to the lighthouse. It was about 2.5 miles to the lighthouse which for some reason seemed to be closed. I went down to the beach which was deserted. The Black Horse Tavern was also closed which surprised me but I supposed it was early in the season. The surf roared on the shore and there was all sorts of rubbish lying there. It occurred to me that I might spot some wreckage from Alpha Lima but there was nothing to be seen. I retraced my steps accompanied only by an occasional aircraft landing on runway 30.

I had a sandwich in the terminal and then went straight down by cab to Hamilton and the operations room. David Roberts was there and he showed me the plots that he had showed me before. A lot of new searching had been done but there was an awful lot to do. Oceanic Engineering was working near where the wreckage had been found and HMS Broadside was still further east looking in the area where Alpha Lima was first thought have dived into the sea.

Roberts told me that the US Navy had stopped searching and that the two Nimrods, which were operating from Bermuda, were planning to go back to Scotland in two days time. I found it all rather depressing but didn't know what to say or suggest. I decided to call Bob Furness at home to see if he could help and picked up David's phone.

"Bob, if the Nimrods leave, the chances of finding any more wreckage will be zero. Remember the position of wreckage will help to pinpoint where the aircraft might be. Won't the R.A.F. allow them to stay for another week or so?"

"I've tried every trick I know but money is short and the Base Commander feels that what is needed is more ships looking for the beacon, not aircraft. Peter, I'm rather inclined to agree. In fact I've been on to the Navy to see if they'll help."

"Any luck?"

"They accepted what I said but said that they would need to look at their commitments and, of course, talk to the political heavy breathers. I expect we'll hear in a day or so. I'm not too optimistic because there is no real British interest."

"Is that quite true Bob? BAE Systems make the wing of the 412. Can't BAE Systems bring some pressure to bear? After all it could well affect their future sales."

"You're right. I will have a word with their marketing people. Now that they've sold their Airbus business to EADS and invested in the European 412 it ought to be in their interest to support European. Still BAE are involved with EADS on other work so don't hold your breath."

"I can't believe that."

"Peter. Don't shout at me. I'm telling you the way politicians look at things. I'll call you the moment I hear something."

"Sorry, Bob. It so frustrating out here. We're making no progress at all."

We carried on for a bit but there was nothing more to be said. I rang off.

"Well at least you tried, Peter." David tried to cheer me up. "Do I gather that Bob is trying the Navy for help."

I nodded.

"Yes, he's doing a great job but I'm not too optimistic."

I left David in the Ops. Room and took a cab back to the hotel. My flight was not until 1700 on the next day so I was at a bit of a loose end. The girl on the desk told me that Capt. Fairclough had not checked out and was expected in very late. I had a solitary meal in the restaurant, which was almost empty, and then spent the evening watching TV.

***

At 6.30 I called Mandy at home since it was Sunday. She was just off to the yacht club. We chatted for a few minutes but there was really not much I could say. I had breakfast and got ready for another walk. The phone rang. It was Charlie.

"Have the police contacted you about the dinghy?"

"What dinghy? What are you talking about?"

"They've found another dinghy on St. David's island."

"How do you know?"

"The police rang Frank who called me. He'd have called you but he didn't know what hotel Susan had booked you into. I promised to call you."

"I'm glad you did. I'll call the police right now. Talk to you later."

I hung up quickly and phoned Joshua Brown.

"It's good that you called, Mr. Talbert. A local inhabitant on St. David's Island found a dinghy on the beach early this morning. One of my men has seen it and it looks as if it belonged to the crashed aircraft. Would you like to see it? Where are you calling from?"

I told him my hotel and he said he'd pick me up in half an hour. He was as good as his word and he then took me to the island which was by the airfield. There was not a lot of wind and the dinghy sat above the high water mark. There was no doubt it had belonged to Alpha Lima. The registration was painted clearly on the side. The dinghy was badly scuffed, in a similar manner to the other two dinghies. On impulse I walked further along the beach. There were some pieces of bulkhead which looked like the other pieces we had seen. I called Joshua over and he said he'd get one of his officers to search the beach very carefully. We collected up the pieces we could find and put them carefully next to the dinghy.

"We'll take all this stuff and put it with the other wreckage. What else should we do, Peter?"

"Well you'd better talk to David Roberts straightaway because they'll have to consider the likely track of the wreckage and whether it affects the likely position of the aircraft. Perhaps the other thing, if you can organise it, is to search some of the other beaches to see if anything else has shown up."

Joshua dropped me off at the terminal and I took a cab back to the hotel. Greg was in the coffee shop, dressed in uniform.

"Have you heard, Greg? Another dinghy has been found."

"No. Whereabouts? Did the Nimrod spot it?"

"No. It was found on the beach. There were some bulkhead pieces as well nearby."

"Well that's good news."

"I suppose so."

"What do you mean, Peter?"

"I'm not sure." Greg looked concerned. I wasn't prepared to discuss the subject until I'd analysed my uncertainty so I rapidly changed the subject. "Where are you off to?"

"Oh. Just back to St. Antony, thank goodness." He looked at his watch. "In fact I'd better rush. See you around."

He looked as if he wished he had time to continue the conversation but I wasn't about to share my thoughts with anyone at this stage, not even with Charlie. I had a sandwich, packed my things, checked out and caught a cab to the terminal. I checked in and we had an uneventful flight back to St. Antony. As luck would have it Mr. Justice was the duty immigration officer. He looked at me, hesitated, and then gave me a week's stay. He clearly did not want another argument and it suited my book to wait my moment.

There was no problem with customs and I got my rental car very quickly. It was dark when I left the parking lot, with no moon. The only traffic was a truck following me with it's headlights full on. I slowed down to try to let it go by but it slowed as well, probably because the road wasn't terribly wide. I began to get worried because I didn't like the truck sitting behind me, uncomfortably close and blinding my rear view. I tried going faster but the truck just went faster as well and I felt uncomfortable on the narrow roads driving so fast. After a few miles we came to a straight piece of road built on an embankment and the truck started to overtake very quickly and then there was loud bang as the truck hit me, the car swerved and I could not keep it on the road. The truck must have hit my offside rear fender very hard and I found it impossible to keep control. The driver had chosen the spot well with the high bank and the car rolled over and over down to the rough field below, finally finishing up facing the opposite way to the way I was going. As it rolled bumping me each time it bounced, with my life out of my control, I seemed to have all the time in the world to review my life, think about Mandy, WAA, the accident, the software and even Charlie.

After what seemed like a very long time, the car stopped rolling and everything went quiet. I took stock of myself and my predicament. I felt as if I had been beaten all over with a heavy stick. Everywhere seemed to hurt but miraculously I was alive. Fortunately the car had finished approximately the right way up. The roof and sides of the car seemed to have been damaged but it was too dark to see anything. The engine was still running and somehow I managed to switch it off. There was glass everywhere where the windscreen was broken. There was a smell of petrol and to my horror my seat belt was jammed by the door. Amazingly I found I could wriggle underneath the strap but not surprisingly in the blackness, I cut myself on the broken glass in the process. I tried to get out of the car but my door was completely buckled and pressing against my leg. Somehow I managed to get onto the back seat and to my great relief I found I could force open the offside door. I scrambled out of the car, crawling over it's side on to the earth. It was marvellous to be lying on firm ground with the stars shining, the warm wind and the insects making their never ending noise.

I surveyed the scene as best I could and tried to decide on the next move. My right leg was bruised but not too badly and my face was bleeding where my head had hit the car. Pieces of glass were all over my clothes but miraculously I was not badly hurt. I very slowly managed to get to my feet by leaning on the car and tried to brush myself down and to remove as much glass as possible but with very little success. There seemed to be even more cuts when I had finished than when I started. One piece of good fortune in the circumstances was that the trunk was smashed open so that I could get at my bags, though they looked the worse for wear. My jacket had finished up on the floor in the back of the car where I could just reach it. I was standing about twenty feet below the road and as my eyes got used to the dark I saw that about two hundred yards further back towards the airport the bank gradually got less steep. Very slowly and painfully I made two trips up to the roadside carrying first my larger bag and then the other bag with my jacket. It seemed to take for ever as I had to stop every few steps. In fact it must have taken at least twenty minutes before I had finished. I was exhausted by the time I reached the roadside a second time and sat down to recover.

There were very few cars and nobody stopped. I forced myself to stand up and started waving every time one came by. Nobody seemed to care and ignored my waves, probably not wanting to get involved but finally one stopped and the driver looked at me very cautiously at first. Finally the driver's window opened.

"What's happened, man?" said a very deep voice, sounding very local.

"I got confused with an overtaking car and drove off the road."

There was no point in saying more than I needed to.

"Jump in, man, I'll take you to the hospital in Cape Harbour for a checkup. I'm Martin Saunders, I look after the airport cleaning."

I protested that it wasn't necessary but in truth I did feel a bit shaken. He drove carefully so as not to shake me up too much and as we got in to the lights of Cape Harbour I could see that Martin was a large cheerful looking man wearing a check shirt with a lightweight jacket on top and the inevitable jeans. He didn't ask me any questions but drove straight to the hospital door marked 'emergencies'. He carried my bags in.

"This feller has had a car accident and needs help."

I looked in a mirror and saw what he meant. My face, hands and clothes were covered in blood and glass. I forced myself to mumble my thanks. He gave me his card with the name of the cleaning company. I thanked him again but he shrugged off my words.

"Glad I could help. See you at the airport, if you're going that way. They'll tell you where my office is."

The duty nurse told me to strip off and she sent for a doctor. She wouldn't let me clean myself up but started bathing and cleaning the wounds on my face and hands, carefully removing splinters of glass.

"You've had a lucky escape, young man. You could have been in serious trouble. I think we'd better x-ray your right leg, though it is probably alright."

I tried to protest it wasn't necessary but she wouldn't hear of it and my protests were not as vehement as they might have been.

"The police will be here in a moment but they can wait until we've taken the x-rays."

I was sat firmly in a chair and wheeled to the x-ray department where the duty radiographer was preparing the films. He took a couple of exposures and sent me back to wait until the films had been processed and the doctor had examined them. They wheeled me in to a small room with a bed and a couple of chairs. My bags and jacket were already there.

"The policeman is here. You lie on the bed and we can get him in. Do you feel like talking to him." I nodded and the policeman came in.

"Well what have you been up to, Sir." I told him an edited version, explaining how I was dazzled by a car behind me as he was overtaking and had gone over the bank. He made some notes on a form.

"You had a lucky escape, Sir. You must learn to be more careful. Just sign this report here and that'll be the end of the matter." I glanced at the form and signed it. He gave it back to me.

"You need to put your address where we can contact you, Sir." I put the name of the hotel and he seemed satisfied.

"Good night, Sir."

By this time the doctor had arrived, this time an expatriate.

"Rupert Stanton is my name, Mr. Talbert. What have you been up to?" He checked me all over very carefully and clearly had no intention of rushing the examination. He took my blood pressure and a sample of blood to be tested. He then looked at the x-rays which had appeared.

"Well you've got no broken bones and apart from some unpleasant cuts and abrasions I think you're going to live. Are you going to stay here to-night or shall we get a taxi to take you to your hotel?" I leapt at the suggestion.

"Well you've been cleaned up very well here. Don't have a shower to-night. You can have one in the morning if you're careful and don't pull off all those plasters. You had better come and see me to-morrow afternoon or Saturday morning before 12 o'clock. Here's my card for an appointment."

I felt pleased to be going back to the hotel. I needed to think carefully about what had happened. Did the truck mean to knock me off the road? It certainly seemed that way but I couldn't be absolutely sure. But if so, why? I chose some clothes from my bag, and the nurse helped me get dressed. She carried my bags out to the waiting taxi and I thanked her profusely. The taxi driver got out of his cab to help me into the car and then load up. It was good to see the back of the hospital and the front of the hotel, not that the staff hadn't been wonderful but a hotel bed sounded a lot more attractive than a hospital one. I paid off the driver in the lobby as he put my bags down. He seemed pleased with the tip I gave him. There was no hiding my dressings and plasters from the receptionist as I checked in.

"Nice to see you again, Mr. Talbert. My my. You look as if you've been in the wars."

I made no comment as she gave me my key. The way I felt I didn't care if Frank complained that I'd kept the room when I was in Bermuda. Something made me turn round. Charlie was watching me, or I thought she was as she was still wearing those dark glasses. I wondered if she wore them in bed so as not to give anything away. She was wearing her brown blouse and matching trousers. In spite of myself I was beginning to recognise her wardrobe.

"Mr. Talbert, I presume?" I bowed slightly but it hurt.

"Ms. Simpson, the talented investigator?"

"The same." She looked concerned. "Peter, what have you been doing? I was expecting you hours ago. I was so worried I rang the police and they told me without any explanation that you would be along shortly."

"Well they were right, weren't they?"

She carried my bags effortlessly to my room, took my key and opened the door. There was no way I could protest. I lay on the bed and she demanded the key of my large bag. I watched her unpack my things and hang up my clothes. I must have been more shaken than I thought. Luckily I wasn't worried that she would see something she shouldn't because there was nothing to interest her and she'd soon realise that the packet of condoms was genuine. Anyway I was sure she'd been through my bag at least once already. At least she knew not to try to go through my other bag, we might have had a disagreement, even in my condition.

I told her the saga of my arrival, from the immigration with Mr Justice again, through the car accident to the hospital. She got the whole truth though it did occur to me that it may not have been all that wise. Perhaps I was shaken more than I knew from the accident. I still hadn't established who was friend or foe but somehow I looked on Charlie as my friend. Mandy would have said that was because Charlie had a fantastic figure and without any clothes on would look like every man's fantasy. She might have been right but I wasn't in a position to check and Charlie had warned me not to make assumptions. She brought me back to my present situation.

"Peter, you may not like my saying this but if your accident was deliberate it is very good news. There would be no reason for you to be attacked if there had been something wrong with the aircraft. Someone must be afraid you know something."

"Or be about to find out something I shouldn't. You're quite right Charlie. That was the conclusion I came to but I'm not absolutely certain it was deliberate."

"Well, you'd better tell me what you've been up to, since it is a basic rule in my business that keeping things to yourself can be a life shortening experience."

"Alright Charlie, you've been very kind looking after me. I'll trust you, I don't have much choice anyway. But before I start I'd better report the accident to the rental people."

Charlie got the yellow pages out and gave me the number. I didn't ask her which firm she had given me. She probably knew the number of the car I rented as well. A sleepy voice answered the phone. I told her the tale and the rough location of the car.

"Did you take full accident cover?" I answered in the affirmative.

"Did you tell the police?" Again I reassured the tired voice.

"What did you say was the number of the plate?"

"I didn't and you're nearer the car than I am."

"What's your name then."

"My name is Talbert and I need another car."

"You'd better come out to the airport in the morning and collect it and you can fill in the accident form. What size car do you want?" The conversation came to a close and I rolled over on my back, exhausted from the effort. I slowly returned to my room companion.

"My journey was probably a waste of time, Charlie. As I told you over the phone I couldn't really shake the met man from the firm belief that the weather on track was good. The Ops. Room was depressing because the area searched was so small. I called Bob Furness to try to keep the Nimrods searching but they're almost certain to be withdrawn. We've just got to hope that the Navy will furnish another boat or two. The only good thing to happen was the dinghy and the wreckage. Mind you, as I told Greg, it was a bit strange."

Charlie suddenly became alive.

"What do you mean, strange?"

"Well as you would say, Charlie, it was terribly convenient for the bulkhead material and the dinghy to be next to each other on the beach. I would have expected the stuff to be spread further apart. In fact I've asked Joshua Brown to search the other beaches."

I paused. The wreckage situation needed thinking through. Perhaps I should talk to Philip Smith of World Underwater Surveys. I relaxed and tried to relieve the aches and pains. I tried to force myself to concentrate but was beginning to feel exhausted and Charlie noticed. Maybe Alpha Lima was never going to be found. I was almost too tired to care.

"You'd better go to sleep now and I'll come back in the morning. Stay in bed until I come, that's an order."

She left and I limped over to the door and bolted it. I checked that the doors to the pool area were also bolted. In bed, I took some pills the doctor had given me and went straight to sleep.

***

I was awakened by the phone. It was 7.30 a.m. I reached over for the phone forgetting for a moment about the previous night but my body soon reminded me that I had been in the wars. I remembered the pills, no wonder I had slept so well. I picked up the phone knowing it was Mandy.

"This is your wake up call."

"You don't know how glad I am to hear you."

"Why? What have you been up to, this time?"

I gave her only a sanitised version of what had happened in case my phone was bugged already. She sounded very concerned.

"My poor love, I told you to be careful. Are you sure your accident was an accident?" She never missed anything. "What are you going to do?"

"I'll be alright, don't worry. I'm going to the airline to-day to see the insurance man and then I can decide when to come home."

"That's the best thing you've said. You know I'd love that but I'm afraid I don't believe you. The moment you start thinking things through you'll decide that you have to find out what happened. Remember what I've said. Be very, very careful."

She rang off and as I replaced the phone I knew she was right. I rolled over on my back to recover but there was a peremptory knocking at the door. I managed to pull some trousers on to find Charlie waiting outside. She breezed in wearing her dark glasses, floppy blouse and Bermuda shorts. I could handle that attire without any difficulty, it was the smooth stuff showing her figure with a dash of perfume that made me stand to attention.

"How do you feel?"

"I'm not sure yet, thank you. My leg is still a bit sore but the rest of me seems to be OK."

"What do you want for breakfast? I'll ring down."

"I'm not an invalid you know. We could go down together and have breakfast."

"Wrong for two reasons. Firstly I've had breakfast and secondly we didn't finish our discussions last night."

"I've been thinking Charlie about our discussions last night. Perhaps we were unwise. Do you think the room's bugged? They even advertise a child monitor in every room."

Charlie looked at me.

"For an amateur you're quite smart. Alright you win. Have a shower and then we can go to the outside bar if it's open. I've got some news for you but it can wait."

She took my complimentary newspaper and sat down in the large chair.

"You don't have to wait while I have a shower, I can manage you know even if I'm not 100%."

She looked at me through the dark glasses, hesitated as if to say something, then got up from the chair she was in and left. I locked the door, bolted it and had a shower. I examined my face and hands as I dried.

The Final Flight

It looked impressive but it didn't hurt too much. Hopefully Dr. Smith would remove a lot of the dressings and plaster. I called him while I remembered and made an appointment for 5 pm. I managed to put on some casual clothes and went to the lobby. Charlie was waiting.

"Let's go into the coffee shop this morning, instead of outside. I don't think it will do you any good to get too hot with all that stuff on."

"Charlie, I haven't spoken to Frank yet to tell him what happened."

I knew I was wasting my breath as I said it.

"I've spoken to him already and he is coming out here later once he has got the airline on the road. Let's go to this quiet table over here," she said avoiding the instructions of the waitress trying to seat us in the middle of everyone else.

I ordered some fruit and coffee for both of us.

"I told you I've had breakfast."

"A big girl like you can manage another breakfast."

She looked at me through her glasses and I decided that I had better avoid personal remarks in the future. She returned to the discussion.

"Peter where did we get to?"

"You told me that you had some news for me."

"*Ocean Searcher* has heard a faint ping from a crash recorder."

I must have looked flabbergasted.

"I thought you'd look pleased. I don't have to tell you I'm not."

"How long is it going to take to find the recorder?"

"Nobody knows. It's in deep water near where the first lot of wreckage was found and the response was very faint."

"Maybe the battery is running out."

"That's what Philip Smith is afraid of. Anyway it seems to settle for sure what happened."

I didn't say anything because I needed time to think. Charlie was talking again.

"You'd better tell me some more about last night."

"Well all I remember was discussing my car going off the road. You know I'm not convinced that truck hit me by accident."

"Nor am I. But you realise that if it was deliberate then the loss of Alpha Lima was definitely not an accident."

"Ah, yes. That's what I meant to ask you last night but I was too tired. Have you checked whether the real paintings were there in customs and were actually loaded on to the plane?"

"Yes. While you were away in Bermuda I did finally have some success. I found out from Westfield in New York that the guards who supervised the paintings coming off the ship in fact did check that the special markings that Christies used while they were packing the paintings and sealing the crates were the same as the ones that were on the crates that went in to the customs shed in St. Antony. I also came to the conclusion it would have been very difficult to switch the paintings as they were loaded on to the aircraft bearing in mind that even if the guards had been 'bought' there were customs and shipping agents around. They would have had to exchange the paintings with dummies and somehow kept the crate numbering correct with the seals intact and not have triggered the warning indicators on the crate."

"So that means the paintings have been lost with the aircraft? But in that case why push me off the road? Anyway it sounds expensive for Westfield. Particularly now the recorder has been heard. Unless of course, one of the customs men were in on it?"

Charlie eyed me thoughtfully.

"It's possible I suppose. That's going to be a delicate area to check. But it would explain why they're so keen to get rid of us."

"Not really unless it was the head customs man stirring it up. Surely there really could only be one customs man in the scam."

She nodded glumly. In spite of her protestations I noticed that both of us had finished our fruit and coffee. We got up to leave and Charlie departed, convinced I suspected that some of the world's masterpieces were fast becoming fish food. For my part I was still feeling a bit shaken up and the thought of lying down for a bit seemed good. Frank called me from the airport and asked if he could come over with John Southern and I suggested about noon. They arrived and woke me up but I didn't mind since I had managed to sleep for at least an hour after breakfast. We met in the coffee shop and they ordered lunch.

"Well, Peter, I've heard all about it from Charlie. You've been in the wars. How are you feeling? You look battle scarred."

"I'm fine Frank, just a bit tender here and there. I reckon I had a very lucky escape."

John Southern joined in.

"You certainly did. Still the accident must have been a coincidence now that they've heard the crash recorder. Let's hope they find it quickly. It certainly looks as if the crew just lost control." John never forgot what his job was. "Anyway did you find out anything interesting?"

"John, I'm not sure you're right about the accident being a coincidence. Certainly Charlie Simpson the Westfield Insurance investigator had made her mind up that my car accident was deliberate. Not sure exactly how she feels now after the news about the recorder. She is still very suspicious." I thought about his question. "Unfortunately I didn't learn too much at Phoenix. Faulty software doesn't seem very likely yet the forecaster is convinced that the weather on track to Bermuda was fine. However, the programmer was so sure that I went back to Bermuda to recheck with the forecasters but it was a waste of time. Still while I was there we got some more wreckage. Mind you, as I told Charlie it's a bit odd to have the dinghy with all the bulkhead material sitting on the beach there. It should have been spread more widely."

"But if it all floats you'd expect it to be together, wouldn't you."

"Possibly Frank. But the dinghy would have been much more affected by the wind."

John Southern joined in.

"I'm thinking about why pilots lose control. Is it easy to change the software? Could they have made a mistake somehow?"

"Installing software in a computer is relatively straightforward, though it can only be done by someone who knows about these things, in WAA's case presumably either Paul Thomas or Tom Mullard. I would expect WAA to download new software releases from Phoenix and then program their computers in the labs. The computer with the modified program would then be swapped with the unmodified one on the aircraft but that's one of things I want to check. But John, if the software was loaded correctly and then there was something wrong with the software itself the pilots would get a warning. Anyway it wouldn't make the pilots lose control."

A thought occurred to me and I looked at Frank.

"With your permission I'd like to talk to Mick fairly soon. I'd like to do a routine investigation in the hangar without alerting anybody. I know an airline runs seven days a week but Mick told me the hangar is quieter over the week-end."

"No problem there, Peter. I'll get him to come over here so that you can talk."

"That's good because I'm concerned that my phone may be bugged." Frank didn't look convinced. I went on. "You know this accident may not have been an accident, but if it was arranged deliberately, what were the instigators of the plot trying to achieve? Was it coincidence that the weather was bad? Was the aircraft blown up, with the freight, including some of the world's best paintings lost forever? But surely that would only make sense if the paintings were not on board at all. Let's call that the scenario number one. But that would mean that despite Charlie's investigations the paintings were not on board. Then Jimmy Morrison gets the insurance money and somebody, presumably Jimmy, gets the paintings.

"Scenario number two has the paintings on board the aircraft but unfortunately the pilots lost control, possibly because something was wrong with the airplane's controls. That has to be the most likely explanation. In that case my car accident was definitely an accident.

"Scenario number three, the aircraft was ditched near Bermuda. Seems incredible, the weather was rough but if the hull was in shallow water some of the paintings might be recovered. I've checked with Charlie and the paintings were double sealed and in crates so they might survive in water for a bit.

"There may be other scenarios but those seem to be the possible ones. However Frank, I don't favour any of them. If scenario number one was the object of the plotters then Charlie had better get on with it and find the paintings. For all I know she probably is. Furthermore, somebody's police had better start looking for murderers but I'm not clear which country's police, which is a real problem. With scenario number two I would be surprised if the pilots would have lost control flying into Angela but conceivably of course, the flying control system could have failed. Whether the scenario was one or two we would still need to find out why they flew in the wrong direction.

"Scenario number three would be impossible in my view. Ditching successfully at night and getting the paintings out of the aircraft after the ditching near Bermuda just isn't on. However, if it were number three then it is possible that the two crew and the other guard are alive and that at a suitable moment the paintings will be raised from the deep if they haven't been raised already. Obviously the Bermudan police need to be involved and Charlie again, though first find your aircraft and the crew."

Frank listened to all this and waited for me to stop.

"It's a mess. We need to get the recorder and later hopefully, find the aircraft. The only firm thing we have is that for the transmitted positions to be incorrect the software must have been faulty in some way, despite what Honeywell say. That's where you're needed Peter. You say it couldn't have been that because the pilots would have noticed." He thought for a moment. "Despite your visit to Bermuda, Peter, perhaps the weather men might have been wrong?"

Frank turned to John Southern.

"John, I know you think the accident is pilot error but from what you've heard from Peter, don't you need to revise your views?"

"Not really. As Peter has pointed out, since the paintings were on the aircraft the accident could not be scenario one and to suggest ditching is ridiculous. The pilots clearly either lost control or had a problem they should have sorted out. Anyway one of the pilots in my opinion should have noticed something was wrong and that the aircraft was on the wrong course. I don't know whether it is relevant but Frank tells me that Hudson had seen Morrison quite recently and let's be quite open about this, Morrison is clearly the prime suspect to have master minded this plot."

I interjected.

"But John, if Hudson had been doing something wrong as you seem to be suggesting then it would not have been pilot error but a deliberate fraud and surely you would have to pay up?" Frank nodded agreement,

"You may like to know that the VOR beacon which should have transmitted check bearings, and which would have enabled the pilot to check his heading, was out of service."

Frank looked at me in amazement, almost with respect.

"I didn't know that. How on earth did you find that out?"

"One of your pilots told me when I was coming back from Bermuda last Sunday. I've got to check with the St. Antony SATCO, Tim Hardcastle, what the problem was but the coincidence is remarkable. If I was Charlie I'd be tempted to say it's altogether too convenient."

"But Peter, if the aircraft did go off on the wrong course shouldn't the pilots have noticed even if the VOR was not working? Couldn't the pilots have checked on the stand-by compass?"

"John, you have a point there but remember it's not on the check list to check the stand-by. Maybe it should be but currently it's left in its stowage since the airframe manufacturer considers an incorrect heading from the computers is impossible."

John thought about things.

"The position of my company will be that we are not going to pay out until we find the wreckage."

Frank didn't look pleased.

"But John. If the hull is at the bottom of the Atlantic we may never ever find it. Still at least we have a chance now we know where one of the recorders is."

John considered for a moment.

"Frank, I don't know all the case law on this thing but I expect that if the aircraft cannot be found after a certain period of time then loss must be presumed. It would clearly be to your advantage to find the aircraft quickly, though possibly not to ours, but it seems to me that to get your money, you've got to prove foul play or that there was something wrong with the aircraft systems. It will be our contention that either the pilots should have spotted there was something wrong or they should have been able to fly the aircraft, regardless of the turbulence. You may have to wait a long time before you get the money or more likely you won't get it at all."

I didn't vote with John and came straight back at him.

"I don't believe you'll make that position stick, John. The VOR was out and the compass could not help them. They steered into a storm and something went wrong. I don't believe you can wash your hands of the matter." Frank nodded agreement.

John looked a bit dispirited probably because, in spite of his stated requirement to find the hull, he realised that his firm might well have to pay West Atlantic Airways the hull insurance money in the end and I had no intention of trying to cheer him up. Frank paid the coffee shop, promised to get Mick to call me, and the two of them left. I got up to leave, saw Jack Wellings with Brian Fletcher from the AAIB in the corner of the coffee shop and went over to join them.

"I didn't know you two were in the hotel."

"We weren't, we've just moved in, we didn't care for the old Anchorage. Peter, what on earth have you been doing to yourself?"

I gave them the same sanitised version I had given the police and asked them how they were getting on.

"Well Peter. It's clearly good news about hearing a crash recorder. Let's hope they can find it and get it up. If they don't move fast the battery may fail. Still they know where the recorder is so that it should be possible to see the wreckage from the towfish returns or even better from the ROV. We still have got no hard facts except the small amount of wreckage. It's all very awkward. We are here because the St. Antony government asked us to help but their aviation people don't seem to be worried, one way or the other. The aircraft was on their register but I think they take the view that if it was a crime of some sort, then the crime was not on their territory so it lets them out. We really need to find the hull and the recorder to find out what happened. Thank goodness the UK Government is prepared to pay the money to get the experts to find it."

"That's news to me. Bob told me the day before yesterday that the Nimrods were going and that was that."

"Well he called me this morning and said that now a recorder has been heard the Navy are sending another boat up from the Bahamas. Luckily they had one visiting Nassau. The St. Antony enforcement people are clearly worried about not letting drugs proliferate on the island and so they would like to find out if this accident is connected with the drug traffic. I'm sure that must have counted with HMG. Our feeling is that the crew made a mistake in that they should have noticed they were going in the wrong direction. I'm not sure whether finding the hull, thousands of feet down in the Atlantic, will really help but we need to keep on trying. It's going to be a long job if we don't actually find the beacon and bring the recorder up. By the way despite the Navy, Bob says he is going to withdraw us in the next day or so if there are no further developments and wait to see what the search brings."

Brian Fletcher took over when Jack Wellings stopped.

"Peter, I'm not comfortable with the ADS positions disagreeing with the probable position of the aircraft. It looks to me as if there was a fault in the software. We sent a signal to Honeywell and are still awaiting their reply. Apparently the experts have drafted a reply but the legal eagles are sitting on it. We've asked Bob Furness to chase Honeywell from England.

"Another thing, did you know the VOR was out of service? If that had been working they would have seen something was wrong."

I nodded.

"Yes, it's a remarkable coincidence."

A sudden thought occurred to me but, rightly or wrongly, I didn't feel like sharing my idea with them, after all they were meant to be the experts. I needed to think things through. We chatted about the search efforts in Bermuda and then I left to go up to my room. The message light was on and the operator asked me to call a Ben Masters and a telephone number.

"St. Antony Police, how can we help?"

It was all a bit unexpected but became even more so when I asked for Ben Masters. A girl answered.

"Chief of Police's office. Who is it please?"

I gave my name and was put through.

"Mr. Talbert. I gather you are coming down this afternoon to see Dr. Stanton, would you like to pop in and see me first? We are only a few doors away."

The bush telegraph seemed to be working well and it sounded like a royal command.

"Sure Mr. Masters. What time do you suggest? You probably know I don't have a car at the moment though I'm trying to find time to go the airport and pick one up."

"Would you like us to collect you or would you prefer a taxi?"

I detected a sense of humour and we agreed a taxi might be more discreet. I got the telephone book out and saw that the immigration department was very close to the police in the main street. I called and asked for the head of the immigration department.

"Dick Bartholomew here."

I gave him my name and asked if I could call in. We agreed 3.15. The message light was still on. Cindy Smart wanted to talk with me.

"Mr Talbert, there's a story going around that you've had a car accident. Are you alright?"

"It's kind of you to call, Ms. Smith. But I'm fine. I was just a bit careless."

"Is that so. I'm getting a different buzz from where I'm standing. Almost as if it wasn't an accident."

"I don't know where you are now but I know what happened. It's not conjecture." I tried to change the subject. "Presumably you've heard the news about a crash recorder being heard?"

"Yes I have. Does that mean everything is now settled?"

"I'm not sure I understand that. The recorder has got to be brought to the surface and in addition we need to find the wreckage. It's all quite complicated."

"That's exactly what I mean, Mr. Talbert. We need to talk."

"Tell you what, I'll call you in a day or so when I feel better."

"Don't forget or I'll call you again. You know I can be very persistent."

I wondered who she'd been talking to and what she was going to write in the Announcer. There wasn't a lot of time left now before I had to go out and getting dressed took a little longer than usual. Shaving would have to wait for another time and I had to put up with my stubble. Mick called and we agreed that he would be in the lobby at eight the following morning. There was a cab waiting at the front of the hotel to take me to Cape Harbour and I was on my way almost immediately to the immigration office. The lady at the desk called Bartholomew's office and his secretary appeared and showed me into his office. Dick Bartholomew was clearly a local and a capable official.

"How can I help you, Mr. Talbert? You look as if you've been in an accident."

I gave him my, by now, standard account of the accident and then explained my various arrivals into St. Antony and my problems with his immigration officials.

"Mr. Bartholomew, why is St. Antony giving me such a hard time? I'm trying to help and, as I told one of your supervisors Mr. Justice, if West Atlantic doesn't get the insurance money the airline will go to the wall and there will be a lot of people in St. Antony out of work."

"Mr. Talbert, we are always very careful about people coming here to work as distinct from being here on holiday. However it does sound to me as if my people have been over zealous."

"That's good news. Mr. Bartholomew, I like to be frank with people. I thought at first that the problems I've been encountering was official government policy and I'm very relieved to hear what you just said. Not to put too fine a point on it, it's my feeling that some of your people have been encouraged by a person or persons unknown, as the saying goes, to give me and Ms. Simpson a hard time. It occurred to me that it could be the customs here if they are fearful of what might come to light as a result of our investigation. Is there any chance of your finding out who it is who is pressurising your people, since it could be very significant in solving what happened to the aircraft?"

Mr. Bartholomew thought about this for some time.

"Alright Mr. Talbert, I will try to help. Here is my home phone number if you need me for some reason. Have you got your passport with you? Where did you say you were staying?"

I gave him my passport and he called his secretary.

"Give Mr. Talbert an unlimited entry without a stay limit valid for one year."

He turned to me. "Let's relax a little and talk off the record. May I call you Peter? Please call me Dick."

He got up and poured some coffee for us both.

"We are very worried about St. Antony being used for drug running and other crimes. The officials here unfortunately are not particularly well paid and a little money can buy a lot of favours. I know you are going to see Ben Masters when you leave here and he will tell you the same story. We try to help him by keeping out the undesirables, but what with our own wrongdoers and the ones that slip in, Ben and his people have to be very, very vigilant. They are doing a first class job but they are up against foreign organisations who are completely ruthless." I nodded. "By the way I suppose there wasn't anybody on the aircraft who shouldn't have been?"

"You're afraid the accident to the aircraft may not have been an accident?" Dick nodded. "Glad to hear that because I've been told that the official policy of your Government is to hope it's an accident. I'm with you. We need to explore the situation very carefully. As usual we need to consider who would gain from the loss of the aircraft. Unfortunately, the body in the water was the insurance company's best man so you can see why we're getting very worried."

"We?"

"The paintings insurance assessor and myself."

Dick thought about this and looked at me straight in the eye. He was giving me a message.

"Peter, one more thing. Let me give you a piece of advice. Remember you're an engineer, not a policeman, not an insurance investigator. Be careful."

I smiled.

"Thanks for the advice, Dick. You're absolutely right but really I need to know the whole story in order to solve my little bit."

His secretary returned with my passport which I put in my pocket without looking at it. We said our farewells and he showed me the police building. Ben Masters was not what I was expecting. He was short, wiry, very weather-beaten and as far as I could judge, originally a white Caucasian but I couldn't be sure.

"Mr. Talbert, come in. I thought we should have a chat." He sat me down in an easy chair and sat in another one. He looked at me carefully. "How do you feel? I'm sorry you've had such an unpleasant experience."

"I'm fine Mr. Masters. 'Shaken but not stirred' if you take my meaning." I liked Ian Fleming's description of how to make a martini. "I'm seeing Dr. Stanton in a moment and I'm sure he'll make me look like my passport photo."

"Peter, may I call you that, since no-one is taking notes of this meeting?" I nodded "Your description of your car accident in my opinion does not accord with reality." I hoped I looked incredulous through my plasters. "I don't believe the lights of the truck behind blinded you and made you leave the road. In fact when I heard about your accident from the policeman who you saw last night, I decided to look at the car myself. Your car had rolled over several times and was severely damaged. However, the damage on the offside of the rear fender was because something had clearly hit you hard. If you ask me your car was pushed off the road by a truck hitting you in the back." I didn't argue but I didn't agree. "Do you know who has it in for you?"

"No Ben, I don't. You know despite what happened it might have been an accident but if it were done deliberately then your question is key. If we could find out who wants to get rid of me, or just frighten me off, we might start working out what really happened to Alpha Lima. Why it fell into the sea. No chance of finding the truck I suppose?"

"Not a hope. The truck will have a bent front fender but so have hundreds of trucks in St. Antony. What I want you to be is careful. Don't do anything that my people should be doing. You are an avionics engineer not a policeman. If you want to look at places in St. Antony that might have interesting things inside, don't feel tempted to have a look yourself. I've made the same point to your Ms. Simpson when I found her looking at the Paragon building in the middle of the night."

"She's not my Ms. Simpson."

"Well that's your problem." He wasn't about to be stopped in full spate. "We can help you. It is no use your learning the truth if you are going to get killed. Here's how you contact me, day or night." I copied the numbers down. "As Dick will have told you, the government here is determined to prevent drug and other illicit traffic on the island. We appreciate your help but we don't want you killed, we'd prefer to hear any information or ideas you might have."

He thought the interview was over but I felt it was too early to leave.

"Ben?" He hesitated. "Do you know a Cindy Smart?" He nodded. "Does she have to be so well informed?"

"She's a good hard working girl and we try to help each other."

"Well it's not going to help if she splashes wild guesses all over the Announcer. Don't you think you should advise her to cool it in return for giving her the inside track if there is one?"

"Possibly."

I couldn't expect any more. We shook hands and I went to Dr. Stanton's office. There were several people waiting so I read the local papers and magazines that lie in doctor's waiting rooms all round the world. My turn finally arrived and Stanton examined my cuts and bruises.

The Final Flight

He expressed himself satisfied and asked his nurse to put plasters on one or two of the worst cuts.

"How's the leg? Is it worrying you."

"A bit sensitive but no real problem. Can I exercise it? I like to swim every day."

"Do whatever you feel like, but don't overdo anything. Come and see me again if you are at all troubled."

I asked the receptionist to order me a cab and was soon back at the hotel. There was no sign of Charlie which pleased me as I was tired. I had soup and a sandwich in the coffee shop and went straight up to my room. Before going to sleep I logged on to America OnLine and asked Mandy for details of the court case which kept the paintings in St. Antony. There was some mail from Jill for me to deal with but it could wait. I lay on the bed trying to go to sleep. Only if Alpha Lima had been blown up or ditched would someone have thought it worthwhile to try to frighten me, or worse kill me. But even then it would only be worth doing if I knew something significant. All sorts of ideas occurred to me and it was ages before I finally dropped off to sleep.

CHAPTER 6

'And sends the fowls to us in care
On daily visits through the air'

In the morning I swam two lengths very gingerly. Mick arrived spot on time and we had breakfast in the coffee shop. Rightly or wrongly I had decided that it would sensible to trust him, not only because I felt that this sort of deceit, which affected the safety of his aircraft, was against his religion, but also because I felt he would be discreet in not disclosing any results in our investigations.

"Well, Peter. You don't look as bad as I was expecting. What's the plan?"

"Mick, I expect Frank told you that if there had been a software fault or if incorrect software had been loaded into the computers the pilots would have noticed straightaway as they taxied out. Which reminds me, when was the last software update from Honeywell?"

"A good point. I asked Paul Thomas that and he said about six months ago. Of course they still have to reload the current software program occasionally into a computer which has had maintenance."

"Well would you humour me? I'd like to check on the whereabouts of all your flight management computers."

As we drove out to the airport and the WAA hangar a thought occurred to me.

"Mick, what happened to the computers on the aircraft that hit the mountain?"

"Good thought, Peter. Unfortunately all the avionics were scrap so we couldn't use any of it for spares."

Mick had got the head storekeeper to meet us and we checked the computers. Each 412 aircraft was delivered with it's own two computers and the airline had ordered six spares so that at one time when the airline had six aircraft, the total computer strength was twelve plus six, eighteen. Two aircraft had been lost so that the total strength should now be eight plus six, total fourteen. We found six in the stores and then we went to the lab where Mullard was doing some work. To our amazement we found another two computers so apparently we had sixteen computers, not the expected fourteen. Mullard had been watching us and looked very nervous.

"I wondered when you would realise that the numbers didn't add up. It's been worrying me for some time but to be honest I didn't like to mention it to anybody."

"You mean there's two extra computers?"

"No, one extra. We've got an aircraft having maintenance on the ramp and one of its computers is here."

"When did you first notice the extra computer, Tom?"

"The day after the accident to Alpha Lima. I've now quietly checked all the serial numbers and they're all our computers. Somebody must have put one computer that wasn't ours onto Alpha Lima before the flight."

"That's incredible." I paused. "But surely one non-standard computer would put a warning up on the flight deck, wouldn't it?"

Tom looked at me thoughtfully before continuing, choosing his words carefully.

"Not necessarily, Peter. You see a computer can be programmed to run as master and the other computer be made inoperative. It's a throwback from the time when aircraft like the Boeing 737 had two displays but only one computer."

The reference to the 737 triggered my memory. I suddenly remembered where I had seen Tom.

"Tom, I've remembered where we met. It's been troubling me for ages. You were at Grand Rapids with Smiths Industries working on the 737 Flight Management Computers three years ago when I was visiting. You showed me round your development labs."

"Quite right Peter. I wondered if you'd remember."

"Tom, have you mentioned any of this to Paul?"

"No, Mick. And when I heard about the car accident to Peter here I wondered if it really was a coincidence. The paintings must be incredibly valuable. Perhaps a crime has been committed though I don't see how. I'm even considering handing in my notice and leaving right now. My family love it here but something strange is going on."

I changed tack slightly.

"Tom, I've looked at your PC which downloads the programs. There are two communication programs, one of which has a Phoenix telephone number. The second one didn't have any numbers in the directory."

"I know. When you looked at the PC the other day I was about to come into the lab. I waited until you had finished and looked myself. The main communication program is with Honeywell over the internet. As you say the second directory was empty but I noticed the last number dialled and copied it down."

He opened a notepad and tore out a sheet and gave it to me. Mick chimed in.

"Tom, I'd prefer you didn't mention any of this to anybody."

Tom nodded heartfelt agreement.

"You bet. Some things are best kept on a need to know basis. Mind you I find it a bit strange that Paul Thomas hasn't checked the computers the way we have done."

Tom was echoing my thoughts as he said that. It was strange Paul hadn't checked. Perhaps he already knew the answer. Mick and I left and wandered over to the coffee area. We nodded to Paul Thomas and Chuck Curtis, the radio supervisor. I showed Mick the number Tom had given me.

"214, that's a Dallas number, one of my sons lives there."

We were both very quiet thinking things over and left for Mick's office. I wondered if Mandy had replied to my last message.

"Well what do you make of all that Peter?"

"Tom's a very good engineer. He's incredibly capable in just the area we're investigating. But where could another computer have come from? They don't grow on trees, not even palms. Anyway they're more valuable than gold dust. What does occur to me is to wonder if there is any chance of tracking a computer coming to St. Antony. Wouldn't it have to come through customs?"

"In theory yes, but there's stuff coming in all the time."

"Are you going to talk to Paul?"

"I don't know what to do for the best. What do you think?"

"Show me the tech log sheet again for Alpha Lima, Mick."

I had a glimmer of an idea.

"Don't talk to Paul or anybody yet. Let me think about it. However, I do think it's worth getting someone to check avionic equipment that's been delivered over the past six months to the airline or anyone employed by the airline. Don't worry about LIAT deliveries but, for example, if Bill Hudson was sent a computer I would like to know."

Mick agreed to put his chief storeman on the job and called him straightaway. Before leaving I asked Mick if he could lend me a standard tape player and we went back into the radio lab where he spotted one doing nothing. Mick then drove me to the terminal and came with me to the car rental desk. They produced a car accident form which I completed. The girl behind the desk didn't care because the car was fully insured. I rented another car and Mick watched me drive off to the hotel where I arrived without incident. It amazed me how hesitant I was at first as I drove away, but my confidence slowly returned.

When I got in I checked my email. Mandy had replied giving me details of the court case that prevented the paintings going on to Bermuda. The case seemed very complicated and was brought by South America Traders Inc. based in Dallas. The plaintiffs suddenly decided to drop the case a day or two before the accident.

The Final Flight

I was still a bit tender from my crash even though I was feeling stronger all the time and another rest seemed a good idea. I lay on the bed, connected up the tape player and put in one of the New York Oceanic tapes. I was expecting to hear the tape I had heard before but too late I realised I had put in the wrong one which would take the best part of two hours. Expecting silence I was just about to change the tape when I heard

"New York Oceanic, this is Speedbird 645. We are at 370 expecting Eltin at 2235Z"

"645 this is New York. We see your ADS position. Call at India for clearance to call Bermuda."

Of course! When I had listened to the tape in New York I had not been able to hear all the other traffic talking to New York. In order to get a short tape and to try to be helpful, the people in New York had cut out not only the silences but also all communication not associated with Alpha Lima. All my desire to sleep suddenly disappeared. I got my notebook out and started to make a complete history of traffic on the satellite frequency. Clearly, the satellite traffic I was listening to was on the frequency dedicated to traffic in the Bermuda area. There must be lots of satellite frequencies and each sector was allocated a different frequency and was controlled by a different controller. The pattern became clear as I listened. All the aircraft I could hear on the tape were flying in the Atlantic in the St. Antony/Bermuda/New York area and controlled by New York Oceanic. All the aircraft were using automatic position reporting. As the aircraft approached their destinations or the continental United States they were transferred by New York Oceanic to the relevant VHF ground based frequency. There were a lot of aircraft going in to Bermuda on the tape. Every so often I heard the calls from Alpha Lima which I had heard before. I guessed that most of the traffic going to the USA had left earlier but there were quite a few business aircraft. I played the tape right through and heard the final message from Alpha Lima. The tape ran on and finished with Paragon 56 making contact with New York en route to St. Antony from Bermuda before the tape stopped. A thought occurred to me and I played the end of the tape from the Nelson control tower for that night which Tim had copied for me. Paragon 56 had landed at Nelson before Tim went to bed. I put my notebook down exhausted and dropped off to sleep.

I woke at 5 p.m. and decided to see if Charlie was in her room but she was out. I left a message 'I've had an idea. How about supper in Cape Harbour?'

I switched on the TV and dropped off to sleep. Charlie woke me about twenty minutes later.

"What's your great idea? In fact I'm off to New York at dawn as my boss wants to talk with me."

"On a Sunday? She's a hard taskmistress."

"We're talking about $100m dollars, not your consultation fee."

"Ouch. You're right. We can talk some other time and I'll keep my ideas to myself."

"Hold hard a minute. I haven't said no. Our meal needs to be early, that's all I'm suggesting."

"That's lucky since I made the reservation for 6.30."

"How did you know I was going to come?"

"I'm quite good at forecasting the future, it's the past I have difficulty with."

"In that case are we going to find the paintings?"

"Join me for supper and all will be revealed."

"Not at supper it won't," she snapped and rang off before I could reply.

We met in the lobby at 6.15. Charlie was wearing a thin jumper with an uplifting bra underneath, which didn't hide her figure in anyway at all. She had chosen a shortish skirt which didn't hide her legs and finally I realised as I got closer, she was wearing some perfume which encouraged me to see if I was missing anything. She had let her hair down to the shoulders instead of keeping it severely tucked away out of sight. She volunteered to drive since she knew I was not fully recovered from my 'accident'.

"Where are we going?"

"The Cape Harbour Bistro in St. Mary's Street but I've never been there so we'll have to find it."

We cruised up and down St. Mary's and Charlie spotted the bistro near the Kensington Hotel. She even managed to park the car in the street, not too far away. The bistro was not full and we got a table in a corner. The waiter lit a large candle in the centre of the table so we could read the menus.

"What are you going to have to drink, Charlie?"

"Is this a business meeting or what, Peter?"

"It's not a what."

"In that case I'll have a spritzer made with Chardonnay."

The waiter who had been listening looked at me and I ordered a Bells and water. We also ordered jumbo shrimps and decided to share a special pizza. I decided to live dangerously.

"Charlie, what would you have ordered if it had been a what?"

I looked at her carefully, probably with some appreciation showing. She steadily returned my gaze.

"Water. I'm a very careful girl."

She gave me one of her smiles which didn't help my concentration and then her face changed as we got down to business.

"Shall we start? Let's hear your idea."

"Well, when we met at breakfast yesterday I think we both agreed with my statement that the paintings had been lost with the aircraft. In saying that I assumed, and I think you concurred, that the aircraft must be under the water somewhere. In fact in all probability that is where it is, now that they've heard a recorder. However, you have always felt and I have never disagreed with you that the whole thing seemed too convenient, too remarkable that on this critical flight the aircraft with the paintings should have disappeared." Charlie nodded. "Good. Well I had chat with Frank and John Southern yesterday and, perhaps more importantly, I spent the morning with Mick checking into the whereabouts of WAA's flight management computers. Charlie, there was an extra computer on Alpha Lima that didn't belong to WAA."

I told her about our visit to the hangar and how we discovered it. Charlie got every excited.

"Surely that proves what I said all along. A crime has been committed."

"Yes, it does look as if you were right but finding the extra computer doesn't find Alpha Lima and the paintings. *Ocean Searcher* may be finding a recorder right now but it hasn't done so yet as far as I know." Charlie nodded. "However, don't you think it is a remarkable coincidence that the aircraft took off so soon after the court case was settled or, to put it another way, don't you think it was very convenient for Angela to be there ready for the accident the moment the case was settled?"

Charlie eyed me reflectively.

"Yes, but what is the point you're making?"

"Well as a result of all these coincidences and listening to the New York Oceanic tape in full, I wondered whether I ought to float another idea of mine in front of you?"

Charlie didn't take her eyes off me.

"Let's have it. I'm not sure I like the 'floating' connotation."

"It looks an almost dead certainty the aircraft dived into the sea, out of control. But there are some curious circumstances about this accident quite apart from the aircraft being in a different position from the one it was reporting. The aircraft had full fuel, the VOR didn't work and, very worrying, your Roger O'Sullivan was found dead in the water. Are we all the victims of a very clever 'find the lady trick'? Until the aircraft is actually found I wondered whether we should be following other alternatives just to cover all the options. Particularly as the crash recorder had a very weak battery."

Charlie observed me carefully through her glasses.

"What has the weak battery got to do with things? What alternatives have you got in mind?"

184

The shrimps arrived and we would have eaten in silence except for the rather obtrusive background music in the bistro and the TV screens on the walls. I ate at my usual 'much too fast' speed and Charlie wasn't far behind. She put her fork down and nodded for me to continue.

"The alternatives? Well suppose your unbribable Mr. O'Sullivan had been spirited away just before the paintings were loaded and a fake guard substituted. Your other guard might have changed his allegiance on the promise of a small pot of gold. We then have an entirely new ball game. Firstly the paintings could have been removed as they left customs and not loaded on the plane, though you say not. Have you considered that the crates could have been switched and the correct number of crates loaded on to the plane?"

Charlie shook her ahead and didn't look too pleased. I carried on.

"Yet another possibility is that the aircraft took off with two guards who no longer worked for Westfield and headed towards Bermuda or rather towards Angela.

"We must then ask what might have happened when all communication was lost somewhere near Bermuda, with all that fuel onboard?"

"You've got my full attention but the pizza is coming. We'd better eat it while it's hot. Do you think you will remember where you're up to?"

I shook my head as the waiter took the shrimp plates away and rapidly substituted an enormous pizza which he had cut in two but the halves were still larger than our plates. I carried on talking and eating as best I could.

"Well clearly we both need to do some investigations. You need to think about extra crates in St. Antony. I need to think about the aircraft taking off with two rogue guards and full fuel."

She looked at me very searchingly but I wasn't sure what she could see.

"Peter, I'm beginning to understand you. You've got some ideas which you are not prepared to share with me. I keep on telling you, and so I suspect do all the other professionals, that secrecy does not lead to a long life. Only amateurs keep things to themselves and, if they're on to something, then as likely as not they get bumped off. You've already nearly been killed in your car."

"But I don't know why."

"Well maybe it was because one of the alternatives you have in your mind but which you are not confiding to me is actually what happened and solves the crime. They're frightened you're going to find the truth and tell everybody."

The Final Flight

We came to the end of our pizza. Charlie had managed to finish her half which impressed me but I supposed she needed a lot of sustenance to swim up and down the pool every day the way she did. She refused my suggestions of dessert and coffee pleading her early morning flight. When the bill arrived she insisted on paying her share and I could see it was pointless to argue. She drove us back and we had a last minute briefing in the lobby.

"I'll call you Peter some time from the office to-morrow. I'm planning to come back Monday night or Tuesday. My secretary does my email so you can check your mail every so often in case I feel the subjects are classified." We shook hands and this time I was certain that her regulation handshake time had been exceeded by a considerable amount, perhaps because she knew she was upsetting me by moving her finger slightly and smiling at the same time. I watched her attractive rear view, not spoilt in any way by her short skirt, disappear as she walked slowly down the corridor.

***

In the morning I called Mandy.

"How are you doing, my love?"

"I'm fine. Reading the Sunday Times and wondering when you're coming home. How are things with you?"

"Making a bit of progress. Can't talk much because this line is not secure. The doctor has taken most of the bandages and plasters off. I managed to swim two lengths to-day and am steadily getting better. Are you coming out to see me?"

"Not while you're working. Possibly if you ever finish."

"It's a wonderful place for a holiday, you'll love it."

"Any idea how long the job will take?"

"I could lie to you but the answer is a definite no."

We chatted on but the conversation was very stilted. It was a relatively short call. After swimming four lengths and having breakfast I drove to the airport to collect the FT. I scanned the paper racks and noticed the Daily Mail. I looked for Aviation Week but I knew it wouldn't be there because it never appeared on the news stands. Back in my room I opened the Mail. Brian had gone to town.

"WAS THE LOSS OF EUROPEAN 412 ANOTHER LOCKERBIE?"

He developed Charlie's theme that it was a remarkable coincidence that the pictures were on the flight. I retired to my room to read the week-end FT which had arrived overnight from New York but I found I couldn't concentrate. Suppose Roger O'Sullivan had been removed before the flight. Was it a coincidence that Alpha Lima had full fuel? Why hadn't Bill insisted on defuelling? Would the flight have taken place if he had? Surely Bill wasn't in the plot, assuming there was one? Regardless of who was in the plot, the one thought that was now dominating everything was that the aircraft could have turned round when the weather got bad and returned to St. Antony or, come to think of it, almost anywhere in the Eastern Caribbean. But what about the crash recorder being heard near the wreckage position? If the aircraft did turn round why not tell New York? There was no way the aircraft was not going to be found if it returned to the Caribbean. It didn't make sense. Did I dream the truck pushed me off the road? But the extra computer was no dream. However, on the balance of probabilities the aircraft must surely be at the bottom of the Atlantic and the paintings never left the ground when Alpha Lima took off. Charlie had better face up to it and start investigating when she got back from her week-end. I wasn't convinced it was only her boss she was seeing. Not that it was any of my business but it was difficult not to speculate.

I pondered my next move and got out the maps of the Caribbean which Frank had sent over from his office. I started thinking the unthinkable. With two rogue guards on board anything could have happened. Perhaps they had made the pilots turn the aircraft round. Could Alpha Lima have returned from Bermuda and not gone into the sea? Surely someone would have seen it return? There were an awful lot of islands, some large with large airfields and some small. Perhaps it was possible. I reckoned with all that fuel on board Alpha Lime could have reached Barbados to the east and St. Thomas to the west. I looked at the possible islands, Barbados, St. Vincent, St. Lucia, Martinique, Dominica, Guadeloupe, St. Kitts, St. Maarten, St. Croix and St. Thomas. Perhaps I should start at one end and work along assessing the places with long airfields and talking to the controllers to see if they had seen Alpha Lima. On the face of it the investigation would be a wild goose chase since if anything unusual had happened, then surely there would have been a report back to St. Antony. However, something unusual had happened and I felt we had to keep searching both above and below the water until the aircraft was found. Before studying all my maps and charts I decided to send an email to Charlie but to my surprise there was already one for me.

"Ms. Simpson has asked me to send you the following message
  'Spoke to Jimmy who said that now the recorder had been heard he was stopping his search. It was now up to Westfield and when would he get paid? He seemed genuinely concerned about losing the paintings. I'm discussing situation with my boss who is

feeling rather glum. Will go to Bermuda on Monday. Unsure of return.

Don't bother to search my room, I've left nothing of value, even in the safe. CS.'

Message from Ms. Simpson ends."

She really had a cheek that girl. Anyway she didn't leave me her master key, assuming she had one. Perhaps she needed reassuring so I sent her an immediate reply.

"Please convey following to Ms.Simpson:-

'Still on job while you're swanning in NY. Beginning to get some ideas.

Best Regards PT. Did you mean to leave your Ysatis behind?'

End of message to Ms. Simpson"

My next move was to call David Roberts in the Ops. Room in Hamilton.

"How are you getting on finding the recorder?"

"Not very well. Hang on I'll get Philip Smith, he's just finished talking to Bob Furness."

Philip came on the line.

"We haven't found the recorder yet. We know from the response yesterday where it is but we can barely hear it now. The ROV is being got ready and it may be able to start searching to-morrow but by then the beacon will be dead if I'm any judge. We may never find the recorder."

"But you should see the wreckage?"

"Yes that's true but there's something strange about this search. For a start I can't make sense of that new wreckage. We've looked at the weather for the last few days and the wreckage should have been out at sea. Of course the sea is never predictable but we certainly can't alter our search strategy."

He discussed a few more details and rang off. I had a sandwich in the coffee shop and on my return found my message light was on, Charlie had called. I called the number she had left on the message and she answered the phone herself, but then it was Sunday.

"Peter, I got your email. I'm not sure if I follow you completely. What ideas? What are you up to, Mr. T?" There was a pause. "You amateurs are all the same. What makes you think I need to carry all my perfumes with me? How did you find out anyway?"

"That's my secret. Anyway I daren't tell you any more over the phone." I had an idea. "Where are you? What's your number? I'll try and call you back in about an hour."

I drove round to Air Traffic but Tim wasn't on duty. The controller knew me and said it would be alright to use one of their lines. My view was that the ATC lines would be secure. Charlie answered straightaway and I explained my plan.

"I'm going to do some investigations to follow up an idea which seems rather unlikely but needs checking. If the aircraft is not at the bottom of the sea, or even in the shallow water near Bermuda, is it in the shallow water of some gorgeous Caribbean island? I know I poured cold water all over your ditching idea but that was because we were thinking of the Atlantic, not some idyllic atoll. With two guards carrying guns we've got a different ball game. I'm thinking of trying to get hold of a small aircraft and flying down the islands, stopping at each significant one, talking to air traffic and maybe flying round. That way I might find out if anything unusual happened on the night of the accident."

"But what about the beacon they heard?"

"I have an idea about that."

"You have an idea about everything. Come to think of you've got too many ideas altogether." She paused. I wasn't sure what she was getting at and I certainly wasn't going to ask. "It's just as well I know you Peter or I might think your latest plan was a boondoggle. I think I'd better go with you."

"Who says? And anyway that would definitely make it a boondoggle."

"No comment." There was a definite pause. "But who's going to pay for your flights of fancy, my friend?"

"Good point. I was going to start with Frank and possibly talk to Greg but if you're offering to pay that's a different matter. She who pays the piper calls the tune."

"Why don't you fly the aircraft yourself. That would save money and we wouldn't have to tell everybody what we were doing. Can you still fly?"

"Depends what you mean by can. Legally I can if I get a valid private pilot's medical certificate, pass a test on US regulations and do some refresher flying with an instructor. Whether I can physically I don't know, even though they tell me that flying is like riding a bicycle, that you never forget. However, it might be expensive getting current again and it would definitely take time. I like your suggestion but reluctantly I wonder whether it wouldn't be more sensible to get a driver. As you inferred it's not unreasonable for Westfield to pay for the trip since you aren't paying for the underwater search."

"Why don't you talk to Frank and get a feel for costs and we can discuss it to-night? Mind you I'd have to get authorisation, it's above my limit."

The Final Flight

"What do you mean to-night? I thought you were away until Tuesday in New York catching up with your social life and seeing your boss. You could only have been in the office two minutes."

"More like two hours and that's all my boss needed. There's a Westfield Board meeting on Tuesday and she needed to be briefed. And Mr T, I'll worry about my social arrangements if you don't mind and you can worry about yours. If there's room on the flight I'll catch the BWIA flight getting in at 8.15 this evening and we can discuss things later."

"Fine. I won't meet you since I imagine you'll be picking up a car. Call me when you get in. Bye."

I decided to call Frank and he invited me over to talk in his house. I went straight over after thanking the controller. We went out and looked out to sea with two cold soft drinks. Pamela was inside but she promised to come out and join us.

"Peter, if I understand you correctly, you're suggesting that one of the alternatives we did not consider last time we were together at the hotel was the aircraft returning back to the islands and possibly ditching near some deserted island. But the crash recorder pinging?"

"They haven't found the recorder yet Frank nor spotted the wreckage. We discussed three scenarios the other morning and this is really scenario number four. I didn't mention it at the time because it was only a wild idea. Anyway, you had John Southern with you and I didn't want the idea to go outside into the wide world. The logical thing is still for the aircraft to be in the Atlantic somewhere near Bermuda and if it's there we need to find it as quickly as possible. But we need to make sure we don't miss other possibilities however remote, so my vote for a start goes for flying over the islands and talking to people."

"But surely it would have been dark? Ditching wouldn't have been possible."

"Not normally, but the stakes were high. Remember that the aircraft has two radio altimeters so a good pilot would be able to make a safe touchdown using the landing lamps. I imagine there would be some identifying lights in the place that was chosen."

"Look Peter, if the aircraft came back to the islands as you suggested, why wouldn't it land on a runway?"

"That's a possibility and I'm going to check all private landing strips as well as the airports. However, surely someone would have seen it and nobody has."

"It all sounds like a wild goose chase to me, Peter."

"You could well be right but I believe that while the aircraft hasn't been found, we should look everywhere possible and clearly with that load of fuel on board the aircraft had the capability to return to the Caribbean somewhere."

"How are you going to do the search?"

"I don't know, that's why I called you. I wondered if you have any ideas to keep the costs down?"

"Well if you were prepared to give up flying round each island looking down for Alpha Lima, then you could fly with LIAT in an old puddlejumper getting out at each stop, talk to air traffic to find out if anything unusual had happened, and then go on to the next island. I could get you a complimentary ticket all the way round. That way it would cost nothing except your time which I would very gladly pay for."

"Well I could do that for a start. At least it would eliminate all the known airfields though ditching is clearly an alternative. I've started checking the maps out to list all the runways, private as well as public, which are not served by LIAT, but not having any luck. If the aircraft did come back and didn't ditch then we've got to assume that it landed somewhere, presumably unloaded the freight and the paintings, almost certainly refuelled and then took-off straightaway. It's got to be like that though no-one has reported seeing Alpha Lima. Goodness knows where it went then, but that would be a good problem to be faced with. However Frank, I think it must have ditched if it did come back from Bermuda else someone would have seen something and we would have heard."

Frank didn't look too sure about anything.

"Listening to you I'm more than ever convinced that the aircraft is way down in the Atlantic with it's crash recorders. However, if you insist..."

I interrupted.

"Could you manage two tickets because Charlie seemed to want to come along? Mind you that was when she thought she was picking up the tab."

"I thought she was in New York?"

"She was until she found out what I was thinking of doing and then she decided to take-off and head back here. I think she's scared that she might miss something and doesn't want to let me out of her sight."

Frank thought about saying something, then seemed to think better of it. I supposed he was thinking what everybody else would think, Charlie and I would be having a high old time if we flew down the islands together but then they didn't know Charlie. On reflection, Mandy wouldn't be too keen either and considering things a bit more I realised that I only knew Charlie superficially. She did have a great smile when she chose to display it and a magnificent body which she didn't choose to display and some alluring perfume which certainly I found rather exciting. It might after all be more sensible to go down the islands by myself.

Frank finally contented himself with, "I should be able to get two tickets, we help LIAT out quite a bit. When will you know for sure what you're going to do?"

"Well if I'm going to do it I'd better start to-morrow going west to St. Thomas. Maybe when I get to the far end, WAA could fly me back here and then LIAT could take me south. Then WAA could fly me back here from Barbados. Charlie flies in to-night and I could call you first thing in the morning with her decision about coming too."

"I'll get two tickets authorised. I'll call Matthew Stephenson this afternoon and set things up. If Charlie doesn't go then they won't actually issue the ticket. All you'll have to do is to call in advance and make your initial reservations and get the reservation clerk to get the authorisation number from Stephenson's office. If you come to my office before you go, I'll let you have open tickets to get you home from either end."

"Thanks very much Frank for all that. If we both go, could you keep tabs on the search operation in Bermuda? The Royal Navy control room in Hamilton can tell you if the recorder and Alpha Lima is found. I'm sure your inestimable Susan can find out for you."

Pamela joined us and we stopped talking about Alpha Lima for a bit. The weather was still perfect and I tried to relax. Margaret Springfield walked over and joined us. Greg apparently had just gone flying somewhere in S.America, Colombia she thought. We had a light lunch and then I took my leave. Back in the hotel there was a message from Charlie saying that she was definitely catching the 4.15 from New York. I got the maps out again and checked the islands very carefully for suitable places to ditch and for private airfields.

I calculated using the European Aerospace 412's manufacturers aircraft performance that, allowing for the need for Alpha Lima to fly low level as it approached the Caribbean islands to avoid being observed, the aircraft could probably get as far as St. Thomas to the west and down to Barbados in the south east. There were quite a few islands where it could have ditched and I realised that the actual length of coastline to be searched was huge. However, it occurred to me that if the plan was to recover the freight as well as the paintings then there would be a real problem because apparently some of the boxes were very heavy. I needed to speak to Greg again to discover what he said was in the freight and whether it was insured. I made a note to leave a message for Greg to call me.

If the apparently invisible aircraft had landed as distinct from ditching it would have needed at least 4,000 ft. of tarmac to land and to be able to take-off again at light weight. It would really have required 6,000 ft. with any fuel and cargo on board but I decided to look at all airfields over 3,000 ft. long to be on the safe side. I went through the maps and the

Jeppeson charts and came to the conclusion that there were fifteen airfields to be visited:-

Island	Airfield	Runway Direction	Length in feet
St. Croix	Hamilton	09/27	7,612
St. Thomas	King	10/28	7,000
St. Maarten	Princess Juliana	09/27	7,054
Sint Eustasius	F.D.Roosevelt	05/23	4,265
St. Kitts	Golden Rock	07/25	8,002
Antigua	V C Bird	07/25	9,003
St. Antony	Nelson	08/26	10,323
Guadeloupe	Pointe-a-Pitre	11/29	11,499
Grand Bourg	Marie Galante	09/27	4,068
Dominica	Melville Hall	09/27	4,800
Martinique	Fort de France	09/27	10,827
St. Lucia	Vigie	09/27	6,201
St. Lucia	Hewanorra	10/28	9,003
St. Vincent	E T Joshua	07/25	4,649
Barbados	Adams	09/27	11,000

The Final Flight

I got LIAT and WAA time tables from the front desk and reckoned that in view of the ticketing requirements it would be best not to be too ambitious but to catch the 1000 from St. Antony, the 1230 from Antigua, the 1530 from St. Kitts night stopping at St. Maarten. On the Tuesday I might decide to do a side trip to Sint Eustasius but in any event I could do St. Thomas and St. Croix on the Tuesday and be back in St. Antony by 1600. On Wednesday I could do Guadeloupe leaving at 0900, possibly a side trip to Grand Bourg, Dominica, then Martinique and night stopping in Vigie in St. Lucia. The next day I could go down to Hewanorra, then St. Vincent and finally Barbados so that I could be back in St. Antony 1730 on Thursday. It would be quite a slog but there seemed no alternative if I was to check on all the movements and see if I could spot something unusual.

I read for a little when I had finished looking at the maps and then lay on my bed looking at the television. Charlie rang at just before nine and we agreed to meet at the outside bar. I put on a shirt and shorts and went out to meet her. She was wearing a bathing costume, shorts, and dark glasses. She had already ordered a spritzer and I decided to have the same.

"Welcome home. Are you sure you can see me through those glasses, Charlie? It's very dark out here."

"Don't worry yourself about me. I can look after myself. What have you been up to?"

"Not a lot. I spoke to Frank about going up and down the islands and went over to see him. Frank suggested using LIAT outbound stepping down the route and WAA for the return flights and certainly it is the cheapest option."

"But you won't be able to look down and check if the aircraft ditched anywhere, Peter."

"I know but at least we will have eliminated the possibility that it landed somewhere. Obviously I'll ask at each place if there were any stories of strange aircraft noises in the night to support a possible ditching. If we draw a complete blank and the aircraft still hasn't been found in the Atlantic then maybe we'll have to charter a plane and fly all round the islands but it will take a long time and it will be expensive."

"How long will it take for you to visit the airfields?"

"I reckon four days using LIAT and WAA going down the islands looking for Alpha Lima and/or looking for something unusual that happened in the air. Frank has arranged the ticketing and I'm thinking of leaving at 10 to-morrow for Antigua."

"By yourself?"

194

"Well I wasn't sure what you wanted to do. It seems a complete waste of time for both of us to do the trip though, of course, it would be nice if we both went."

Charlie took her glasses off and looked at me carefully. She grinned.

"Yes, Peter, you're right on both counts. It would be nice but it would be a waste of my investigative time. I think I had better rely on your detective skill in this matter."

"But I'm only a poor avionics engineer."

"I know but we have to prioritise our efforts."

She put her glasses back on.

"So I'll tell Frank you won't be requiring the ticket he did for you?"

She took her glasses off again and looked me up and down.

"That was a bit sneaky, Mr. Talbert. You didn't tell me it was all arranged for both of us. Perhaps I could come at least one way, as a holiday."

"Your boss doesn't expect you to take holidays when you're doing a job."

"I don't think you want me to come. My boss trusts me implicitly."

"And so do I, Charlie. Let me make my position clear. There is nothing I would like more at this particular moment than to have you come down the islands with me. However, is it sensible? Would it help or complicate the investigation? Would it complicate our lives, Charlie Simpson? You live in New York with your social life and I live in London with mine."

"Only you can decide matters like that, Peter Talbert." She considered the situation. "I tell you what. Cancel me off the first half of the trip and we can have another drink out here on Tuesday to decide whether I should come with you on the second half."

"Sounds good to me, Charlie. Let's have another drink to confirm the deal." I made the necessary arrangements while Charlie replaced her glasses. "Now what have you been doing to pass the time?"

"Peter, you always ask questions which are all embracing, to coin a phrase. I'll give you selected replies. I saw my boss who read my fortune with Westfield Insurance and encouraged me to get a move on and find the paintings though she knew that now the recorder has been heard the paintings would be in the Atlantic. Maybe that's where I should go if they really are lost."

"Don't do anything like that in a hurry. The Atlantic is very wet."

"Then I told her how you were almost certainly pushed off the road which cheered her up on the grounds that if the paintings had been drowned nobody would have bothered to try to kill you. I went on and told her about your idea of the aircraft not diving in to the Atlantic. She liked the thought of the aircraft returning to the islands and ditching and, you will be pleased to hear, I warned her not to mention it to anyone at Westfield or anywhere else as you were a nut case full of wild ideas. She told me to keep close to you since you seemed to keep things moving and I asked her to rephrase her instruction. Finally she told me to ask you about the recorder beacon if the aircraft was in the Caribbean. From what I had told her about you she felt sure you would have an answer." She stopped. "Have you."

I grinned at her.

"What do you think?"

"It doesn't matter what I think. It's what you think that matters." She was getting cross. "For God's sake tell me what you are scheming."

"I'm not scheming but I think it may be worth counting how many crash recorders WAA have and whether they have lost one, with a flat battery."

Charlie looked at me and considered what I had just suggested. She sipped her drink and watched me carefully over her glass and I decided to stare back without comment.

"Peter, I also checked on how the search for the recorder was going with the Navy Control Center in Hamilton and was pleased to find that they hadn't found it. Let's keep our fingers crossed that they don't find it and that your wild and improbable theory is right."

"I don't mind them finding the recorder." Charlie looked surprised. "The records will show whether my theory is correct. The way I feel at the moment, if they find the wreckage on the sea bed I will be very surprised. We'll just have to keep all the balls in the air at the moment. Anything else to report?"

"Nothing that need concern you. New York is cold by the way. There are compensations for being down here."

"Did you eat on the plane?"

Charlie said she hadn't so we looked at the menu. I looked at it carefully but it hadn't changed in the last few days.

"Is there a Mrs. Talbert?"

I considered her remark carefully as I tried to decide whether to have prawns or tuna.

"Is there a Mr. Simpson?"

Charlie was also finding the choice very hard indeed.

"Not at the moment."

"Well there was a Mrs. Talbert but she disappeared." I decided to tell Charlie about Diana and our searches and then, on the spur of the moment, decided to bring her up to date. "Two week-ends ago there was a call out of the blue which might have been her when I was staying with my girl friend in Bournemouth. I checked on the number and it was a hotel in New York. I want to go there some time and look through the guest list but the chances of spotting her must be remote."

We ordered some food from the bar and some spritzers.

"Was there ever a Mr. Simpson, Charlie, apart from your father?"

"No there wasn't, but there have been one or two close run things. The problem is that I'm very determined and men don't like it. They think that what they see is what they get and suddenly they realise life isn't that simple, not with me anyway. That's why I don't encourage them by not letting them see very much."

"I had noticed, Charlie."

We both grinned and I could feel yet again that being irradiated by Charlie's smile and being contemplated by her questioning gaze was definitely becoming more than just a rather delightful experience. However we didn't stay long after we had eaten. As I came to my door in the corridor she suddenly leant forward and kissed me rather slowly on the cheek. I could smell her perfume and her body and felt her lips moving on my skin. As I turned to respond she walked down the corridor leaving me to go into my room and prepare for my trip.

***

In the morning I watched Charlie finish her swim and then did my ten lengths. Charlie was having breakfast at her table and indicated through her dark glasses that I might join her. She was reading the Economist and I was still perusing the week-end FT.

"I'm staying in St. Maarten to-night if all goes according to plan. Air Traffic will know where I am if anything breaks. Otherwise see you to-morrow night."

I went back to my room, gathered up my case and drove out to the airport. I collected my return tickets from St. Thomas and Barbados from Susan in Frank's office and then went to the LIAT desk to ask for the supervisor and sort out my reservations. It seemed to me that the best way to get help from air traffic was to warn them in advance and advise them of the purpose of my visit. Consequently, I asked the supervisor to signal down the line asking all the other station supervisors to advise air traffic of my likely arrival time and saying that I would like to chat to the senior controller on duty. The aircraft left on time and I was in Antigua in 25 minutes. I went to the information desk and got the girl to call the Tower. She said they were sending someone over.

I didn't have long to wait. A friendly looking man, very tall about 6ft 3ins. introduced himself.

"Peter, I'm Henry Livingstone the SATCO here. I got a message you were involved with that terrible accident to the WAA 412, Alpha Lima."

"Yes, Henry. I'm checking up on aircraft movements on the night of the disappearance of Alpha Lima and for the next few nights."

I explained that I was looking for anything unusual that might mean something and be significant. Just to avoid some cross questioning I emphasised that the aircraft was being searched for by Oceanic Engineering off Bermuda but that there were some loose ends that we needed to tie up. Henry took me through a side door of the terminal building, across a short walk outside in the tropical heat, and then into the tall control tower building where we were back in air conditioned comfort. The building was very new and we went up by elevator to radar room level. From there we walked up a central staircase into the local control room with an amazing view all over the airfield, the island and some sea beyond.

"What a fantastic tower."

"Yes, we are lucky, Peter." He had opened the daily log. "Why don't you look through the book here to see if you spot anything interesting or unusual."

I looked at the book but there was nothing special that I could spot. On the night of the accident there was nothing after 2200 local except for a Paragon aircraft taking off at midnight.

"What happened after the Paragon aircraft took off, Henry."

"As it happened I was on duty that night and the airfield closed. However, we did not get any sleep because of the emergency and the messages coming in, which we were having to acknowledge and respond to."

"Were you in your office or up here?"

"I have a portable bed up here but I didn't have a chance to use it."

I had clearly drawn a complete blank so I made my farewells, went down the elevator and back into the airfield terminal. I was in plenty of time to check in for St Kitts and we arrived on time. The airfield was smaller than Antigua and I was able to make my own way over to the control tower where I was well received by Ted Linklater, the senior controller.

"Well Peter. I got a garbled message from LIAT that you'd like to talk to me. How can I help you?"

I went through the same explanation as I had given to Henry Livingstone. Linklater didn't have anything special to report but he got out his movements log which I looked down. There were the normal scheduled flights but very little else, not even a Paragon flight. The airfield had been closed from midnight to 6 am.

"Do you leave your lights on when the airfield's not open? Why couldn't an aircraft land in the middle of the night?"

"Yes we do leave the lights on, but someone would have heard an aircraft landing. And any way it would have had to take-off again as there was no extra aircraft on the ground in the morning."

I wasn't entirely convinced but there was no way I could check further, on this trip anyway. We chatted for a bit and I asked him to ring his opposite number at St. Maarten to let him know what I was after. We had a sandwich together in the terminal and I asked Ted if there had been any reports of unusual aircraft flying in the middle of the night from anywhere in the island but he said none had come his way. He wasn't on duty himself that night but, as at Antigua, there was a lot of traffic relating to the accident.

The St. Maarten flight left St. Kitts punctually at 1530. Twenty five minutes later I was entering the Princess Juliana control tower talking to a controller with a pronounced Dutch accent. I explained my quest and he had nothing to report. He called the senior controller in F D Roosevelt on Sint Eustatius but the story was the same. I didn't have the same problem as at St. Kitts since both airfields were open all night. However, as at St. Kitts I checked if any strange aircraft reports had come of flying over the islands and again, as at St Kitts, they didn't know of any.

Feeling a bit depressed I went to my hotel, a rather nice European style business hotel in the French part of the island which had been booked for me by LIAT. I had a very quiet meal and went to bed. The following morning I went on to St. Croix and then St. Thomas but again I had no success at either place. I was back in St. Antony as planned at 1630 feeling thoroughly cheesed off. I drove back to the hotel and left a note for Charlie that I was back. Up in my room I called Frank.

"I'm glad you called. Charlie is with me. The Oceanic Searcher launched its towfish. Amazingly it found something almost immediately about sixty miles east of Bermuda but the echo seems a bit weak. They're putting a TV Camera on it first thing in the morning. So we should know something by midday. How did you get on?"

"Abysmally thank you. I feel like cancelling to-morrow and Thursday, especially if the sidescan sonar has shown something."

"Don't do that yet, Peter. Hold on a moment." There was a pause, Charlie came on the line.

"Don't forget our drink to-night but in view of the news from the Oceanic Searcher you had better carry on island crawling by yourself."

I called Mandy to check all was well and give her a situation report. She still didn't know if or when she was coming out. Charlie called from the lobby and said thirty minutes. She was wearing a different bathing costume from our last meeting at the bar which seemed to show her figure off more than her last one, a distinctly briefer pair of shorts, some perfume but the same dark glasses. She had already ordered her spritzer and I decided to have the same. I recounted my lack of success. Charlie had not really achieved anything either apart from gathering the news about the ROV.

"What are we going to do if the underwater return is a false one and you get nothing Peter?"

"I've been thinking about that. Obviously the search carries on in the Atlantic and we'd better think how we are going to search the shallow bays and insets for the aircraft around here. I'm not clear whether we can do it at relatively high altitude or whether we need to be near the water. Instinctively I feel we should be at about 3,000 ft. with an aircraft that has a reconnaissance camera fixed underneath the fuselage."

"How are we going to find one?"

"Couldn't you get your office to do the walking and to look for aerial survey firms in the Yellow pages and the other classified directories? There's bound to be a small aircraft with a camera in Florida somewhere." I looked at her carefully. "Now you're sure you don't want to come with me to-morrow? It might bring me luck."

"You feel quite safe in pressing me to come now you know that I'm going to say no."

"I'd be delighted if you said yes. I told you it might bring me luck or something."

She took her glasses off for a moment and looked at me without giving me any clues.

"What do you mean by 'or something'?"

"I plead the fifth amendment."

"You can't. You're British."

"In that case you couldn't possibly expect me to comment."

"Where are you staying to-morrow night?"

"Vigie in St. Lucia. I requested LIAT to see if they could get me into the St. Lucia Beach hotel but it is not yet confirmed. Why? Are you thinking of joining me for the last leg?"

Charlie took her glasses off again and smiled at me.

"I thought I'd stay in case there was some news from Bermuda."

"I hope there isn't. Then perhaps there will be something to be discovered in the islands."

We ate at the bar again in the tropical night and this time when we finished we decided to walk a little way along the beach in the dark. Charlie was not wearing her dark glasses. There was no cloud but there was some moon. The stars were shining brightly. We kept our distance and said nothing. We both knew there was a black hole ahead of us which we were going to find very difficult to avoid and I had the distinct feeling that neither of us was putting up much of a struggle. She decided to kiss me good-night again, this time on the lips but held my hands down by my sides. She stood just close enough to feel me pressing against her and then retreated once again along the corridor.

***

In the morning I caught the 0900 to Guadeloupe and savoured the first of the completely French islands. The pattern of each visit was the same as when I went west and I finally made St. Lucia without anything to show for my efforts. The St. Lucia Beach was sensibly unchanged from when I was there with Diana many years before, soon after we were married and I was a Captain with Britannia. The small bay was beautiful though I didn't have much time to enjoy it as it was almost dark when I arrived. Charlie was in her room when I called and came straight to the point.

"There was an aircraft down there, Peter, but would you believe it's not Alpha Lima. They found half a fuselage and, fairly close by, almost a complete wing off an old aircraft with two piston engines apparently. They're not going to waste time searching for any more pieces. The bits they did find were half buried in rubbish but luckily the bottom was very rocky. They were amazed to find the airplane after all these years; they spoke to the AAIB in Farnborough and their best guess is that it was an aircraft that was lost in 1948, an Avro Tudor, G-AHNP called *Star Tiger*. Apparently it was an aircraft, the loss of which was never explained, and therefore credited to the Bermuda Triangle. It's probably mentioned in that book you have."

I was pretty sure I'd never mentioned the book to Charlie but she could have seen it that night of my accident. On the other hand she would have seen it if she'd searched my room. In spite of my problems it was fascinating to learn that the wreckage had finally been found.

"You see. I told you, Charlie. There are no mysteries, the Bermuda Triangle is just a convenient way of dealing with unexplained losses. We could solve them all if we had enough money and time." I returned to the matter in hand. "Charlie are they going to carry on searching?"

"Yes they are because though they can't find the crash recorder, they think Alpha Lima must be close by."

"Maybe and maybe not. We shall see. Anyway I'm looking forward to seeing you to-morrow evening sometime."

She didn't reply. I left early in the morning by coach to Hewanorra at the other end of the island and did not get to St. Vincent until 1300. I followed the usual pattern and went straight to the control tower. Philip Statler was the senior controller and he invited me to his office.

The Final Flight

"Peter, it's good to meet you. I understand that you are looking for any unusual events about the time of the loss of the European Aerospace 412?"

"Yes Philip. Basically I'm interested in air traffic movements on the Friday night of the disappearance and the next few nights though it does not have to be restricted to those dates. Do you have anything?"

"You must judge. On the Saturday morning when I came on duty there was a Paragon G3 sitting on the ramp. There was a telephone message to call the Paragon Corporation in St. Antony and the Operations guy there was full of apologies. Apparently the aircraft had been doing cross country night flying training including landings at Guadeloupe and St. Lucia and the trainee set up a landing at St. Vincent. We were closed but, of course, all the lights are left on and the aircraft touched down but as bad luck would have it, they had a brake problem. They decided to stop the night. I was furious with them. They said they had engineers on the way over and asked if we would stay open until they had fixed the problem. I stupidly agreed as they had given the statutory 12 hours notice to stay open after 2200 hours. In the event they weren't able to leave until Sunday morning 0230 when the aircraft left for Belem in Brazil. I closed the airfield after the aircraft took-off and thought nothing more about it. I'm only mentioning all this to you Peter because the flights did not seem normal but I'm not sure exactly what's worrying me. I think it is the combination of the aircraft suddenly appearing on the ramp combined with the fact that it left for Belem."

"Did you check whether it landed at Belem?"

Philip looked uncomfortable.

"I'm afraid not. I was taking a week's leave and my wife and I were leaving very early in the morning."

"Can we check now? What was the flight number, by the way?"

"Only by going through all the AFTN messages which will have been filed. It came in using its tail number, VP-GPA, but left for Belem as Paragon 45."

I looked at my watch and thought about what Philip had been saying.

"Could you have a check and let me know? I need to follow up every lead even though that probably means wasting your time."

He was obviously embarrassed and keen to make amends for not checking the Belem flight and agreed straightaway. I thanked him and left for the terminal. As I relaxed in the plane it occurred to me that perhaps I should go on to Trinidad after Barbados, even though I wasn't getting anywhere. Alpha Lima would have had very little fuel left if it had tried to land at Port of Spain so it was a most unlikely port of call, nevertheless for the sake of completeness? My luck was in. The stewardess told me that the aircraft went on to Trinidad but that they did a crew change at

Barbados so that the aircraft was on the ground for an hour. She agreed to get a message to the supervisor at Barbados to get Frank to ask LIAT to let me go on to Trinidad and get me a flight back to St. Antony as late as possible. At Barbados I was met by the LIAT agent who gave me a ticket to Port of Spain and a ticket for a WAA flight leaving Trinidad at 2000 direct to St. Antony.

William Hatton, the Barbados SATCO, had come in specially to meet me in the Tower. He considered my questions about unexpected aircraft movements and looked through the logs.

"No Peter, nothing strange seems to have occurred and my controllers haven't mentioned anything to me."

I definitely wasn't making much progress and the St. Vincent movement didn't seem to be leading anywhere. The LIAT aircraft left on time and we landed in Trinidad at 1730. The senior air traffic control officer, Wally Roberts met me. He took me straight to the tower and I asked him the normal questions. He got the log out.

"No, there's nothing special about Saturday night, Sunday morning. Apart from the normal scheduled flights, Paragon 72 landed at 0330 from St. Antony and left at 0930."

I looked over his shoulder and had copied the details down before I saw that it was the wrong day.

"Wally, you're looking at the next night. What happened on the Friday night/Saturday morning."

"Sorry, you're quite right." He turned back. "Only scheduled flights that night I'm afraid."

There didn't seem any point in staying on and I didn't want to miss my flight. As I was leaving to go to the terminal Greg Fairclough appeared. He appeared to be surprised but pleased to see me. He was on his way back to St. Antony in one of his G3s and seeing me he offered me a ride back.

"It'll save you some time and it's no problem for me."

"Thanks a lot but Frank has been to a lot of trouble in the last few minutes to change my ticket so I think I'd better keep to the agreed plan. You've been working hard since I saw you last by all accounts. Margaret told me you were in Colombia the other day."

"No, I didn't go in the end. I managed to offload the trip."

"By the way, Charlie asked me to ask you. What exactly was the freight that was lost on Alpha Lima?"

"It was some machinery, lathes and the like, destined for S.America when we could find a buyer. St. Antony were charging us so much for storage in the transit sheds that it seemed sensible to move the machinery to Bermuda while we were waiting, where the cost would be halved."

"Are the insurers going to pay, Greg?"

"The stuff wasn't insured. It didn't have any real value." He must have sensed my next question before I asked it. "Showing hindsight it would have been more sensible to have 'landed' the stuff in St. Antony."

Greg left to go to his aircraft. I glanced at the log and noticed it was the one that had landed in St. Vincent on the Saturday, VP-GPA, and that he had just flown in from Barbados. They clearly hadn't kept the aircraft in Brazil very long.

I made my excuses to Wally and left to catch my 2000 flight to St. Antony which landed at 2045. I was back in the hotel at 2110. Charlie wasn't in her room and I went to the bar for a drink and supper. I saw her there in a hideous blouse, baggy trousers and unattractive glasses. When I appeared she looked slightly uncomfortable.

"Welcome back, Peter. I wasn't expecting you so soon. They told me you had been delayed in Trinidad and would be staying the night. Did you have any luck?"

"I'm not sure, but I can see you weren't expecting me. Have you eaten yet?"

Charlie grinned and shook her head. I ordered a whisky, another spritzer, some large prawns and two steaks, medium rare. Charlie took off her glasses and looked at me sternly.

"You are keeping something to yourself, Peter. I'm beginning to recognise the signs. Why did you go to Trinidad? Don't you think you should confide in me?"

"You're wrong. I went to Trinidad to make absolutely sure I didn't miss anything." She look unconvinced. "Has Oceanic Searcher found anything more?"

"No. And don't change the subject. You know you shouldn't keep things to yourself."

"I'm not. Anyway you wouldn't want to tell me everything. What have you been doing to-day?"

"Why should I tell you anything if you don't exchange information?" She was getting rather annoyed but then she paused and changed the attack. "And anyway, how did you know I wanted prawns and steak?"

"You looked as if you needed prawns and steak. Am I allowed to say I like your method of making sure nobody joins you at the table?"

"No, you most certainly are not." She stopped, frowning and hesitated. "Do you think I would enjoy my meal more if I got changed?"

"I've no idea but since you ask me, I know I would, but please go easy on the perfume. You've got a very good idea what it does to me." She grinned. "And Charlie, how many spritzers had you had before I arrived? I only want to know to see if I have to catch up."

"You don't."

Chapter 6

Charlie left and returned in about five minutes wearing a particularly becoming bathing costume which seemed to accentuate her breasts and cleavage and an even shorter pair of shorts, if it were possible, than the one she was wearing at the bar last time we met. There was also the distinct smell of a different perfume that I found extremely disturbing. The food had arrived and we had a very enjoyable meal followed by another walk along the beach. I told her a bit more about my trip to Trinidad and the aircraft at St. Vincent.

"I met Greg at Trinidad. He had just arrived from Barbados and offered me a trip home."

"But you came back with West Atlantic."

"I know. Frank had gone to a lot of trouble on the ticketing and I didn't want to be rude."

"I'm glad you did that, Peter, it's given us more time to talk."

"Actually it would have been quicker with Greg, it was one of his G3s. The same one that was at St. Vincent just after the accident on the Sunday and went on to Belem."

"I know what I wanted to ask you. Did you ask him about the freight?"

"Yes I did. He said it was machinery, 'lathes and the like', and he told me the same story as Jimmy told you. I asked him if the insurers were going to pay and he told me that the freight was not insured."

Charlie reached out and took my hand to make sure we kept on walking. However I turned round after a bit and led the way home.

"What's the rush, Peter?"

"I'm only human Charlie. Don't let's even discuss it. You're putting me under great pressure. I can't think what I should be doing."

"Well I've certainly no intention of telling you."

She didn't seem to want to go back and to be truthful I didn't want to either. Maybe it was because of the exploratory way she held my hand and my index finger. I wasn't sure we were going to be able to get back but we finally made it.

"See you in the morning." I left hurriedly as I needed to think out my plan for the morning and with Charlie looking the way she did on the beach and then touching me, I was finding it quite impossible to think of anything except Charlie which, while in some ways she was a puzzle, wasn't the mystery I was being paid to solve.

***

Charlie was late so I had to swim my regulation ten lengths while she was finishing her twenty. For some reason she had decided to wear a bikini which was not particularly abbreviated but certainly did her figure no harm. I decided to miss breakfast and called Tim Hardcastle to suggest a meeting.

"No problem. I'm on duty this evening at 1800 local. Would that be alright for you or do we need to meet earlier?"

"That'll be fine."

I decided to go for a drive and went towards the WAA hangar. The gates were open and I parked at the back and opened the windows to enjoy the breeze. It was hotter than I really wanted but it seemed a shame to run the engine and use the air conditioning. I could see the ramp of the business operation, St. Antony Fliteline, and considerably further down near the start of the runway I could see the Paragon ramp and hangar. I decided to get a bit nearer and moved down to the St. Antony Fliteline parking lot, and hoped nobody would move me on. The Paragon engineers seem to be preparing a Beech 420 for flight. Some boxes were being brought out of the hangar and loaded on to the aircraft. It must have been a brave decision for the St. Antony government to build several hangars in order to develop the airport, hoping to rent them to the airlines and anybody else they could get hold of. As Mick had explained, LIAT and WAA clearly got a good deal but I wondered if it really made sense for smaller companies like St. Antony Fliteline and Paragon to rent such expensive hangars.

Paragon seemed busy. The Beech 420 left and a Cessna Citation landed and taxied in. A plain red Honda Accord drew up beside me and the policeman who had been at the hospital got out. He was wearing an open necked check shirt and blue shorts. I unlocked the doors, closed the windows and started the engine. He got in.

"How are you to-day, Mr. Talbert? You are looking much better than when I saw you last."

I protested my good health but I was not convinced he was listening to my answer. There was silence for a few minutes as we both watched the activity on the Paragon ramp.

"You don't need to run the engine on my account, Mr. Talbert."

I dutifully switched off and opened the windows. It occurred to me that his desire to have the engine off might not have been to save me money but to get a better view through his binoculars without having the window in the way. I began to suspect that Ben Masters picked his team with care. We watched for some time as the Cessna left, another Beech taxied in and a Gulfstream 4 was towed out of the hangar. The policeman started to leave.

"My name is Rick Welcome, Mr. Talbert." We shook hands and he looked me in the face, very carefully. "Mr. Masters hopes that you are just concentrating on your engineering investigation and leaving the policing to us."

He went back to his car and I looked at the steady stream of cars moving along the road outside. Greg Fairclough drove by into the Paragon facility. He must have opened the gates remotely and shut them behind him. I saw Mick's car drive by and go on to the WAA ramp. Tom Mullard got in his car and left, followed shortly afterwards by Paul Thomas. It was all go. A Gulfstream 3 landed and a short thin man got out who might have been Jimmy Morrison. Greg Fairclough appeared and they shook hands and disappeared inside.

I decided I had had enough and drove back to the hotel and lay by the pool for half an hour as part of my recovery treatment, reading my notes. I soon started to go brown and realised that Mandy would immediately want to check me all over. She thought that hard work precluded getting a sun tan.

Back in my room I looked at my watch. It was 5.30, 2.30 in Phoenix. Jessica should be back from lunch. I called Tim and asked if it would be alright if I arrived early and used his phone. He let me in and I went into his office which was empty. It took a little time to find Jessica but she finally came on the line.

"Jessica, there's something you should know. There was an extra computer on Alpha Lima." There was a long silence. "Are you still there?"

"Yes, I am. I've been afraid of this for some time, ever since you left the other day. You see the computer may be one of our development ones."

"I don't understand. When I left you the Wednesday before last you told me that there couldn't be anything wrong with your flight management system and the computer software. You said that I'd better recheck the weather. In fact Jessica, I did what you said but it really does seems as if the weather was probably as they forecast, just high cloud."

"Peter, what we actually agreed was that if there was an error with system software then the pilots would be bound to notice. I haven't changed my position on that. However, let me tell you something which has been concerning me. Are you sitting down?"

I was sitting down but I got my notebook out.

"Peter, my best programmer was a guy called Steve Rodriguez. I think he got his initial training in Bogota and then he became a Citizen and got his master's degree in Dallas. To be honest, I didn't like him very much and I certainly didn't trust him but he was brilliant. I had no reason to complain, quite the reverse, until one day I unexpectedly went to talk to him about an urgent job that had to be done and looked at the development rig he was using. The heading on the navigation display was north east but the positions on the line all had the same longitude so that heading should have been due north. I asked him what he was doing and he said he was trying out some new code which wasn't working correctly. I didn't make an issue out of it since it just could have been true, but he looked very shifty."

"What happened then Jessica?"

"Well he left the firm soon afterwards. He told me that he was going back to Dallas. Then some weeks later we started making an inventory of all our test gear as we had just certificated the 412 software and we discovered that we were a program loader and a flight management development computer short. The back-up program listing CD was also missing. I suspected that Rodriguez had taken the equipment with him but I couldn't be sure."

"Why didn't you get the police to check his apartment?"

"There was absolutely no proof and the police would have needed a reason. I did call his apartment but he was no longer there. Then it occurred to me that he might have been approached by another firm wanting to get into the Flight Management business. The investment in developing the algorithms and writing the software is enormous. Honeywell are the most successful followed by Smiths Industries at Grand Rapids, Rockwell Collins and perhaps Thales, though I think they are working with Smiths now. With all the information that Rodriguez took with him he'd be worth a prince's ransom to one of the General Aviation firms or even to Thales. I've been watching our competitors very closely to see if one of them suddenly announced a new product or made unexpectedly fast product developments. So far there's been nothing."

"Well what's worrying you then?"

"We're all very busy here as I'm sure you appreciate. I thought no more about it until this accident occurred and then I became uneasy again, particularly after your visit. You see it would be impossible to write and test any new program, rogue or not, unless there was a development rig. On Thursday after you'd gone I checked that there were no rigs missing. In fact there is no way a large electronic rack could go missing but it did occur to me that the rig drawings could be removed and to my horror my worst fears were confirmed, I could not find the working drawings that we used to use. The master drawings were there but not the others. I asked around, asking the rest of the team but they all looked at me blankly."

"So you think that Rodriguez not only took a computer, loader and listings with him but also the drawings so that he could make a development rig?"

"Yes I do. I don't believe he would have to make the whole rig, but he would know exactly the parts he needed to test his software."

"Wouldn't that be expensive?"

"Yes, and very time consuming. But it wouldn't have been difficult if he had been planning the thing carefully."

"So you think this guy, Rodruigez wrote a rogue program, loaded it into the computer he pinched and then he, or someone, sent it to St. Antony to fit in Alpha Lima?"

"Yes I do, but it still leaves the problem of fooling the pilots. I'm very worried Peter but I'm not sure what to do."

"Well if you take my advice you'll talk to Max. He's very reliable in matters like this."

There was not much more to say. I thanked her and told her I would keep in touch. By the time I had finished it was getting dark. Tim was doing local control with an assistant and there was not a lot going on.

"Nelson, this is Paragon 76, request taxi for Bermuda."

I looked over to the Paragon hangar and saw the anti-collision light flashing on the Gulfstream 3 I had seen earlier. Tim gave him permission and the lights started moving in front of the hangar. The floodlights on the ramp outlined the G3 for a moment as the aircraft went through the gates and on to the taxiway. It turned left for 06 and we could barely see it as it went down to the holding point on the far side of the runway.

"Nelson, this is 76, we have our clearance from San Juan Oceanic, request take-off."

Tim gave 76 the take-off clearance and the aircraft lined up and took off turning right towards Bermuda.

"That'll be Jimmy Morrison going home."

"How on earth do you know that, Peter?"

"I was over at the WAA hangar this morning and saw him arrive, or at least I think it was him and Greg Fairclough met him."

"You seem to be getting very knowledgeable about our goings on."

LIAT and WAA had quite a few aircraft returning from the islands and Tim handled the traffic by himself. The assistant kept the log going and wrote out the cards for each aircraft. Tim was only using the tower frequency and didn't bother with 121.9 for taxiing. He said it was a waste of time when the traffic was light and it had the advantage that the aircraft arriving and leaving knew what was happening. Different controllers did it differently, he liked a relaxed atmosphere if the traffic permitted.

"What happens at night, Tim, do you close down."

"No, we man the tower 24 hours a day but there is a room down below where the local and radar controllers can sleep. If there are any unexpected movements the phone goes down there and they come on duty. We keep all the facilities on all the time of course, the lights, the ILS, the beacon and so on. Why do you ask?"

"I'm not sure. I suppose I like to know everything that's going on. I'm always looking for odd things. It's my training."

Tim thought for a moment.

"I'll tell you an odd thing. I should have mentioned it to you when we first met but there was somebody listening and I didn't know you. Funnily enough I was just chatting to Greg Fairclough about it in the golf club to-day. That G3 that took off just now started transmitting on the emergency frequency the other night when it was coming in from Bermuda. He was transmitting on the proper frequency at the same time."

"Did you tell the pilot?"

"Not at the time. It took me some time to notice what was going on. They must have the same equipment as the WAA 412s. They do that occasionally, apparently when the pilot leaves a switch in the emergency position. I called somebody in the hangar after he'd landed to warn them of the problem. There was something else strange about that flight which I was going to tell you but I can't remember. It's old age getting to me I'm afraid."

"Did you go to sleep after the aircraft landed?"

"Yes and no. There was nothing we could do to help in the search for Alpha Lima so I switched the VHF alarm down to the room with the beds and tried to go to sleep. In fact the phone rang quite a bit with various enquiries on Alpha Lima."

"Did you get up again?"

"No, I just dealt with the calls down below as they came in."

"I seem to remember from what you told me the first time we met that you've got the tape of the communication that night. Are you going to keep the emergency tape when the four weeks is up?"

"Yes we are. I've already given instructions to the engineers to let me have the tape."

"Do me a favour. Lock that tape away in a safe. If you haven't got one, give it to your bank manager. It might be important."

"I'll do what you ask in the morning. You obviously know a lot more than you're letting on."

"Not really but I've got a feeling that we don't want to lose that tape."

The traffic had just about dried up and Tim poured some coffee.

"Are you on all night?"

"Yes. In fact there's the Paragon Gulfstream 4 at midnight and that's it."

"They keep some strange hours. Where's it going to?"

"Bermuda. It's like a milk run. Goodness knows what they do. I suspect they are carrying some of Jimmy's freeloaders home after they've been in the Casino here for a night out."

"Tim, that night when Alpha Lima disappeared. The VOR failed that evening. Did the engineers tell you why?"

"I wasn't on duty but apparently just before the aircraft took off the VOR alarm went, that one over there. We phoned the duty engineer and he drove out to the site and told us that the main power cable had been cut by a truck or a digger apparently carrying out some maintenance work."

"Seems a strange time for a digger to be working."

"That's what we thought and the engineers could not find any digger. It took several days before the cable could be reconnected properly."

"Tim, can I look through your arrival and departure log for the Saturday and Sunday following the loss of Alpha Lima?"

"Be my guest. By the way you asked one of my controllers for the logs of those few days. They're here in an envelope." He passed me a thick buff coloured package.

I got my notebook out and checked through the flights. Then I left Tim to it and went towards my car which was next to Tim's in front of the floodlit building. As I unlocked the car there were two muffled bangs and a noise of breaking bricks. I threw myself to the floor as two more thumps took place and more brickwork seemed to explode. Instinctively I knew that I was being shot at though nothing like it had ever happened to me before and I moved to put the car between me and the direction of the shooting. There was a ping and everything went very quiet. My mind told me this was just like I'd seen on a film set. What I had never realised was how frightening the real thing was. I was scared. But my luck was in as Tim had heard the bullets hitting the bricks and opened the door.

"Peter, what on earth's going on."

"Keep down. There's someone having shooting practice and I'm the target."

Neither of us moved. There was a noise of branches breaking in the middle of a clump of palm trees next to the terminal car park. I very cautiously looked up and saw a large truck driving away. I couldn't be sure but it looked strangely familiar. Perhaps I'd have recognised it if I had looked at it through my rear view mirror.

I crawled into the tower entrance door while Tim stood back keeping the door open. I stood up and brushed the brick splinters from my clothes.

"What was all that about, Peter? Are you alright?"

"I think so, Tim. That's twice in three days."

"What do you mean, twice?"

"You heard about that car accident of mine?" He nodded, there were no secrets out here. "Well it probably wasn't an accident. I was pushed off the road." There didn't seem much point in saying that it was probably the same truck.

"I'll call the police."

"I'd rather you didn't. They'll tell me to leave the island and I want to finish what I've been doing."

"Alright, if that's what you want." He paused. "Peter, it seems to me that you clearly know something that somebody doesn't want to be generally known."

"The thought had occurred to me." I smiled rather ruefully. "I've got a lot of ideas but there's no aircraft and no paintings. I must be stupid because my attacker clearly thinks I know."

"More likely he thinks you're just about to find out, or work it out, and wants to kill you first."

"Yes, could be. Please do me a favour. I'd appreciate it if you didn't mention this shooting to anybody. You know how it is, word always gets around and in no time at all it will be front page news in the Announcer."

I had decided it would be better for Tim if I did not confide in him so I left him in the tower waiting for the Paragon aircraft to leave and went out to my car. There was nothing obviously wrong with it and I drove back to the hotel and went to bed without seeing Charlie. I didn't trust myself with her on the beach and I couldn't make up my mind for sure exactly what game she was playing with me.

CHAPTER 7

'He cast (of which we rather boast)
The Gospel's pearl upon our coast'

In the morning I managed my normal ten lengths and got back from the pool to find two messages, the first from Ben Masters. He'd appreciate it if I could find time to call in. I checked that it would be alright if I went round after breakfast. The other message was from Laurence Darling, the commercial attaché. Would I like to go round to the High Commission for drinks at 6 that evening and then go out for a meal. I called the number he had left and accepted the invitation. Laurence apologised for giving me such short notice but he had only just realised what I was doing in St. Antony and felt it might be useful if we met. I went round to see Ben. He was wearing uniform less his jacket and looked very formal. The air conditioning was going full blast.

"Nice of you to find time to come round, Mr. Talbert. Bearing in mind our last meeting, I wondered if we were being completely frank with one another."

"What do you mean, Mr. Masters?"

"Well I was looking at these notes this morning and it set my mind wandering."

He pushed over a copy of Charlie's email to me and my reply.

"But this is from America OnLine. They didn't give you that. You must be filtering all the mail on the internet spine into the Island. Did you get permission?"

I looked accusingly at him but wondered how the hell he'd done it. St. Antony must have quite an elaborate telephone computer setup on the island. I'd have to scramble all communications in future, though if they were really clever they could refuse to receive or send scrambled text.

Ben looked slightly embarrassed.

"Well Peter," I noticed he had suddenly gone informal. He clearly hadn't got permission, "it's like this, we like to keep a watching brief on villains on the island and the internet is quite useful."

"I'm not a villain and you've blown your scheme by showing it to me."

"If we thought you were a villain I wouldn't have shown it to you. It is your reply to your Ms. Simpson that caught my eye."

"She's not my Ms. Simpson."

"Well that's your problem. However, I noticed your statement 'Beginning to get some ideas,' and that really troubles me. I don't like people doing things I don't know about and, in my experience, it is seldom good for their health."

"You're reading more into that message than was intended. It's quite simple. I decided to look for an alternative explanation for the disappearance of Alpha Lima."

"Peter, I need to know your alternative explanation."

The phone rang and Ben listened without saying anything. A moment later Rick Welcome came in and Ben invited him to sit down.

"You know one another I believe?" I nodded. "Rick tells me there's a long scratch along the side of your car and a crack in your rear fender. Did you know that?"

I cursed myself for not examining my car in the daylight. There had been a loud noise from the car last night during the shooting but I had forgotten to look this morning in the daylight. Even Inspector Clouseau would have got that right!

Ben went on.

"Rick thinks the marks could have been made by bullets." He suddenly became stern. "Peter. We can't carry on like this. What the hell's been going on?"

I decided the time had come to share some of what I had gleaned with Ben. I mentioned my concerns about the Flight Management System software and my various other concerns. I also told him about the shooting the previous night.

"Ben. It's a ridiculous situation. My attacker thinks I'm going to find out something very shortly and it's a killing matter. I almost wouldn't mind his attacking me if I had worked everything out."

Ben nodded.

"You're lucky the attacker is not a professional killer. It looks like a spur of the moment decision to take you out or frighten you at the very least so that you'll go away. Peter, what did Tim Hardcastle tell you in the tower last night?"

It was a good question.

"He obviously told me something but I must have missed the significance."

I didn't mention about the double transmission to Ben or that Tim knew something more, but had just forgotten what it was. If Ben knew that, he'd be camping in the tower trying to help Tim to control the traffic until Tim remembered and I didn't think that would be helpful. I also didn't tell him that the log was quite interesting.

"Alright Peter. The facts seem to be that Alpha Lima has been lost in suspicious circumstances. They have heard but not found the crash

214

recorder in the Atlantic. They are looking for it and the aircraft but meanwhile there's something going on here. If you find out something you're to contact me straightaway. Remember, I don't want you discussing it first with your Ms. Simpson. You are to call me, day or night. You understand?"

I nodded.

"She's not my Ms. Simpson."

"So you keep reminding me."

"Ben?"

"Yes Peter?"

"I want you do to me a favour."

Ben looked at me and said nothing. I carried on.

"Stop bugging my phone, searching my room, looking at my email. It slows me down and I can't concentrate…"

He smiled and finished my sentence, though not the way I'd intended. "… on the electronic engineering. Anyway, how do you know it's me and not your Ms. Simpson or somebody else?"

"I don't for sure. At least if I know you've stopped, it narrows the number of people listening to my phone. Ms. Simpson I can handle."

"But I thought she wasn't your Ms. Simpson." He grinned. "OK Peter. I'll give it a rest. If you'll excuse me I've got a lot of work to before I have to leave for an official lunch."

So the fancy dress wasn't for me, that was something. Rick showed me out to my car and pointed out the scars. We shook hands and I went back to the hotel. Ben had forgotten to ask me what my alternative plan had been. Presumably he knew I'd been flying up and down the islands.

Back in my room I called the airport manager.

"Lionel Brown here."

"My name is Talbert, Peter Talbert. Is it possible to come and see you? I'm helping WAA on this accident investigation and there are one or two points I need to find out. I'm sure you'll be able to help me."

"Of course. Come up now and if you've got time we can have a sandwich. Ask at the information desk and they will tell you where my office is located."

I drove to the terminal and parked the car. The terminal was not too busy as I went through to Brown's office. His secretary showed me in and we shook hands. He was a large, local St. Antony man wearing a striped white shirt and brown trousers. His jacket was hanging at the back of the door. I looked out of the window over the ramp and most of the airfield down to the WAA hangar.

"Why don't we go up to the restaurant? It'll be less busy than the coffee shop and they need the business." He smiled. "I'm not taking my jacket."

"That's fortunate, I don't have one."

Lionel was right. The restaurant was almost empty. I watched a LIAT aircraft taxi in to a finger at the terminal as we sat down.

"You've made some great improvements since I was here last, Lionel. To this terminal for a start. And all the new buildings and taxiways."

"Tourism is our chief product and always will be, so the Government is very supportive of our plans and we got some money from the UK Government after the last lot of hurricanes. Not all the islanders like the idea but I'm sure it's the right policy. We've cleaned up the area over here a lot by building the maintenance hangars and the business terminals on the other side of the runway."

"It's about the hangars that I wanted to talk. They're your hangars aren't they?"

"Yes, we built them and we lease them out. They are a bit large for Paragon and the Fliteline operation in St. Antony but it was cheaper to build identical hangars than getting the architects to design four different buildings."

"How long have they been there? And a supplementary, were they built by a local firm?"

"About two years and partly. We got a London firm of architects to do the design and Taylor Woodrow actually had responsibility for the construction, though they did use our biggest local firm, St. Antony Construction, to do a lot of the work. Why do you ask?"

"Well I'm interested in any special modifications made by the users."

Lionel stopped for a moment. He looked at me.

"Peter, are you really a policemen in disguise? Your interests seem to be a lot wider than black boxes on aircraft."

"No, not at all Lionel. But you know how things go during an investigation. It's difficult to keep to just one area. I'm trying to establish what extra facilities WAA or Paragon for example might have over LIAT or Fliteline."

"Well, we were fortunate in that we had lessees for the hangars before they were even finished which pleased my bosses. The architects had drawn up a list of priced optional modifications. Any other modifications had to be approved by me before being sanctioned because obviously we couldn't allow uncontrolled developments on the site. I seem to remember that both St. Antony Fliteline and Paragon wanted to be able to prevent any access to their area without going through gates and we allowed the extra fences. Of course no aircraft can get on to the taxiway from any of the hangars without going through airfield gates. That's to prevent animals and unwanted vehicles getting on to the airfield.

216

We allow the hangar operator to control those gates, though we have the option of taking control if we think they are irresponsible."

"Have you got a copy of the final plans of the hangars?"

"I'm afraid not. We sub-contracted that responsibility to the builders. You'll have to see them if you need something more. They are down in the town and I can let you have their number and a name when we go back to my office."

We finished our sandwiches and went back to his office. He opened a drawer in his desk.

"You need a Mr. Sampson, Tom Sampson, and the office is in St. Mary's Street. You can use my phone."

He gave me the number and Mr. Sampson agreed to see me at 3 o'clock that afternoon.. I had a few minutes to spare so I thanked Lionel and asked him where I could find the guy who helped when my car went off the road.

"Martin Saunders? He's a hard working feller and he keeps his cleaners under control which I like and why we let him have the contract. Rather than my trying to explain to you, ask information in the terminal. They'll point you at the door."

The terminal was getting busier as the European flights were expected. The man at the desk showed me the door and corridor for Martin and I found him at the second attempt. I thanked him for rescuing me.

"I didn't recognise you, Mr. Talbert, without all that blood and glass. It was a pleasure to help. How are you getting on with your investigations?"

"Are there no secrets here, Martin?"

"'Fraid not Mr. Talbert. This is a small island and we all like to know what's going on."

"Well we are making some progress but we haven't finished by a long chalk."

"Take care Mr. Talbert. We don't want you going off the road again."

I looked at him. His face was impassive and I couldn't decide if he was telling me something or not. It was hot outside and I was glad to get the air conditioning working in the car as I made my way down to Cape Harbour. I found St. Antony Construction in St. Mary's St. after two runs up and down the street and then asking a local by-stander. Mr. Sampson was waiting for me.

"Yes we keep the plans of the hangars. I've got them out ready. What did you need?"

There were four big piles of drawings completely covering Tom Sampson's table.

"Well could I see the list of optional modifications and find out who took what?"

There was a file on top of each pile and he looked at the LIAT file. He showed me the complete list of optional modifications and there was a mark against the modifications that LIAT had taken.

"May I study the four modification files for a moment?"

"Go right ahead. Excuse me while I carry on with these papers."

I compared the hangar standard for the four operators. The extra fences and gates were shown for Fliteline and Paragon. At the back of each file there was a list of special modifications for each hangar.

"Who has to give permission for the special modifications to the hangars? For example the avionic labs in WAA and the extra rest rooms in the Fliteline hangar?"

"Theoretically Lionel Brown and his people but in practice as long as the changes comply with the building regulations no formal application has to be made."

I made a list of the differences between the hangars. The Paragon hangar seemed to be identical with the WAA but the LIAT and Fliteline hangars seemed to have less interior extras apart from the extra toilets. It might be a waste of effort on my part but only time would show. I went back to the hotel and had a message to call the control tower to speak to Chris Mattinson.

I rang straightaway..

"Tim said you wanted to talk about the radar coverage on the night Alpha Lima left for Bermuda."

"That's right. Was there anything unusual about the departure? Did you watch the aircraft?"

"Well to be honest I didn't bother. The aircraft had been cleared out of our area and I was working an inbound from Colombia so I wasn't watching. I'd love to be able to say that it left on the wrong heading but I'm afraid I don't know and, of course, we don't record the radar."

"Fair enough Chris, but I had to check. Were you on duty all night?"

"In fact I was. The watch normally changes at 8 o'clock but I agreed to stay on all night because one of the controllers wanted to be away that night. As you know, there is not much on usually after about 1 o'clock and we go to sleep unless the alarm goes off. That night was no exception in spite of the emergency to Alpha Lima. We saw Paragon 56 land and then Tim and I went to the room with the beds as there was nothing more we could do. In fact he had a pretty disturbed night answering telephone calls."

"What makes the alarm go off?"

"Any Mayday, Pan or Securité call on the emergency channel or any calls on our working frequencies."

"You must get a lot of false alarms?"

"Yes we do but that's fair enough. But there wasn't an alarm that night."

"Thanks Chris."

It was a great pity the radar had not tracked Alpha Lima. However, even if it had and the aircraft did go off on 030° or whatever the heading was, it wouldn't explain what had happened subsequently. I decided to call Jack Maynes and luckily found him at home.

"Jack, it's Peter here."

"How are things going? I read you got one body in the wreckage. Have the rest come in? Did you find the answer."

"No, not yet. That's why I called. I need your help."

"Off you go."

"The night that Alpha Lima disappeared, you kept the ADS tape?"

"You bet we did."

"What time does the recording stop?"

"I don't know exactly but I can find out. Why do you need to know?"

"Well there was a flight, Paragon 56, which left Bermuda for St. Antony and arrived at about 0300Z. I need you to examine the tape for that flight from about 0200Z onwards and see if anything strange occurred?"

"Are you going to give us any clues?"

"I can if you like. Is the reporting regular? Does it jump or hesitate?"

"Leave it with me. You do realise that the aircraft was in San Juan airspace and not ours? Luckily for you we tape all the ADS reports, for San Juan as well as for New York so we can find out what you want to know. What's your number? It may take some hours to find the answer depending on finding the tape, finding somebody I can trust to look at the records and also on the availability of a playback facility. It'll probably be to-morrow before I can get back to you."

"Send me a message on my mobile when you're ready and I'll call you."

After my shower I put on my first tie for a long time and got ready to go round to the High Commission in St. Mary's St. once again. I found the Commission first time and managed to park the car. It was obviously a formal do and I got the impression that most of the guests were accompanied by their partners as we made our way to the entrance of the building. Mandy would have loved the occasion and I wished she had been with me. Very sensibly, everybody was checked in at the reception desk as they arrived so that the men could have a badge pressed onto their lapels. There were badges for the ladies as well and I noticed that most of them wanted the badges even though they might mark their dresses. The High Commissioner and his wife welcomed us all as we arrived.

"Mr. Talbert. You've come to help Frank Westbourne. We're glad to see you. It's a bad business and we need to have it sorted out as soon as possible. It's such a shame for all those wonderful paintings to have been lost. Good Luck."

Lawrence Darling was watching for me to arrive and button-holed me the moment I left the reception line. He was a typical young career diplomat and presumably had asked me to drinks because he liked to keep his ear to the ground.

"What can I get you? We've got most things here."

I settled for a scotch and water.

"How are you getting on with the investigation? It's a strange business but it certainly looks as if the aircraft went into the sea, especially as they've now heard the recorder beacon. Any chance of finding it?"

"I don't know. You've obviously got the news that the Bermuda Triangle is not quite as mysterious as it was. After all these years the ship searching for the WAA aircraft found what is believed to be the wing and part of the fuselage of an Avro Tudor named *Star Tiger* that belonged to British South American Airways. The aircraft disappeared en route from the Azores to Bermuda and, as you can imagine, the accident really hit the headlines at the time. No trace of the aircraft was ever found and there were all sorts of theories about what might have happened. My guess would be that it was a failure of the cabin structure due to pressurisation. After all, I think it was the first airliner to be pressurised. However, unlike the early Comets, which had square windows and therefore had a weakness due to metal fatigue at the window corners, the aircraft had round windows. Curiously, later Tudors had square windows. It would be very interesting to look in detail at the structure of the window cut-outs but I'm afraid that information is lost in history.

"Whatever happened to the Tudor must have happened very suddenly since there was no MAYDAY emergency call and yet up to the time of the accident the aircraft had been communicating regularly with the Azores and then Bermuda. The fact that the fuselage was not in one piece tends to support my theory that the hull split. I hope they have some good photographs so it is possible to see the edges of the fuselage. It would be fascinating to find out after all this time why it crashed, if that's possible. Perhaps it will be too difficult. What has always puzzled me is that, when the results of the Comet inquiry were published, nobody ever re-looked at the Tudor accident enquiries."

"Enquiries? Was there more than one accident, Peter?"

"Yes there were two, the second one a year later and the aircraft *Star Ariel* also had round windows. I haven't been able to find out why some aircraft had round windows and some square. As I mentioned, to really understand the fatigue situation on the aircraft we need to be able to see the structural drawings or at the very least talk to someone who knew the issues. But of course that is not possible since it happened so many years ago. When I get back I'm going to try to go through the archives of Flight International since they used to produce splendid cutaway drawings of aircraft structures."

"But surely people must have understood about metal fatigue at the time? Why did the firm that made the Comet use square windows?"

"de Havilands. A very good question. I don't think they did understand about stress concentration at square corners and the weakening effect of fatigue. Anyway I'm afraid I've come to the conclusion that we are unlikely ever to find out the answers. It might have made a huge difference to the success of the Comet and the UK aircraft industry if Avros had suspected that round windows were safer than square ones but, as I said, later Tudors had square windows so they were probably no wiser than de Havilands. We'll never know."

I could see Lawrence was trying to recall something.

"Peter, I seem to remember reading a book by Nevile Shute all about metal fatigue. Wasn't it written before the Comet accidents?"

"Yes, Lawrence. The book was called No Highway and quite remarkable in its foresight. It was published in 1948, between the two Tudor accidents. Wouldn't it be wonderful to be able to talk to Nevile Shute now and also the Avro engineers to find out what they knew?"

I forced myself to come back to the matter in hand.

"Anyway, the point is now that if the boat doing the search can find the Tudor then it should be able to find Alpha Lima if it's down there."

"Alpha Lima?"

"Sorry. That's the name we give to the European Aerospace 412. The full phonetic name is Victor Papa, VP for St. Antony, and Whisky Alpha Lima, the registration letters. It's just as well HMG agreed to help the St. Antony Government by paying for the underwater search. In fact as I'm sure you know there are now two RN boats out there helping plus *Ocean Searcher* which found the Tudor. Of course, if the aircraft is thousands of feet down, the paintings will already have been ruined. I can't imagine the company which insured the paintings will pay any money for the search."

"Surely the pictures were protected?"

"Sure, but not down to a depth of thousands of feet. Perhaps they should have been but they weren't."

"Shouldn't the aircraft manufacturer pay some money to clear its good name?"

"Possibly. I'm beginning to wonder whether we've all missed something, and are searching in the wrong place. Jimmy Morrison who, as you know runs Paragon as well as owning the lost paintings, chartered an aircraft with a magnetic sensor on the back plus a boat with a hydrophone to try to help and search inshore but it didn't find anything. The obvious scenario is that the aircraft must be somewhere near where the beacon was heard and this scenario is supported by HMG, the AAIB and the St. Antony Government, but it's strange nothing's been found."

"Have you any other ideas?"

"None that I feel can be credible. It's not really for me to suggest scenarios to the accident investigators. I just look at the aircraft systems, try to decide if they have malfunctioned and, if so, why, and possibly the effects of the malfunction."

He didn't looked convinced.

"Peter, from what I hear, you are doing a lot more than that. Luckily nobody has asked my opinion yet, thank goodness. If they do I'll call you straightaway and hopefully you'll give me good advice. By the way I've booked a table at the Kensington Hotel. You are joining me for dinner rather than eating all these bits and pieces?"

I accepted gratefully and we walked down the street. The menu was typically American and we had salad and steak. Clearly Lawrence regarded St. Antony as a stepping stone on a diplomatic career and as far as I could judge he was quite young to be a commercial attaché. His degree was in languages but he met the mandatory first class honours requirement demanded by the foreign office. Nevertheless it seemed to me his qualifications to be commercial attaché were distinctly questionable. I preferred the French system where government commercial representatives had worked in industry and understood the pressures in winning business worldwide. However, I promised to keep in touch with him and went back to the hotel.

There was a message in my key rack, 'See you for breakfast, 8 o'clock sharp, CS'.

***

Charlie was cleaving her way through the water at 7 o'clock when I looked out. I was pleased to see that she was wearing a very conservative bathing costume. I gave her a few minutes start while I shaved and ventured out through my poolside doors. Charlie finished her twenty lengths or so halfway through my leisurely ten; we met, as she had planned, at the poolside.

"What's been happening Peter? You seem to be avoiding me for some reason."

"Nonsense. I've been very busy. I was planning to ask you if you would care to join me for breakfast but you got in first."

"Good recovery. Where shall we go?"

"Your choice. How about inside for a change?"

"Twenty minutes."

As usual it was no effort to watch her go to her room. I managed to get to the coffee shop before her and I was relieved to see she was wearing a rather unattractive blouse and bermuda shorts when she appeared. I tried to help her sit down but she waved me away.

"Thank you. Now then what have you been busy at?"

There seemed no particular reason to answer her in a rush. I called the waiter over and we ordered our breakfast. However, Charlie seemed to be getting a bit impatient and so it seemed advisable to start.

"Well first of all I saw Ben yesterday morning. He's been reading our email."

"Our email! Is that legal?"

"He did look uncomfortable when I challenged him. However his heart is the right place so I shared some thoughts with him about the flight management computer software. He told me if I had any more ideas to share them with him and not you. However, he's not to know what I'm sharing with you."

"You're sharing very little with me at the moment, Peter."

"Well don't tempt me."

There was a pause and by mutual consent neither of us said anything for a moment. I thought it was as well that Charlie had kept her glasses on.

"Well Charlie, I've been thinking." Charlie looked at me through her dark glasses. She knew when I was being serious. "Your guard Roger O'Sullivan. Let's assume for the moment that he was correctly identified. Did you check by the way?"

"Yes I did and our man swears it was O'Sullivan."

"OK. You said O'Sullivan was a good guy. Maybe it was because he was a good guy that he got killed and a substitute guard was put in place. You see providing the other guard didn't object, Westfield would not find out for sometime that they had lost O'Sullivan and in fact the switch, if there was a switch, would have been done just before the aircraft was to be loaded.

"Wait a moment, Sherlock. If Roger was killed before the flight he would not have died from drowning."

"Right. He must have been kidnapped and held over Friday and Saturday nights and then sent to Bermuda and deliberately thrown into the water."

"That's awful, Peter."

"I know Charlie but that's probably what happened if Alpha Lima didn't dive into the Atlantic. Its disappearance is not a game. Roger O'Sullivan is dead, I've been attacked and where are the crew of Alpha Lima not to mention the guards?"

A bell boy went by paging a call for me. I went to my room by the poolside door and asked the operator to put the call through.

I answered the phone. "Peter, it's Tim Hardcastle. I've remembered what it was I meant to tell you."

"That's good. Shall I come over or is it some thing we can discuss over the phone?"

"Oh, as it happens I don't think it's anything particularly special. It was just that Paragon 56's approach was very low and the aircraft made a very short landing so that it could taxi straight in to the Paragon facilities. I've known small aircraft to do that but not the G3s or the G4."

"Have you mentioned this to anybody?"

"No. There's nothing really to tell."

"Good. As I said the other day, please keep it to yourself. Don't tell anybody." He agreed, albeit I thought a little reluctantly.

Charlie looked at me as I came back to the table.

"Who was it? Anything interesting?"

"Only Tim in Air Traffic. He just remembered that the aircraft did a very short landing that night."

"Why did he call you?"

"I think because when I saw him in the tower the other night just before someone had a go at me, he said that he noticed two strange things but at the time he could only remember the one about the aircraft transmitting on both frequencies. So when he remembered about the landing he felt he had to tell me."

Charlie looked at me very sternly.

"What do you mean someone had a go at you?"

"Ah yes. I forgot to tell you. When I left the tower after talking to Tim some bullets whistled by me and hit the tower. I saw a truck drive away, I think it was the same one that pushed me off the road."

"Peter, you're the limit. Why didn't you call me?"

"Well I didn't see you that night and, as I was a bit shaken, I decided to go straight to bed. Then I missed you in the morning so I forgot. However, Ben's sidekick inspected my car when I was talking to Ben and spotted the bullet marks. Ben gave me a roasting. I had to tell him all I've told you."

224

"Well that's not very much. My sympathies are with Ben. Getting information out of you is like getting blood out of stone, to coin a phrase." She looked at me again, very carefully. "You know Peter, I think you've got a theory which you're not sharing with me. The time has come to unburden yourself or I'll tell Ben you're holding out on him."

"You play tough, Ms. Simpson. Alright, I'll give you a possible scenario, but not here. Where shall we go?"

"Why not in the shade by the pool?"

We left the coffee shop and got two chairs under an awning.

"Charlie, at the moment it's probably true to say that pretty well everybody is convinced that Alpha Lima dived into the sea because the pilots lost control. The scenario is that the pilots flew the wrong way, got involved with a tropical storm and, once there, the view is that the aircraft was doomed due to a variety of possible causes, either pilot ineptitude, bad avionic design, faulty flying controls or the Omnipotent Being operating the Bermuda Triangle wanting another victim." Charlie nodded and I carried on. "The cynical amongst us however, and I suppose that means just you and me, thought it was a remarkable coincidence to lose the aircraft on the flight with the paintings on board and with Angela in position to muddy the water. Your first thought was that the aircraft had been ditched to get the paintings out, but we all shouted you down."

"Tell me about it. You were all so rude, if not to my face, behind my back."

"Well Charlie, my problem as you would expect was an avionic one; how on earth could the automatic reporting system be telling the air traffic controllers in New York that the aircraft was on track while the pilots were happily flying the wrong way, thinking all was well. I didn't believe in ditching so, at first, I was forced to think the aircraft had indeed dived into the sea. Well, as you know I consulted the experts in Phoenix who made the flight management system and I discovered that it was most unlikely to have been faulty software. For the aircraft to have gone off in the wrong direction and yet transmit the correct ADS position would need special software and it would have been impossible for the pilots not to notice as they taxied out. Then we had the two strange occurrences, that Alpha Lima had been refuelled 'by mistake' to full tanks and the VOR failure. There were just too many coincidences."

"You can say that again."

"I believe that the over fuelling was deliberate. I'm sure we were all meant to think that the aircraft had been lost at sea in the best traditions of the Bermuda Triangle. You see, there was another remarkable coincidence which was that the weight of the aircraft with the required cargo and with full fuel exactly equalled the maximum permitted take-off weight. Only a very knowledgeable person could have calculated how much the aircraft could carry and I don't believe in fairies. Now we come to the guards. If they were not Westfield's guards then clearly they could have gone up to the flight deck and made the pilots turn round and fly back to the Caribbean somewhere. It's clear that the aircraft must have landed somewhere or even ditched, Ms. Simpson please note, just as we thought."

"We thought! You've got a cheek. Anyway there's no aircraft. How are you going to show what actually happened? You've already been down the islands and found nothing."

"That is indeed the problem. And furthermore I'm worried we may never find it. But I did find something though not what I expected. I found that there was some night flying problem on a Paragon aircraft which landed at St. Vincent."

"OK. Then what?"

"I'm not sure. There could be one or two explanations."

"Don't give me that. We're meant to be partners. You know a lot more than you're saying."

"Well I've got some more things to check."

"Well don't call me, I'll call you."

Charlie got up and went round the pool to her room. Her back was showing resentment in every movement but it didn't seem to spoil the view. Perhaps I was being a bit unreasonable but I didn't want to make a fool of myself by advocating some impossible scenario. As I was musing on the situation a bell boy came round with my name on a placard. I went to the outside bar and picked up the phone. It was Ben's secretary. She put Ben on the line.

"I think we may have found your truck."

"How do you know?"

"Well you're not the only detective on the Island, Peter. You see I kept the rear fender from your car and it had some paint marks on it. The truck was discovered early this morning at the bottom of a cliff near Full Moon Bay I thought of you and asked to see the front fender. The paint samples match exactly and, of course, the fender has some fairly fresh deep indentations and scratches which would be expected if it pushed your car off the road."

"Who does the truck belong to?"

"Well that's why I called you. You'd better come over and bring your Ms. Simpson with you."

"Ben, she's not my Ms. Simpson."

"You know best but bring her anyway, or shall I phone her?"

"You'd better phone her. I'm not her flavour of the month for some reason. She thinks I know more than I've told her."

"And probably a lot more than you've told me. See you in ten minutes."

I did a quick change into something more suitable for a Police Headquarters, grabbed my bag and went out to the car. As I left the parking lot I glimpsed Charlie making her way to her car. Luckily I managed to squeeze into the last slot in visitor's car park. As I locked up Charlie arrived looking very business like and not wearing her 'keep off' outfits. She surveyed the situation and parked in the reserved slot by the entrance door. I reflected that life being what it was, if you looked like Charlie you could be like the proverbial elephant and park where you wanted.

I waited for her to get out of the car and opened the entrance door for her. She swept in as if I was the doorman. I followed her to the desk and we signed in. Ben's secretary came out and took us in to his office.

"Thank you both for coming over. Please make yourselves comfortable."

I offered Charlie a chair which she ignored and took another one. I sat in the one she had refused and caught Ben's eye for a brief moment as we sat down. He didn't miss anything and decided to make matters worse.

"Did Mr Talbert tell you about our recent conversation, Ms. Simpson?"

She shook her head and Ben repeated what he had just told me and carried on.

"We've checked the registration of the truck. I suppose you know who it belongs to Peter?"

"I'm not sure. If I had to bet I think I'd go for WAA."

Charlie looked at me with surprise but somehow I felt Ben expected my answer.

"Yes you're quite right. The problem is, who has been driving it?"

"Is it a pool vehicle, Ben?"

"That's what they tell me down at the hangar."

"Any finger prints on it?"

"Now that's a very interesting question."

He looked at me expectantly.

"Because there's none on the steering wheel or door handles?"

"Yes, Peter, you're quite right again. Anyway I decided to put my pride in my pocket and have a discussion with you two in case you've got some suggestions."

Charlie butted in.

"You leave me out of it, Ben. It's Peter who's trying to commit suicide not telling us what he thinks is going on."

"I don't know exactly what's going on. I do have some ideas but I'm waiting for some more information. Why don't you get Frank over if he's not away flying. He may know who has been using the truck. Perhaps Mick Flanagan could help too. Another thought. It would be interesting to hear Greg Fairclough's views on loading the paintings and freight."

"You're at it again, Peter. Trying to organise my business."

"I thought that was why you asked us over."

He ignored me and called his secretary in and asked her to see if she could find Greg, Frank and Mick.

"Where's your new information going to come from?"

"I'm expecting a call from Oceanic Control. Also I need to check something with Honeywell. May I use your phone?"

"Why not? You seem to be in charge here. Use the one in the office across the corridor."

I called Honeywell and spoke to Max Postwick. He told me I'd better talk to Jessica. As usual she had slipped out of the office but they soon found her. I asked her some detailed questions about the flight management computer software and the way the two computers were interrelated which had only occurred to me after we had spoken the other day. I rang off and began to feel that some of my suspicions were being confirmed. When I got back to the office Greg and Mick had arrived and apparently Frank was on his way. Ben asked me to expound my ideas.

"Well Ben, Charlie seems very certain that the paintings were loaded onto Alpha Lima. So there are two alternatives. Firstly, the loss of the paintings was a complete coincidence and there was a genuine accident with the pilots losing control in the storm because of the weather or because they were unable to deal with a serious fault with the aircraft. The aircraft then dived into the Atlantic and that was that. The alternative was that the loss of the aircraft was an insurance scam and somehow the paintings were recovered. I suppose for the superstitious amongst us there is a third Bermuda Triangle explanation, but not for me, anyway."

Frank Westbourne came in and I carried on.

"Now then, once the wreckage was discovered it was possible to identify the body as Westfield's best guard, Roger O'Sullivan. The body had died from drowning but the doctor could not be sure that the death had occurred immediately after the crash. It occurred to me that there might be another explanation. Was it possible that Roger O'Sullivan was not on the aircraft when it crashed?"

I looked round. There was no doubt I had everyone's attention. Charlie of course, was not surprised and I had the feeling that she had got over her anger by the poolside. Greg looked very interested, Mick was taking notes and Frank was trying to catch up with the situation. Ben was making sure the tape recorder was on.

"You see, as Charlie here said right at the outset, there were just too many coincidences. The storm, the aircraft having full fuel on board, the weight of the aircraft exactly matching the maximum permitted take-off weight, the court case being settled, the paintings being released to coincide with the poor weather and the failure of the VOR at take-off. And don't let's forget the navigation error which must have occurred. It was that that really bugged me. If the software was deliberately tampered with then the pilots would have been bound to notice it. But then I established with WAA's help that there must have been an unidentified computer on Alpha Lima, so there was certainly something very strange going on. However, I might have given up trying to explain what had happened until I was attacked, not once but twice. There had to be an explanation for all the coincidences.

"So I dreamed up a scenario of the guards taking over the aircraft and making the crew turn round, back to the Caribbean. Plenty of fuel, they could have gone almost anywhere. But why did no-one see the aircraft? I flew along the islands without any real success except that there was a Paragon aircraft which had landed at St. Vincent on the night in question while doing night flying training.

Greg joined in.

"Yes you're quite right. That was VP-GPA. The crew should never have landed as the airfield was closed, even though the lights were on. As bad luck would have it they had a mechanical, problem with the brakes. We managed to get them away to Belem the following night after we had repaired it."

"Yes, Greg. That's what the controller told me." I turned back to the others. "And then I remembered something. When I was listening to the tape of the Alpha Lima satellite conversations I heard Paragon 56 flying to St. Antony. In fact it was the last flight out of Bermuda that night. It struck me as curious that we had lost Alpha Lima but we had found another aircraft, a G3 VP-GPA, at St. Vincent. I began to think the unthinkable; would it have been possible for Alpha Lima to have swapped with Paragon 56? I got the log out which James Donald, the Bermuda SATCO had given me and my suspicion was confirmed. The registration of Paragon 56 was VP-GPA."

Greg butted in looking understandably very cross.

"Ben, this is absolute nonsense. I'm not going to stay here and listen to this rubbish. I've got a business to run."

He got up and made for the door. Ben looked undecided.

"Greg, I thought you'd like to hear Peter's theories."

Greg stopped with his hand on the door.

"Talbert is wasting all our time. Alpha Lima is at the bottom of the Atlantic and it's only a matter of time before it's going to be found." He turned to Charlie. "You should stop encouraging him and face up to the fact that your company owes Jimmy Morrison $100 million dollars." He turned back to Ben. "You know where to find me."

The door slammed behind him. It was Charlie's turn to be put out. Perhaps she didn't like being accused of encouraging me.

"He seems very sensitive. Why couldn't he wait a bit?"

Ben didn't seem to be perturbed at all. I suppose he'd seen it all before.

"Is that it, Peter?"

He knew very well it wasn't but that was the way he played the game.

"Not quite. I did have one hard piece of evidence, Paragon 56 was transmitting on both the normal and emergency frequencies when it landed in St. Antony. Now I was fairly sure that the G3 didn't carry the type of VHF that could do that. Only the European 412s of WAA carried the right radio sets. So I persevered with my idea. If Alpha Lima had substituted for Paragon 56 would it have been noticed?"

They were all looking at me with various degrees of disbelief. Mick decided to speak.

"Somebody in our hangar would have done. Remember my guys were working out on the ramp."

"I'm not sure about that, Mick. For a start the routine would have been upset by the news of Alpha Lima having been lost. I suspect a lot of your people would have been inside waiting for news. Furthermore, Tim told me that Paragon 56 did an exceptionally short landing and taxied straight into the Paragon facility. Assuming it didn't have any fin lights on and also assuming that the normal lights on the ramp were off, would anybody know the type of aircraft that had landed?"

"But why would the ramp lights be off?"

"That's an important point of course, since it narrows down the people who might be involved in this scam."

"It's much more than a scam, Peter." Ben looked at me very sternly. "If you're right, and I suppose it is just possible you may be, this is a crime. At least one person has been murdered." He added "But Peter why did no-one see the aircraft in the morning?"

I could see Frank thinking.

"It might just be possible. Peter might be right. Our hangar can be split down the middle shutting off the back from the front." He paused. "But of course, our hangar is special."

"No it's not Frank. I checked with the builders and Paragon have the same dividing doors as you have."

Ben looked at me and shook his head.

"You really get around, Peter. If you ever become unemployed I might offer you a job as a trainee detective."

"Thanks Ben. Anyway as Frank has suggested, the aircraft could have taxied straight into the back of the hangar and be hidden completely from view."

It was Charlie's turn to come in.

"But the Customs, Peter?"

"Well I've thought about that." I saw Ben grinning in spite of himself. "I don't believe it would have been a problem. Customs allow Paragon a lot of latitude. Paragon and business aircraft do not have to land and go to the terminal to be inspected before going over to their hangars. This is a deliberate act of policy to stop congestion on the airline ramp. The Paragon Operations room tell customs what they have and generally they just take the paper work over to the customs office though, of course, customs can inspect the aircraft anytime they wish. Significantly in this case after the aircraft had landed, someone from Paragon took round to customs a list of some mundane household goods to be dispatched to Europe."

"Wait a minute. How do you know he did that? Who went round?"

"I checked with Richard Sebble, the chief customs man when I was up at the terminal the other day. He showed me the log of the incoming aircraft that night and the following morning, unfortunately with an indecipherable Paragon signature but the aircraft registration was VP-GNE. The goods were cleared in and straight out into a couple of large crates to go in a container to Europe to catch the next available ship. Had the customs gone round to Paragon they would have seen the large crates ready for trans-shipment in the front part of the hangar."

Mick burst out.

"But there would have been no G3."

"That's what I thought but I've checked the Air Traffic log and the other G3, would you believe VP-GNE, was in St. Antony and because of the wrong registration on the flight plan the customs man would have been quite satisfied had he checked the tail number."

"Surely Air Traffic would know something was wrong?" Mick was again the questioner.

"Not really. It was a very short landing. There was no way Tim could have seen the type of aircraft. And it's not Air Traffic's job to check all the aircraft on the airfield. They just bill the operators with take-off and landing fees. In fact Tim went to bed after Alpha Lima landed and there was no-one on duty. I thought at first that Paragon 56 had landed later on, when the controllers had gone below, doing a very steep low power approach without landing and navigation lights and landing without anybody noticing. Remember the runway lights are left on all night so the G3 wouldn't have needed landing lights. The people on the approach are used to aircraft at night and would have no reason to comment. The crash crew were right at the end of the runway, also asleep."

"If the Gulfstream could do that, why didn't Alpha Lima simply land later on in the night?"

"Because Alpha Lima didn't have the endurance to fly that long. Remember Alpha Lima had to fly out and back while the G3 took off nearly two hours later and was only going one way."

Charlie looked at me.

"Can a G3 do a short landing?"

"No, it can't." I looked appreciative. "The G3 would have used more runway than the 412 and it might have been noticed. It would have had to backtrack and perhaps somebody outside the WAA hangar might have noticed it. That's why I favour the idea that the aircraft landed at St Vincent and Paragon gave the controller that cock and bull story."

Frank had an idea.

"OK then if you're right why don't we go and look in the Paragon hangar now?"

"Well that's up to Ben. Presumably he'd need a search warrant." Ben nodded. "But anyway I don't believe the aircraft's there."

"Well if it's not there, where the hell is it?"

"I don't know."

"But you have an idea. Right, Peter." I nodded at Ben.

"Yes I have. Remember the aircraft at St. Vincent. It left just after midnight the following night to fly to Belem but no-one knows if it got there because the airfield closed the moment the aircraft left. However, I had a stroke of luck when I was in Trinidad, the controller inadvertently showed me the movements for the following night and Paragon 72 landed from St. Antony in the early hours of the morning."

Charlie asked for the aircraft type and registration.

"As you've guessed, it was a G3 and the registration was VP-GPA. My feeling is that Paragon 72 was really Alpha Lima when it left St. Antony and the aircraft switched with VP-GPA somewhere near Trinidad."

"But surely somebody would have reported VP-GPA as missing since it didn't fly to Belem?"

"Yes, Charlie. A very good point but it was Paragon 45 that left for Belem and what almost certainly happened is that the aircraft cancelled it's plan saying that it was returning to St. Vincent and if anybody had tried to contact St. Vincent there would have been no reply."

She persisted.

"OK. But surely Bermuda would have known that it was the wrong G3 that left for St. Antony the previous night?"

"It wasn't the wrong G3 that left Bermuda. What was wrong was that the G3 on the ground at St. Antony was VP-GNE and there was no reason for St. Antony air traffic to realise this. Anyway as far as they were concerned VP-GPA left as Paragon 72 the following night."

Frank looked very worried.

"But you still haven't told us where's Alpha Lima now?"

"Yes I'm afraid that's the key question. Where are the pilots, the guards and the freight?"

"And the paintings, Peter?"

"And the paintings, Charlie. Well I suspect that the aircraft is somewhere in S.America, probably Colombia. I think it was carrying arms which was being sold illicitly to rebels."

"But why?"

"Good question. First and foremost it was necessary to get rid of the aircraft or it would have been discovered. He couldn't leave it in the Paragon hangar. My hunch is that South American Trading sold the guns and ammunition in advance in S.America, perhaps to some rebels, probably Colombia but could be somewhere else. They would have no difficulty arranging such a deal. Remember they would have had excellent contacts in S.America. Selling the arms got them not only some money but it enabled them to get rid of the aircraft. The plot has clearly worked since we've heard nothing of the aircraft at all."

Frank butted in.

"Well surely we can find out? I want my pilots and the aircraft back."

"I'm sure we can find out in time but we will need the help of the United States Government, their intelligence network and, possibly, their reconnaissance satellites. However, I have to say I'm very worried about the pilots. They may have been killed having served their purpose."

"What do you mean?"

"Supposing my reconstruction is correct. The guards were no longer Westfield guards. That's alright as far as it goes but there was no way that the guards could have made Bill Hudson and Jim French do what I have described. One if not both of the pilots would have to be accessories to the scheme. Otherwise it could not work."

There was a complete silence in the room. I'm sure Ben and Charlie had already worked out what I had just said but it was one thing to think it, quite another to hear it expressed quite definitely. Frank looked disbelieving.

"Peter, that's an awful thing to say."

"I know but there really is no other construction one can put on the events. You see, for the G3 and Alpha Lima to change places the pilots of the two aircraft would have to be co-operating completely with a very well laid out plan. I thought at first it would need both of the WAA pilots but then I realised that since the guards had guns presumably only one pilot would be needed. The other could be made to help or be disposed of."

"Are you saying that Bill or Jim had agreed to all this?"

"I'm afraid so and I think it was Jim French. Remember he used to work for Paragon. The rogue software was needed to ensure that the aircraft flew out, almost all the way to Bermuda, without Bill Hudson knowing there was anything wrong. My guess is that Bill had no alternative but to watch while Jim took over. Interestingly, Paragon 56 was transmitting on both frequencies when it landed. Perhaps Bill selected this feature without Jim noticing to try and tell us something was wrong."

"But the false ADS position reports? Bill would never have taken-off if something was wrong on the ground."

"You're right and this point worried me for a long time. As I told you, Jessica had suggested that the pilots would have noticed incorrect software. But she missed a point. I wondered if the rogue software could have been set up so that everything would work normally on the ground but it could be changed in the air. When I called her just before this meeting started, she realised for the first time that this could have been done by having a special page on the flight management computer to select a heading error so that the aircraft could be steered into Angela. Chuck would have fitted the rogue computer into the right hand side so Jim could control it. It would have been programmed to be the master one by selection on a special page. Once selected, the aircraft would turn gradually on to the wrong heading and transmit the wrong position reports on ADS. This new page would never ever be found unless you knew it was there and anyway it would only have been visible on Jim's computer."

"But surely Bill would have checked his heading on the stand-by compass?"

"Mick, you know as well as I do the stand-by is never used. It's folded away out of sight on Airbus and European type aircraft. My guess is that the stand-by heading would have been tampered with anyway, so that when eventually Bill did check when things started to go wrong, everything would look okay. Of course, if he had asked Jim to check the stand-by Jim would have said it was OK."

"You seem to have thought of everything. But if you're right where's Bill?"

"Frank, if you were masterminding this plot you'd probably arrange for both pilots to be killed once their job had been done and the aircraft landed in S.America. Bill would almost certainly have realised this. The

234

flight to S.America must have been incredible in spite of all the sophisticated satellite navigation equipment. I'm not sure Jim could have done it by himself. He probably needed Bill to help him. If Bill had refused I suppose they would have killed him in St. Antony. Perhaps Bill reckoned that if he helped he might be able to persuade Jim to change his mind, who knows?"

Ben had remained very quiet during my narrative. However I was sure he was following every word from us all.

"Wait a moment, Peter. You've been going on so long the tape has run out. I've got to change it round." He switched the cassette round. "You know for an engineer you've got very romantic ideas. All this sounds very unlikely. Have you got any evidence at all? Is it all that easy to swap two aircraft in mid-air? And anyway the aircraft registrations don't match for a start and what about the crash recorder beacon in the Atlantic near the wreckage?"

"Ben, these days aircraft have to carry equipment called Traffic Collision and Alerting System, TCAS for short. The primary object of carrying this equipment is so that if an air traffic controller makes a mistake, the pilot is warned if there is likely to be a collision. There is a small screen which shows aircraft which are in the vicinity and the pilot is told to climb or dive to avoid a collision if the two aircraft are very close. What almost certainly happened here is that the two aircraft used TCAS to manoeuvre themselves so that they were very close to one another and, at the appropriate moment, Alpha Lima called itself Paragon 56 and carried on towards St. Antony. The G3 would have dropped down to be out of radar cover."

Charlie joined in.

"But Peter, surely VP-WAL needed to turn round at a certain time for the two aircraft to meet up?"

"That also worried me for a bit. My guess is that at the time contact with the aircraft was lost either Bill decided to turn round because things were getting too difficult or one of the guards must have made him."

"But don't they have automatic reporting?"

"Yes Charlie, they do." I'd taught her lot about aircraft, more than she'd taught me about paintings, or anything else for that matter. "Jim French must have turned off Alpha Lima's ADS C transmitter when the aircraft turned round and then turned it on again as Paragon 56 turned its transmitter off. In addition, Alpha Lima would have started using Paragon 56's transponder code."

"Surely it would be noticed."

"I'm not so sure if the switch was done properly. Remember the ADS transmissions are not continuous. That was why I called the Center on Long Island. I wanted them to make a very careful examination of Paragon 56 ADS position reports. I'm still waiting for their report."

Ben shook his head.

"You've still got some more explaining to do. For a start who dreamt all this up? Was it Jim? Surely not."

"Not in my book. It has to have been Greg. Only he could control all the things that needed controlling."

"But you just let him walk out of the room!"

"Not me, Ben. You did."

"He can fly away at any time and escape."

"If you say so."

Charlie looked at me thoughtfully.

"You don't seem very worried."

"To be honest I'm not. You see as long as Greg is here, the paintings are almost certainly here. Once he goes you need to be worried."

Ben drummed his fingers on the table and nobody else said anything. He noticed we were all looking at him.

"Peter has made his outrageous fairy story sound very credible. But I have a real problem. There is no aircraft and no paintings. I'm going to be laughed, literally out of court, if and when I ask for a search warrant. If I charge Greg now I'll be a laughing stock. He's got a lot of friends in the Government. What do you think Frank?"

"I agree Ben, you do have a political problem." He looked at me.

"Surely Greg couldn't have done all this by himself? You said that there was some special software put in the flight management computers to fool Bill."

"I'm afraid almost certainly your Chuck Curtis changed the flight management computer when he changed the radio before the flight. Oh, he must have altered the stand-by compass at the same time. And he arranged to let Greg have a crash recorder with a flat beacon battery."

"Why don't you think Jimmy Morrison was in on the scheme?"

"Very fair question. I believe, notwithstanding what anybody else may think, that Jimmy Morrison was not in on it. His actions to try to help Charlie searching for Alpha Lima were genuine. He believed that the paintings were being delivered back to him. I think Greg Fairclough was working with a firm in Dallas called South American Trading and they saw the opportunity for this trick months ago when the paintings were taken to London. Incredible though it may seem, there are always people who will buy stolen masterpieces. South American filed the suit to keep the paintings in St. Antony until they were ready with the software and suitable weather. In fact their opportunity came much sooner than they were expecting due to the early arrival of the first hurricane. Greg worked in Geneva before he joined Paragon and I wondered if he had contacts

236

there. The firm was Geneva Aviation. You could start some investigations to see if he has a wife there or a girl friend."

"You're letting your imagination run wild, Peter."

"Maybe, but it's worth a try. Shall I carry on?" Ben nodded. "I believe that he paid an ex-Colombian programmer, who was at Honeywell, for the rogue software. This programmer had contacts in Dallas and there was a Dallas telephone number. You could try to trace an address. I can also give you a name of a Honeywell programmer who knew the man in question. South American Trading must have arranged for the programmer to send a flight management system loaded with this software to Chuck in St. Antony.

"Before the aircraft took off everybody knew that some of the world's finest paintings were on their way to Bermuda. What nobody knew except South American Trading plus Greg and Jimmy was that the aircraft was also loaded with a lot of arms and ammunition in freight boxes which he had ordered to be taken out of customs and put on the plane. Greg arranged the total amount of weapons so that the aircraft would be on its maximum take-off weight."

"How do you know that, Peter?"

"All the arms were in boxes labelled machinery but as the goods were in transit St. Antony customs didn't care. Both Jimmy and Greg told us that the machinery was lathes and things and I think we need to ask some searching questions of both Jimmy and Greg. I told you I checked the aircraft's take-off weight and it was at the maximum permitted. If you subtract the weight of the fuel and the paintings there just had to be a lot of so called machinery on board to make the total up. It's true I'm guessing the machinery was arms but I think customs may be able to help confirm my conjectures. These arms were scheduled to be sold by Paragon salesmen to firms and governments in S.America in exchange for goods and Jimmy had agreed with Greg that the machinery could be moved to Bermuda to reduce the storage charges. So Greg took the opportunity to use the trip to get a lot of arms as well as the paintings out of customs on the pretext that the transit shed charges in St. Antony were too high and he was going to store the 'machinery' in Bermuda. After the flight, everybody assumed that the paintings had been lost for ever and Jimmy naturally enough was very upset and crying for the insurance money. In fact Greg now had both the paintings and the weapons in the Paragon Hangar. It was a very elegant plan."

"You're right about Jimmy, Peter. If he was in on the plot and that sort of man, which we have no reason to believe he is, he'd have had you killed by now. He's a real professional at whatever he does."

"Presumably Ben, it must have been Greg who had two attempts at killing me. It was curious that the truck belonged to WAA but I guess Greg was taking precautions. He must have got a key, I don't know how."

Mick's face suddenly cleared.

"I can explain that. You know we bought the truck from Paragon some months ago and once or twice at night it's been reported missing, but we never really sorted things out as whenever I tried to do a careful check it was always in position."

"But Peter, what happened to the paintings?"

"Well Charlie, my guess is that Greg took the paintings away in the truck, the same truck he used first to try to kill me by pushing me off the road and then to try to shoot me. He wouldn't have risked sending them to Colombia in my opinion. The paintings are probably still here on the island unless he has managed to smuggle them out already. I imagine he will have taken the painting packages out of their crates because that would make them much easier to store. He would then have had the crates burnt. As I mentioned, the significant thing is that Greg is still here and I don't believe he will leave until he has spirited the paintings away."

My mobile vibrated, there was a message to call Jack Maynes. I got Ben's permission and called Jack from Ben's secretary's office.

"Peter, you must be on to something. We looked at all the ADS reports. In the San Juan area the ADS only reports every 10 minutes but for some reason at about 250 nautical miles from St. Antony there were two reports timed a minute apart which as you know is not possible."

"What about the positions of the two reports, Jack?"

"I was just coming to that. The position of the two reports was the same; I would have thought that they would be at least 8 miles apart. Can you explain all that Peter?"

"Yes Jack, I think I can but it makes a strange story. Do you mind if I wait until I can confirm what happened?"

"Not a bit. I'm just delighted that you're making some progress."

"Jack, one more thing. How many people know about this?"

"Just myself and Francis Devere, why?"

"Keep it to yourselves at the moment. The situation is very delicate and we don't want the story to break until we're ready for it. Please keep the press out of it. Thanks for your help. I'll keep in touch."

Charlie had followed me into the opposite office and had been listening to my end of the conversation.

"So you were right? There was a swap?"

"It certainly seems so. We'd better go and tell Ben or he'll come and get us."

I told Ben about New York Center and the significance of the timing and of the identical positions. I stopped but Ben carried on making notes. He suddenly looked at me.

"But Peter. The wreckage? The body?"

"What I haven't told you yet is that the same G3 VP-GPA left Trinidad on Sunday morning, flew to St. Antony and then flew on to Bermuda. Ben, I found out that Greg's son flies for Paragon, but based in Bermuda. Did you know that?" Ben nodded. "Greg's son would clearly be flying the G3. My bet is that that evening the G3 went inside the hangar, the doors were closed and then the dinghies, life jackets, partitions, bottles etc. were loaded. In addition, I suspect that Greg also loaded into the aircraft a handcuffed Roger O'Sullivan, who had had to be removed under duress just before the paintings were loaded and replaced by a guard who was working for Greg. He would have been keeping him handcuffed in a cellar below his house for about 36 hours.

"The air traffic log then shows the aircraft taking off for Bermuda landing at one o'clock the following morning. Presumably Greg's son immediately drove off with the dinghies etc. plus Roger O'Sullivan to St. Georges Harbour because I've discovered he kept his large high speed cruising boat there. He must have forced O'Sullivan on board somehow, knocked him unconscious and then dropped all the stuff and O'Sullivan, with a partially inflated life jacket, into the water 50 miles or so off shore. O'Sullivan would have drowned almost instantly from the water temperature and the son would have returned to the harbour the same night or the following night depending on the weather.

"Incidentally they must have kept some wreckage back in the son's house, possibly because they didn't have room in their transport. When I mentioned to Greg in Bermuda that there should be more wreckage he must have driven out the next night and put the dinghy and the rest of the smashed bulkheads in position on the beach. In fact I saw him leave the hotel after we got back from a night club. I thought he was going back to one of the girls but, of course, he really left to go to his son's house."

Charlie decided to comment.

"I told you not to jump to conclusions. And it was no wonder he tried to shoot you." I raised my eyebrows. "You told him the wreckage was in the wrong place at lunch just before he left for St. Antony. He probably realised that you might be smarter than he thought."

Ben summed things up.

"Peter, that's quite a yarn you've told me. You've stitched in fact with fiction so that I don't know whether I'm coming or going. Is this really all credible? Would you solemnly swear that you really believe the story you've just told me?

"Yes Ben. I'm absolutely convinced that the main events happened as I've described."

"But Peter, from all that you've said it means that if we do go into the Paragon hangar we won't find anything."

"Yes, I think you're right but you'll still have to go in."

"Peter, do you have any evidence at all to support your theory?"

"Well firstly, remember the evidence of New York Center showing the glitch in the position reporting. Secondly, you can check all the G3 movements with the various airfields. Thirdly, the landing Paragon aircraft on the Friday night was transmitting on both the emergency frequency and the correct frequency. The Gulfstream 3 cannot do this but the European Aerospace 412 can. Unfortunately, this double transmission was such a common event that the air traffic controller did nothing except talk to someone in the Paragon hangar after the aircraft had landed, possibly Greg disguising his voice."

"Anything else?"

"Well we have the two voice tapes of that night, one from New York and one from Nelson here. I'm no expert on voice recognition but I think that on both tapes the voice of one of the pilots of Alpha Lima and the voice of the Paragon 56 pilot, though disguised, is the same. We would need to get that checked."

"Anything else?"

"Yes, the life jackets. I believe they were partially inflated so that they would be found. If they had not been inflated they would have sunk to the bottom. Furthermore, they put a life jacket on the body to make certain it would be found. It was a bad move on Greg's part because it made me suspicious right from the start."

"OK Peter. You say the bad guys are South American Trading and Greg. Who in St. Antony were in on the whole plot?"

"My view is that only Greg's son knew the whole plot including the killing of Roger O'Sullivan. The rest knew what they needed to know but no more. That way Greg did not have to disclose the whole plot. Jim had worked for Paragon for many years and Greg persuaded him with money to do the flying. The guards knew their part which in my view included killing both the pilots in Colombia or wherever the aircraft actually landed. Greg told Chuck Curtis what he had to do and he would have given Chuck some cover story. Chuck must be a very frightened man, ever since Alpha Lima disappeared and the body was found. The only other person in the plot must be the other G3 pilot but I suspect that Greg's son flew the aircraft on his own. By the way, I expect you'll find that South American Trading is a front company consisting of just Greg and the real brains of the operation. I don't believe Greg would have thought it all out himself or organised the software, he doesn't strike me as being smart enough. You'll be lucky to find that person, he'll have gone off with the money they received for the arms."

"What about the guards and engineers in the Paragon hangar?"

"As I told you, I think that there was no-one on duty on the two nights in question, that is Friday night and Saturday night, and, of course, during the day no-one could get inside the rear part of the hangar. Anyway as I've just said, I bet Greg arranged for no-one to come in to make doubly sure."

"If Greg is going to get away with this he'll need to remove Chuck, the other pilot of the G3, and the people on Alpha Lima."

"Greg must have paid Chuck an advance and promised him a ransom in due course. I agree he won't really be safe while Chuck is around but it may be a risk he will have to live with. The other pilot of the G3, if there was one, clearly will need dealing with by Greg but again he is probably being very well paid as well as being blackmailed, perhaps he has a false passport. You might try and find out if there was anyone with Greg's son. That leaves the crew of Alpha Lima and I'm not sure what Greg will need to do with them because at the moment I doubt whether even he knows what has taken place. Perhaps you should talk to Colombia and the other possible countries. Even if we find the aircraft we're not going to find the crew. Not unless a miracle happened and Bill persuaded Jim to give up. You know it might be kinder for Bill's wife to let her think the aircraft was lost at sea, if we can, anyway for the moment."

"Where do we go from here?"

"Well Ben, if I were Greg I'd be trying to get the paintings out of the country as quickly as possible. There is however a complication."

"I'm beginning to realise there always is with anything you do." I saw Charlie nodding.

"Well I'm just a little worried about Tim Hardcastle. He and Greg are quite friendly and they play golf together regularly. Despite the fact that I asked him not to, I'm pretty sure he will have mentioned to Greg about the short landing and, of course, about the double transmission. Unlike me, he is a material witness who could testify against Greg. I think that if Tim was questioned closely he might remember that he heard Jim's voice from Alpha Lima taking off and something like Jim's voice in Paragon 56. Do you think you had better warn him, or watch his house in case Greg tries to do something stupid?"

Ben nodded reluctantly and called Tim in the Tower. Apparently he had gone home. Ben called his home and there was no reply. Ben called Rick in and told him to find Tim quickly and then call him back to let him know where he was.

Ben looked at me and then said slowly,

"Peter, you do realise that we cannot prove a crime has been committed. How would you like to be me trying to get a search warrant from a judge?" He thought some more. "If we could find the paintings we would know that your theory is right." Ben looked at Charlie "You must be used to looking for lost and stolen paintings, Ms. Simpson. What do you suggest?"

"The paintings belong to Jimmy and he wants them back and we want him to have them back as otherwise we will have to pay the insurance money. We could tell him our suspicions and get him to complain to the St. Antony authorities to find out why you aren't searching Greg's place and the whole of St. Antony. Perhaps Peter and I had better go to Bermuda and meet Jimmy Morrison and see if we can't think of a way of getting him to pressurise the St. Antony government to search for the paintings." She looked at Ben. "Shall I call Jimmy and try and set something up?"

Ben nodded. He looked at me as I started to speak.

"Ben, you need to watch Greg and see what goes on. However, you have an impossible problem in that he earns his living flying in and out of the country. Can't you stop him leaving St. Antony?"

"Tell me about it! You're doing it again telling your grandmother what to do.

"I've been thinking as you've been talking. We've just got to keep our eyes peeled to prevent any paintings being exported. I'll alert customs to be doubly on their guard. But there's no way at this stage that I can prevent Greg leaving."

Charlie left and went back to the hotel.

"Ben, let's look in the Paragon hangar before I go back to see how Charlie has managed with Jimmy. Will they let you in?"

"Good idea. We can make sure the aircraft isn't there. My badge should do the trick to get inside."

We got into Ben's car and drove over to the hangar. Ben put his siren and light on as he drove up to the gate. There was a pause and the gate slid aside. Bill turned the siren off and we went into the building. A nervous mechanic appeared.

"Is Greg Fairclough in? May we look around?"

Ben pushed by the mechanic without waiting for an answer and we went down a corridor into the hangar. The layout was almost identical to West Atlantic Airways. We entered the front half of the building and the inside hangar doors were open so we could see the whole hangar. There were no aircraft there at all. I asked Ben if we could walk round the inside at the back and Ben led the way followed by the mechanic. There was only one other mechanic visible but it was lunch time. There was a washroom at the back and another room without windows next to it. The hangar had rooms above the ground floor like the WAA one but there were two solid doors, one each side, so arranged that if the inside doors were closed no-one could go from the front of the building to the back. We went into the washroom and the other room which had a table, a couple of chairs and a single bed. There were two or three cupboards with all sorts of aircraft pieces lying around. I could see Ben was getting impatient.

"Come on Peter. Let's get out of here. I haven't a search warrant and I bet Greg will be here in a moment."

"Wait a moment Ben. Have you seen this?" I pointed inside the cupboard to a type of key on a piece of string. "Surely that clinches it?"

"What do you mean?"

"Ben, this key is a compass adjustment key. I bet you this was the key that Chuck used to alter the compass and handed on to Jim to correct the alteration. Checking the stand-by compass is not part of the normal check list. The heading on the main display would almost certainly have been correct when they lined up for take-off. When Jim entered the false course to be steered the program would have been arranged to turn the aircraft only very slowly so Bill wouldn't have noticed, particularly as they were in cloud. Then when Bill realised there was something wrong he would have pulled down the stand-by compass and, of course, it would agree with the aircraft's indicated heading since this little device would have made the stand-by compass read the wrong heading."

Ben reached out for the key but I held his hand for a moment.

"Ben, I know there is not much surface area on the key but there may be finger prints on it. Presumably you can get hold of Jim French's finger prints from his home and try to match them up?"

Ben looked at me in a way which showed respect combined with annoyance, possibly with himself. He didn't say anything but took a length of paper off the toilet roll and very gingerly used the paper to pick up the key and wrapped the rest of the paper around it. I took an envelope out of my back pocket, removed the note inside and handed Ben the envelope. He placed the paper and key inside it and we went back to the car. As we drove out of the parking lot Greg drove in. Ben waved but did not stop. He took me back to his office and I returned to the hotel for a quick sandwich. I told Charlie where I was and she appeared at the table a moment later.

"Dinner with Jimmy and Samantha, eight o'clock sharp. Jackets and ties. Hopefully, Frank is right now fixing the tickets and reservations for us."

The Final Flight

CHAPTER 8

'But apples plants of such a price,
No tree could ever bear them twice'

Jim reached up into the roof panel and then turned the aircraft on to a reciprocal course as Bill had asked. He asked Bill to fly the aircraft for a moment. Bill tried to transmit to New York Oceanic on the satellite radio but nothing happened. He saw Jim lean over and adjust the flight management computer. Bill glanced down and saw the navigation display showed 202°T instead of the 162°T he had been steering. He checked with the stand-by compass which still said 173°M. Something was seriously wrong. Bill turned and saw the smarter of the two guards, Roger O'Sullivan, looking at him, holding a very small revolver with a surprisingly large bore.

"What the hell is going on?"

The guard ignored him and turned to Jim.

"You know what to tell him."

Jim looked at Bill in a rather unpleasant way.

"I'm afraid Bill you are no longer Captain of this aircraft. As long as you do exactly as you are told you won't be harmed. Robert here is liable to use the gun at the slightest provocation. He shoots first and asks questions afterwards." Bill looked at the man he thought was called Roger O'Sullivan; Robert stared back at him impassively. "We are now going to return to St. Antony."

Jim pulled a compass adjustment key out of his pocket and set the magnetic compass to read 10° more than the aircraft's True heading. Bill's mind was racing. Everything began to make sense. The flight management system and the stand-by compass must have been fixed in some way to fool him and the air traffic oceanic centers. He had been steered deliberately into the tropical storm, Angela, presumably to make everybody think that the aircraft had been lost, out of control. Jim must have turned off the satellite radios. But surely the ADS would tell New York where they were. He reached down for the flight management control and display unit.

"Don't touch anything without permission Bill. I've switched the ADS off from the Flight Management Controller if that's what you're wondering. I've also switched off all our external lights, flashing beacons and pulled the breaker for the cabin lighting."

Robert said nothing but was clearly in charge, after all it was he who had the gun. Presumably Robert realised he'd be crazy to use it since the bullet might depressurise the aircraft or, more likely, cut the fly-by-wire control and the aircraft would be uncontrollable. Robert must have seen him looking at the gun.

"In case you get any ideas, Mr. Hudson, the gun I am carrying has been very carefully chosen." Robert's accent was from the Southern United States with a hint of an Eastern European accent; he spoke very slowly. "It will incapacitate you but not damage the aircraft, providing of course, it hits you first. You may know that terrorists use them quite a bit these days in these situations." He paused. "Now, unplug your microphone and give it to me with your headset."

Bill did as he was told. They clearly weren't going to let him talk to anyone over the radio. Bill looked at the radar and saw that the weather ahead was improving. They could be at St. Antony in one and a half hours and letting down in about an hour but surely Jim wouldn't be so foolhardy as to go back there in spite of what he had just said. He must be going to a private airfield with all the freight. Jim switched on the VHF to St. Antony approach frequency.

"Nelson approach, Nelson approach, this is Paragon 56 en route to St. Antony from Bermuda. We are currently flying at 330 our ETA Nelson is 0320Z."

There was very weak and disembodied reply, clearly not from Air Traffic.

"Paragon 56 squawk 1342 and confirm."

Jim answered immediately, as if it was the answer he had been expecting.

"Paragon 56 confirms."

Automatically Bill looked at his watch. It was 0120Z, the aircraft would be miles away from St. Antony, way out of VHF range. Why on earth was Jim using the wrong callsign, Paragon 56? Whoever had replied to the transmission it couldn't have been Nelson Approach. It was pointless transmitting to St. Antony and anyway why talk to St. Antony?

Jim adjusted their transponder to 1342 but did not switch it on. Next he started operating the FMC and Bill looked down to see what was happening. Jim entered the tail number VP-GPA as the aircraft registration instead of VP-WAL and Paragon56 as the flight number instead of VPWAL. Bill said nothing but for the first time he had an inkling of what might be going to happen.

Jim selected Flight Level 330 on the glare shield, pressed execute and the aircraft descended from 350 to 330. Jim then selected a waypoint on the inbound track from Bermuda to St. Antony at 21°N 62° 15'W and turned the aircraft towards it. They were now on a heading of about 240°

and Bill estimated they would be at Jim's waypoint at a range of 250 miles from St. Antony, which he realised would be outside St. Antony's radar cover.

"Jim, you're taking us on a collision course with the other aircraft."

Jim looked at him and said nothing. He switched on the Traffic Caution and Alerting System but there was nothing to be seen. Bill knew that whatever was happening had to be due to the freight, presumably the paintings. It was the only explanation. Perhaps he was going to find out why the freight was so heavy. With a sickening feeling he realised that he was expendable and was almost certain to be killed the moment they had finished with him, presumably after they had landed. Faced with that reality he was surprised to find himself comparatively calm. He realised that subconsciously he was saying to himself 'while there's life there's hope'. He had never been tested in this way before but it had always been his view that the human race in general reacted to do everything possible to stay alive, no matter what the duress. Survival was what life was all about and Bill supposed he was typical in struggling to find a way to survive. The first thing he decided that he wanted to do was to alert the authorities. A thought occurred to him. The European Aerospace 412 had an option which permitted dual simultaneous transmissions and reception both on the selected frequency and on the emergency frequency of 121.5. It worked for both pilots irrespective of who selected it. All the pilots hated the option since people were always leaving the dual transmission selector switch in the wrong position and then transmitting inadvertently on the emergency frequency. However, Ron Gibbons, the chief pilot, felt that they should have the modification because they did so much flying over water.

Bill started working out how he could select the dual position. His interphone box which controlled the headset and the microphone selections was next to him, behind the side stick controller position. His hand was already down there on the controller. He would wait his moment. An aircraft appeared on the TCAS display at about the 'three o'clock' position. It came closer and closer and its bearing did not change. They were on a collision course. The high cloud from Angela cleared as they headed south and Bill saw the lights of the aircraft which was showing on the TCAS. The time seem to pass very slowly but gradually Alpha Lima approached Jim's waypoint as the range of the other aircraft reduced and then became dangerously close. Just as the TCAS gave a climb warning Jim turned the aircraft on to 177° for St. Antony. Jim kept looking at his watch. Two minutes after getting to the waypoint and turning on to track, Bill heard another aircraft call, presumably the aircraft showing on the TCAS display.

"Nelson approach, Nelson approach, this is Paragon 56 en route to St. Antony from Bermuda. We are currently flying at 330 squawking 1342, our ETA Nelson is 0320Z."

Jim altered the Flight Identification and enabled ADS reporting on the FMC controller. He switched on the transponder so that St. Antony's secondary radar would see them as the aircraft came within range. Jim also switched on all the lighting again and started to transmit.

"Nelson approach, Nelson approach, this is Paragon 56 en route to St. Antony from Bermuda. We are currently flying at 330 squawking 1342, our ETA Nelson is 0320Z."

Bill suspicions of what was going to happen were now confirmed. Alpha Lima was going to take the place of the aircraft which left Bermuda as Paragon 56 and actually land back in St. Antony. What chutzpah! If it wasn't so desperate Bill would have laughed in disbelief. They would never get away with it. He guessed that Paragon 56 had a moment before switched off its ADS, transponder and turned off its lighting. Jim started to repeat the transmission and Bill saw that the guard instinctively was watching Jim. Bill selected the dual transmit function. A weak warning light confirming the dual selection glowed on his selector box and there would be one on Jim's box. Bill prayed he would not notice.

The timing of the two flights for the changeover had been extremely fortuitous until Bill remembered that he had noticed Jim using his mobile just before they had strapped in. Presumably he had phoned the pilot in Bermuda.

Bill guessed the repeated transmission was not for St. Antony but for the real Paragon 56. It had to be either a Gulfstream 3 or 4 since only those Paragon aircraft had the height and speed performance to match the European Aerospace 412. What the hell was that aircraft going to do? Presumably it was going to land somewhere else, maybe on a private airfield, perhaps in South America. It wasn't his problem but, of course, in a way it was.

Jim adjusted the weather radar and he could just see Lundy coming into view. Bill wished he'd looked on Lundy on the way out, he might have spotted they were on the wrong track. Jim repeated his transmission, this time expecting and getting an answer.

"Nelson approach, Nelson approach, this is Paragon 56 en route to St. Antony from Bermuda. We are currently flying at 330 squawking 1342, our ETA Nelson is 0320Z."

"Paragon 56, this is Nelson. Stand-by"

Inexorably Lundy got closer and St. Antony started to be painted by the weather radar.

"Paragon 56, press ident." and a moment later *"Roger 56, we see you at 150 miles, descend when ready to 3,500 ft., altimeter 1027, cleared for approach to Runway Zero Seven. VOR out of service, weather at Nelson, 070° fifteen knots, visibility 15 miles, temperature 27°C."*

"Paragon 56 this is Nelson. There is a full scale emergency in progress. A European Aerospace 412 VP-WAL disappeared flying from here to Bermuda at about the same time as you left Bermuda airspace. Did you hear any transmissions from Alpha Lima?"

"Nelson this is Paragon56. I'm afraid not."

"Paragon 56 how about the weather en route?"

"Nelson this is Paragon 56. Weather was smooth but we were in high cloud most of the way as forecast because of Angela."

Jim prepared to do the let-down briefing and looked at Bill.

"I shall fly this approach and landing. You are to read the check list and make the necessary selections. Be very careful not to be clever." Bill could feel Robert pushing the gun into his shoulder. "One more thing. Don't switch on the fin logo lights or you're in trouble."

Bill called out the approach checks and Jim positioned the aircraft as if for a straight-in approach on Runway Zero Seven. The lights of Cape Harbour were very clear below and Bill could make out the faint lights of the runway and the green/white aerodrome beacon flashing near the tower. Jim called for the first flap setting as they left 2,500 ft. and slowly reduced speed. At 1,500 ft. he called for approach flap. The navigation system showed they were 8 nautical miles from the field. Bill switched the landing lights on. At 4 miles the aircraft was down to 1,000 ft. and the radio altimeter voice called out the height. Up to that point Jim had been doing a standard approach, but after he had told Bill to lower the landing gear and full flap Jim allowed the aircraft to descend well below the correct glide slope. Bill could see that the Precision Approach Indicator lights were showing four red lights but he realised that as it was deliberate it was pointless complaining. The check heights from the radio altimeter voice warning happened much further from the airfield than usual because the aircraft was so low. It occurred to Bill that if it had been a real voice there would have been some nervousness if not emotion as the voice called "100 ft.", "50 ft." and finally "30 ft." so far away from the runway threshold with the shadowy ground illuminated by the landing lights flashing by underneath. Bill saw that Jim was not only very low but also 5 knots below the correct approach speed. As the landing lights showed that they had crossed the airfield perimeter and were barely over the runway Jim closed the throttles immediately so that they touched down firmly well before the correct touch down markers. He selected full reverse thrust as they touched down and applied full brake on the brake pedals overriding the smoother automatic braking. The aircraft seemed to stop in a few yards and Jim was able to release the brakes and cancel reverse thrust well before the turn off to the Paragon hangar. Bill had always known that Jim was a good pilot but he rather wished he had been spared watching such a superb display of skill. The aircraft was a long way from the airport terminal so the duty controller would have had great difficulty seeing it touch down so early.

Bill switched off the emergency frequency transmitter on the last bit of the approach while Jim was concentrating on landing.

"Nelson Tower, this is Paragon 56, may we switch to 121.9 and call Nelson Ground."

"Paragon 56, Roger. Stay on this frequency."

"Nelson Ground, this is 56, may we exit to the ramp. Please tell customs we'll be right over with the paperwork."

"56 this is Nelson, cleared to ramp, will advise customs, good night."

The gates were open so that Jim could taxi straight into the Paragon facility but the normal floodlights were not on. Bill realised that they had been deliberately left off so that it would be difficult for anyone to see the type of aircraft. The hangar doors were open and Jim taxied right into the hangar to the back wall and applied the parking brake. Bill looked out of his window and saw the internal hangar doors closing. The Auxiliary Power Unit was still going which was extremely dangerous but Jim rapidly completed the shut down checks and stopped it. It was deathly quiet.

"Well, we made it."

Jim sounded exuberant. He clearly believed that they had managed to fool the air traffic system into believing that Alpha Lima had disappeared. The lights on the flight deck were still on as Jim had left the emergency battery connected. Jim now took his emergency torch out of his flight bag and got out of his seat. Bill noticed that Robert had not relaxed at all but kept his gun pointing at him. Jim opened the front entrance door and lowered the aircraft's steps. He must have gone down into the hangar because shortly afterwards the hangar lights came on and then after a bit ground power was plugged in. Jim reappeared on the flight deck.

"Bill, if you take my advice you'll do exactly as we tell you. Take your flight bag and overnight bag and then leave the aircraft. You're to sleep to-night in the room at the back of the hangar."

Bill looked at Jim's face. Jim had obviously planned this conversation very carefully and looked uncomfortable. Bill turned to Robert.

"Why don't you kill me now? Your job is done."

CHAPTER 9

'And does in the pomegranates close
Jewels more rich than Ormus shows'

We reckoned if we didn't stop we'd catch the 3.30. I threw some clothes in my bag and waited for Charlie to appear with her bag. She was wearing a thin jumper and trousers with a matching colour bra underneath which I found difficult not to notice. We took her car to save time, collected the tickets, rushed through immigration and the doors shut behind us.

"Peter, we seem to be making a habit of this. Where are we sitting?"

"Frank's spoilt us and put us in the front again. There're no other passengers. We can sit where we like." The stewardess nodded agreement. "By the way where are we staying?"

"In the Morrison household, where else?" Charlie decided to sit opposite me across the aisle. "By the way I'm not coming back with you. My boss wants to see me again to find out what Westfield can do, if any thing, to get our government to put pressure on the St. Antony Government to try to find the paintings."

"Charlie, what are we going to do about the search in the Atlantic? We can't very well tell them to stop until we've got some firm evidence."

"Well the search is controlled by your Government and the AAIB, not by Peter Talbert Esq. private investigator, so until the solution to the accident becomes official I would have thought the search must go on."

I reluctantly agreed. There was a pause as we contemplated the happenings of the last few days. Charlie suddenly leant over and squeezed my arm.

"Peter, I'm glad you didn't accept a lift back from Greg the other night. We might not be on this plane together now."

"Charlie, you didn't have to worry. I told you, I was suspicious even then, particularly as he had apparently followed me from Barbados. He must have known I was on to something."

"Well, Peter, since it's confession time, Greg asked me out to dinner when you were in Phoenix."

"I'm not surprised, the way he acted at Frank's. He thought you were the greatest thing since Cleopatra or was it Juliet? How did you put him off?"

"I didn't."

"And you talk of how lucky it was for me to be here on this flight." I leant over and squeezed her arm in turn. "Where did you go? Not to his house I trust?"

"Certainly not. He suggested his house but I countered and proposed the best restaurant in Cape Harbour and he couldn't very well back out once he'd invited me. He offered to pick me up from the hotel, to coin a phrase, but I said I would meet him there."

"What happened next?"

"I don't normally answer questions like that but in your case I'll make an exception. We had a very pleasant evening. We discussed the accident of course, and you got lots of mention."

"Why me?"

"We agreed that you should be getting on with sorting out the electronics and not interfering with matters that didn't concern you. And what did you know about paintings anyway?"

"Did he invite you back to look at his etchings since he would value an opinion from an expert?"

"No, it would have been a smart idea. Clearly that's what you would have done in similar circumstances. Actually he inferred that we both had had too much to drink and why didn't we get one of his cars to drive us back to the hotel and his house. However, I politely refused his charming offer."

"Do you think he would have tried to bump you off?"

"I don't think so but perhaps he was going to try and get hold of both of us and stage an accident or a suicide pact! You can never tell with that sort of person."

"Well Charlie I think you had a lucky escape."

"Not luck Peter. I was just as careful as you were. Anyway that's behind us now."

She took my hand and absent mindedly starting tracing a pattern in my palm. It was just as well the cabin attendant came round to offer us another drink.

"Charlie, I've been thinking."

"Peter, that's your biggest fault in our relationship."

"You wouldn't like me to be impetuous?" She decided to ignore my question. "How long are you staying in New York?"

"I plan to catch the 9.30 and be downtown by 12.30 for a working lunch. I'm booked to return on the 5 o'clock getting in 9.15."

"Why don't I come with you to New York? I could have lunch at the Adelphi where Diana's phone call came from and then chat up the manager."

"That's a brilliant idea. The Adelphi is very close to our office. We can share a cab. Here's my tickets for the flight and seat numbers so that you can make the reservations."

I made a note of Charlie's tickets and then asked the cabin attendant for the phone. I got through to WAA at Bermuda and got them to change my return reservation and book my flights to and from New York.

About three quarters of an hour before landing the hostess asked Charlie if she would like to visit the flight deck. She accepted with alacrity and didn't reappear until we were taxiing to the ramp.

"That was absolutely super. I really enjoyed looking at the flight deck."

"Did they show you how the automatic reporting is done?"

She looked surprised.

"Yes they did as a matter of fact." A look of comprehension came over her face. "You really are the absolute limit. You fixed that didn't you, Peter?"

I nodded and she squeezed my hand and kissed me rather slowly on the cheek.

"Don't you think we should keep moving and let the other people off?"

Charlie grinned and we collected our bags. We were through customs and immigration in no time. Phil Mancuso met us, took my tickets and told me to pick up the new tickets at the WAA desk in the morning before departure. He gave me a message to call Ben Masters.

It was cold compared with St. Antony but there was a driver standing just outside the customs exit point holding a large sign saying 'Ms. Simpson and party'. He took our bags and led us to a very long stretched Cadillac with darkened windows so that it was impossible to see who was inside. Charlie obviously approved and she took her glasses off as we went in. The car was parked, engine running, where cars are never allowed to park in front of the terminal but nobody seemed to mind. We looked inside as we got in and I recognised Jimmy Morrison. He beckoned us to sit down on the palatial seats. Charlie opted to sit next to him and I sat opposite.

"Mr. Talbert, I've heard so much about you. This is indeed a pleasure." I looked at him to see if he was pulling my leg but he had a completely straight face. Perhaps he had been hearing a lot about me but I would have liked to know who was his informant.

"I read, of course, about the inquiry on the crash at Heathrow. When I heard that Frank had hired a consultant it took me a moment or two to realise that you were the star witness at that inquiry. You haven't had much of a rest?"

"I never like turning jobs down Mr. Morrison. You never know where the next one is coming from. As you know, if you're self employed there's no-one else to rely on."

He smiled at me.

"If you say so. Charlie here tells me that you've made some progress on the loss of my paintings?"

"Well we have a theory but proving it is going to be difficult. That's why we're here. We need your help talking to people in St. Antony. Would you like me to start telling you the tale? You may think it is far too fanciful."

"To reach my position in the business I'm in, you become aware of the deceitful nature of people. However, I would like my wife to hear the story as well so why don't we let it wait until we've had an aperitif before dinner."

I wondered if Charlie had given him some warning of what I was going to say or whether he had been suspicious for some time. We arrived at large double gates which opened as we approached and we drove up to the impressive entrance. We were shown upstairs to our rooms which were adjacent and had, I discovered when I went inside, a connecting door. Our bags appeared and a hostess who seemed to be in charge told us that we were to meet downstairs at 7.45, forty minutes time by my watch. I reckoned there wasn't going to be a lot of time for Charlie but that wasn't my problem. However, I needed to call Ben. He had left his office but I got him at home.

"The Hardcastles were on their way to have dinner with Greg when we found them. They came round to my office and I persuaded them to spend the night in the Kensington Hotel. I had to tell him enough to make him wary of Greg and he looked appalled. However, I remembered what you said about Jim being on both Alpha Lima and Paragon 56 and when I mentioned this to Tim I could see all the cogs click into place. He was very embarrassed he'd not noticed Alpha Lima as Paragon 56, but I told him to forget it and keep his mouth shut. Of course we've got a problem still because I can't keep Greg on the island."

"Ben, don't worry. You know my view. If Greg hasn't left already the paintings must still be on the island."

I rang off and got changed as quickly as I could. Charlie was waiting for me as I came out of my room. She clearly hadn't wasted any time either. She was wearing a white blouse and long skirt and looked extremely smart. She had used the same perfume as the one she used at the Westbourne's. My blazer and grey slacks, presentable though they were, didn't match her elegance. We were shown in to a reception room where Jimmy was with a very smartly dressed lady who I assumed correctly to be Samantha, his lovely and legendary wife.

Charlie had her normal spritzer, Samantha had a diet coke and Jimmy and I both had scotch on the rocks. Samantha saw Charlie looking round the walls of the room which were covered with wonderful paintings. "As I am sure you will be able to see Ms. Simpson, a lot of them are not the real thing. In order not to spoil the room decor we had copies of all our valuable paintings made so that when we loaned them for exhibitions there wouldn't be blank spaces on the walls. As you can imagine we are desolated by the loss of our best paintings. Now we'll never be able to substitute the real ones again for the copies."

Charlie wandered round the room examining the paintings.

"Well Mrs. Morrison they are fantastically good imitations. If I didn't know, these two Monets here would have fooled me completely. As for the Renoir, unbelievably good. Obviously, careful testing would find the copies but to be frank, for pure enjoyment, these paintings look as good as the originals. However, you don't have to give up hope yet. Perhaps we are going to get your paintings back."

Charlie started looking at the paintings again.

"I'm so glad you asked us here. I know it wasn't to look at your collection but for me it is a wonderful opportunity to see some paintings I've known about for years but never had the opportunity to see."

I saw Samantha looking slightly impatiently at her watch and then talking to the waiter who seemed to be in charge of the dining arrangements. Much to Charlie's obvious disappointment her inspection of the collection was interrupted by being called into dinner. We went in to a dining room that had to be seen to be believed. Antique table and chairs, superb modern paintings. Even the wine glasses looked antique, though luckily the wine was only vintage. I was almost afraid to drink but I did manage to get over my worries. We started by discussing trivia like the abundance of rain in Bermuda and then Samantha came to the point.

"Peter, may I call you that? Jimmy tells me you may be able to throw some light on the loss of the West Atlantic Airways aircraft carrying our paintings. I had assumed that despite all Jimmy's efforts searching in the shallow waters, the paintings were lost for ever."

"Well Mrs. Morrison…"

"Sam, please."

"Well Sam," it didn't sound as good as Charlie, "the paintings may well be lost for ever but I'm not sure. It's possible that a very clever fraud is being committed. I've already warned your husband that he may not agree with my theory at all. I don't want to accuse people of things they didn't do but there are some very peculiar circumstances in this matter. I think we need to be frank with one another. Charlie asked your husband what was in the freight boxes and," I looked at Jimmy, "you told her that it was machinery." Jimmy nodded. "I got an identical answer from Greg.

However, because the freight was so heavy I just wondered whether it was actually guns, weapons, ammunition, that sort of thing that you were selling, quite legitimately I'm sure, to countries in S.America, possibly in exchange for commodities."

"Yes, Peter. You're quite right. Obviously because the stuff was being kept in transit in St. Antony we didn't want to advertise what was in the boxes. However, the St. Antony Government suspected what was inside and they bumped up the storage charge so we were forced to start moving the stuff elsewhere. That's why Greg took the opportunity to load the aircraft with the freight as well as the paintings."

"Greg told me it wasn't insured."

"That's true. The premiums would have been so high I decided to take the risk."

"Well Charlie and I don't believe the paintings have been lost and we believe that the so called freight has been sold in South America somewhere. The paintings might never have been loaded of course, but we favour another explanation." I explained about the rogue software, the VOR failure, the court case coupled with settlement as Angela appeared, about Paragon 56, the double ADS transmission to New York Oceanic, and the short landing at St. Antony. I also explained about the transmissions on both the normal and emergency frequencies which could only be done by a European Aerospace 412 and not by a Gulfstream 3.

"I've come to the conclusion that the paintings actually came back to St. Antony that same night and were removed from the aircraft, which was then ferried to S.America somewhere the next night, doing another switch and the weapons were presumably sold. Goodness knows what happened to the four people on board. We may never know."

They had both been listening intently. Jimmy decided to probe some more. "But who put Jim up to it? Who flew the Gulfstream 3? Who switched the Flight Management Computer?"

"The mastermind was someone at South American Trading working hand in glove with Greg Fairclough. I think you'll find Greg's son was flying the G3. Chuck Curtis must have switched the computer and to be honest I don't think I'd like to be in his shoes. He knows too much but perhaps he's left a statement with his solicitor in case of a suspicious death."

Sam turned to Jimmy.

"I warned you some time ago. I never trusted Greg. I had a female intuition about him."

"Yes, dear. It looks as if you were right. Now Mr. Talbert if you're correct the paintings are sitting in St. Antony, or I hope so. Presumably we can get an order to search Greg's house or anywhere else he might have put the paintings?"

"Not as simple as that because everybody thinks the aircraft is in the Atlantic somewhere and we've got nothing concrete to convince the judge that there should be a search warrant. We were hoping you might be able to pressure someone, Mr. Morrison," I could manage Sam but Jimmy seemed out of place, "with all your contacts here and in St. Antony. As I told you earlier, that's why we're here. It needs someone with clout to make the St. Antony authorities move."

Jimmy looked at Charlie.

"Any ideas?"

"It's difficult Jimmy," she didn't have a problem with what to call him, "at the moment we've got four missing people, a missing aircraft and the missing paintings. What we don't have is an obvious crime. It's a chicken and egg situation. Ben will only be allowed to search everywhere for the paintings if it can be demonstrated that they are almost certainly on the island. We can't very well expect the St. Antony police to be allowed to have search warrants on the evidence they have. The judge might say 'But what about the crash recorder beacon they heard near Bermuda? Hm, very interesting but maybe the Bermuda Triangle has struck again.' "

We went round and round the problem for hours. Jimmy told us where he thought Greg might have hidden the paintings. "Don't forget to look in his girl friend's house. I know there are several storage rooms underneath which they put in when they built the house on the sloping ground, because Paragon Corporation sold the land to the developers. There's also a cellar in Greg's house, but that's a bit obvious."

"Mr. Morrison, what we need is a St. Antony Judge to permit Ben Masters to have a search warrant. Being blunt, you must know a lot of influential people in St. Antony. Don't you think talking to them might help?"

"It's difficult unless we know a bit more. I'll think about it. Maybe I will talk to the Chief Minister. He's a good guy of course, but as you inferred, it's getting a judge to agree."

We made no further progress. Charlie and I retired upstairs towards our rooms after liqueurs and coffee.

"Well, we had a nice dinner but I'm not sure we achieved anything else."

"I'm afraid you're right, Peter. Let's hope he will talk to his buddies in St. Antony. Of course he may be afraid that they might think he's involved." She thought for a moment. "Anyway, it was worth coming just to see the paintings. They were fantastic."

She stopped outside her door, looked at me and came slowly forward and kissed me on the lips. I put out my arms to hold her close and then, as I started to pull her towards me she backed away.

"Sleep well, Mr. T"

I wondered about the adjoining door to Charlie's room. I made sure my side was unlocked in case Charlie needed me but it seemed most unlikely that I was going to find out whether her side was locked or not.

***

In the morning the four of us had breakfast at 8 o'clock in a room overlooking the Atlantic and the rain which they had in abundance, but was desperately needed in St. Antony. We made our farewells and Jimmy promised to talk to someone in St. Antony. He did not accompany us to the airport but we had the same car. We were at the airport in plenty of time for me to pick up and pay for my tickets and then clear customs and immigration. The British Airways 767 left on time and we landed at Kennedy ten minutes early where the weather was cold and very windy.. I wasn't dressed for winter but reckoned I'd probably manage. The business class tags worked and we got our bags quickly from the conveyor. For once there wasn't a line for the cabs and we were soon heading for Charlie's office, taking the Mid Town tunnel to Manhattan. I dropped Charlie off with our bags, agreed to meet at the airport and then I went a further three blocks to the Adelphi.

Lunch time was clearly a good time to arrive. The bulk of the overnighters had long since left and the new wave were not due until later. I asked to see the manager and an assistant manager appeared. I explained about Diana and the call that I had received at 3.05 in the morning, Eastern Standard Time.

"Well Mr. Talbert. I'm not sure I can help you. We only let the police look at our records if they produce a court order so you would have to convince your police in England to contact ours to see the register. But quite frankly I don't see how that would help you. As we've been talking I've checked the computer and there wasn't a Mrs. Talbert registered that night."

"How about tracking the telephone call?"

"Yes, that might be possible but our current computer program is not set up to do that type of search. You would need to talk to Western Union who are our phone company here. I suspect that they would need our permission to search the records which again we would not give without a court order. I'm sorry I can't be of more help."

He didn't look very sorry but I supposed that that was understandable. However, I felt he was being a little bit more than unhelpful. Of course he had a hotel to run and didn't need people like me trying to get information for reasons which might be absolutely fictitious. Still, he didn't have to be quite so unfriendly. I looked at my watch. It was still only 1.30 so I went into the coffee shop for soup and a sandwich. The room was crowded and I had a short wait to be seated before being shown to a table at the side of the room. It was not the table I would have chosen, being close to the door where the staff came in carrying the food but, as the place was full, there was no point in complaining.

The menu was standard and I ordered a tuna salad and coffee and then tried to read USA Today while I was waiting. My thoughts kept returning to Diana and the fact that the telephone call was at 3 o'clock in the morning East Coast time. I watched the assistant manager come into the room and talk to one of the staff and then I had an idea which could explain the manager's attitude. My waitress returned, a darkish girl, possibly of Cuban extraction to judge from her accent. She started to put the food down.

"Could you call the person in charge over who looks after the coffee shop?"

"You're not going to complain are you?"

"No, of course not. I just need some help."

The waitress finished putting the food down and went away. I was halfway through my salad when a smart lady appeared wearing the hotel uniform, looking as if her ancestors had lived in the Far East. However her accent was pure New York.

"Is there a problem, Sir?"

"Not at all. I'm enjoying my lunch but I wondered if Diana is on duty to-day? I'm visiting from England and I haven't seen her for ages."

"Hey, we've got several Diana's."

"Well, this one has a British accent."

"You must mean Diana Carstairs, one of the deputy managers. She's just gone off duty but I know she's still here as some big cheese has called all the managers together for a meeting a 3 o'clock and they're all complaining amongst themselves."

"Any chance of your getting a message to her, telling her Peter Talbert is here?"

"I'll see what I can do."

She disappeared and I carried on with my salad and USA Today. My waitress reappeared holding a coffee jug.

"Would you like me to warm your coffee up? Susie asked me to tell you that she found Diana and gave her your message."

"Is that all?"

"'fraid so." She raised her eyebrows and filled up my mug. "What were you expecting?"

I drank my coffee slowly, I still had plenty of time to get back to Charlie. Just as I was wondering whether to search for Diana, she appeared, not in uniform. She was still a very attractive woman, nearly as tall as Charlie, and I realised that the very light brown hair, instead of the dark hair she used to have, didn't do her looks any harm. She looked around, saw me and smiled. I stood up to help her to the seat opposite mine.

"How on earth did you find me, Peter? Was it the telephone call? I realised too late I should have selected no number transmission." I nodded. "The manager told me someone was looking for me and then the coffee shop manager came along confirming my suspicion it was you. I was in two minds whether to come here and see you but I knew you'd be paging me over the loudspeaker system in ten minutes if I didn't come." She looked at me to see what the missing years had done to me. "Why didn't you contact me?"

"What do you mean, Diana? Contact you? How? One day you were there and the next you weren't. We never heard a word from you. Your parents and I thought you were dead. We searched everywhere."

She hesitated, looking uncomfortable.

"I know, I should have contacted you earlier. But I did write when the divorce came through."

"What divorce? What letter? Have you gone mad?" I could feel myself getting annoyed the way I used to do when we were together. Diana had very little consideration for others then and nothing seemed to have changed. "Divorce is like marriage, it needs two people."

"Calm down, Peter. Whether you like it or not we're no longer married. Do you remember Ken Carstairs?" I shook my head. "Well you did meet him once at one of the Britannia parties. We started going out when you were away overseas. Things weren't going well between us, Peter, and he persuaded me to leave you and return with him over here. He got me a green card and after two years I filed papers for a divorce and as it was uncontested it went straight through."

"But I never got any papers."

"Well I don't know about that. I left it all to Ken's lawyer. We've been married now for two and half years. He's a dispatcher with United and works at Kennedy. I'm a deputy manager here and I like the job."

My mind was racing. Diana seemed to think she was divorced but I wasn't too sure. Anyway, there was nothing I could do about it over lunch. As far as I was concerned I was well out of it, but everything needed to be tidied up and I knew just the person.

"You had better give me the name of your lawyer, Diana. We've got to get things put on a more formal footing."

"I don't know her name. I told you, she's Ken's lawyer."

"Well will you get them to write to me? You must see that what you have done is irresponsible in the extreme and you should have spoken to your parents at the very least, not to mention me, your husband. When we got married you vowed for better or for worse, not until something better came along. What am I going to tell your parents?"

"Nothing if you don't want to."

"Yes, that's your solution for everything. If you've got any decency at all you will call them immediately." I looked at my watch. "It's not too late. And I warn you, Diana, if you don't fax or email me your lawyer's name, and make no mistake she's your lawyer in this divorce, not Ken's, I shall get my lawyer to serve a document of some type on you here, in this hotel, with the maximum publicity."

I stood up and walked out of the coffee shop without looking back and out of the hotel into the strong wind, inadequately clad but I didn't care. I walked the three blocks back to Charlie's office and took the elevator to Westfield on the 34th floor. I gave the receptionist my name and she said that she would let Charlie know I was in Reception waiting to meet her to travel back to the airport. I sat down and picked up the Financial Times and drank some coffee. We didn't need to leave for about an hour but it was too cold for me outside and it was simpler to wait in the office than wait at the airport. I was fuming inside and out, and an hour not speaking to anyone would probably give me a chance to cool down. I felt a tap on my shoulder and looked up to see Charlie.

"You found her then?"

"How on earth did you know that?"

"You should look at yourself in the mirror, Peter. Don't tell me anything now. I've got about another 30 minutes here and then we can leave early and wait in the Executive Club lounge so that you can get smashed if you think it will help."

She left without waiting for an answer and returned as promised accompanied by a lady I correctly assumed to be her boss, probably fifteen years her senior. Charlie introduced Wendy Greengrass.

"Mr. Talbert, I'm delighted to meet you. Charlie's been telling me all about you."

"I hope not, Ms. Greengrass, I'm just the electronics specialist, Ms. Simpson's the investigator. I'm sure she's been telling you about the paintings and discussing how she's going to get them back. We are making quite a lot of progress in the investigation of the disappearance of the European Aerospace 412, but without finding the aircraft or the paintings it's difficult to say we've got the solution."

"Well Mr. Talbert, you and Charlie seem to be working well as a team without going in to who is doing what." I didn't dare look at Charlie. Ms. Greengrass ploughed on. "Perhaps I could have expressed that better. I'm sure between you we're going to get the paintings back."

"Yes, I believe that. I'm more worried about Bill Hudson, the Captain of the aircraft. He seems to have been drawn in to something he had no part of but, of course, we don't know anything for certain yet. As I'm sure Charlie mentioned to you, we don't want the press involved at the moment. Everybody except for about five or six people believes that the aircraft is at the bottom of the Atlantic and until we find the paintings we need to keep up that belief."

Charlie put on her coat and we took the elevator down to the street level. I flagged a passing cab, put our bags in the trunk and we set course for the airport. The traffic was beginning to build up but we had plenty of time.

"How did you get on, Charlie? Did your Ms. Greengrass have any ideas?"

"To be honest, not really. It's going to cost Westfield a lot of money if we don't get our hands on the paintings."

"I'm sure we'll get them as long as Ben watches Greg very closely. He won't leave without the paintings."

"Peter, how did you get on?"

"I don't know. I found Diana and she claims we're divorced which sounds fine, but I'm not convinced. I'm sure it takes two to split as well as two to wed. Anyway, my girl friend's a lawyer so she can sort it out."

We checked our bags kerbside, got our boarding passes and Charlie led the way to the lounge. I noticed her dark glasses were not used on home territory.

"Coffee, tea or?" she raised her eyebrows enquiringly with a very straight face.

"Scotch please Charlie, but only a single malt and two lumps of ice."

Charlie poured herself a white wine and added some soda. We raised our glasses.

"You're looking better, Peter. You should have seen yourself in our office."

"Well, I was livid but on reflection it may work out quite well for me. But it's rotten for Diana's parents. I don't think she realises how cruel she's being."

"How on earth did you find her, Peter? The Adelphi's a big place."

"Well it was luck really. The manager I asked seemed unusually unhelpful and I wondered whether he was covering up for Diana. It then occurred to me that since her call to England was in the middle of the night here, she might be working in the hotel. That way she wouldn't have to pay for the call. She always was a bit careful. So I took a gamble and asked my waitress for her by name. The rest as they say was," I paused "… most unpleasant but I suppose it will be alright in the end."

"I'm not sure everybody would call that luck, Peter. Some thinking seems to have taken place."

The flight was called on time and we were served dinner almost immediately after we took-off.

"I feel choked after eating a tuna salad in that hotel. Mrs. Carstairs, as she chooses to call herself, has ruined my appetite. What did you do about lunch, Charlie?"

"I stuffed myself full of sandwiches but I'll manage to nibble something." I nodded my agreement.

The flight passed very quickly as Charlie extolled and discussed, almost ad nauseam, the real and imitation paintings she had seen at the Morrison's.

Going through immigration Charlie got involved having to explain what she was doing on the island again but I waltzed through. She grabbed my passport and saw the unlimited entry stamp.

"That's new. That wasn't there last time I looked," she said accusingly. "How did you get that?"

"It's who you know that counts." I didn't enlighten her but I could sense she wasn't exactly pleased that I had managed to solve the problem while she was still being cross questioned every time she came to St. Antony.

Charlie drove us back to the hotel and we had a council of war in the coffee shop before we went to bed. We'd given up talking in our rooms as it meant whispering.

"Why don't we drive round to Greg's house and see what's going on. I know where he lives."

It sounded sensible but not really my scene. However, I didn't want to be a spoilsport so we drove in Charlie's car to Greg's house in Seaward. It was 11 o'clock as we parked outside and watched with the car lights out. There were no lights in Greg's house that we could see. A car appeared out of nowhere driving slowly by and Charlie suddenly turned towards me, held me firmly and started to kiss me with some deliberation. She put her tongue inside my mouth and checked it in a way that would have made my dentist proud. However, it was a distinctly more pleasurable experience than going to my dentist, but I couldn't tell if Charlie was enjoying the experience as much as I was, though I did my best. The purpose was clearly to make the onlooker think our intentions were purely amorous. I felt it important to make our performance as convincing as possible but I was fairly sure that Charlie must have been looking over my shoulder while she was conducting her oral examination as the embrace ended as abruptly as it had begun leaving me hanging in the air.

"I think there's somebody in that car watching the house."

"Perhaps it's Greg's guard. I think we'd better not risk it."

Charlie reluctantly agreed and drove back to the hotel. We went to our rooms. My phone rang. It was Charlie.

"Peter, there's a message from Ben Masters. It says 'Leave the house watching to the professionals.'"

"It must have been his man driving by watching the place." She didn't say anything so I continued. "You know Ben seems to know our every move, Charlie. A thought has occurred to me."

"Go on, I'm not sure about your thoughts."

"If you are still decent I suggest that we look more closely at your car."

We met in the lobby and she was decent, though still wearing her glasses which she let me remove. We went out to the car and I started examining the car with my torch. I felt all round underneath and then round the engine and in the trunk. I found it underneath the spare tyre. That was the advantage of plastic cars, you could transmit from inside the car. It wasn't very big but it clearly did the job. I showed the bug to Charlie and put it in my pocket. It had a magnet but it wasn't needed where it had been placed.

"I would never have thought that St. Antony would have had that sort of monitoring equipment."

"It's because of the drug war, but clearly they can use the equipment to track people like us. I must check my car in the morning."

We went inside and standing outside her room she looked at me thoughtfully. "You know Peter, I'm going to have to be careful where you're concerned. You have certain rare attributes which I find disturbing," she paused, "like brains. Good night." She was gone.

In the morning Ben was on the phone. "You two had better come round."

We went round and got told off.

"You have just got to be patient. We'll get a break in the end. We always do."

I had to bend down and do up my shoe laces leaning against Ben's car as we made our way back to Charlie's car. Back at the hotel we felt frustrated. I left Charlie and did some mail. I decided I'd better call Mandy and tell her about meeting Diana.

"How on earth did you find her, Peter?"

"Well I think she called me when I was at your place but I couldn't be sure and I didn't want to raise our expectations. She sounded as if she'd been drinking. However, I did ring back. It was a hotel in New York,"

"You never told me."

"I know. I didn't know what to do."

I went on and told Mandy how I found Diana in the hotel.

"Isn't that good, Peter? We can sort things out."

"I think so but it will need a lot of chasing to get all the papers we need. The real trick is not losing her again. Do you have a partner firm in New York to help?"

"No problem. I'll start straightaway."

I told Mandy that we had come to a sort of impasse and would let her know what was happening. Frank called and suggested we went to the Atlantic Reef for dinner. I asked Charlie who agreed reluctantly. She'd been talking to her boss in New York who was being pressurised by the CEO of Westfield. He said Jimmy Morrison should be talking to the St. Antony Government, he couldn't see why he wasn't and insisted that Jimmy should be doing that instead of demanding the insurance money. Her boss had told the CEO that she couldn't see why St. Antony didn't send the cavalry in and search everywhere on the island.

I was in the lobby in plenty of time. Charlie appeared wearing a thin dress without a slip. Her legs looked superb when the light shone through. She had a white bra, which certainly didn't do her cleavage any harm, and the outline of her brief panties was clearly visible. I didn't know if it was the type of bra that was constantly advertised, but certainly I found that initially the effect was all the advertisement claimed; it was difficult to look her in the eye, dark glasses or no dark glasses, without looking down first. And she had that perfume on again. We went out to my car and I held the door open for her so that she could get in. She seemed to show a lot more leg than was necessary as she got into the car, but I didn't feel like objecting. She took her glasses off when she was in the car and I tried not to look at her. It was more than flesh and blood could stand, mine anyway and she knew it. I think she wanted to see if she could get me to make the first move.

We had a very pleasant evening, just the four of us. I noticed that Charlie was drinking spritzers without the soda water and was relaxing visibly. I only had one scotch and one glass of wine as I was doing the driving. We left at about ten; there was a clear sky and the moon was rising. Charlie said nothing as we drove home. I held my breath. We got our keys and she took her glasses off, put them in her bag and then we went by the pool area so she could drop her bag off in her room. She gave me her key to look after and led me to the beach to look at the stars. We both knew what was about to happen.

"What a superb night. Let's walk along for a little."

We walked slowly along and she reached out for my hand and started stroking it.

"If you carry on stroking my hand like that you may get more than you bargained for."

"How do you know what I'm bargaining for?"

The Final Flight

We stopped walking and as she turned towards me I put my arms round her. She started kissing me very gently at first and then more seriously as I responded. This time I put my tongue in her mouth and there were no complaints. I pulled her very close and she seemed to like it. She moved her body against mine as she felt me. She murmured reflectively in my ear as I pressed her bottom against me.

"Peter, I've been thinking. You know when we first met at Bermuda on the way back here you suggested that we should stop calling each other Ms. Simpson and Mr. Talbert as we were going to see a lot more of each other. Well I've decided now is the time. I'm going to let you see a lot more of me and I'm looking forward to seeing a lot more of you."

It didn't seem worth arguing. I allowed myself to look all over her in a way that I had avoided up to that moment because I knew the inevitable consequences. She had a fantastically athletic body and a superb figure. She was the stuff that male dreams are made of. She kissed me sensuously on the lips as I stroked her.

I managed to whisper.

"Where do you suggest this examination should take place? And when did you have in mind?"

"I'm not sure Peter that I like the concept of an examination but I leave you to decide what would be desirable. I think my room would be a good venue, don't you? Why don't you go to your room and get rid of all those clothes and come round to my poolside door?"

However, notwithstanding her suggestion she pressed her body ever closer against mine and we carried on kissing until I had to advise her to stop what she was doing. We went back down the beach to the hotel and I left her to go to my room. I put on some bathing shorts and a bath robe, took a large bath towel, locked my door and went out to the pool area which was bathed in moonlight. I knocked on Charlie's door and she let me in. There was no light on but there was enough light from the moon to see she was wearing a slip and nothing else. Some people might have thought it was two sizes too small for her as it was very short and I could see her breasts were thrust forward with the nipples showing through clearly, even in the semi darkness. As she turned round to lock the door I came to the conclusion that it would have been a pity if the slip had been any longer and it occurred to me that Charlie had not after all bought a slip that was too small for her. In fact she had probably bought a very, very expensive slip, probably from some well know lingerie house to make sure that when she wore it her body was shown off to perfection. I wondered whether I should ask her the maker's name, it fitted her so magnificently, but thought better of it.

"What on earth have you brought a towel for, Peter? I don't think it will be necessary, do you?"

She came up to me, holding her body away from mine and kissed me very gently on the lips.

"I'm a boy scout. With you I like to be prepared for anything. You may have wanted to go swimming."

"Well it's nice of you to be prepared. I don't know about you but swimming wasn't what I had in mind. Talking of your being prepared, I think it would spoil the enjoyment for both of us. I don't think we need to bother. What do you think?"

She undid my trunks which fell to the floor and moved slightly closer to hold me, perhaps to make sure I wasn't being a boy scout. I moved forward and kissed her neck. There was no way I was going to argue with her in my condition. I whispered in her ear.

"I have to say that I think you're right."

"You're talking too much, as usual."

Charlie took her hand away and went over to the side of her bed and sat down. I went close up to her and took her slip off. It didn't seem the right moment to examine it. Instead I held her breasts which were magnificent and then stroked her nipples while she stroked me. She moved back on the bed so she could lie back and I gradually put my weight on her, thrusting myself inside her. She wrapped her legs round me so that I could not escape. She was incredibly strong and I felt encased within her. We came together and later I wondered if there had been anyone in the next door room, not that it mattered. After what seemed like forever she slowly relaxed her legs and we got up. Charlie hung on to me very tightly indeed and I held her in my arms. After a time she loosened her hold.

"Let's have a shower and go to bed."

She turned the shower on and clearly expected me to join her. It seemed churlish to refuse. We dried ourselves off and lay down on the bed. I held Charlie close to me and dozed off, but only for a moment.

"Charlie, I've had an idea."

"Peter, you've had one good idea to-night. I have to tell you I'd be very surprised if you had another in your condition." She wriggled her bottom. "If you've got an idea it's not obvious."

"Charlie, be serious."

"I'm being very serious."

She started to kiss me. She must have felt me respond. "That's better. Perhaps your idea is better than I thought."

I decided it might be sensible after all to delay what I had in mind for what Charlie had in mind. I whispered in her ear "I feel a proper Charlie."

"This is not the time for British jokes. We are not amused," she paused, "and what are you are doing is definitely not proper," she wriggled closer "but don't stop." And I didn't.

Later we both lay on our backs and I realised that my idea still hadn't gone away.

"Charlie?"

She rolled over and buried her face on my chest.

"What is it now?"

"I've still got the idea I had before you sidetracked me."

"I've never heard it called that before. What other idea have you got?"

"It's about the possible whereabouts of some of the missing paintings and I'm not sure I like the answer. Charlie, where have you looked for the missing paintings?"

It was like an electric shock. She rolled over on her side and looked at me intently, her breasts hanging forward. I had her full attention.

"Well, nowhere really. You know we can't get a search warrant."

"You remember I told you that Paragon 56 had a few items of household belongings which had been put into shipping crates. I seem to remember that they were being sent to Europe somewhere by boat. Doesn't the Canberra leave to-morrow?"

She leapt off the bed, threw my bathing shorts, bath robe and towel at me and unlocked the poolroom door, pushing me outside before I could get the shorts on. We met in the lobby a few minutes later, neither of us dressed to perfection. Her car was nearest and she was in her Fangio mood. We broke the record to the airport but it was late at night and only a junior customs guard was on duty. Charlie called the duty customs officer and finally managed to track down Richard Sebble, the chief customs officer who, judging from Charlie's end of the conversation, didn't seem too gruntled. He grudgingly agreed to come down straightaway when Charlie pointed out that he would get all the credit.

We only had to wait ten minutes before he appeared. Charlie explained the situation and he got out all the books.

"The flight you mention, Paragon 56, only had a few items of household equipment and they were added to some crates which were sent to a freight agent in Cape Harbour for shipping in a container to Europe to Ms. J.Fairclough, Apt 323, 24 Rue Vittoria, Zurich."

"Please, the name of the shippers."

Sebble went back to the entry in the book. It seemed to take forever to find the name. "Albert Smith & Son."

"How can we find them, please, quickly?" Charlie was getting frantic.

Sebble looked at us, considered the situation, without any urgency.

"You won't get anybody there at this time of night."

"Where's their office? Please hurry."

"On Valley Road, Number 15."

I looked the number up in the telephone book and called it. There was an answering phone with an out of hours number. I called the number and a sleepy voice answered.

"What is it?"

I tried to explain that we needed to know the whereabouts of some household belongings.

"Why can't it wait until the morning?"

I knew I didn't sound too convincing so I decided to spend some of Charlie's money.

"There's a hundred US dollars if you come to your office now and tell us about the goods."

My offer seemed to help break the log jam and we agreed to meet in fifteen minutes at the office. We went to Charlie's car. She had heard my end of the conversation.

"You're being very free with your money, Peter."

"Yours actually, but I didn't think you'd mind in the circumstances."

"We'll just have to see when we both send in our expenses."

"Do I send mine to you or to your boss?"

"You send yours to Frank."

"Drop me off on the way home will you Charlie? I thought I was getting paid overtime for helping you."

Charlie stroked my face as she drove.

"You're not such a bad guy really."

"Please keep both hands on the wheel or stop."

"That's called Hobson's choice."

We arrived at Valley Road just as the duty manager did and Charlie explained what we needed. We gave dates and he got his books out.

"Ms. Simpson, we shipped the container out to-day to the Canberra."

Charlie was aghast. "When does it leave?"

"Five p.m. to-morrow."

I decided that Charlie needed help. I called Ben Masters at home. It didn't take me long to give him the highlights.

"OK Peter, you've got a deal. I'll send my deputy to get an order from Judge Brown on the grounds of suspected robbery. I'll warn the Captain of the Canberra now what is happening and he will have to choose between delaying the boat or releasing the container. The boat is under our jurisdiction. In fact if he acts quickly it might be possible for him just to off load the household belongings. It's up to him. Anyway I'll wake him up now."

There was a pause.

"Oh, Peter!"

"Yes Ben?"

"You'd better be right. The Judge will kill me if he has been woken up for no reason at all. I'll get the stuff taken to the customs shed at the harbour. Why don't we meet at eight if the Captain has agreed and sent the goods ashore."

"Ben?"

"Yes Peter? I can feel another crazy suggestion coming."

"Well if you'd rather I kept quiet."

"Out with it."

"Ben. Do you think Greg knows that we are on to him?"

"Almost certainly."

"Then I should check the passenger manifest of the Canberra very carefully if I were you. There may be a single male traveller whose name you may not recognise but whose face you most certainly will. Greg will have worked out it is only a matter of time before we find the paintings wherever they are. If I'm right he will think that at least he has got some paintings on the Canberra and that's better than nothing. He will have hidden the rest of the paintings somewhere to be recovered later."

"Peter. I'll buy you dinner if you're right."

"You're buying me dinner anyway if you get the paintings. Getting Greg requires another reward."

"Alright then, I won't have you arrested for putting two bugs on my car."

Charlie walked over to the phone.

"Peter, what did you do?"

I told her about Ben and the Canberra.

"I told you. It's not what you know but who you know. You've got to have friends, Charlie. What do you want to do now? The Captain may not play ball until the court order arrives. I reckon the earliest we'll get the stuff will be about six in the morning. It could drag on if the Captain chooses to be difficult. I don't think he will because the Canberra comes here regularly. We have now two choices. Your room or mine?"

The shipping agent knew what had to be done. Charlie told him to send the bill to her firm. We got into her car and drove back to the hotel.

"While you were talking to Ben I was chatting up the agent. He was the freighting agent when the paintings first came to St. Antony and he also organised the loading on to VP-WAL. He told me that he didn't trust the guards when they loaded the aircraft but since they were supplied by Westfield Insurance there was not much he could do. He checked that both guards had Westfield's identity cards."

"What did you say to that, Charlie?"

"There wasn't much I could say. We clearly need to improve our system. Two guards may not be enough for our type of work. The problem is that we are talking about such large sums of money and the amount of money we pay our guards is comparatively small, so they can be bought very easily. Of course someone like Roger O'Sullivan is very special. He couldn't be bought and so the poor man was killed. We need better guards, more of them and pay them more, and then our customers will scream when we put our premiums up."

Charlie parked her car and we went into the lobby and collected our keys. We walked down the corridor to our rooms. Charlie let me take her in my arms.

"I'm too tired to do anything but sleep, Peter. Good night."

We kissed and she almost changed her mind, but she didn't. I went to bed and very soon dreamed that the whole building was falling down. There was frequent thunder which turned into Charlie banging on my door at 6 a.m.

"Come on Peter. We've got to go."

"You should have rung me."

"They told me they were going to. See you at the customs shed."

I had a shower and shave and got dressed. There was no real urgency in my opinion so I decided to keep cool. I got to the shed at 6.45 as Ben arrived. Charlie was fuming since the Canberra had managed to offload the crates and the goods were there waiting. Understandably, the duty customs would not open up the crates without permission from Richard Sebble which Charlie had accepted with bad grace. Ben called Sebble and it was agreed that the ceremonial opening would be at 8 o'clock. We went to a dockside cafe and had breakfast. I felt ready for it and Ben and I didn't do too badly but Charlie refused to eat. She was on tenterhooks. I understood and decided not to pull her leg. She squeezed my hand and Ben winked at me when he thought Charlie wasn't watching. But you can never be sure with dark glasses. Certainly she withdrew her hand very rapidly after the wink.

Finally 8 o'clock arrived and we were all assembled in the custom's house inspection room. The two large crates which had been unloaded from the container were forced open and the contents laid out on the floor. There was crockery, cutlery, pots and pans, towels, blankets and finally a few photographs in some very large ornate frames. I was afraid to look at Charlie because I knew she would be so disappointed. She took off her glasses, laid them on a side table and looked at the framed photographs, two of which seemed extremely thick. She turned one over and placed it flat on the table. She went to her bag, took out a very sharp knife and started cutting the sealing tape at the edge of the frame. I felt she had done this sort of thing before. The back came off very carefully and there was a stiff fairly thick package behind the photograph.

"This is the way the picture was sealed by Christie's before it left London. Here's their number and seal."

We all looked at the package except Ben who had gone out to tell his policeman to pull in Greg, his son and Chuck Curtis.

"Charlie, do you have to open it?"

"I don't think so Peter. I can't possibly seal it properly once we have checked the painting."

Ben rejoined us.

"Ms. Simpson, you obviously know that this is one of the missing paintings. That's all I really need to get search warrants. I'm trying to find Fairclough and his son right now. Are there any more paintings here?"

Charlie looked at the other photographs in their frames and selected the other thick one. She opened the back and took out another similar package with a seal and reference number.

"Right Ms. Simpson, you come with me to the Court House and make a signed statement to the Judge. I can get the warrants and we'll pull the island to bits."

In fact Ben didn't have to pull very hard as he found the rest of the paintings in their sealed packages as Jimmy had foretold under Margaret Springfield's house. She said that she had agreed that Greg could use the space for storage but had no idea what he had put in it. I believed her but Ben cautioned her. All the packages were taken to the custom's shed. Charlie examined the seals on all of the packages and declared that the packages had not been opened but that there was one missing. She was very upset. Ben's men carried on searching but had no further success. It spoilt our celebrations. She called Jimmy and told him the news and judging from her end of the conversation he was delighted, even though he was one painting short. Then she called her boss who seemed ecstatic in spite of there being one missing, but remembered to pass on her thanks to me.

Ben came back and told us they couldn't find Greg but he had managed to find Chuck who denied everything. The Bermuda police had been unable to find Greg's son. It seemed to me that if Chuck said nothing Ben wasn't going to be able to make anything stick. Perhaps he would offer him a deal if he told all but I did wonder how much Greg had actually told Chuck. He probably just gave him money. I guessed that Chuck must have wondered what had happened to Alpha Lima when it disappeared and must have been very alarmed when the body was found. Perhaps the body might possibly make Chuck talk, not wanting to be an accomplice to murder.

A long discussion then took place in the customs shed as to whether it was necessary to open each painting and Charlie took the position that it was not necessary. Her company was satisfied that the paintings had been recovered and they could now be shipped to Jimmy Morrison. Sebble finally agreed provided that one painting was opened so that the press

272

could be called in to record the success of his department. Charlie insisted on having a room with controlled temperature and humidity and I suggested that there might be such a room in the hospital. Charlie looked at me, I hoped with thanks rather than exasperation, and got customs to see if the hospital could help. The whole entourage moved off to the hospital and as the operation looked as if might be going on for hours I went back to the hotel. I called Jack Wellings and told him what had happened and to call off the search. He didn't sound too pleased about the way he had been kept out in the cold and asked how could we be sure that the paintings had actually been loaded in the first place. I invited him back to the hotel for a chat.

I then called Mandy to tell her the good news. As usual she was in court but I told her secretary. I relaxed on my bed, wondering what I should do next. There was a tap on my door. Charlie came in, sensibly leaving the door open and hugged me.

"Ben called me when I got back."

"What did he say?"

"Well we were talking about getting the paintings safely to Bermuda. He sent his apologies to you because he didn't have time to congratulate you properly before you left and would you call him straightaway. He promised he'd catch up with you later and buy you a drink. By the way he said he was considering charging me as well as you because 'my man had put two bugs on his car'. Of course I told him straightaway you weren't my man and do you know what he said?"

"That's your problem."

She stopped in her tracks.

"Sometimes Peter I think you're far to clever for my own good."

I grinned. She looked carefully at me.

"What did he mean about the bugs?"

"Perhaps he was referring to the fact that the two bugs that he had attached to our cars had somehow found their way onto his car. It was just a convenient way of returning them."

It was Charlie's turn to grin.

"Now I know why you had to tie up your shoelaces as we left Ben yesterday. If he hadn't found the paintings he'd probably have arrested you for interfering with the course of justice."

I called Ben.

"You were right again Peter. I confirm my offer of a job as student constable. I got one of my men to look at all the St. Antony passengers as they checked in and he decided to interview Herr Weissmann who had a Swiss passport. The man was bald, wore a black trilby, and had a moustache. Somehow my man felt he wasn't genuine since he couldn't answer all the questions correctly when he was asked about how he arrived on the island. In addition he had only booked the journey last night. The man tried every trick in the book and called for the Captain who said that in the circumstances he was sure that Herr Schmidt would not mind being examined in the ship's hospital to check the moustache and the baldness. As they went to the hospital Schmidt tried to escape and in the scuffle my man pulled the wig off and revealed Greg Fairclough. I like to think that we would have checked all the passengers anyway Peter, but your advice was not untimely. Thank you once again. I'm working on Chuck Curtis now to get him to turn into a prosecution witness. Really well done, Peter. See you very soon."

He rang off. I looked at Charlie.

"Could you hear what Ben said? They caught Greg on the boat."

"Only because of you. And we only got the paintings back because of you. I want to kiss you." I shut the door. She seemed to want to congratulate all of me and in the circumstances I decided to co-operate. However the phone seemed to keep on ringing, starting with the local press and then from the States followed by Europe. They mostly wanted to talk to Charlie though Flight, the FT and Aviation Week wanted to talk to me. The media decided to join in and we gave up the unequal struggle.

"Peter, we'll have to get dressed. This would have been a super way of spending the afternoon but it's difficult to concentrate when the phone keeps on interrupting. I've had to agree to let the local press photographer take my picture at 5 o'clock. Then I'm going to buy you dinner somewhere. Just the two of us. Where shall we go?"

We chose The Inn overlooking Paradise Harbour. It wasn't the best place on the island but we never got tired of looking down on the boats below and the cliffs above. She'd managed to find a dress I hadn't seen before and seemed to have more on than the previous night at Frank's. She wasn't wearing perfume but it didn't seem to matter. She still smelt gorgeous. It was my turn to drive again.

"My boss is over the moon. She's so delighted."

"Quite right too. You've saved her nearly \$100M in insurance money."

"I feel a bit of a fraud. I did very little. You did all the work. You sussed out not only what must have happened but you found the paintings."

"Don't worry about it. It was my pleasure."

"But Greg might have killed you."

"Let's dance."

We moved slowly over the floor. She was not a girl I had to look up to but it was a close run thing. She danced beautifully. She could feel me pressing against her and seemed to like it.

She whispered in my ear. "It's a shame."

"What's a shame?"

"Us. It wouldn't work."

"It's been fun trying."

She moved back for a moment so she could look at me. "Yes, Peter, it really has. I'm not used to meeting men like you. Most of them are wimps or think that I should roll over on my back for them. That's why I wear dark glasses and dress the way I do with all those awful clothes."

She came close again.

"Charlie, the music has stopped."

We went back to our table and drank some more wine. Charlie seemed to have given up Spritzers for the real thing and it wasn't even Lent.

"You didn't argue, Peter."

"About what?"

"Us. When I said it wouldn't work."

"Well Charlie, you know I like to look facts in the face. We are like strangers in the night. You have your roots in the North East United States. Mine are in England. It's almost a paradise location here where the climate can do no wrong, but it's not real. It's not for us. If we were both multi-millionaires perhaps we would have places together in New York, London, here, who knows where, and walk roughshod on our past. But we aren't and we can't. We are both doers. We would find it difficult to be subservient to each other. At the moment you know I can't keep my hands off you, I lust after you, but we both know it wouldn't work long term."

"Let's dance some more."

We glided over the floor. We held on to each other and tried to forget the world outside.

I whispered in Charlie's ear.

"I've had an idea."

"Can't we finish our dinner? It's so good and we can try your idea out later. The way I feel, any way you like."

"I'll rephrase that. I've got another idea."

"Let's go back to the table so I'm ready for it."

I led her back and held her chair to help her to sit down.

"I like that Peter. Why can't more men do that?"

"Charlie I have to tell you that my guess is that there are very few men in the world you would allow to do that. I feel privileged."

She took my hand and kissed it.

"You're right. What about your other idea?"

"Well you think you're one painting short. Are you going to pay the insurance on it?"

"I suppose we'll have to."

She suddenly came to attention and was watching me like a hawk.

"Have you got any better ideas?"

"I might have."

"Come on. Don't tantalise me."

"Why not? You've been tantalising me ever since we met."

"Not last night. Not to-day and I won't to-night." She reached out and stroked me.

I swallowed and held my breath.

"Look Charlie. On second thoughts don't look. It puts me off. Put your glasses on."

"I can't."

"Why not?"

"I haven't brought them. Come on Peter, let's have your second idea so we can concentrate on your first."

"Well I have a theory. The day after the aircraft disappeared Jimmy heard about the ADS and the storm and was truly heartbroken. He wanted to have those paintings on his walls. Samantha also heard about the ADS and the storm, but unlike Jimmy she decided that Greg had pinched them. The loss was altogether too convenient. She didn't know how but she knew Greg and had never trusted him. She had never liked Jimmy agreeing to Greg's son flying for Paragon either. So she called Greg. It was a difficult conversation because she knew that their phones could well be bugged. She told Greg that unless he 'found' her favourite Renoir he would be in trouble, and it wouldn't be with Jimmy, she'd tell the police. He protested he didn't know what she was talking about but that he would see her when he was next in Bermuda.

"Greg was in a spot but as I told you he was planning anyway on sending the G3 back to Bermuda with the 'wreckage'. He decided to fly in the aircraft with his son. Very convenient as they didn't need another pilot. He managed to get the Renoir into a very large suitcase. Greg stayed in his son's house that night after his son had gone to place the wreckage and Samantha came round to see him in the morning. She took the Renoir away with her."

Charlie could hold herself in no longer.

"Do you really believe any of that? It's a wild guess. Samantha looked surprised when you were telling her the story the other night."

"Maybe, but wasn't she an actress before she met Jimmy? I'm sure Samantha almost certainly reacted like you when she heard the aircraft had disappeared. The loss was altogether too convenient."

"But what has she done with the picture if you're right?"

"Oh, that's easy. You were looking at it. It was on the wall. You said yourself it was unbelievably good. She swapped with the copy when Jimmy wasn't looking and put it where the other copies were stored."

I kept a straight face which she examined carefully. She didn't know whether to believe me or not, to laugh or cry. I wasn't going to make it easy for her.

"Are you making this up?"

"Charlie, I'm surprised you didn't notice that Samantha was fidgeting when you were looking at the Renoir. She was trying to get us into dinner as quickly as possible." I could see Charlie remembering. "Shall we take bets? Remember I also looked at the Renoir."

"No we shan't. And don't give me that about your looking at the Renoir and knowing it was the real thing. You don't know the backside from the front." She paused and grinned as she saw that I was going to interrupt. "Stop being coarse. You really are the limit. I'm talking about paintings. I have a pleasurable feeling going right through me, just like when you're stroking me. You might just be right. In fact the more I think about it the more convinced I am that you have got it right again. Peter's luck again. Alright, it wasn't luck, bighead. But why did she do it?"

"What's the Renoir worth, $12-$18m? Well Jimmy's business was not in too good a shape and she needed a personal pension fund which Jimmy wouldn't know about. You people would pay Jimmy the insurance money and she would always be able to flog the painting to unscrupulous collectors if she needed to." I paused. "Charlie, presumably the moment Jimmy asks for the Renoir insurance money you will want to visit chez Morrison and discuss the matter?"

"You bet we will. The problem is that if you're right Samantha will hide the picture when she knows I'm coming."

"Do you want my advice?"

Charlie grinned at me.

"You're going to give it to me anyway."

"When the claim comes in, call the lovely Samantha yourself and say you really appreciated dinner the other night and looking at the pictures. Particularly the Renoir. In all the circumstances which she and you well understand, your company is not prepared to pay the claim. Will she explain the real situation to Jimmy or does she want you to come up and do it?" I could see Charlie savouring the situation. "She'll have a real problem but it won't be yours. She'll know very well that the claim for the lost Renoir is bound to fail. She'll just have to tell some cock and bull story to Jimmy about Greg returning the picture." Charlie clearly liked my plan. "Now if you want me to make the call and pretend we have extra information I'll do it but it will cost you."

"No, Peter. It won't be necessary. As usual I like your ideas. Why don't we have our last waltz?"

Charlie held on tight. All of a sudden she realised that she was going to get 100% for this job. She'd go back to New York smelling of roses. Her mind was racing.

"I don't know what to say, Peter.

"Then don't say anything. Just relax and enjoy the music...."

"... and the company."

We looked for the last time down into the harbour with lights twinkling below and left the hotel. The stars were still shining, the breeze was still blowing, the insects were still making their noises and the night was still warm. We held hands and walked to the car. I helped her in and then got in to drive home. She pulled me over and kissed me. Her face was wet with tears.

"You should be up there, over the moon, not crying."

"I know but I feel like crying. There's only you I can do it with."

I drove home slowly while she held my hand. We walked into the lobby together. There was an envelope for me with a fax inside. We collected our keys. She stopped as we came to her room and she put out her hand.

"Do you think you'd better spend the night in my room, Peter, in case you get another idea?"

I held her quietly in my arms and for a moment was perfectly still, inhaling the smell of her hair and her body.

"I don't think so, Charlie. We've come to the end of my ideas, my darling. What is it the song said? 'I wouldn't have missed it for the world'." She squeezed my hand. "You've got all your paintings. I'm afraid we've got to climb our own separate ladders now."

She turned her head up and we kissed, not passionately, but knowing it was for the last time. We separated slowly.

"Good night, Ms. Simpson."

"Good night, Mr.Talbert."

She turned round and I watched her go into her room. I opened my fax as I walked down the corridor.

'Marvellous news. Have told clients I have problems as well as them. I need to have a Commonwealth consultation. Arriving St. Antony BA flight 452 1500 hours to-morrow. Looking forward to seeing you. Love Mandy.'

CHAPTER 10

'Oh! let our voice His praise exalt
Till it arrive at Heaven's vault'

Bill considered his predicament. Surely someone must have seen them. He couldn't believe the audacity of the operation. The sums of money involved must be huge to mount such a risky operation as this and to deliberately kill people, because he was convinced that neither he nor Jim would be allowed to survive and there must be others who, like them, knew far too much. He looked around him in the room. There was a trestle bed, a table, four rather ramshackle chairs and a couple of metal filing cabinets full of old manuals. He took most of his clothes off and hung them, as best he could, on one of the chairs. He lay down on the bed and tried to go to sleep but he could hear a lot of noise which sounded like people moving boxes and sliding them on the floor. Then he could hear hammering. Finally, after what seemed like forever but actually was only about an hour, he dropped off to sleep.

In the morning Jim appeared with Claudio, the junior guard, who was holding a pistol. Jim looked defiant but was carrying some breakfast on a tray and tried to apologise.

"Good morning, Bill. I'm sorry we got you involved in this thing. You know we can't let you go until the job is finished."

Bill started to put his survival plan into action and tried to sound a lot more confident and aggressive than he felt.

"Don't give me that Jim. You know and I know that I'm never going to be released and if you think that they will let you get away you must be mad. I suggest you think again."

Jim look unconcerned.

"I'm not worried. I've taken precautions. I've written a letter. They wouldn't dare do anything."

Bill knew he must make Jim feel unsure of the situation.

"Well I hope you're right for your sake but I'll be amazed if they don't kill you when they kill me however much you promise to keep the story to yourself. They wouldn't risk it. Just think about it."

Jim looked as if he was trying not to listen but Bill had a feeling, and he hoped he was not deluding himself, that Jim was not as confident as he pretended. Bill asked to go to the rest room and Claudio took him along. As he went along the side of the hangar he saw that the aircraft was still inside with the interior doors closed. There were some open empty crates on the ground which he could tell from the markings had contained the paintings. Bill assumed that the heavy crates were still on the aircraft since they were nowhere to be seen. He noticed that three of the aircraft dinghies were next to the crates plus some life jackets, assorted bottles, seat cushions and a couple of polystyrene bulkheads which seemed to have been deliberately smashed. There were also a couple of very large open freight crates, full of all sorts of household junk, which seemed more suitable for trucks or ships rather than aircraft.

He went into the toilet and Claudio waited outside. The guard was not worried as there was no way he could get out. When he'd finished he washed himself as best he could and Claudio let him go back to the room and locked the door behind him. Bill toyed with the rolls and coffee but he felt so sick with worry that he couldn't manage anything. Jim returned after a bit and Bill decided to keep asking questions, he'd nothing to lose.

"How are they going to get rid of the aircraft?"

"We're going to deliver it either to-night or to-morrow night to Colombia."

So that was why the freight was so heavy. There must be guns, ammunition and the rest in the heavy boxes. Bill became very alert. Perhaps there was a remote chance, because he suddenly realised that Jim needed his help.

"Whose we? You surely don't imagine I'm going to have anything to do with it?"

Jim looked concerned.

"I've got authority to say you'll be allowed to go once the flight is over."

"I find that hard to believe, I'm afraid Jim. Anyway you don't really believe the aircraft can get to Colombia from here without being detected? It must be right on the limit of the 412's range capability. It'll never get that far."

Jim was on the defensive.

"It will get there and we won't be seen. We've worked it out very carefully. However there won't be a lot of fuel to spare. That's why we need you to help and why we're going to let you go when we get there."

"But I'll tell everybody, how can they possibly let me go."

"What will you tell them, Bill? I'll have disappeared and you know nothing about who has planned this operation."

Bill didn't believe Jim for a moment. Last night's flight had been planned very skilfully so that unfortunately for him, the chances were that everybody was convinced that the aircraft had crashed in the sea. Still he decided not to challenge Jim on that point since it suited his plan to keep his counsel.

Jim carried on persuading.

"Are you going to help us? It's going to be a very long and difficult flight. It needs two of us."

"What happens if I say no?"

"I don't know."

"But you can guess, can't you Jim?"

Jim looked shamefaced.

"I've told you. Come with us and they'll let you go."

"I'd feel more confident about that if there was a letter for me as well, Jim."

He let Jim sweat a bit. He doubted Jim could manage by himself but perhaps he'd get another pilot. Possibly the one who flew Paragon 56, though he'd be needed if there was going to be another switch.

"Jim, let me see what you've planned."

Jim relaxed slightly. He clearly wanted Bill. Perhaps there was a disagreement between the mastermind who planned the job and Jim. Perhaps the mastermind was not convinced that Jim needed Bill. Jim went out of the room and returned with some maps and charts. Bill got up and laid them out on the table. The track lines went south to the north of Trinidad and then went to Colombia via Guyana, Brazil and Venezuela. The route avoided the airways, the big airfields and Bill reckoned the route was chosen to try to reduce the chance of being detected by the ground radars. The altitude for each leg was written down in red. By going on the airway to Trinidad the altitude would be kept high and therefore the fuel burn had been minimised. For some reason there was a low level bit from north of Trinidad, between Tobago and Trinidad, and then south for about 100 miles. From there the plan showed the aircraft climbing to maximum altitude, to minimise the fuel burn, going due south across the mouth of the Rio Grande down the disputed Venezuelan/Guyana border to Brazil at 5°N. Then the plan showed the aircraft turning onto 252° and flying for 643 miles to the equator, at first flying along the Brazilian/Venezuelan border, then north of the border in Venezuela and back into the north west part of Brazil in the headwaters of the Amazon. Finally the aircraft was to fly for another 187 miles to a landing strip on the Rio Yari just north of the Equator. There was a planning sheet showing the fuel burn and time for each leg.

Bill looked at the total fuel planned and saw that there was only going to be 45 minutes fuel left at the landing strip, hardly an adequate contingency for the weather and the winds. The whole thing looked ridiculous but he supposed it might just be possible to make the planned landing strip. Bill saw that the nearest Colombian Air Force base was at Puerto Leguizamo and clearly by hook or by crook he had to persuade Jim to land there. However, he doubted there would be enough fuel to make it.

"Jim, it won't work. What happens if there's a navigation error or a strong head wind? The reserve is inadequate."

"You know we've got the latest Global Positioning System on the plane so we won't get lost. The flight would be impossible without it but with GESS it should be straightforward. We're checking the wind right now. It looks as if it's going to be alright. If not we'll wait until tomorrow."

Jim looked him.

"Will you come?"

Bill decided that he might as well keep alive as long as possible and nodded. At least he'd live a few more hours. Who could foretell what would really happen? Jim left him saying that take-off would be at 1 o'clock in the morning and took the maps and charts with him. The day dragged on very slowly. He managed a bit of sleep during the day. Jim returned at 4 p.m. with a club sandwich and some coffee.

"We'll have some food on the aircraft, Bill, but I've asked for a meal before we go."

Bill guessed that Jim didn't have a lot more freedom than he had. Nobody could be allowed to see Jim either or the game would be up. The guards must have instructions to watch Jim as closely as they were watching him and Jim must be feeling the pressure. Bill was more than ever convinced that he must make Jim think that he was going to be killed at the same time as he was, which would be, he guessed, the moment the arms were delivered to their destination. He forced himself to eat a little food and drink some coffee. At about 8 p.m. everything went quiet. All those not in the plot must have gone home. He asked to go to the restroom but he was told he would have to wait. He heard the noise of a tractor and some other vehicles. Presumably they were refuelling the aircraft and getting ready to take it outside. The warning horn for the inside doors sounded and he heard a tractor, probably moving the aircraft. The horn went again and shortly afterwards he was allowed to go to the rest room. To his surprise the aircraft was still in the hangar but it had been turned round. He supposed they wanted to reduce the possibility of it being seen to a minimum. They would want to taxi straight out on to the taxiway, down to the holding point and take-off without any delay. He imagined that they were going to use a Paragon call sign again and do a switch somewhere: the plan clearly suggested it would be just north of Trinidad. He wondered how they were going to satisfy air traffic because there would be an extra aircraft in the air which had to be got rid of, but then he realised the beauty of using Paragon flight numbers and not tail registration letters, as was usual on private flights. Air Traffic wouldn't notice because there would be other Paragon aircraft on the ramp which they couldn't see and anyway they wouldn't care about the tail letters. It wasn't their responsibility.

Jim returned at midnight and said they were to go into the aircraft. Jim got in the left hand seat to show he was in command and Bill strapped himself into the right hand seat. Robert and Claudio followed them into the aircraft and Jim raised the steps and closed the doors while Robert watched Bill, being careful as ever holding the pistol. The inside hangar doors slowly opened and Bill saw that the outside doors were already open. The ramp was completely dark with no floodlights. Jim started the aircraft's auxiliary power unit inside the hangar which was highly unsafe and not permitted, in order to get electrical power without having to connect up to a rig or a long land line. A tractor appeared to tow the aircraft out but Bill couldn't see who was driving it.

As the aircraft was being towed Jim asked for taxi and take-off clearance for Paragon 72 to go to Trinidad. Bill looked down at his navigation display and it showed the route which he had seen that morning drawn on the maps which Jim had shown him, starting to go down normally to Trinidad and then going between Trinidad and Tobago and disappearing into S.America. Jim must have programmed the flight management systems when electrical power had been on the aircraft while it was being refuelled. The clearance came immediately, not surprising at that time of night, and Jim started the engines. Robert kept watching Bill like a hawk, holding the gun almost touching the back of his head. Bill had no doubt that the slightest sign of lack of co-operation and he'd be dead. There seemed no point in sacrificing himself to stop the scheme when there was just a chance of his surviving.

Bill called out the checks and Jim told him not to switch on the logo light or the beacons. They taxied out and got take-off clearance immediately. Jim selected the maximum take-off flap setting which was more than was permitted for the weight of the aircraft in that warm temperature in case an engine failed. Bill knew Jim had decided to ignore the possibility of engine failure. All Jim wanted was to get airborne and climb as quickly as possible so that the aircraft was well above the control tower and could not be identified. The chances of an engine failing on that particular flight were infinitesimal. Bill knew it wasn't worth arguing about the flap setting. Thinking about it, Bill wondered whether an engine failure might not be the best solution.

They got permission to enter the runway and Jim opened the engines to full power on the brakes before releasing them. The aircraft surged forward rapidly and Bill called out the take-off speeds which Jim had given him as the aircraft accelerated. The engine powers looked good and at rotation speed Jim pulled the aircraft up steeply and banked it slightly so they flew over the control tower and well above it. Bill reckoned it would have been impossible for the controller in the tower to see them.

Bill automatically went through the after take-off checks. The whole thing was incredible. They had got airborne from Nelson without any problem at all. Bill would never have believed they could have done it without someone in Air Traffic noticing, but it was 1.30 in the morning. Paragon often did flights in the middle of the night so the flight itself would not have been considered unusual. Bill wondered whether anybody had ever checked why Paragon found it so necessary to carry out flights round the Caribbean in the middle of the night. He supposed that since it didn't break the laws of any of the islands, they just didn't care.

Jim turned the aircraft on course for Trinidad, climbed to Flight Level 330 and as they cleared Nelson control he switched the TCAS on and the aircraft flew steadily down the airway towards Port of Spain. Bill watched the lights of Guadeloupe go by on their port side, probably he knew for the last time for him on this earth. It was a wonderful night, full moon, and in the distance Bill could see the lights of Martinique and all the other islands. There was no other traffic at that time of night, the atmosphere was completely still and the aircraft seemed suspended in space as the islands drifted by underneath.

Bill's mind came rapidly back onto the flight deck as Jim called for descent clearance from PIARCO approach as they approached Grenada and they were cleared down to Flight Level 50 on course for the PIARCO VOR on the far side of Port of Spain. Jim took the auto-pilot out and let down much faster than would be normal for an aircraft approaching from the north and Bill noticed that Jim had switched the transponder off, presumably so that PIARCO would not know either their position or altitude. Jim switched the landing lights on and levelled off at one thousand feet above the water, well below the hills to the north of Port of Spain and, Bill realised, the visibility of the PIARCO radar. There was an aircraft on the TCAS display on their starboard side and as it turned through 360° Bill could see it also had its landing lights on. As the aircraft turned in front of Alpha Lima, Bill noticed from the TCAS that it started to climb very rapidly and then he heard it transmitting to PIARCO approach.

"PIARCO Paragon 72 we've been having trouble with our transponder. We are now using our reserve set transmitting 1316, are you receiving the squawk?"

"Thank you Paragon 72, this is PIARCO. We see you on course PIARCO at flight level 50 range 30 miles, you are cleared to make an ILS approach on Runway One Zero, call at SHARK."

Jim reduced altitude to 500ft., turned the landing lights, navigation lights and cabin lights off and then turned on to 143° to steer between

Trinidad and Tobago. In the moonlight Bill could make out the land masses on either side and the sea below. He turned to look behind his left shoulder and Robert was still very vigilant, standing guard holding the pistol and pointing it at his head.

***

There was no turning back. They were beyond all communication with the world as Bill knew it. Jim must have been mad to ever agree to take part in the plot. They were on their way to South America on a venture that was as crazy in its inception as in its execution. Not for the first time in his life, but now probably for the last, Bill wished he could see what the future had in store for the four of them. He was not a religious man but he prayed that he might survive and be reunited with his family again and all that he held dear.

"Jim, who did you give your letter to?"

They were flying steadily for a few minutes at 39,000 ft. above the Rio Cuyuni in Guyana. The whole thing seemed unreal, surely a nightmare and Bill would wake up in a moment, safe in bed.

"My solicitor of course, with strict instructions to give it to the police if I disappear. My instructions are that he should try and contact me once a month and if he cannot establish where I am then he must release the letter."

"Which solicitor? Does he live in the States or the UK?"

"No of course not, I gave it to Williams of Smith and Williams in Cape Harbour."

"Jim, Paragon uses most of the solicitors in Cape Harbour. Isn't Williams a member of the Golf Club?"

Jim nodded, Bill thought slightly uncomfortably.

"He plays with Greg a lot doesn't he? If Greg is in the plot I don't give much for your chances."

Bill could see the guard was listening to the conversation, but not really understanding it. He could also see that he'd finally got through to Jim. So Greg was the mastermind. No wonder all the details had been planned so thoroughly. He wondered if Jimmy Morrison was in on the plot. Jim was looking very indecisive and not concentrating as much as he should be doing on the operation of the flight.

They reached the turning point at 5°N, 60° 30' W and the auto-pilot turned the aircraft towards the Equator and 70°W. Bill marvelled at the power of the Galileo European Satellite System. They were up to 41,000 ft. now since Jim had been able to let the aircraft cruise climb for maximum range, because for once in their lives they did not have to worry about air traffic rules and other aircraft. Below, the moon shone down on the black jungle and Bill could see an occasional light or fire in the darkness. On the flight deck everything was warm and comfortable, an unreal existence in a hostile world. Bill looked at Robert who was beginning to look sleepy. Jim looked in torment.

Bill calculated the fuel for the umpteenth time.

"We'll make our primary destination with 45 minutes fuel, we'll make our secondary one with ten minutes to spare, if we're lucky."

Bill marked Leguizamo and pointed it out to Jim on the display. Jim got his Jeppeson landing charts out and then looked at the topographical map. Bill wondered if Jim was ever going to do anything. Suddenly Jim told the guard he had to go to the toilet and the guard kept his eyes even more closely on Bill as Jim squeezed by him. So closely that he did not see Jim take the fire extinguisher down from the bulkhead and hit him with all his might. It probably killed him as the man slumped onto the central console. Jim managed to pull him clear as Bill watched the auto-pilot. Bill saw the gun on the floor by the man's hand. He grabbed it and managed to put it in his pocket.

"Jim, lock the flight deck door and tie up Robert with the cockpit escape rope, though to be frank I don't think he'll ever move again. Let's hope the other guard is asleep."

Jim looked dazed but did what Bill told him.

"Jim, I've put in the Leguizamo waypoint and we've got 200 miles to go on 260°M. It looks good. I think we're going to make it."

Jim nodded. He was absolutely shattered. Bill realised that, unlike Jim, he had found some hidden strength. It was just getting light. They appeared to be above some thin cloud and he gradually reduced the aircraft's height. Bill became more and more concerned as he let down because they seemed to be getting into thicker cloud and there was no sign of the ground. He checked the map to make sure that they were nowhere near high ground and prayed that the satellite positioning system was accurate. Just as he was beginning to give up hope he saw patches of jungle through the cloud and he was finally able to level off at 3,000 ft. with the cloud above them and the dark green menacing trees beneath.

Bill tried calling the airfield on the emergency frequency but there was no reply. Below them the jungle stretched all around them as far as the eye could see which, unfortunately, wasn't very far and the situation rapidly became much worse as the visibility deteriorated. The jungle got nearer and started rushing by underneath. Bill checked the fuel, he reckoned they would still just make it even though they were lower than he really wanted. He saw the shape of the Rio Putumayo on their left and he realised it was going to be touch and go because the gap between the cloud and the jungle was getting narrower and narrower as the cloud tentacles went into the trees. At last, ahead, after what seemed like an eternity a change in the colour of the green appeared in the jungle and he could see a clearing and a short runway. He slowed the aircraft right down and lowered the slats and some of the flaps. As they lined up with the runway he selected the landing gear and the rest of the flap. Jim seemed to be in another world.

The Final Flight

EPILOGUE

'Which then perhaps rebounding may Echo beyond the Mexique bay!'

"She was a funny girl."

I grunted.

"Who was?"

It was difficult trying to catch up with all the periodicals and technical articles I needed to read and carry on a conversation at the same time. We had only just returned from St. Antony after spending an idyllic week in the best hotel on the island. We had swum, lain in the sun, gone snorkelling, sailed in the catamarans and even found time to go to bed. It was a holiday to savour, the first for both of us for longer than we could remember.

"Mandy, did you see that the Paragon stock has recovered and is up to 20."

"Don't change the subject, my love."

"I'm not. Apparently the markets regained their confidence and guess what?"

"What?"

"Jimmy Morrison bought a whole load of stock back at 7 on a dawn raid so that he's now got his 50% again and he's made a profit in spite of losing quite a bit when he sold on a falling market. Men like him are survivors. I suppose he'll buy some more paintings. Mind you he'll have to build a larger house to get them on the walls."

I picked up the most recent copy of Aviation Week and turned the pages. Suddenly something caught my eye and I shivered.

"Darling, listen to this. 'A persistent story in Bogota that Colombian rebels downed an airliner as it was landing at the Colombian Air Force base of Puerto Leguizamo about three weeks ago has been confirmed by the army chief of staff. The aircraft caught fire when it hit the ground and was totally destroyed as ammunition and grenades, which the aircraft was carrying, exploded keeping all the rescuers at bay. Four bodies were discovered in the wreckage. The army chief of staff said that the aircraft seemed to be a modern jet but did not know what type it was or where it had come from. It was hoped to get experts to identify it. The rebel band which shot the aircraft down had been killed outright.'"

"That was them, wasn't it Peter?"

"Yes, I'm afraid it must have been."

Mandy held my hand. "You're very upset, aren't you?"

The Final Flight

I nodded. It was such a shame. Poor Bill. He'd done nothing to deserve what had happened to him. And Jane too. Somebody would have to break the news to her. She probably knew Bill was dead but didn't know how he had died. We were both very quiet thinking about what had happened. I wondered why the aircraft was landing at an air force base. It didn't make sense. It should have been landing on a rebel controlled strip.

The police had caught Greg but he wouldn't say anything even after Chuck became a prosecution witness. They'd found Greg's son in New York with his wife's parents. He'd admitted that the aircraft left for Colombia and that Bill had agreed to go on the last flight but he wouldn't say anything else. Perhaps Bill had agreed to go on the flight in order to get Jim to change his mind. He must have won in the end if they were landing at Puerto Leguizamo, only to be defeated by cruel circumstance. No-one would ever know for sure.

"By the way did I tell you that the St. Antony police had one bit of luck; the Dallas police found Rodriguez in the Offices of South American Trading and when they searched his apartment they found the rig drawings but not the rig. He said that he was approached by South American Trading who asked him to quote for writing some special software for the European Aerospace 412. They sent him the spec. and he realised it was going to take a lot of work. Furthermore, he would have to pinch a computer, get hold of the rig drawings and get a rig made. He quoted a very high price and said he would need to be paid cash before he would proceed. The guy at South American Trading agreed and he was told to send the computer to WAA attention Chuck Curtis when it was ready. That was what made Chuck finally give evidence. Honeywell are trying to get the police to prosecute Rodriguez."

"What for, Peter?"

"You're a lawyer. You should know. For pinching their copyright of all things."

"That would have to be a civil case and the legal costs would be more than Rodriguez has. Forget it. They would do better to get the police to prosecute for pinching the program loader and the computer. Can't they have a go at South American Trading?" She paused. "By the way what will happen over the insurance money? Will Hull Claims really pay Frank, bearing in mind that the aircraft was never found?"

"I think they'll have to. After all the aircraft has been found, even though it is in little bits, all burnt and charred. I imagine they will send someone to Leguizamo just to be certain. They will find it very difficult not to pay Frank in full. They may wriggle a bit."

In fact I did wonder if they would pay out completely. If I was representing Hull claims I think I might try to persuade them to withhold some money because Bill might have spotted with the radar that the aircraft was not tracking over Lundy correctly, but it would be a difficult point to argue since he would probably have been using the radar looking upwards in cloud.

"…but she was funny."

Mandy brought me back home from the New World. I knew I'd have to forget Bill and what had happened but I found it very hard. There was an enormous lump in my throat.

"Who was?"

"You know perfectly well who I mean. She seemed to have no dress sense. It was almost as if she was deliberately trying to look unattractive."

"Who?"

"Charlie of course."

"Oh, Charlie."

I knew who she meant alright. At least I thought I did but I wasn't taking any chances in case she had done a flash back to Liz. It couldn't be Diana because Mandy had never met her. Not unexpectedly we had not heard from Diana's solicitors though it could only be a matter of time. Unusually, we were spending the week-end at my house in Kingston instead of going to Mandy's flat in Bournemouth, but it worked out better for both of us from a work point of view, both before and after the week-end.

"Don't 'Oh Charlie' me, Peter. I know your technique. I mean why did Charlie Simpson avoid us? You asked her to dinner and she wouldn't come, said she was too busy packing up the paintings for shipment."

Bill disappeared again for a moment and I was back in St. Antony.

"Mandy, she came to Frank's thank you and farewell party to me."

"Only for a moment, and then she barely talked to us."

"She was at the Ambassador's cocktail party."

"But she didn't really chat."

"She was at the United States embassy reception."

"Same as our Ambassadors. She never really said 'thank you' to you. If it hadn't have been for you she'd never have been promoted to a vice-president of Westfield Insurance. You did everything and got nothing apart from your consultant's fee from Frank."

"Well, she sent me a cheque for $1,000,000, that was quite a good thank you."

"Peter. You are the absolute limit. You never mentioned it."

"How else do you think I could afford to cosset you in the most expensive hotel in St. Antony? Most of it's gone."

She dug me in the ribs.

"Come off it, it wasn't that bad. I looked at the final bill."

"But the bill was in my brief case. You're as bad as Charlie."

"Now just what do you mean by that?"

"I mean what I said. She was always looking through my things to make sure I wasn't hiding anything from her."

"I'm not sure I like the sound of that. There are some things you need to keep to yourself, or for me anyway."

"That's just what I told her."

She thought for a bit.

"Who signed the cheque?"

"She did, and someone else, presumably the chief financial officer."

"For services rendered I suppose?"

I decided to ignore her inference.

"It was the advertised reward. She is a vice-president of the firm and apparently has the power to sign cheques."

"I hope you're right."

"I know I'm right because I cashed the cheque the moment I got it in St. Antony and checked on Friday when we got back that the cheque had been cleared."

"You know you really are an expert witness."

"On what subject?"

"You know what I mean. You are doing it again. You are an expert as a witness. I mean you always answer questions exactly, and I have no reason to believe untruthfully, but you never answer questions in a way that lets the counsel go on a fishing expedition. To coin a phrase 'you are economical with the truth'. You are the most secretive man I know."

"I'm not secretive at all. I tell you everything you ask."

"But you don't volunteer things like a normal man."

"Wait a moment. Now we're getting down to it."

I put the Aviation Week down that I was trying to read and looked at her. "How many normal men do you know?"

"In the biblical sense? That's my secret, my love."

She kissed me in a way that suggested that the cross-examination I was going through was for information only to enlarge her knowledge base, and that it would not be used in evidence against me. I managed to say "Do they all get this treatment?" as she ran her hands over my body but I couldn't rise to Mandy's expectations. I just couldn't stop thinking about Bill. But that was the nice thing about Mandy, she understood.

The Final Flight

The Final Flight

Printed in the United States
100054LV00006B/34/A

9 780955 385605